Marvellously untouched by twelve years of formal education, Sylvian Hamilton has been at different times a secretary, mother, lexicographer, journalist, farmer, second-hand bookseller and antiques dealer. She is a devoted *Star Trek* fan. Since arthritis clipped her wings, she spends much of her time at home, a tiny cottage in the Scottish border country, with a very patient husband, two cats and about five thousand books. *The Pendragon Banner* is her second novel featuring Sir Richard Straccan, the bone-pedlar.

THE PENDRAGON BANNER

Sylvian Hamilton

ORION

An Orion paperback

First published in Great Britain in 2001
by Orion
This paperback edition published in 2002
by Orion Books Ltd,
Orion House, 5 Upper St Martin's Lane,
London WC2H 9EA

A CIP catalogue record for this book is available
from the British Library.

ISBN 0 75284 800 3

Printed and bound in Great Britain by
Clays Ltd, St Ives plc

In memory of Michael. Shine on, Michael.

Prologue

Mid-winter, and the wind still came scything from the east, its howl drowning the chanting of monks and nuns shivering in the church. Candle flames dipped and swayed, flaring in the draught and casting strange shadows. If only it would snow, said the farmers and thralls huddled round their fires – snow would dull the bitter edge; but although the clouds massed heavy and dirty yellow, the snow that should have fallen still held back, and nothing softened the stone-hard ground or the sharp vicious outlines of leafless trees.

Mid-winter, and day by day for weeks the ice had spread and thickened until now the island of Avallon was an island no more; folk could walk dryshod instead of poling their flat boats to the convent's jetty.

Mid-winter, in the year of Our Lord five hundred and sixty-five, and in her stone cell on a narrow bed lay an old woman, dying hard. For thirty years she had lived within these walls and the world outside had forgotten all but her name, which men would remember for ever. Her confessor prayed, a tall dark rook of a man; and two nuns tended her, wiping the death sweat from her face and chafing her cold hands.

She was not aware of them. Behind her flickering eyelids she was young again, bride of Arthur, the warlord who called himself king. He was in her dream, seated in his hall with his captains. There they were, Bedwyr, Cei, Drustan, Gawain; she could see them, she could even smell them – leather, iron, sweat, and blood.

She woke, heart hammering, fearful eyes staring past pools of candlelight into the shifting shadows. Her fingers plucked at the coarse blanket and her cracked lips moved.

'Who's there?'

'Dear Mother,' said Sister Berenice tenderly. 'Be at peace. We are here and God is here.'

Of course He was. God was everywhere, even in Camlodd . . . Camlodd! Sinking back into the dream she rode again through muddy vennels between traders' stalls, where little brown pigs rootled, grunting around folks' legs. She could smell the throat-catching reek of dung, tanning, brewing, rancid fat, sour milk and smoke, and heard again the sounds of battle, horses neighing, men shouting, women screaming and the shrill cries of children.

But the stronghold of Camlodd was gone, laid waste long ago, destroyed so thoroughly that no one was even sure where it once stood, or could say, 'Here was Arthur's hall, here Guinevere's bower.' It had become legend: Camlodd, that had been no more than a squalid huddle of huts and stables around Arthur's hall, with the heads of enemies stuck on the stockade posts, stinking and shrivelling until at last the skulls of kings and warriors fell to the ground to be kicked about by little boys.

Camlodd was gone, Arthur too, and his captains. Gone, Cei and Bedwyr, Gawain and Gwalchmai, and – so they said but Guinevere knew better – Medrawt. Sometimes, when her shields of prayer and penance were lowered in the unguarded moments when sleep took her, or as she woke, she heard his bodiless voice calling her name.

For thirty years she had mortified the guilty flesh that had yearned for Medrawt, lacerating her skin with the lash, tormenting it with a hair shirt, ulcerating her knees to the bone on cold stones, praying for the souls of those who had died because of her lust; all but one. She did not pray for Medrawt.

Something touched her face. Warm, wet. Tears. Sister Gruach was weeping. Guinevere touched the young nun's hand. 'My daughter . . .'

These were her only children, no child had been born of her body. If she had given Arthur a son, would men still have turned from him to Medrawt? Thousands might have lived; Camlodd itself might still stand had she not been barren. But she was not to blame.

Virgin she had gone as bride to Arthur's bed, and ten years later, virgin to Medrawt.

Medrawt . . .

'*Still here, old woman? Not dead yet? I am waiting for you.*'

'Lord Jesus, protect me . . .'

Father Magnus bent, his ear to her lips to catch the faint breath.

'The Banner,' she whispered. 'Bring it to me.'

He fetched it from the altar, Avallon's treasure, in its precious case of garnet-crusted gold, the dragon-blazoned war banner of Arthur; and more precious still, stitched between its doubled layers of heavy silk, a relic beyond all price: a linen cloth stained with the blood of Christ.

Reverently Magnus placed the reliquary in Guinevere's hands. She fumbled with the clasp, and as he bent to help her the distant chanting stopped and the screaming began. There was a clash of weapons. Nuns and priest stared at one another in sudden terror. They knew what it was, they had all heard it at some time in their lives.

'Raiders!'

'God have mercy on us!'

Berenice slammed the door and leaned against it – there was no bar. Magnus bent over the dying woman, touching her eyelids and lips with his crucifix and holy oil.

There were shouts and rushing feet in the passage. An axe blade split the door which fell inward under blows that burst its hinges, crushing Berenice beneath. The raiders pushed into the room, a nightmare of helmets and grinning teeth, brandishing swords and axes oily with blood.

'Don't hurt her,' Magnus cried, standing between death and the dying with arms outspread. 'She is a most holy lady, and was a great queen!'

But in seconds the cell was a shambles, the priest speared to the wall, the old nun's worthless carcass hacked, kicked aside and trodden underfoot. Gruach flung herself across Guinevere's body, but was seized and stripped, her value as slave or bedmate expertly, brutally assessed: young, fair, virgin – worth keeping.

The chief of the raiders snatched the reliquary from the dying woman's hands, laughing with pleasure at its weight and richness. The plain silver ring on her swollen finger was a paltry thing, but Borri let nothing pass, not even a trifle such as this. He cut off the finger.

Guinevere died.

Borri opened the reliquary, discovering the fabric rolled within. 'What's this?'

'That's a treasure of the Cross-God,' said a thrall, one of the convent's kitchen slaves and fellow-countryman of the raiders whom he had let in at the back door. 'They keep it on the altar. A mighty talisman. Very magical.'

'Magic?' Borri shook out the heavy silk, and the scarlet embroidered dragon quivered as if it breathed. 'What does it do?'

The thrall questioned Gruach and turned triumphantly to Borri. 'Long ago,' he said, 'their god was murdered. The night before he died he was in a garden. He was afraid, she says,' he added disgustedly, 'and the sweat of his terror turned to blood.'

'Gods fear nothing,' said Borri. 'But I have heard this Cross-God is a womanish thing that fears blood and battle and the business of men.'

The thrall nodded. 'True, master. One of the god's servants, *Yosif* by name, mopped up the blood with a linen clout. Christians value such stuff. That,' pointing at the pennant, 'has a bit of the cloth sewn inside it.' He jabbered at the nun again, heard her reply and continued. '*Yosif* came to this land, and that talisman brought him great wealth while he lived. That was long ago, but later Arthur Pendragon, the one called the Bear, had it sewn into this pennant to give him victory in battle.'

Borri snorted. 'He was defeated.'

'That was because he lost the talisman and his luck with it. His sister's son Medrawt stole it. There was a battle where each slew the other. After that the talisman was brought here. It has great powers, this woman says.'

'I'll keep it,' said Borri after some thought. 'Let it bring wealth to me, my kin and my friends.'

Gruach snatched at his arm mouthing nonsense. He shook her off, looking at the slave for translation.

'She wants someone to bury the old woman. She says she was once queen of this country.'

'Torch the place,' said Borri. 'We dig no holes for their carrion.'

'She says the old one was Arthur's queen.'

At that there was an uneasy silence. Arthur had been dead for thirty years but his fame was very great.

Borri frowned. 'It would not be wise to offend such a ghost as his. We will bury his old woman.'

They buried her in the leafless winter-bitten orchard and heaved the great altar slab off its base to lie over her grave. They fired the convent, took their captives and plunder and moved quickly onto the next settlement, the next rich church.

A trail of bloody destruction led back to their ships in the river called Sabrina. Two nights ago they had landed there and marched inland to Avallon, leaving a smoking spoor of crows and corpses. They met no defence for in winter no one feared sea raiders; like everyone else, they stayed at home by their firesides. But a spae-wife had told Borri to fare forth over sea and win great fortune. She gave true rede. When at last they turned back, their plunder filled three long carts.

Two ships foundered on the way back, but Borri's, carrying the talisman, was spared. At home, he set it in the place of honour, but was careful to placate Odin with a blood offering.

A man needed all the gods he could get on his side.

Chapter 1

It began like any other Showing Day. Who could have foreseen it would end in the abbey's ruin?

Pilgrims had been turning up since dawn. Laughing, chattering, singing and cheering, some drunk, some weeping, some propping along others in worse case than themselves. By midday the queue had grown quite long, a hundred or so. Some brought food, others fasted. A few of them seemed whole, but mostly they were a collection of the afflicted – harelipped, wry-necked, club-footed, goitrous, pocked, scrofulous, limbless, blind, deaf, mute, palsied, tubercular, deformed and insane. Some walked, some limped, some crutched and some crawled. Some were self-propelled on little trolleys, paddled along by the hands, or else levered themselves forward on hand-trestles. Others were led, pushed, dragged or carried; the hopeful, the hopeless, young and old, the living, the dying and occasionally – carried by friends or relatives – the already dead.

The great doors of the church opened and the queue began to shuffle forward. They were let in a few at a time and looked over, shut up, exhorted, and suitably intimidated by the sacristan, Brother Harold, whose skull-faced severity put the fear of God into the most obstinately cheerful spirit. The senior brethren had seen the uninhibited goings-on at many another shrine and they weren't having any of that *here*, thank you very much! Pilgrims the worse for drink were weeded out at the door, and any misbehaving once inside were collared and hauled away by burly Brother Simon.

By the time the hopefuls had been inspected, sorted, preached at, rebuked, dusted and tweaked into tidier presentability, most of them were quite deflated. Then they were made to kneel and only managed a timid cheer when the relic, the hand of Saint Derfel, was held up to their eager eyes; creeping out afterwards like chastened children while the next bunch was admitted.

The hand had a notable history of miracles in the past but in recent years its reputation had fallen off. Fashions come and go, in saints as in garments, and Derfel was no longer popular. Like many other shrines throughout the realm this one had lost out to Becket. Fifty years ago there would have been a thousand or more pilgrims here. The flood had become a trickle. Nevertheless, twice a year on the Showing Days some pilgrims still came, and from midday to dusk the relic lay in full view on the altar.

It was not imposing. Its original reliquary, a jewelled silver gilt casket in the shape of a hand, had been sold, for with the decline of offerings the priory was feeling the pinch. Now, when not on show, the hand was kept in a plain wooden box. The priory had grown disenchanted with its relic; instead of locking it carefully away with the prescribed ritual and prayers at dusk the brethren more often scurried off to their suppers and left the hand lying on the altar, sometimes all through the night until Prime.

There it lay, claw-like, mummified, brown. Most pilgrims were permitted merely to touch the faded purple silk bands tied round the stump of the wrist; these hung down over the edge of the altar for that purpose, their ends blackened and frayed from innumerable fingers, kisses and tears. The more pitiable, however, were privileged to be touched with it.

Outside, a fashionably dressed man had been watching the queue. Fine clothes strained around his broad belly, and the brimmed and feathered cap pulled well down over his eyebrows and shadowing his fat face couldn't hide the ugly red pits and furrows left by smallpox. Not until evening did he join the queue. By then the crowd was thinning and drifting away, locals heading for home and travellers for the Maison Dieu or more interesting places to spend the night. Small parties had set off already to reach other towns before nightfall.

The dandy tipped a boy to hold his horse, and tacked on at the end.

It was damp and perishing cold inside the church. The candles had burned low and the fiery sinking sun shone through small panes of precious coloured glass in the centre of the western window, splashing rainbows over the stone floor. As the pilgrims shuffled, some on their knees, towards the altar, their flesh and garments were tinted violet and emerald, ruby and amber. A child crouched, patting the coloured flagstones, smiling at the play of colours over his small scabby hands. His mother yanked him to his feet, whispering loudly, 'Don't let them bloody monks see you muckin about!' Harold scowled at her. The child's upturned snotty face, lit red and green, was marred by a harelip.

This was the last group and the guardian monks, chilled through, were stamping their cold feet, yawning, scratching and huffing warm breath on their fingers, their minds on supper. The pilgrims were relieved of their offerings, mere fourthings and half-pence for the most part, before they trooped out. The dandy came last.

As he bent his knee at the altar he glanced back over his shoulder; the monks were already vanishing through the door into the slype, which led to cloister, wash house and refectory. The door squeaked shut behind them and the dandy heard the key turned in the outside lock.

Now only one monk remained in the church to herd the pilgrims out, the dandy coming last with the gaunt figure of Brother Harold right behind him, ready to close and lock the great doors.

The dandy unhooked a flask from his belt and handed it with a coin to the boy waiting with his horse. He made a shivering noise with his lips.

'Brrr! Is cold, no? Get this filled. Wine, not ale, and urry!'

A Frog, thought Brother Harold with instant Saxon dislike. The boy handed the Frog his reins and ran to the nearest pothouse. The Frog gave Harold, who was hoping for more, two pennies, then clapped a hand to his belt for his gloves and found them missing. He turned back to the doors which Harold, coming forward to take the pennies, had left ajar.

'*Sangdieu! Mes gants!* I ave forget ze gloves. Old ze orse!'

Before the monk could object the Frog had shoved the reins into his hands and darted back inside. The horse shifted its feet, stamped, sidled and snorted. Harold eyed it with irritation and clung on. After only a few moments the Frog emerged, pulling on one elaborately embroidered and tasselled glove and carrying the other.

'*Merci, mon frère.*' Heaving himself into the saddle, he trotted towards the Maison Dieu where the boy, coming with his flask, met him.

When he had closed and locked the doors Brother Harold, blissfully unaware that he'd be kicking himself for ever more, hurried around the side of the church to the warming house.

Tuppence, he thought disgustedly. *The fat Frog was a miserly sod.*

The fat Frog trotted sedately southward. After he'd gone a mile or so, he hooked the uncomfortable wax plumpers from inside his cheeks and tossed them aside into the bushes. Under his padded garments he was neither fat nor French but English: Sir Richard Straccan, former crusader but now buyer and seller – and not for the first time stealer – of precious relics.

Five miles from Cheringham he turned off the road, urging his hired nag to an unwilling gallop over rough country to Belmarie Wood. Dismounting, he led the horse in among the trees along ever narrower paths until he came to the clearing where his servant, Hawkan Bane, sat comfortably cooking sausages over a small bright fire. Two hobbled horses whickered softly in greeting as Bane scrambled to his feet.

'You're late,' he said. 'Any longer and I'd have scoffed the lot. How'd it go?'

'Give me a sausage, for God's sake,' said Straccan. 'Here.' He passed the relic to Bane and seized the skewer of sausages from the flames.

'Mind,' said Bane. 'They're – '

'Ow!'

' – hot. Any trouble?'

'Not so far, but we'd best put a few more miles behind us while the moon shines, and get rid of this nag. Someone might recognise it.'

No one was likely to recognise him. He peeled the lurid flour-and-paint scars from his face and wolfed six sausages before shedding the Frog's garb and donning his own breeks, shirt and jerkin. Wadding the discarded hat, gloves and padded clothes into a tight bundle he shoved them well down into the middle of a tangle of brambles.

Wrapping the relic with great care, first in a piece of silk and then in sheep's wool, Bane stowed it in a leather satchel which Straccan buckled to his belt. They packed up the small camp and put the fire out, careful to cover all traces.

The moon was right overhead when they struck on the worn and muddy line of Watling Street. Barring accidents they expected to reach Bromfield the day after tomorrow.

Prior and community at Bromfield would be well pleased and not a little astonished. The relic had been stolen from them – they said – seventy years ago, when the Empress Maud's army sacked the priory and burned the church. Some years later, the thief, dying, had bestowed his looted treasure upon the abbey at Cheringham, hoping to bluff his way past Saint Peter with the aid of the monks' prayers. Civilised requests over the years from Bromfield's Benedictines for the relic's return had been met with scorn, insults and even blows from Cheringham's Praemonstratensians. Hiring Straccan to steal it back had been a final act of desperation; the brethren of Bromfield never really expected to see the holy hand again.

That wouldn't stop them trying to screw the price down!

Chapter 2

Darkness had settled on Ludlow town. Wan glints of light seeped out around the edges of ill-fitting hide shutters, but only when the moon slipped out between the clouds were walls, doors, kennels and middens briefly revealed. There was still activity in certain parts of the town though, as the criminal fraternity – thieves, housebreakers and such – got ready for business. At the approach of two riders and a packhorse dark shadows faded into darker corners. Horsemen with swords were not the prey they favoured.

'Hear that?' Bane reined in. 'Over there.'

They stopped.

'There!'

The sound, a groan, came from the midden ditch in the middle of the road. Straccan nudged his horse towards it, pausing when he saw a long bundle.

Bane drew his sword. 'Watch out.'

Straccan got down and pushed the bundle with his foot. It rolled over heavily. A body. Moonlight showed a pale face and the dark wet gleam of blood, but the man was breathing and the pulse at his neck beat strongly.

'Better take him with us,' said Straccan. 'Jesus, he's soaking wet!'

'Niffs a bit too,' said Bane critically.

'Can't be helped.' Grasping the man's jerkin, Straccan heaved him over his saddle and led his horse up the steep road to the castle.

'He's been set upon,' said Straccan, when the castle's surgeon bustled into the dormitory followed by his apprentice. 'His head's still bleeding.'

The surgeon leaned over the unconscious man, parting the bloody hair to peer at the seeping wound and raising the closed eyelids to examine the eyes. He sniffed at the mouth. 'Not been drinking,' he said. 'I'm surprised they left him his clothes. Must've heard you coming. Let's get em off, see the damage.'

'They took his shoes,' said Bane as he and the surgeon stripped the man. There was a large rough and ready darn in one stocking.

The surgeon ran his hands over his patient's ribs, belly and limbs with casual efficiency.

'Hmm. Lot of bruising. Had a good kicking, by the look of it. Nothing broken. Bruising over the liver though – might be fatal, might not. Heartbeat's strong, he'll probably be all right. Though you never can tell,' he added hastily, just in case. 'Internal injuries aren't always obvious so soon after the event. The head wound needs cautery.'

Putting his satchel on the bed he took out a cautery iron and handed it to the apprentice, who stuck it in the coals of the brazier and fell to picking his nose while waiting.

'Took his purse, did they?' the surgeon enquired.

'Purse and anything else he had.'

'Lucky for him you happened along, or they'd have taken his life as well, I shouldn't wonder.' He snapped his fingers and the apprentice jumped, handing him the cautery iron glowing cherry red. The surgeon spat on the iron, approved the hiss and clapped it to the wound. Bane winced. There was a deep groan from the patient and a stench of burning hair and skin. 'Two, three, four, five,' intoned the surgeon. He removed the iron and inspected the damage. 'That's stopped it,' he said with satisfaction.

Straccan dug into his purse and gave the surgeon some coins.

'Thank you, sir. He should come round before long. There may be some fever; there often is after cautery. I'll bleed him if there is.' He took his satchel and departed, followed by his apprentice, scowling because he hadn't had a tip.

Bane hung the man's hide jerkin on a peg by the bedhead and draped the rest of his wet, bloody clothes over the drying-rail by the fire, investigating pockets as he did so.

'Aha!' There was a small pocket, roughly but solidly stitched, inside the shirt on the left. Bane's probing finger hooked something out – a glossy wisp, a curl of dark hair tied with a scrap of blue wool. Sweetheart, wife, daughter?

'Look at this.'

'And this,' said Straccan with the man's belt in his hands. Its lining was split, neatly and deliberately, to make a safe place to tuck a few coins or any other small thing of value. 'A bit of parchment.' He smoothed it out and angled it to the candlelight. 'Latin,' he said, surprised. '*Cymbium* something. *Cymbium Vulstani sum*.'

'What's that mean?'

'It says, *I am Wulstan's cup*. Sounds like an inscription.'

'Maybe that's his name. Wulstan.'

They looked at the unconscious vulnerable face in the narrow bed. It was young, pleasant, square-chinned, straight-nosed, with dark curly hair. Beard shadow darkened the jaw and there was a small crescent-shaped scar on the chin. By the fire, the steady dripping from his clothes had made small puddles on the flags.

'I wonder how he got so wet,' Straccan said. 'He was soaked to the skin.'

'Perhaps he fell in the river,' Bane suggested.

'Maybe.' Straccan yawned hugely, picking up his saddlebags. 'We'll find out when he wakes up. Will you doss down here and keep an eye on him? If he comes round he won't know where he is. I'll see you in the morning.'

Leaving the dormitory he found the small room he was to share with two other knights in transit; they were both snoring. Resigned to a bad night he got between the dubious blankets and pillowed his head on his empty saddlebags. It had been a busy day. He had delivered the relic to Bromfield and squeezed his payment from the monks' coffers – not without a struggle – but his hard-won silver was safe now in the Templars' keeping. He closed his eyes.

As sleep continued to elude him, Straccan remembered the curl of hair in the young stranger's pocket. A sweetheart most likely. Lucky man. Straccan's hand closed on the charm he wore on a thong round his neck, given him by Janiva, the woman he wanted to marry.

Last summer he'd told Sir Guy, the lord of Shawl manor and in some sense her guardian, that he wanted to marry Janiva.

'Good luck to ye, me boy,' the old man had wheezed. 'When's the weddin?'

'Ah,' said Straccan, catching a shrewd glance from Dame Alienor. 'As soon as she says yes. Do I have your permission?'

'If you needed it, aye, but she's a free woman, and—'

'Wilful,' supplied his wife.

'Hard to please, I was goin to say,' said Sir Guy. 'She wouldn't marry our son, ye know. If ye win her round there's a mark of silver for her dowry, I'll buy back her house and land and ye'll have my blessing. I'll be glad to see her safe wed before I die.'

And now he *was* dead, that kindly old man. The widowed Dame Alienor still lived at Shawl but the manor belonged to their son Roger. Roger, who not so long ago had wanted to marry his foster-sister Janiva.

With his eyes closed Straccan conjured her image: oval face, smooth sun-flushed skin, gold-brown eyes, generous lips, red-brown hair. Last summer when he'd asked her to marry him she'd refused, for reasons that seemed good to her but not to him. She was still of the same mind when he had seen her last, at Easter, but he was not giving up, then, now or ever, although their last meeting had ended badly.

He still didn't know why. She was glad enough to see him when he arrived, yet soon it seemed he could say nothing right. She put him off at every turn. He pressed her too hard, she said; besides, Dame Alienor, new-widowed, was ill and needed her. How could he talk of marriage at such a time? Her place was here. Every clumsy thing he said only made it worse, and in the end they'd parted unfriends, Janiva tearful, himself angry.

He couldn't leave it like that. Now the Bromfield job was done he could go back. He'd start tomorrow.

Chapter 3

It was warm in the still-room at Shawl and the fine fragrant dust of herbs hung in the sunbeams that slanted through the narrow windows. This had always been Janiva's favourite place. Her earliest memories were of her mother and Dame Alienor talking and laughing together in this room, the dust of herbs on their hands, sweet scents clinging to their sleeves and aprons; two young women, one born unfree the other noble, mother and foster-mother united in their care for the son they shared and loved – Roger, Janiva's foster-brother.

The two babies shared the same cradle, fed from the same breasts, played together, squabbled, made up and loved each other, until at the age of seven Roger went away to begin his long training as squire and knight. In due course his parents would choose a wife for him, a girl of noble birth with a manor or two and money. Ten years later it really threw the cat among the pigeons when Roger announced he wanted to marry his foster-sister.

His parents so doted on their only living child that against all good judgement they would have permitted it had not Janiva, to their relief and astonishment, refused. Before Roger could get his breath a suitable match was swiftly arranged – Richildis was heir to three manors – and the marriage had taken place last summer.

Since the wedding the young couple had been away touring the dowry manors but now they were expected at Shawl any day. Troubles never come singly, and hard upon Sir Guy's death arrived bad tidings: Roger's cousin had laid claim to Shawl and was even now with the king, in favour, and likely to win his case. Roger would need to squeeze Shawl manor until it hurt if he was to raise the funds necessary to contest the claim.

'. . . coltsfoot,' finished Alienor.

Janiva looked blankly at her.

Dame Alienor laughed. 'I thought so! You were miles away. I said, with all these coughs we have almost run out of coltsfoot.'

'There's plenty of horehound; it's just as good with a little honey in hot water. What is it, my lady?' for Alienor was watching her, smiling.

She looks ill, Janiva thought with a pang of worry. Grief for her husband and anxiety for her son's inheritance had aged the lady of Shawl. Her round cheerful face had fallen in, the flesh on her sturdy bones had thinned and she looked ten years older than she had last summer.

'I'll lay odds you were thinking of your sweetheart,' Alienor said. 'And don't tell me he's not, for he means to marry you. My lord made enquiries last year, discreetly, of course. Your Straccan is a good match.'

'Madame—'

'He's well with the king, too; that's useful while it lasts. He has a good estate, unencumbered my lord said, and only one daughter; so your son will inherit with no ill will. That's fortunate; the sons of a first wife mean trouble.'

Half laughing, half annoyed, Janiva interrupted. 'Madame, I have told him no!'

'So? He keeps coming back, doesn't he? You can always change your mind. Not a bad thing,' she added with an approving nod, 'to begin by saying no.'

'I meant it!'

'Did you?'

Alienor gave her a shrewd look. Janiva felt herself blushing. Did she? She'd been sure enough at first. But now?

'You should think on the future,' said Alienor, reaching to pat her hand. 'You are still young.' She looked fondly at Janiva. 'Do you really see yourself here years from now, an old woman alone?'

Old? She had never thought about it. Youth seemed to stretch ahead, an eternal Now, unchanged by the years' passing. Alone? Before Straccan came she had been content, self-sufficient, an entire being. That completeness was gone, no use pretending otherwise. Her life went on as it always had; she was busy and useful here in her own place among people she had known all her life.

Nothing had changed.

Everything was different.

'It's not at all like I thought,' she said, and was surprised to hear herself saying it aloud.

'What? Love?' Alienor smiled and the ill, weary look was gone briefly from her face. 'Bless you, girl. It never is.'

Chapter 4

The king had arrived at Bristol last night, several hours ahead of his baggage train and with only a handful of attendants. Most of the lords and captains summoned to meet him were there already, and the rest – if they knew what was good for them – would be there today.

It was scarce five in the morning when the courier from Dublin was shown into the royal bedchamber, but the king had been up since three and the room was full of people: knights of the royal household, squires and pages, captains and guardsmen, servants, clerks, petitioners and place seekers. The king and his captains were grouped around the bed on which a great map of Ireland had been spread, three of its corners weighted down with small coffers and the fourth with the king's brass pisspot.

Blocks of colour on the map marked the holdings of the Anglo-Irish lords; the king's left hand rested on William Marshal's great expanse of blue as he jabbed with his right forefinger at the yellow splash of the de Lacy lords, Hugh and Walter. Other holdings were coloured green, purple, brown, grey, pink. There hadn't been time to prepare a new map and the former holdings of the renegade lord William de Breos, appropriately blood red, eclipsed all but Marshal's.

The king took the letter and broke the seal. While he read his captains continued to argue, pointing here and there at the map, shaking their heads or nodding agreement as each made some point. Hearing John's exclamation they turned expectantly.

'Kilkenny,' said the king. 'Breos is in Kilkenny. Or was, when this letter was written. Well, my friends, now we know where we're going. From Crook we march on Kilkenny.' He bent over the map, tracing the route from Crook through Newbridge and Thomastown with the point of his dagger until it reached Kilkenny. 'There,' he said, and drove the steel through map, coverlid, blankets, feather bed and all, right to the hilt.

John's captains exchanged furtive glances in which gleamed secret satisfactions. Breos had lorded it over them far too long before he tripped over his own arrogance and folly. He had it coming. They would outdo one another in baying at his heels, each thankful *he* was not the subject of John's vengeful campaign.

'He'll know we're coming,' de Breauté said.

'So much the better.' D'Athée grinned. 'He'll run. More fun.'

'Not for you, Gerard,' said the king. 'Sorry, old chap, but I want you here. He'll run all right. I think he'll run back to Wales, to my son-in-law Llywelyn, and try to raise the Welsh against me. He'll be out of luck there. One of these days Llywelyn will do it, but not yet; he's not ready. He'll give Breos hospitality but no money and poor William must have money. There's only one way he can get it: he'll call up his knights and sworn men. He'll have a raiding force, not a great one but enough to be a nuisance. So that's your job, Gerard. You can have a hundred men. I'll chase him out of Ireland; you hunt him down.'

'I will, sire.'

John dismissed them and read the letter again before crushing it in his fist and tossing it into the brazier where it wriggled like something alive before bursting into smoky flame.

He stared into the glowing coals, thinking.

To buy his way back into royal favour – some hopes! – to pay the vast sums he owed the king, to regain at least some of his former holdings and safeguard the inheritance of his sons Breos would need a great deal of money. A raiding party in the Marches, unhindered for a time, could sack rich towns and abbeys, extort money from travellers and hold wealthy prisoners to ransom. Given his head for a month or so, Breos stood an excellent chance of raising more than enough to pay his debts.

I'll let him do it, the king thought. *I can do with the money, Christ knows. Give him enough rope before I hang him. Tell d'Athée to make some show but hold off until I give the word. It's only Wales, after all.*

There had been one other matter in the letter, which he had not shared with his captains. Breos had sent his wife and sons into the safekeeping of his son-in-law Walter de Lacy, in Meath, but was not without feminine company in Kilkenny. Another woman had joined him there – John's former mistress, the witch Julitta de Beauris.

The king watched the parchment writhing in the brazier and smiled. It would give him great pleasure to meet the lady Julitta again. Just a year ago her involvement, and her husband's, in a plot to murder him had come to light; her husband had paid with his life but Julitta had somehow managed to escape to Brittany. Now she had thrown in her lot with Breos. Why?

He would know soon enough.

John watched the last blackening shreds of the letter curl and fall to grey feathers on the charcoals. Just so would Julitta burn when she was delivered into his hands.

Chapter 5

On the dungheap a cock – gaudy, randy and proud – crowed exultantly. At four in the morning the stables, ward and bailey of Ludlow castle were already busy with grooms attending to the horses, carrying feed and water, boys shovelling dung, early travellers calling for their horses, kitchen sluts hurrying to and from the well, men-at-arms changing watch, dogs yapping and hens scratching in the straw and mud. The great gates stood open, cows had already been milked and taken out to pasture, and the daily stream of hawkers was pouring over the drawbridge into the bailey carrying fruit and vegetables, butter and lard and cheeses, chickens, ducks, geese and sucking-pigs and anything else the castle cooks might buy.

Bane found Straccan in the stable. 'Our drowned rat's asking for you.' He produced an apple from his sleeve, took a bite and offered the rest to Zingiber. The stallion lipped it from his palm and chomped, nuzzling his sleeve in hopes of more.

Straccan looked up from the hoof he was examining. 'All right, is he?'

'A bit quiet. I think his head hurts.' Bane reached for the rasp Straccan was using. 'He's in the dormitory. I'll finish this.'

Gold and rose light touched the towers – painting them for a few moments with the hushed splendour of legend – until the cock seized and trod an indignant hen, and somebody swore and threw a stone at the squawking pair.

The man was sitting on the edge of his bed in his rough-dried soiled clothes, shoeless, pale and looking rather frightened. He stood up as Straccan came in.

'Good morning, sir.'

'How do you feel?'

'My head aches, but . . . Sir, Master Bane said you brought me here. It was good of you. Thank you.'

Decent manners. Whoever he was, he was used to the civilities and his English had a slight Welsh accent. 'Who attacked you?'

'I don't know. I . . . Sir . . .' He sat down again suddenly, as if his legs had given way.

'What's the matter?'

'Something's wrong. I don't *know* anything! Who am I? What am I doing here? I don't know *anything*!' He put his face in his hands and turned away, trembling.

Straccan hooked a stool with his foot and sat down. 'You've lost your memory.'

The man nodded miserably.

'I've known a couple of men it happened to after a wallop on the head. It came back after a few days.'

The man looked hopeful. 'Did it, sir? I'll be all right, then?'

'I'll have the surgeon take another look at you.'

The surgeon, when he came, gently felt the man's skull all over, peered into his eyes and made him look to left and right, up and down. He shrugged. 'Well, sir, I could tell you he'll come to himself tomorrow or next week or never, but to tell you the truth I don't know any more than you. I've seen this before, as you have yourself. All I can say is he'll probably get his memory back in time. In bits and pieces at first most like, then one day' – he snapped his fingers – 'it'll be there like it was never lost. His skull's not cracked. It'll just take time.'

After the surgeon had gone Straccan said, 'Let's see what we *do* know about you, shall we?'

'What do you mean, sir?'

'Simple things first. You're not a monk or a clerk – no tonsure. You're not a beggar. Your clothes are of decent stuff, not expensive, a bit worn but not worn out; they fit properly so they are your own, not cast-offs. You're too old to be an apprentice so you're probably in someone's employ. You're not married—'

23

The man looked up, amazed. 'How d'you know?'

'A wife would make a better job of darning.'

'Oh.' He regarded his foot as if he'd never seen it before. 'Fancy that!'

Straccan warmed to his deductions. 'Until very recently – when they set on you, I suppose – you wore a ring.'

'I did?' He looked at the pale patch round his middle finger and rubbed it. 'So I did.'

'You look to be about, oh, twenty. And we'll have to call you *something* until you remember your own name. What d'you fancy?'

The man frowned. 'I don't know.'

'William? Henry?'

'Well . . .'

'No? What about David? Or Wulstan? Two mighty saints to choose from.' There was not a flicker of recognition at the last name. Straccan sighed. It had been worth a try. 'I like Wulstan myself,' he said. 'Let's call you that for the time being.'

'Right, sir.'

'Two things you had on you,' Straccan said. 'This,' producing the scrap of parchment, 'and in your left-hand pocket, something else.'

Wulstan found the curl and looked at it without recognition. The words on the parchment left him equally blank.

Straccan laughed. 'Never mind, lad. All's not lost. You remember your left from your right.'

Chapter 6

Lepers weren't allowed to enter churches, of course, and most of them didn't give a toss anyway. God had abandoned them; as far as they were concerned He could get stuffed. But this wet morning one of the accursed had left crutch, bell and pack at the foot of the steps and clambered awkwardly to the squint, where he could peer into the church itself. Wisps of white hair clung wetly about his shoulders but he was not old. Just dead.

Not all corpses were decently hidden under the earth. In the lazar houses up and down the country dead men still breathed. Officially, legally, they were dead although they walked, talked, laughed sometimes (but cursed more often), dreamed, suffered and despaired. Cast out from homes, families, communities, rejected with full and appalling ritual by the Church, as abhorrent to God as to mankind. Forced to attend their own funerals – the solemn Mass for the Dead, the symbolic burial, grave dug, priest gabbling – then driven out, often with stones, while priest and kinfolk, smug in their bodily well-being, went home to their hearths, bacon and ale, warm beds and warm bedmates.

Lepers must either beg on the roads or enter that fearful abode of the living dead, the lazar house. So dreadful was the hopeless finality of its walls that many, even the old and feeble, preferred to chance it and beg, always on the move, starving, freezing, ringing the bell or rattling a wooden clack-dish for alms. Shunned, loathed, imploring charity, praying for compassion. Waiting for the final death.

There was no one within the leper's limited field of vision inside the little church but candles burned as always on the altar and through the squint he could see the Holy Rood. It was veiled, of course; the whole of England being under Interdict the face of Christ might not be gazed upon until the Pope lifted his ban. But the cloth had slipped a bit and one spiked hand of the crucified Christ reached towards the leper. His own right hand, clumsy in bandages, moved to sign the cross on his breast.

Back in the cell the leper had left behind in Scotland, a crucifix had hung over his bed. He longed to take this one loved, familiar thing with him, but might only take his crutch and alms dish, bell, and water bottle. In addition to the clothes he wore, his pack held a change of drawers, clean bandages and some food. Round his neck, under the scratchy hospital-issue shirt, hung his purse and a small cross made of olive-wood from Jerusalem: God and Mammon on a single thong.

'Comrade,' he whispered through the grille to the wooden Christ, 'lend me your strength to go on. There's work for me, after all.'

His hands pressed the rolled letter in a pocket inside his shirt. He had its words by heart. It had taken more than half a year to find him, sent at first all the way from Wales to the lazar house at Sainte Colombe in Normandy, which he had left long ago. There it waited until a traveller could be persuaded to take it back across the Channel. Sainte Colombe was too poor to pay anyone to do this service but at last a pilgrim agreed to carry it in exchange for the monks' prayers. On the journey the pilgrim fell sick, the prayers not being sufficient to keep him in health, and was delayed until Christmas. After that the letter made its way in fits and starts whenever anyone could be bothered with it, until at last it reached Scotland, coming to Garnier's hands at the lazar house outside Stirling just before Easter.

From Sulien of Cwm Cuddfan to Garnier the leper, greetings, trusting to God His mercy that thou livest yet. I pray thee, for our old friendship, to come to this our community and take upon thyself the task of Master of the lazar house, and the charge, bodies and souls, of our lepers here.

His old friend would probably have given him up by now but the letter had given Garnier a new lease of life, and with God's help he would get there. He had said his farewells at the lazar house at Stirling, and the medicus had given him an innocent-looking bottle containing the combustible whisky normally reserved for snowbound wayfarers, and only then if they seemed at death's door. The medicus made it himself from an old family recipe; it would raise blisters on a boot.

Garnier stared at the shrouded head of Christ, bowed beneath its wreath of thorns. 'Comrade, you carried your cross. Help me to carry mine. It is a weary way.'

More than three hundred miles he had come already, a weary way for a dead man.

'Comrade, I'll be glad of your company when you're not too busy.'

Descending the wet steps cautiously, he settled the packstrap over his shoulder under the cloak and made sure his mask was securely fixed before picking up bell and crutch. Head down against the wind, he crossed the graveyard. The porter, who had popped inside for a warm, scuttled beetle-like out of the little gatehouse, cursing weather and leper alike, and tugged the heavy gate open once more, just enough to let him edge through.

Garnier looked at the road ahead. Strung alongside it, straggling downhill like irregular lumpy beads on a cord, loomed a few squat thatched huts, each with its bit of ground, chickens, a goat or two and sleeping pig. The houses clotted into a small village at the foot of the slope and here and there light gleamed around the edges of shutters. Picking a way through ruts and refuse, skirting puddles, he started down.

This early there were few folk about and they ignored him. A dog snarled and lunged at him, but a prod from his crutch gave it second thoughts. A child, running from his door, saw the big cloaked figure limping quietly past and whooped happily, looking around for something to throw. Dog turds lay handy, missiles satisfactory to both parties, giving the boy the pleasure of flinging them and his target relief they were not stones.

The road ran south to Shrewsbury where there was a hospice for his kind; he would rest there for a day or two. He had run more than half his gauntlet but the worst lay ahead: the Welsh Marches, the dangerous territory known as Murderers' Country

Chapter 7

Like most travellers, on his journey Straccan picked up letters and messages for delivery at later stopping-places, among them letters for Engelard de Cigony, one of the king's trusted mercenary captains and temporary constable of Ludlow castle since the hasty departure of its former castellan, William de Breos.

Cigony greeted Straccan with an enormous sneeze, flipped the letters to his clerk and invited his visitor to share breakfast, regaling him with an account of his latest bag of outlaws.

'Thick as fleas in a whore's bed,' he said. 'One thing you have to say for Breos—' He paused and Straccan eyed him expectantly, but the constable was in the throes of another massive sneeze. '*A-a-aratcha!*'

'That's a nasty cold you've got, my lord.'

Cigony mopped his nose with a square of linen. 'Damn funny thing, I get one about this time every bloody year and it lasts the whole bloody summer! My wife's tried every remedy she can think of. Nothing works. Where was I? Oh yes, outlaws. Breos did at least keep em down. They don't know me yet; they think I'm a soft touch. Ha! They'll learn! Forty-three we've rounded up this week, and that's just for starters. I've got two new alaunts, splendid dogs, brave as lions, can't wait to try em! The forest'll be safe as a nun's garden by the time I'm through.' Another sneeze hovered, making his eyes water, but came to nothing after all. He wiped his eyes and jammed the hanky up his sleeve.

In his turn Straccan related the story of the man who had lost his memory, and they swopped anecdotes of similar occurrences.

'Yves de Pontgarron,' said Cigony. '*You* know him. Lost an eye at Mirebeau. Farts like a trumpet! Lost *his* memory after his helmet was split in the tilt yard. *Aratcha!* Bugger it! Chinon, it was, in ninety-eight. Got it back but turned nasty. Started knocking his wife about. Mind you, she *was* Welsh. She bolted. Messy business. Big scandal. And what about Auberi d'Umfraville – remember old Dummy?'

Straccan searched his memory and found a cheerful, thuggish face very much the worse for wear.

'No teeth? Broken nose?'

'*That's* the chap! Lost his memory *and* his wits. His wife fetched him one with a cook-pot; caught him at it with their son's wet nurse. Poor sod! Got his memory back after a while but never the same man. *Hell* of a wallop,' the constable said reverently with an oddly nostalgic look in his eye. 'Splendid woman, Constance, splendid . . .'

Time passed amiably, punctuated at intervals by Cigony's ringing sneezes, and Straccan confided to the constable his concern for the man he called Wulstan. 'My business is done and I hardly like to leave him here alone.'

'Not your responsibility, old boy.'

'No.' Straccan fell silent, his memory casting back to his meeting with Bane six years ago when Bane had insisted that by saving his life Straccan had assumed responsibility for him. Now there was another injured man on his hands. Wryly he recalled the sorcerer Rainard de Soulis taunting him, last summer in Scotland, about the 'misfits' he'd gathered round himself, his friends and companions. He grimaced at the thought of Soulis' dreadful death and came full circle again to the matter of Wulstan. Another misfit!

'Tell you what,' Cigony offered, 'I'll have a word with Prior Anselm. The monks'll take care of him until he gets his senses back. Meanwhile I'll have enquiries made, see if anyone knows him.'

'Thank you, my lord.' Straccan got up to go, seeing the constable's squires hovering impatiently by the door. 'I mustn't delay you any longer.'

'Right enough! Things to do, outlaws to catch. Like to come along? I can promise good sport.'

Straccan declined the offer and took his leave, hearing another shattering sneeze as the door closed behind him. The outlaws would have a better than even chance, he reckoned; they'd hear the constable coming a mile off.

A light shower sprinkled him as he crossed the inner bailey. In the stable their horses stood saddled and ready but there was no sign of Bane; he must be fetching their packs. Zingiber wuffled a greeting. Straccan stroked the velvety nose and rubbed the stallion's ears then, stooping, checked the hoof he'd left to Bane and the other three. All well there. Zingiber shifted impatiently, smelling the rain and eager to be away.

'Sir Richard Straccan?'

He turned and saw a man wearing royal livery over his hauberk, a blocky young man, fair-haired with a jutting jaw and intent, intelligent blue eyes. The sword at his hip was plain and businesslike, its leather grip and scabbard well worn. A professional, this one.

'I'm Straccan. Who are you?'

'Bruno von Koln. I come from the king, Sir Richard. He bids you attend on him at Bristol.'

Hell and damnation, thought Straccan. 'Now?'

'*Ja*. I am to escort you there, with your servant Bone.'

'Bane,' said Straccan. 'What does the king want with Bane?'

'Pardon. *Bane*. The king said he must come.' Von Koln shrugged. 'I do not know vy. I see you are ready to ride. *Das ist gut*. Ve lose no time. Vere is Bane?'

Fuming, and with the German mercenary at his heels, Straccan returned to the hall. No Bane, but there, on a bench against the wall, wearing a clean shirt and breeks Straccan recognised as his own, was Wulstan, looking lost.

'Just a minute,' Straccan said. As he made a beeline for Wulstan the German grasped his arm.

'No vun must know the king has sent for you.'

Trailed by Captain von Koln, Straccan crossed the hall and sat down. 'How are you, Wulstan?'

The young man looked up with a shy smile. 'Well enough, thank you sir. My head's healing.' He touched the seared patch gingerly.

'Did you get any breakfast?'

'I don't feel like eating. I keep thinking I ought to *be* somewhere, or *doing* something. Perhaps somebody's worried because I haven't turned up.'

'Be patient. It'll take a while.' He glanced up. The mercenary was right behind him and paying close attention. 'I have to leave Ludlow today. Will you be all right?'

Wulstan's face fell. 'Oh, I . . . Of course. You've been very kind to me, sir. Master Bane gave me these clothes, he even managed to find some shoes to fit me. If, when, I'm myself again I'll repay you somehow.'

'Never mind that. You can put up at the priory until you get your memory back or until someone comes looking for you. The constable has promised to arrange it. I'll see you when I get back.' *Whenever the hell that is*, he thought sourly.

Wulstan looked down at the table. 'You are very good, sir, to be concerned.'

Straccan clapped him on the shoulder. 'Cheer up, lad. It may seem strange but it's better than being dead.'

Bane wasn't in the dormitory either, nor in Straccan's pokey bedchamber. With a sigh, and shadowed by the German, Straccan headed for the kitchen. He should have looked there first.

'Don't be daft,' said Bane, stowing bread and cheese in his already bulging scrip. 'Pass that ham, will you? Ta. He can't want *me*! He doesn't even know I exist! What would he want *me* for?'

'I don't know! *He*' – with a jerk of his head towards Bruno, whose expression of faint amusement was becoming annoying – 'won't say. Have you packed our stuff?'

'Course. I was just getting some extra supplies for the journey.' He stared at the German. 'I hope he's brought his own. We won't be going to see Mistress Janiva now, then?'

'No,' said Straccan, with a face like thunder, 'we won't!'

Chapter 8

The king had left Bristol three days ago.

'No matter,' said Captain von Koln calmly. 'Ve vill follow.'

'Where to?'

'The host sails for Ireland from Cross-on-Sea.'

'Oh, Jesus!'

Bruno smiled thinly. 'Don't vorry, Sir Richard. Ve vill catch up vith the king tomorrow or the day after.'

'Where?'

'Neath, perhaps. If not then Cardiff.'

Straccan groaned.

'Look at it this vay, Sir Richard. Sooner Cardiff than Vaterford, *nein?*'

'Are you serious? Not Ireland!'

'You do not vish this meeting vith the king,' the German observed.

'Noticed that, did you?'

Bruno grinned.

'No,' Straccan said ruefully. 'It's not that; it's just that I had other plans.'

'Involving a lady,' said the German with a sympathetic nod.

'Yes.' Oh God, yes, and what would she be thinking of him now? He'd said he'd come back. Now God alone knew when that might be.

'Vell, the faster ve ride, the sooner you may return.'

Two days later, in a dripping Welsh dawn eight miles or so outside Cardiff, they caught up with the tail end of the royal baggage train and began slogging slowly past.

The servants and functionaries of the royal household straggled over three miles of road, reduced to crawling pace by the heavy wagons which churned and rutted the road to clay-pit consistency and sank to their axles every few yards. It had rained non-stop since Bristol, and the escorting knights, men-at-arms and archers, soaked to the skin and dripping, cursed monotonously as they struggled through the sticky quagmire.

At the front were the king's hawks and dogs, precious creatures most tenderly transported. Then came the lumbering sumpter wagons carrying beds and bedding, coffers full of hangings and draperies, the trappings of the royal bedroom, the king's chairs, cushions, jordan, livery cupboard, bath and all essentials. Next came the wardrobe, with the king's clothes folded in chests, layered with rue and fleabane and sprinkled with pieces of costly amber-gris to perfume the precious fabrics. Tucked somewhere safely among the royal shirts, drawers, robes and tunics were the king's books and jewels, hidden where only his valet Petit knew to find them.

Two long carts were necessary to transport the royal chapel, altar, candlesticks and candles, priest's vestments and the Halidom. Cooks and kitchen clanged and rattled along, pots and pans dangling and jangling, swathed hams and bacons smelling strong, barrels of dried fish and dried fruits, salt and the valuable spice chest, all surrounded by men armed to the teeth to defend the king's dinner.

Workers in the fields straightened and stared. Some waved, some made rude gestures, and when the noisy, seemingly endless procession reached a village small children ran alongside shouting, and bony limping dogs left off scratching to bark the gaudy creaking show along.

The din was unbelievable, and when they had passed it and the train was long out of sight Straccan could still hear the confused noise of shouting, clanging and rumbling wheels. It sounded like a distant battle.

'Not too much off,' said the king.

The barber had finished trimming the royal beard. There was more grey in it now than a year ago but the king's hair was still predominately red. The barber moved round to tidy the curls at the back of the royal neck. A puppy with hair of much the same colour slept in an abandoned position on the king's lap. John's fingers gently circled its tight pink belly in a continuous caress. Beside his chair in a basket slept a reddish long-haired bitch and the rest of her litter, snorting and twitching in snug security.

The last time Straccan had been summoned to the royal presence he'd been kept waiting four days before John found time to see him. This time Bruno von Koln took them straight to the king's private solar, without so much as a bite of breakfast or a chance to wash.

It was pleasantly warm in the room. Scented candles and a brazier cheered the relentlessly dismal morning. There were only a couple of clerks and a brace of pages in attendance, and in one corner a Welsh minstrel played his harp softly.

'Am I getting thin on top?' the king asked.

One of the clerks said hastily 'Your grace's hair is as thick as ever it was.' Over the top of the royal head the barber shot him a may-you-be-forgiven look and winked. Sauce! The clerk stared coldly back.

Outside, rain lashed the shutters, but within the chamber the only sounds were the murmuring harpstrings and the soothing, competent *switch-switch* of the scissors as the barber, snipping, circled the king.

'I once found my father sitting on an upturned bucket in the yard, with a stable boy cutting his hair,' said John suddenly. 'At Chinon, it was. No sense of dignity, my father, yet no one ever dared bugger *him* about the way they do me!'

The barber made a sympathetic sound.

'Even *he* couldn't live for ever, though,' said John. 'Ah, Straccan, there you are! Have you seen his tomb?'

'King Henry's, my lord? Yes. Very fine.'

'All there, they are, at Fontevrault: Dad, Mother, my glorious brother. All very dignified and peaceful and quiet. God's feet, that's a laugh! I can't remember them *ever* quiet! They never talked, you know. Just screamed at one another. My brothers too. Henry used to shout at everyone, Geoffrey was always yelling about something and as for Richard, well, you know what he was like. I remember them all *purple* with fury! I thought it was the normal colour for grown-ups, when I was small.' He nibbled at a scrap of loose skin on the side of his thumb, pulling until it tore sharply into the quick flesh.

'I've seen my father so mad with rage he'd roll on the floor and bite the rushes.' He kicked at those underfoot. 'And they weren't kept sweet and clean like mine. Months old and full of dogshit. No wonder they call us the Devil's Brood! Do you believe in ghosts?'

Startled, Straccan said, 'I don't know, my lord. I've never seen one.'

'Haven't you? Lucky man. They're everywhere. That's why you won't catch me lying at Fontevrault when my time's up. Imagine the squabbling that goes on when there's no one there to hear them.'

The barber finished and was waved away. John set the puppy back among its siblings and the bitch wagged her tail and licked his fingers lovingly. As he took a handful of dates from a silver bowl a page darted forward to offer a perfumed napkin. The king wiped his sticky fingers and turned to Straccan.

'Thank you for coming, Sir Richard. You've had a wet time of it. That's Wales for you. I don't know why I bother with it. You've brought your man, I see.'

Bane shifted uneasily as the king's green gaze fixed on him.

'As you ordered, sire.'

'Ordered?' John looked surprised. 'Did I? I can't think why.'

I can, thought Straccan. *You didn't want anyone to find out you'd sent for me. Your captain kept us together so Bane couldn't tell anyone. Why's that, I wonder? What's going on?*

The harper paused to tighten a string and in the sudden silence Bane's belly gave a long loud rumble. Straccan had never seen him blush before.

36

The king laughed. 'Forgive me, Master Bane! You are both soaked and haven't had a chance to break your fast. Bruno, take them to the bath house and get them some dry clothes. I'll see you later, Straccan, when you've had something to eat.'

'He knew my name,' Bane muttered uneasily as they followed Bruno across the hall. 'How'd he know my name?'

'It's nothing to vorry about,' said Bruno, overhearing. 'The king vants to know everything about everyvun he meets. He vill know vere you ver born, who your father vas—'

'Huh! He knows more than my mum did, then,' growled Bane.

When Straccan returned the king wasted no time.

'Relics are your business, Straccan; have you heard of the Pendragon Banner?'

'Of course, sire. It belonged to Uther Pendragon and after him to Arthur his son. But like the Graal it has been lost since King Arthur died. That's all I know.'

'Fortunately Wace here has learned a bit more,' said the king, crooking a finger at one of the clerks. 'Come, Robert, tell us all about it. Sit down, Straccan, and pay attention.'

Robert Wace came forward, bringing with him an overpowering scent of violets and an air of suppressed intensity. Peering at his note-tablet, he cleared his throat importantly.

'The Banner was indeed King Arthur's. In Nennius' writings it is described as a swallowtail pennant of white silk, embroidered with a scarlet dragon. The saintly Abbot Gildas wrote that it was borne before Arthur in all his battles, and that while he had it he could not be defeated, for stitched into it' – Straccan looked up curiously at the sudden quaver in the clerk's voice – 'was a linen n-napkin stained with the sacred b-blood of our Lord Christ.' He crossed himself as did Straccan and, after a moment, the king also.

'There can be no greater relic,' Wace said eagerly. 'None more precious! Only the Crown of Thorns could equal it!'

The king had taken an orange from a silver dish at his elbow and was peeling it, popping segments into his mouth as Wace continued.

'Saint Joseph the Arimathean brought the relic to Glastonbury, where it was kept for many years until Uther sacreligiously tore it from the altar and took it for his own. When Arthur became king he had the precious thing sewn into his war pennant, and was never defeated until the traitor Mordred stole the Banner and slew Arthur in his last battle. After that no one knows what became of it.'

'Until now, perhaps.' The king leaned back in his chair and took up the tale, the harper's chords providing an apposite accompaniment.

'At Eastertide,' John began, 'a woman died in the hospital at Cwm Cuddfan in Wales: a Danish lady called Ragnhild. She came to England ten years ago to marry an English lord, and as part of her dowry she brought a relic that had been treasured in her family for hundreds of years: the Pendragon Banner.

'But there was a storm. The bride-ship was wrecked in the Severn Sea and all aboard perished save Ragnhild and Hallgerd her maidservant. They were taken to a priory of the Penitent Sisters near Avonmouth. The river warden sent word to me of the wreck and the maidens, and *I* sent word to Ragnhild's father in the Danes' land to let him know his daughter was alive. But once he'd seen her safe aboard – as he thought – her father had raised rebellion against King Valdemar and he and all his kin had been put to death. So the lady had neither home nor family, all her goods were lost with the ship and the man she was to marry repudiated her for a wealthier bride.'

'What became of her?' Straccan asked.

The king shrugged. 'It was a bad time just then. I was busy elsewhere, new-come to my crown. There was trouble in Brittany – there's *always* trouble in Brittany, and there was rebellion in Poitou. What with one thing and another I'm afraid the Danish maidens slipped my mind. The pity of it was they believed themselves to be prisoners at the convent and ran away.' John spread his hands in an eloquent gesture of helplessness.

'The winter was hard that year. They were caught in a blizzard. They found some poor shelter but with no food, no fire . . .' He sighed. 'Men hunting wolves found them but by then the maid was dead.

'Ragnhild however survived. When I was reminded of her I made what amends I could – a dowry, a husband. When she fell ill she was taken to Cwm Cuddfan, to Sulien's hospital. Before she died she told him about the Banner.'

There was more to come. Straccan waited.

'When the ship struck, they feared what might befall. Ragnhild was a great lord's daughter; if they were rescued she might be held for ransom or forced into a demeaning marriage. Such things happen. So she stripped off her rings and Hallgerd put them on. Until they knew themselves safe, the lady would pretend to be the maidservant. If they fell into honest hands and were delivered to her betrothed, that would be the time for truth.

'With the ship sinking beneath them Ragnhild took the Banner from her dower chest and tied it round her neck under her cloak, and buckled her girdle around herself and Hallgerd so they should not be lost from each other and the power of the relic would save them both. And so it did.

'But when they found themselves captive – as they thought – and learned that Ragnhild was penniless, without kin or home and cast off by her betrothed, they kept up the pretence. To the end. The maid who died in the snow was the lady Ragnhild, and the one who survived—'

'Was the serving-maid,' said Straccan.

'Yes. Quite like a ballad, isn't it? So sad. I must get Madoc here to set it to music.'

'Is that why you sent for me, my lord? To get the Banner for you?'

John arched his eyebrows. 'You're the expert. I apologise for the short notice. I've only just found out about all this, you see.'

Straccan frowned. 'How *did* you learn about it, my lord, after all this time?'

'That doesn't concern you.'

'I think it does, sire. You may not be the only one to know about it. That makes it my concern.'

John smiled. 'You will just have to get to it first, won't you?'

'*Is* someone else after it?'

'I shouldn't be surprised; word gets around. There's no time to lose. It wouldn't do at all, politically you understand, for this relic to fall into the hands of, oh, the Bretons, for instance, and become a rallying point for traitors. There are traitors everywhere.' John paused, his green gaze cold. '*Straccan*,' he mused. 'Curious name, but of course it was *Estraccan* at one time, wasn't it? A Breton name.'

Straccan's stomach gave an uneasy twist. 'My grandsire's father came over from Brittany in Red William's time, more than a hundred years ago. I've no kin there now and no allegiance. You speak of traitors, my lord,' he said boldly. 'Do you think I'm one?'

John got up and walked to the window, pushing the shutter aside and scowling at the rain. 'No . . . No, of course not. God's feet, what a climate! But talking of traitors, do you know William de Breos?'

'I've heard of him.'

'Who hasn't?' said the king bitterly. 'He's in Ireland just now, brewing treason, but I'm going to chase him out. He'll run back to Wales where he still has friends. Somehow I don't think it'll be long before he starts looking for this thing. You may run into him. And although you don't know *him*, I'm sure you'll recognise his companion.'

'Who's that, my lord?'

'An old acquaintance of yours – mine too – Julitta de Beauris.' He saw Straccan's face change. 'I see you remember the lady.'

Shock had frozen Straccan for a moment, but in the same instant a blazing core of rage lit within him. 'Sire, do you think I could forget? That hell-witch kidnapped my daughter! She tried to murder her!'

'There you are, then – a chance to settle old scores,' said the king lightly. 'I'm sure you'll think of something suitable. As long as she's still alive when you've finished with her.' He grinned wolfishly. '*My* turn then.'

'Where—' Straccan's voice broke hoarsely. 'Where is she?'

'Still in Ireland, but not for long. He *will* be looking for the Banner. You had better get to it before he does.'

'Where is it, then, my lord?'

John looked speculatively at him. 'That's an interesting problem, Straccan. You see, Ragnhild hid it. She never told anyone where.'

Chapter 9

Janiva filled her scrying bowl with water, signed the cross over it and cupped her palms against its rough sides. Emptying her mind of the day's small happenings, breathing deeply, she gazed into the water and waited.

There was her reflection, oval face framed in russet hair, braids plaited with green wool. For a moment she looked into her own brown eyes and then it was as if she gazed into a deep bright well. Far down was a swirl of movement, where glints of colour, and then images began to rise. Small, bright, they swam up one after the other to the surface, where each was broken and scattered by the next.

Once again, as she had for weeks now, she saw . . .

Fire, and herself in the midst of it.

Rivulets of flame licking her bare feet, rippling up around her body . . . her gown catching fire, gone in an instant, leaving her naked in the flames . . . her outstretched hands trying to push the fire away . . . her hair blazing in an aureole of flame around her head . . .

It was gone. There was just water in the bowl.

But when she signed the cross over the water it felt as if someone was hanging onto her arm to prevent it.

'Blessed Mother, protect me!' Even her tongue seemed stiff, the words hard to shape. Chilled, trembling, she sat for a while before carrying the bowl into the garden where she tipped the water onto the earth. For an instant she thought she saw glints of green, like the glance of green eyes through the splashing water, but they were only wet leaves gleaming.

Her hand jerked, and the bowl that had been her mother's, and which she valued more than anything else she possessed, slipped from her grasp, fell and smashed on a stone.

'Oh no!' She bent, touched the broken pieces, picked up one, and another, then let them drop. Softly she said, 'I'm so sorry!'

It was just a common black glazed bowl but she had treasured it. Its breaking seemed an ill thing. *Another* ill thing, for nothing had gone well at Shawl since Sir Guy's sudden death. Dame Alienor ailed though she denied it. The bones showed sharply in her cheeks and wrists, and her gowns hung loosely on her body and had to be taken in. Now and then she had to fight for breath, and at such times her lips and cheeks took on a bluish tinge. A bad sign, Janiva knew: the sign of a worn and failing heart.

And there was Richard; what did he expect of her? Last year she had refused to marry him but at Easter he had asked her again. She had put him off with scant courtesy, her grief for Sir Guy still raw and anxiety for Dame Alienor gnawing at her. Father and mother they had been to her since her own mother died. Was that why she had been so sharp with Richard? Because his presence was an intrusion into her grief and fear? Or was it because her treacherous body had wished for nothing so much as to fall into his arms and be held and comforted? And if she had, would that have been so bad a thing?

Too late to fret about it now. He had not come back. So why did she feel so desolate? Wasn't that what she wanted?

Tears overflowed. '*Absit omen,*' she murmured, and began to pick up the pieces carefully with cold fingers that still shook.

At the sound of hooves approaching Janiva stood up, cradling the shards between her palms. There were two riders, strangers: a woman, richly dressed, short, plump and blonde, attended by a boy. The woman's palfrey snorted alarm at Janiva's sudden appearance, flinching and sidling until its rider, wrenching cruelly on the bit, got control.

'Damn you,' she cried angrily. 'You frightened my mare!'

'I'm sorry,' Janiva said. 'Do you want me?'

43

The woman – no, she was just a girl, not more than fourteen or so – stared. Her prominent blue eyes were unfriendly. She snapped her fingers and her attendant slid from his pony, running to help her down. To Janiva's surprise this stranger walked straight into the cottage, gazing around curiously. Janiva followed. A pot simmered over the fire and the girl peered into it, sniffing.

'Mass, but you eat well. There's meat in there,' she said incredulously. 'Where's your husband?'

With sudden dismay Janiva realised this must be Richildis, her foster-brother's bride.

'I am not married, madame,' she said.

Richildis walked around the room fingering things. She picked up the spindle and put it down again, touched the wooden cook-spoons, even lifted the dividing curtain and stared at the second bed.

'Who sleeps there, then?' she asked, raising an eyebrow.

'Whoever is sick. Whoever I am tending.' Janiva lifted the pot to a higher hook, away from the flames.

'You are a leechwife?'

'I have some skill in healing,' Janiva said.

'Do you sell love potions?'

She couldn't help laughing. 'No! I make medicines for the sick.' She heard another horse outside and a man's voice, the lad answering. Her foster-brother appeared at the door.

'There you are,' said Roger to his wife, panting. 'I've been looking for you. You mustn't gallop like that, you might get hurt. Good day, Janiva.' Beaming, he took her hand.

Richildis looked from her husband to Janiva and flushed unbecomingly.

'I'm glad you've met,' Roger blundered on, man-like, noticing nothing. 'I was going to bring you here, sweetheart, but you rode ahead so fast I lost you.'

Richildis scowled. 'Why should you bring me here? Are we to visit all your villeins?'

Roger said, 'Janiva is my sister, my foster-sister,' and stood there looking large and stupid.

Richildis recovered quickly, her frown smoothing out. 'I see.' She walked to the door, passing Janiva without a glance, tossing the words back over her shoulder. 'Well mistress, still unwed? We must find a husband for you.'

'You are kind, madame,' said Janiva, 'but I do very well as I am.'

Richildis laid a possessive hand on her husband's arm. 'Surely there must be one among your servants who will marry her?'

Roger looked embarrassed. 'My sister will do as she pleases,' he snapped. He took his wife by her elbow and pulled her out of the house. 'Say no more on that,' he hissed into her resentful face. 'Janiva's a free woman. Apologise to her!'

The girl's face was scalded with colour but she turned obediently to Janiva.

'Your pardon, mistress. My lord rebukes me.'

Before Janiva could reply Roger's wife had scrambled into her saddle and driven spurs into her mare's sides. The horse squealed and galloped away, its hooves sending leaves and sods of earth flying, with the servant dashing after her.

Roger leaped onto his own horse and sped after them, shouting back to Janiva 'There's to be a feast! I'll see you then!'

'Oh, Roger,' said Janiva wretchedly to his retreating and oblivious back. 'Why did you make so much of it? Better to have laughed it off. Now she will always dislike me.'

And hard on the heels of that came the chill thought: *She is mistress here.*

Chapter 10

'I don't like it,' Bane said as they rode out of Cardiff, their cloaks already sodden and heavy by the time they reached the gate. 'Why us? He's got a whole army after the lord de Breos.'

'He wants Julitta,' Straccan said. *She made a fool of him*, he thought, *and of me, too.* 'He won't rest until he gets her.' *Nor will I.*

'What about this Banner thing? Is it true, d'you think, or just bait for Breos?'

'God knows!' He'd been wondering that himself, turning the story over and over in his mind and coming up with nothing but more unanswerable questions.

It was a fine tale, and parts of it – the shipwreck, the rescued girls – had to be true. But the Pendragon Banner? Could the Danish bride's relic really be the battle pennant of King Arthur, lost for seven hundred years? Or was the whole thing an intriguing fabrication, bait, as Bane said, for Lord William? Why would Breos want it, anyway? What was Julitta's part in all this? And why had the king suddenly flung Straccan's Breton ancestry at him and talked of treason? If it was meant to warn him, he was warned! He had his orders, to find the Banner 'with all speed', and by God he'd have to try. In John's service, failure wasn't an option.

'Are we going to Shawl first?' Bane asked.

'Ludlow first, I'm out of money. You'll have to go to Shawl alone and tell Janiva what's happened.'

'What's the chances of finding this Banner?'

'Small!' But however small, the king had commanded him to find it. Even if the whole thing was no more than the fevered ravings of a dying woman, he had no choice; it was a royal command. He must obey.

What did he have to go on? Precious little. The shipwrecked maidens had been taken to a priory of the Penitent Sisters near Avonmouth; that much was fact. The river warden, Maurice de Lacy, had notified the king, wrecks and anything of value found in them being royal perks. If there *was* a relic Ragnhild had somehow managed to hide it, and then died without revealing its hiding place even to her faithful companion.

All right, he thought. *Supposing it's true, where could she have hidden it?* Somewhere in the priory seemed most likely; he'd have to start there. But no, the girls had run away. Surely Ragnhild would have taken it with her. They had wandered off and got lost in the forest and if she had hidden the relic somewhere in the greenwood that was that. It was lost for ever.

The more he thought about it, the more hopeless the task seemed.

For the next two days the rain never stopped. Flooded roads slowed their progress, impassable fords and washed-out bridges forced them miles out of their way, compounding misery and frustration. But there was worse to come: during the afternoon of the second day massive thunderheads piling up in the west spread and raced towards them, growing ever darker until with a fierce bellow of wind the storm broke upon them.

Lightning rent the sky followed by a great cracking roll of thunder and within moments rain was falling so densely that it was impossible to see anything ahead and so heavily that grass and plants were smashed flat. Water ran in streamlets down every slope, frothing, treacle-brown, and filling ditches and gullies to overflowing.

Bane, splashing ahead, shouted something which the wind whipped away. He pointed, and Straccan, wiping the rain from his eyes, thankfully saw the shelter of broken walls and part of a roof, an old deserted shrine.

They urged the horses in an awkward scramble up a steep bank, pushing in through the bramble and nettle camouflage of years.

The broken flagstones were thick with emerald moss and ivy clothed the walls. Rowans had forced their way up through the floor.

Presently they were joined in their refuge by a hare, which crouched quivering at Straccan's feet, its fur flattened and soaked but its blue-glazed eyes dark and calm. He was careful not to move.

There were fluttering sounds and presently Straccan realised that the branches of the stunted sturdy rowans were crowded with birds of all kinds: finches, redbreasts, sparrows and starlings, titmice and blackbirds, dunnocks, even an owl. They clustered in rows like feathery fruit, with occasional small stirring of wings, puffing of breasts and soft chirps. Their bright dark eyes glinted like small beads and he could hear the scrape of tiny claws shifting their grip on the twigs and branches.

The steady roar of the falling rain continued. Bane, asleep now, snored gently. Straccan gazed wonderingly at the creatures about him and wished Janiva could see this.

Rain battered relentlessly at the shelter and thunder rolled, further away now. Zingiber snorted softly and the fawn tensed, but relaxed again. Straccan looked round their sanctuary once more, marvelling, then leaned his head back against the wall and closed his eyes.

Jesu, of your mercy, watch over my daughter.

Gilla . . . she was safe, thank God, in the convent at Holystone, where the nuns had cared for her since her mother's death eight years ago. Straccan smiled at the memory of his last visit there, when they'd picnicked in the priory garden, making plans for Gilla's homecoming at the end of this year. She would be twelve in November. Time to think of her future . . . he put the thought away. Not now. There was plenty of time. He would lose her soon enough, to a husband or to the convent, if that was her choice. *And Jesu, of your mercy, keep Janiva from scathe.*

Janiva . . . he couldn't go to her now. He had no doubt John's paid eyes would be watching his every move. When they got to Ludlow he'd send Bane to her with a letter. Saying he loved her, that the king's command, unexpected and unwelcome, kept him from her; that he was sorry; that he would come as soon as he could.

Jesu, of your mercy . . .

He slept.

Chapter 11

Bridges were always in need of repair. They cracked and crumbled, were penetrated by rain and split by frost. Gaps were bridged by planks which rotted and fell, or broke under the weight of carts. Rivers swelled and swept away trees which buffeted the piers and often broke the arches above.

The wonder was not that so many bridges fell but that any stood at all, given their age (a lot were Roman), the hazards of the weather and the reluctance of those who collected the tolls to fork out for any maintenance. The bridge across the Wye near Clasbrig was the responsibility of the bishop, who had shrugged off the inconvenient matter of repairs for years, and last night's storm had finally done for it.

Three people had the ill luck to be crossing when the flood-waters hit the bridge. A wall of muddy water several feet high and filled with tumbling debris had surged down the river with a great roaring noise, striking the old bridge with tremendous force, carrying away an entire arch at one end, together with the toll-collector in his hut and a pedlar with his pack mule who had just paid to cross. Almost at the same time a great tree trunk bashed the pier at the other end, and it vanished in the boil of water as if made of sand. The central arch stood a moment longer, then slewed and fell away, leaving the two central piers jutting up above the torrent about twelve feet apart, and on one of those piers two other travellers – a young woman with a black palfrey, and a leper.

The leper crouched beneath the palfrey's belly, bandaged hands over his ears – or where they would have been if he still had any – eyes shut, lipless mouth behind his mask mumbling prayers. The girl, white with shock, held the horse's head and bound her veil over its eyes. It trembled but stood rock-still. She looked at the leper, horror overwhelmed by pity, amazed that life should still be so dear to one so dreadfully afflicted. She wondered how long it would be before their shuddering pinnacle of safety also succumbed to the continual blows of trees and tumbling rocks.

'Don't be afraid,' she said to the pitiful creature, trying to keep her voice from shaking. 'Someone will surely see us. We'll be saved.'

Over his mask, the lashless blue eyes creased at the corners as he looked at her. She had the ridiculous feeling that he was actually smiling!

'Bless you, mistress, I'm not afraid,' he said huskily. 'It's your safety I pray for, and the souls of that luckless pedlar and the tollman.'

It was so dark that the coming of night made little difference. Regular bolts of lightning illuminated the strange tableau – horse, girl, leper – as still as the stone they perched upon.

Straccan woke to an unaccustomed silence and a smell of burning. The rain had stopped. The wild creatures had gone and so had Bane. Wet branches showered drops all over him as he pushed his way out of the shelter. The horses stood ready saddled and Bane had a small fire going, with a pot of ale suspended over it, and was making toast, hacking chunks from a loaf he'd liberated from the royal kitchen at Cardiff and offering them to the flames on the end of a long stick. A pile of calcined pieces lay beside him.

'When you entered my service,' Straccan said, eyeing a black-ened crust critically, 'you told me you could cook. Gave the truth a bit of a polish there, didn't you?'

'They just want a bit of a scrape.' Bane seized a knife and suited action to word. 'There!'

Straccan inspected the cindery nugget. 'I suppose I've had worse.'

Breakfasting on toast dunked in hot ale, they looked about them at the tide-wrack of the storm. The stony track they'd been following was lost under a steady flow of brown water. The storm had turned hillsides into cataracts, bowling rocks and stones from their beds, washing shallow-rooted bushes and heather into tangled heaps sometimes too high to get over. Drowned rabbits, moles and hedgehogs lay about, and marooned on a small mound, grumbling, was a cross and scruffy badger.

They led the horses, picking their way delicately among tumbled rocks and barriers of brushwood, skirting boiling streams where none had been yesterday, and wading through knee- and thigh-deep torrents when there was no easy way round.

After a wild and terrifying night, dawn found the swollen river running high, overflowing the lower bank and flooding the land on that side. The gale and rain had abated during the night but a stiff wind still blew. The stranded travellers were half dead with wet and cold. The leper thought wistfully of the flask in his satchel; he really could do with a couple of mouthfuls but as the young woman couldn't share it he must go without.

Now and again came the thud of something hitting the piers but incredibly they still stood, and around them a tangled mass of roots, tree trunks, broken branches, bushes and other flotsam – the sodden bodies of sheep, a broken boat, pieces of thatch – had accumulated. They were on a little island in the middle of destruction and as far as the eye could see there was no sign of habitation or humanity.

As the morning wore on the mass of rubbish caught and held even more debris, considerably slowing the force of the water which found its way round the blockage by pouring over the lower bank. Shallow floodwater now covered the land on that side, with trees and bushes and small mounds rising out of it, and a few surviving sheep clumped together bleating mournfully on small soggy islets.

The leper grunted, and reached across the horse's back to tug the girl's mantle. Raising her head she saw a large flat-bottomed boat rowed round the bend past a clump of dripping willows. The boatman came to rest against the mass of flotsam, holding onto it to keep the boat steady, and shouting up at them.

'I don't do this for love, you know!'

'How much?' the young woman cried.

'Shillin.'

She gasped with shock. It was an absurd sum. 'That's too much!'

'That's inflation for you. There's an Interdict on, you know.'

'I've only got ninepence.'

'That'll do.' He leered at her. 'Seein as it's you. Jump down.'

'The others too.'

'What?'

'My horse and this man,' she said stubbornly.

'Bugger that! You'll never get the horse in!'

'We can if you help.'

'Well, maybe. But I'm not taking *that* thing,' pointing at the leper.

'If you want the money take all of us.'

'Stuff your money,' snarled the boatman. 'I'm not having any filthy lepers in my boat! You'll sing another tune by night-time!' And he pulled slowly away, past the obstacles, and let the boat drift out of sight around the bend behind the willows.

The girl burst into tears, but presently wiped her eyes and nose on her wet mantle and met the leper's lashless inflamed gaze over the horse's back.

'God will reward you, mistress,' he husked.

She wiped her nose on her mantle. 'Let's hope he sends us another boat, then.'

'Who are you, mistress?'

'Alis of Devilstone.'

'My name was Garnier.'

During the cold grey day the flood subsided until the river no longer overran the banks but poured, still swift and muddy, between them, occasionally adding another bush or dead sheep and once a drowned man to their barricade. The wind died away in the late afternoon. It was dusk and a gauzy mist was thickening when they saw the boatman returning. The mist hung over the water so that he seemed to float eerily on cloud. He didn't bother to come over to the pier but hung onto some of the debris alongside the bank and bellowed, 'Changed your mind?'

'No!'

'Rot, then!' He began to drift away downriver, but just then two horsemen, one behind the other, came slopping through the flooded meadow, round the river's bend into the reeds at the bank. Reining in, they stared first at the pier and those upon it, and then at the boat on the far side.

'Ferry!' shouted the foremost rider.

'Shillin!' the boatman bawled back. 'Each!'

The man gave a snort, half amusement, half disgust, and beckoned the boatman across. The broad clumsy craft surged heavily over the water, grounding in the reeds, and the first rider led his horse, uneasy but obedient, into it.

On the pier they watched the boat's passage and saw the rider lead the animal ashore, up the steep bank on the far side, while the boat went back for the other man and deposited him in turn on the bank. The watchers on the bridge saw the first passenger spring down the bank back into the boat, heard a screech of dismayed surprise and saw some sort of scuffle. Presently the boat was rowed towards them, and as it drew close they saw the traveller sitting with his sword drawn, its point waving gently between the chest and throat of the boatman as if uncertain which to pierce first.

The boat bumped into the flotsam, and their rescuer made it fast to a protruding root.

'Get up there and help them down,' he said, giving the boatman a shove.

Whining, cursing, the man clambered over the heaving tangle of branches and rubbish. His nose was bleeding and blood from his split upper lip had sheeted his chin.

It wasn't easy getting the palfrey into the boat, terrified, stiff and awkward, but the girl jumped, scorning the boatman's hands, and the leper slid unaided. As the boatman made to jump back down the stranger slipped the rope off and the boat swung away from the pier. The boatman hit the water with an enormous splash and surfaced, grasping at the tangled branches and swearing horribly. The stranger seized the oars and thrust the boat towards the bank.

'Folk'll be along in the morning,' he shouted, adding in a normal voice, 'more's the pity!' To his new companions he continued, 'There's a village just over the hill; there'll be food and beds, and we can get dry there.'

Alis said, 'Who are you, sir?'

'My name is Straccan.'

The boat jarred against the bank. Straccan made it fast and helped Alis out, Bane reaching an arm to pull her up the slippery bank. The leper managed well enough, using his crutch to haul himself up the bank. They looked back at the ruins of the bridge. On the pier, silhouetted against the last westering light of the evening, a little figure leaped and waved its arms; its howling could faintly be heard even above the steady rushing of the river.

Chapter 12

Janiva had put on her best gown and a brave face, and taken her place at one of the tables below the dais. This feast, the first since Sir Guy's death, was a chance for friends and neighbours who had missed the wedding last summer to see the young couple and bring gifts, besides wishing Sir Roger good fortune before he left in a few days' time to put his case to the king.

Sir Guy's death had cost the manor dear. Sir Roger must win royal favour if he hoped to keep his inheritance. That meant thrusting himself forward to gain the king's notice, taking expensive men-at-arms to join the king's Irish expedition and parting, inevitably, with substantial sums of money to ensure the king's goodwill.

To finance this and outfit its new lord in style the manor had been tallaged and some minor properties sold. One way or another Shawl was feeling the pinch, but Dame Alienor had done her best at short notice to put on a show. Course after course came in to the uncertain accompaniment of a wobbly trumpet, and there was even professional entertainment.

The tumblers were out of puff now, having a rest in the rushes, swigging ale and sneaking out one at a time to try their luck with the kitchen girls. The musicians still piped and squeaked, though they'd drunk too much to know or care what they were playing, but that didn't matter because the feast had gone on for hours and most of the diners were too drunk to notice.

Several ladies had retired behind the vomiting cloths held up by their attendants. Two of the male guests were fast asleep, one with his face in his pudding. Under the table the dogs snarled over bones and scraps. Dame Alienor rummaged secretly with both hands at the side-lacings of her gown, trying to ease it, but the damned cords had gone into knots and she couldn't work them loose.

Bride and groom sat side by side. At Richildis' other hand sat her chaplain, Benet Finacre, a thin pallid man made for candlelit closets and dark corners. A limp ring of ash-coloured hair circled his tonsure and the bare skin atop his head showed no sign of outdoor weathering. He and Richildis leaned together to speak over the general din, and from time to time he glanced down at Janiva as if she was the subject of their talk.

Richildis was overwhelmed by her finery. There were so many rings on her plump fingers that she could not bend them to pick up food and, like a baby bird, she opened her mouth obediently for her husband to pop in titbits. Roger was very drunk and had missed her mouth several times, spilling sauces and custards down the front of her gown.

From her seat below the dais Janiva could see sweat standing like blisters on the bride's brow and the bloodless flesh around her lips. When Richildis' eyes rolled back to show their whites as she slid from her seat to the floor in a faint, Janiva was there before Roger could sort his legs out and stand up.

Women pressed round, elbowing Finacre out of the way. Janiva loosened the tight lacing at the girl's throat and breasts, blotting the sweat from the waxy face with Richildis' own veil. Red glossy faces ringed the tableau, bending over the fallen girl, reeking of food, wine and vomit and giving off enough heat to fry an egg. Murmurs of alarm were rising.

'Roger,' Janiva said sharply, 'get her out of here. Get someone to carry her to bed. Let her lie in her shift. Bathe her face with cool water.'

Her foster-brother was on his knees patting ineffectually at his wife's limp hand.

'My lord Roger!' This time her voice brought a gust of sobriety to him; his slack mouth snapped shut and he stood to bawl orders.

'Stand back,' said Janiva, getting up. 'Give her air.' Obediently they shuffled aside, just enough to let Lady Alienor through.

Alienor grabbed Janiva's shoulder. 'What's the matter with her?'

'It's all right,' Janiva said quickly, seeing the fear in Alienor's eyes. 'It's just the baby.'

Richildis' eyelids fluttered open and her eyes fixed on Janiva. With a weak sob she clutched her husband's arm as he leaned over to raise her.

'Don't let that witch come near me,' she said. She said it very clearly.

Flushed avid faces stared at Janiva, eyes shifting uneasily aside as she turned away. Alienor and the other women were supporting Richildis to the stair, Roger flapping uselessly in their wake. Family and guests thronged at the foot of the stair passing the good news from mouth to mouth.

'An heir!'

'With child already!'

'Well done! Good old Rodge!'

Janiva stepped down from the dais and walked quickly out of the hall. Benet Finacre, following in the women's wake, paused on the stair and watched her leave. Back in her cottage she lit the fire, the dry kindling flaring fast to throw her stooped shadow on the wall. Humped, black . . .

Witch!

She fed the bright little flames until the fire burned steadily, holding her shaking hands to the heat, spreading the fingers so they seemed edged with flame, clasping them together until the trembling stopped. Outside an owl hooted, answered by another farther away. A vixen yapped and a rabbit, dying, screamed. She shivered.

Witch.

It was only a word, a good word in the old days. It meant Wise One, whether man or woman. But now few used the name in the old way, as a term of respect and trust. Now, more and more, *witch* was a foul name, a term of abuse used in fear.

It was the reason she'd given Straccan when she refused to marry him: '*It will do you no good to have a wife whom folk call witch.*' That was true, but wasn't there another truth? Wasn't the deeper reason that she feared to hand herself over – heart, mind, and body – into another's keeping?

The precious time she needed to learn, to practise and grow in power and become more than a village spaewife, would instead be spent here, there and everywhere in diminishing ways, if she was wife, lover, mother . . .

Her own mother had said it, that the wise grew strong in solitude, just as God's holy hermits did, away from the distractions of human love. Power stretched thin when the mind must be divided between love and learning. Already she had not that single-minded devotion to her craft and skills which had always come naturally; her heart and mind were tugged two ways, off balance.

Easier for a man, of course, she thought wryly. *Wise men can wed. Wived and cared for, they still have all the time they need to pursue their art.*

Her mother, villein-born, part of the manor livestock, had no choice – she wed and bred at her lord's bidding – but Janiva, being free, was also free to choose. Power or love? It was not possible to have both. The chill suspicion she was afraid to face and kept pushing away now surged up and overwhelmed her. She could deny it no longer. Her powers were failing.

Scrying, that simplest of her abilities, now brought only horrifying visions of burning. The spells she spoke over her medicines, charging them with energy to increase their healing properties, no longer worked. When she tended those on the manor who were sick or injured she no longer felt the glow that had always until now burned like cold fire, passing from her hands into the ailing or damaged body of the patient.

She was losing her magic and felt suffocated by an unbearable sense of loss and despair. Close to tears, she clenched her hands until her nails dug into the flesh of her palms and the sharp pain focused her thoughts once more.

She had thought to stay here all her life (but had not thought to grow old), here where she knew everyone and thought of all as friends. Would they still think of her as *friend* now that Richildis had called her *witch*?

Why did Richildis dislike her so? Could she have learned that Roger had wanted to marry her, his foster-sister, and had only agreed to marry Richildis when reluctantly convinced that Janiva would never marry him? Was it jealousy that goaded her?

I must make the best of it, she thought. *When she's here, I'll keep out of her way. There's no need to be upset because of a fainting girl's spite.*

To give Straccan the answer he wanted would mean leaving Shawl, her home, her work, Dame Alienor, all the people she knew and cared for. It would also take her away from Richildis and her malice. Yet for her foster-brother's sake and for the girl's own, she could not leave without trying to righten Richildis' ill will.

The quick fire had dwindled and gave no heat. Janiva shivered. It had never crossed her mind that she might not be safe in her own home.

Chapter 13

With everything else out of season hunting outlaws was a welcome pastime, having the double advantage of pleasure and profit for there was a shilling bounty on each man's head, dead or alive, as for a wolf's head; outlaws and wolves being in law one and the same.

The hunting party assembled in the inner bailey of Ludlow castle, where the horses stamped and snorted and their dung was shovelled up as it fell. Hounds strained at the leashes, whining with eagerness. Friends of the constable, servants and hangers-on mingled, waiting for Cigony to join them, passing the time comparing outlaws' reputations and damning their chances.

Having left Alis in the care of Cigony's wife – the leper had taken himself to the lazar house outside the town – Straccan came upon the constable on the stairs.

'I won't delay you, my lord. I just wondered if there was any news of Wulstan.'

'Who?' The constable looked no better. His nose was red and his eyes watering.

'The man who lost his memory, my lord.'

'Oh, him! God's teeth, yes!' Leaning through the window Cigony bellowed, 'Hang on, you lot, I'll not be long!' As he turned back to Straccan one of his massive sneezes caught him unawares, making him stagger and lean against the wall. 'Oh God!' He mopped his nose. 'Your man's a bad lot, I'm afraid. He's in prison.'

'What's he done?'

'Murder. And theft.'

The victim's widow had come to Ludlow to report the murder, and the coroner had gone back with her to examine the body of her husband and find the murderer. Suspicion pointed at the one man missing from the manor – Wulstan.

'Who *is* Wulstan, then, my lord?'

'Real name's Havloc. Steward at some little pisspot manor in the March. Killed his master.' Cigony snapped his fingers irritably. 'What was his name? Drogo, that's it!'

'Has Wul— Has Havloc got his memory back?'

'Not a glimmer.'

'What's he supposed to have stolen?'

'A gold cup, entrusted to him to sell.'

A cup. There had been something about a cup. What was it? Of course – the scrap of vellum in the unconscious man's hand. *Cymbium Vulstani sum.*

'My lord,' said Straccan urgently, 'who can tell me more about this accusation?'

'See the coroner. He knows all about it.' Cigony pulled a handful of tow from his pocket and blew his nose. It bugled like a hunting horn and in the bailey below the dogs raised eager heads and gave tongue.

'Thank you, my lord. I won't detain you now, but may I speak with you when you get back?'

'Sup with me tonight.' Cigony hurried downstairs. Shouts and laughter rose to greet him and looking through the window Straccan watched the hunters clatter out of the gate.

'What's up?' asked Bane when Straccan found him in the hall.

'Trouble.'

'The king?'

'No. Wulstan.'

'What's he been up to?'

'Murder.'

The coroner had other murders on his plate and had been called away, taking his clerk with him. In a small dark office Straccan found a sergeant-at-arms hunched, disconsolate, over a parchment, clutching his quill as if it was a dagger and shaping the letters with both tongue and pen. He looked up, grateful for any interruption.

'Yes, sir? What can I do for you?'

'You have a prisoner called Havloc.'

'That's right. May I ask your name, sir?'

'I'm Richard Straccan. What's he charged with?'

'Murder. Worse, petty treason, for it was his lord he killed, Drogo of Devilstone.'

'Devilstone?' That was where the girl on the bridge came from: Alis of Devilstone. What had she to do with this?

The sergeant was still talking. 'There's a matter of theft too. Interesting, that. Bit of a problem for the justices. Should he be boiled for the killing or hanged for the theft? Can't do both! Now the *old* constable, Lord William de Breos, that was,' he went on chattily, '*he'd* have said boil him. Always liked a good boiling, did Lord William. But this *new* constable . . .' He sucked his teeth reflectively, musing on the differing tastes of men. 'Well, who knows? We'll just have to wait and see.'

'Who accused him?'

'The coroner, of course.'

'When was Drogo killed?'

'He disappeared when Havloc left Devilstone two weeks ago, but it was a while before they found the corpse.'

'And where was that?'

'In the forest, barely a mile from his hall.'

'How did he die?'

'Hard to say, sir. The face was black and hugely swole.' He sniffed. 'Crows'd been at him – one eye was gone.'

'Why did the coroner accuse Havloc?'

'His ring was found near the corpse. And he'd scarpered. With the cup.'

I am Wulstan's cup. There *must* have been some sort of cup.

'I want to see him.'

The sergeant shook his head. 'Can't do that, sir. He's in the pit. More'n my job's worth.'

'Sergeant,' said Straccan earnestly. 'Havloc was attacked when he came to Ludlow. He was unconscious when I found him. He couldn't remember anything when he came round, not who he is, or where he came from, nothing! The surgeon at the castle attended him, he'll tell you the same. Look, I'll pay all charges if you'll have him taken out of the pit and housed in a cell instead.'

The man looked doubtful 'I dunno, sir. It's not customary.'

Straccan laid a purse on the sergeant's letter. His eyes brightened and the purse vanished into his pocket with a rapidity a conjuror might have admired.

'Right you are, sir. I'll see what I can do.'

'Not the common gaol,' said Straccan. 'Let him have water to wash and a cell to himself. I'll pay for bedding and food from a cook-shop. Oh, and no irons.'

'Have to be irons, sir, even for a privileged prisoner. Petty treason's a cut above plain old murder.'

'Not your biting irons, then. Decent irons that don't cut, and a walking length of chain. There'll be another purse in it if I can rely on you.'

'I'll see to it meself, sir.'

The cook had decimated the population of the dovecote and the kitchen was full of feathers, some of which were still floating about in the inner ward and even in the outer bailey, and clinging to the clothes and shoes of the servers at supper. At the high table, Straccan picked one off his blancmange and continued his conversation with the constable, while below the dais a pair of tumblers went through an unenthusiastic routine, ignored by the diners.

'He's been accused, my lord, but it seems there's no proof, nor any witnesses.'

'There is a witness,' Cigony said. His wife had insisted on rubbing his chest with some concoction of her own; he smelled strongly of wintergreen but it seemed to have done some good. He'd hardly sneezed at all during supper.

Straccan's eyebrows shot up. 'Who, my lord?'

'Drogo.'

'But he's—'

'Doesn't matter, apparently. They've brought the corpse here from Devilstone for a Hearing. Coroner's idea, not mine!'

Straccan found he'd gone off his pudding. He pushed it away. 'When's the Hearing?'

The constable spat out a small feather which had escaped his vigilance. 'Tomorrow.'

Tomorrow. Well, he couldn't leave anyway until the floods went down. Nothing would be moving in or out of Ludlow for the next two or three days. South of the town, Leominster and miles of surrounding country were under water. Even the king wouldn't expect him to swim to Avonmouth.

Cigony leaned back in his chair, waving away the dish of sweets a server offered. The tumblers finished their turn and stood sweating, holding out their caps for coins. None were thrown and after an embarrassed moment or two they backed away, muttering.

'The young woman I brought here, my lord—'

'Oh, her,' the constable said glumly. 'Alis. She won't go home. She says the prisoner couldn't have killed her father.'

'Is she Drogo's daughter?'

'Yes, and the prisoner's sweetheart.' Cigony sighed heavily. When it came to dealing with young women he hadn't a clue. Alis could not be permitted to see the prisoner, of course, so must either be sent home again – which she strenuously resisted – or kept somewhere safe in the town. The constable had looked resignedly at her – rough-dried, muddy and stubborn. He knew determination when he saw it and handed her over to his wife.

'Why bother yourself with this business?' Cigony drained his cup. 'He's not your man.'

'I found him, my lord. I feel responsible for him.'

Straccan leaned his elbows on the board and watched the next turn, a juggler, new to it and nervous. The lad began tossing a few coloured balls, dropping some and sending a couple shooting into the diners' puddings. When he graduated to daggers Straccan judged it prudent to leave before any blood was shed.

Chapter 14

At the sound of the key in his cell door Havloc jumped to his feet with a clank of chain, slumping back in relief when he saw who his visitors were.

'Are you all right?' Straccan asked, looking hard at him for cuts or bruises. The young man was pale, unshaven and noticeably thinner. He was chained by one leg to a staple in the cell wall, and there were scabbed shackle-galls on his wrists, although the gaoler had kept his promise and removed those chains. Other than that, though, he seemed unmarked.

'I'm well, sir, and thankful to be out of the pit. Sir Richard, what's going to happen to me? Do you know? They say . . . they say that I killed a man.' The knuckles showed bone-white in his clenched fists. 'I don't remember,' he said desperately. 'I *can't*! Sir, what will they do to me?'

'There's to be a Hearing,' Straccan said. 'The coroner will present his reasons for accusing you.'

'Then what, sir?'

'That'll be up to the jury. If they say you're innocent you'll be a free man again.'

'And . . . if not?'

'Then the constable will decide what to do with you.'

Havloc shivered, wrapping his arms tightly round himself for comfort. 'Am I a murderer?' he whispered. 'God help me, I don't know! I can't remember. One of the guards told me to pray to Saint Leonard, patron of all prisoners.' He looked at Straccan with desperate eyes. 'I *do* pray, sir, day and night, but nothing's changed.'

'You ain't in the pit, at any rate,' said Bane.

'Forgive me,' said Havloc contritely. 'I'm not ungrateful. But I'm afraid!'

'Take heart at this, then,' Straccan said. 'On our way back to Ludlow we met with a young woman coming here to speak for you. She says Drogo was still alive; she saw and spoke to him *after* you left Devilstone.'

'Who is she?'

'Alis of Devilstone. If her name doesn't mean anything to you you're in for a nice surprise. She says she's your sweetheart. Don't look so scared, lad. She's on your side!'

The constable's wife clucked over her new charge, tut-tutted at her ruined clothes and ransacked chests and coffers to outfit Alis with the necessities. A motherly woman whose daughters were grown and long gone to husbands of their own, she tucked Alis under her wing, and that night in their bedchamber badgered her husband on the girl's behalf, much to the annoyance of his squire who slept on a pallet at the foot of the great bed. *No consideration, the great folks*, he thought crossly, as Lady Margery's strong and carrying voice went on, and on. He wished she'd shut up and let him get a bit of kip. So did his lord.

'I can see her mother in her,' the lady mused. 'She has Eloise's eyes and the same firm chin. Poor Eloise, I knew her quite well before she married that pig Drogo. Nothing of *him* in the girl, thank God! It's a great pity she's compromised herself with this murderer of yours.'

'My dear,' protested the constable, roused by this injustice from the first fuzzy layers of sleep. 'He has not yet been found guilty. And according to this girl . . .'

'Alis.'

'Alis, yes. Her evidence must be heard and judged. Havloc *couldn't* have killed her father, she says. He was with her all the night before he left Devilstone, and Drogo was still alive after he'd gone.'

'Oh!'

While Lady Margery digested the implications and the squire

found a sudden interest in this aspect of the tale, Cigony resumed his interrupted descent into the soft well of slumber only to be jerked up again by his spouse's knuckle in his ribs.

'Cigony. *Cigony!*'

'Eh? What? Oh, for pity's sake, Margery.'

'If she's not a virgin any more we will have to say they are betrothed.'

The constable thumped his pillow. It had seemed soft enough minutes ago but now he couldn't get comfortable. He turned on his side with a sigh. His ear felt as if it was resting on a log.

'*Are* they betrothed?' he asked.

'They'd better be,' muttered Lady Margery ominously. 'Father Ambrose will have to marry them as soon as you let this Havloc go.'

'I *can't* let him go, woman! He's been accused, there's to be a Hearing. Oh God,' he said as an unpleasant thought struck him. 'I hope it's not hot tomorrow.'

'After all that rain I hope it *will* be hot,' said his wife. 'I've never known such a summer. I found mould on your clean drawers in the linen chest this morning. *What* Hearing?'

'Didn't I tell you?' he asked, knowing full well he hadn't. 'The corpse is to witness against the slayer.' It was dark, but he could *feel* his wife's disgusted glare. 'It's Paulet's idea, not mine.'

'Paulet! He's a fool.' Lady Margery's voice dripped contempt. The king's coroner, Sir Brian Paulet, was from Aquitaine and considered himself superior to the rest of mankind. Lady Margery couldn't stand him. 'Anyway, if Havloc was with Alis . . .'

'*If* ! That's the whole point, Madge. There's only her word for it. *A-a-aratcha!* Oh, God!' His cold was usually better in bed, but all this talking must have got it going again. 'The word of a girl in love,' he continued, wiping his nose on the back of his hand. 'Possibly with child, have you thought of that?' His squire was all ears now, and smirking in the dark. 'Her word won't carry any weight by itself.'

'She's a truthful girl.'

'You've only just met her.'

'I knew her mother.'

'Oh, well, that's all right then. That'll go down well at the trial.

"She must be telling the truth, my lords, I knew her mother!" '

'Don't be sarcastic, Cigony!'

'Sorry,' muttered the constable. He banged his pillow with his fist and sat up, leaning back against it. Blessed welcoming sleep had beckoned, been denied and fled. He could talk all night now if that's what his wife wanted.

'Can't Paulet let the man go, if Alis swears to his innocence?'

'Even if the corpse fails to accuse Havloc I don't think Paulet will take her word, Madge.'

'Then tell him *you* believe her!'

'Do I?'

'Sir Richard does.'

'Straccan?'

'Didn't he tell you how he found her?' Lady Margery launched into an account of the rescue from the broken bridge. 'You see?' she finished. 'She wouldn't go to safety without her horse; she wouldn't even desert that wretched leper.'

'Well, yes, I grant you that was admirable.' *Stupid*, he thought, *but* – he had to admit – *admirable*.

'If she was a man you and that wretched Paulet would take her word without question!'

'You're probably right, Madge.' He fidgeted with the pillows, shifted his legs – the whole bed seemed lumpy, hot and uncomfortable. He could do with a drink. Waving down his squire who scrambled up to attend him, Cigony swung his legs out of bed, padded to the livery cupboard and poured a cup of wine. 'Would you like a wafer?'

This minor attempt at distraction was ignored. It took more than a wafer to deflect Lady Margery.

'You'll talk to Paulet, then?'

Back in bed, carefully keeping his cold feet away from his wife's warm ones, the constable sighed and accepted his lot in life. 'I'll talk to him.'

'Cigony!'

'What?'

'You've got crumbs in the bed again!'

Chapter 15

There was only one witness and he was already dead, but that didn't matter; he could still give evidence.

So many had come for the entertainment that there wasn't room to swing a cat. Some had even bagged places the day before, bringing food and drink and camping overnight on their chosen spot; and for those with less forethought a vendor had set up a pie stall and was doing a brisk trade, in spite of the smell that pervaded the enclosure, ripening as the sun rose higher.

Brought to Ludlow in a cart, the body lay on a plank supported on trestles placed where any breeze would serve to carry the odour away from the kitchen nearby. Unfortunately there was no breeze. The fine morning was already hot, and the corpse lay beneath a glistening pall of humming flies. A brazier burned beside the rough bier, but the fragrant herbs sprinkled on the charcoal stood no chance in the olfactory battle.

Inside, in the great hall, the prisoner's sweetheart waited. The corpse would have its say first. If that proved the accused guilty, there would be no need to hear the woman. God would have spoken. The cheerful noise of expectation died down as the constable and his officers made their appearance, only to rise again in a tide of boos and hisses as the prisoner was brought out.

'Get a move on,' said the constable. 'I haven't got all day.'

The clerk of record wrote busily in Latin Officialese on his parchment roll:

Drogo, lord of Devilstone, being slain wickedly in the peace of the lord king, is brought hither according to custom and the law of God to bear witness. And Havloc, Drogo's man, taken for the slaying, comes. And the corpse is asked, is this man guilty? And . . .

Father Ambrose seized Havloc's right hand, held it up like a trophy for all to see and slapped it down hard upon the corpse's breast. A bubbly belch burst from the dark puffy lips, and a pregnant woman who had elbowed her way to the front so as not to miss anything fainted.

There was a moment of silence, and then a general groan of disappointment when it was seen that the corpse neither rose in miraculous accusation nor mutely bled. Some tried to argue that the belch was significant but Father Ambrose said it didn't count.

The constable beckoned the coroner, who had kept as far back as he could from the proceedings with his nose buried in a prophylactic posy of flowers. 'Well, Paulet? Now what?'

The coroner glared at the uncooperative cadaver. 'It may be that the corpse is too old to bear true witness, there being no liquid blood,' he suggested.

'Rubbish,' snapped Cigony. 'God can liquefy blood if there's need. Can't He, Father Ambrose? Yes! There! You wanted this filthy ritual, Paulet. Don't tell me now you won't abide by it!'

The coroner gestured broadly with his nosegay and the constable sneezed violently as if orchestrated. 'There is still the theft to be considered,' Paulet said. 'That is a hanging matter, although not in my hands.'

The clerk's pen scratched, scribbling fast.

. . . it bore no witness against Havloc, and he is . . .

He looked up at the constable. 'Is he innocent, then, my lord?'

'Yes,' said the constable and 'No,' said the coroner together. The clerk of record made a blot and swore.

Cigony swung round upon the trembling jury. 'All right, you lot, out with it!'

Heads leaned together, whispering anxiously, and eventually

one, shoved forward as the reluctant spokesman for all and pale with the responsibility, pulled off his cap and mumbled, 'Please, me lord, pardon an all, but we reckon as we oughter hear what yon young wumman's got to say.'

'You've made me waste a good hunting morning with your stinking mummery,' said Cigony, turning on the coroner. 'Either he's guilty or he's not! It won't do, Paulet. The girl will *have* to be heard now. I'll see you in the hall.' He made swiftly for the damp coolness indoors, calling over his shoulder, 'Take the prisoner back to his cell until I decide what to do with him. The rest of you wait in the hall.'

'Well?' said his lady when her husband, glossy with sweat and panting from the stairs, entered her bower. 'Sit down, my lord, do. Pah! How the stink clings to you! Well?'

'A farce,' said Cigony, sinking onto a low stool at his wife's side, breathing hard, his face and neck an alarming colour.

Lady Margery unbuttoned the neck of his tunic and laid cool fingers against the bulging veins in his forehead. She nudged a serving woman. 'Bring ale,' she said, 'and a basin of water for my lord to wash.' And to her husband, 'I don't mean that Godless charade outside. Did you talk to Paulet? Has he heard Alis?'

One of her women came in with a basket of fresh-picked strewing herbs and scattered them over the floor. Cigony gave a tremendous sneeze. Funny, he thought, he hadn't sneezed *once* while outside just now. Why was that? Could it be something to do with the stink? Would other stinks have a similar effect? Come to think of it, he never sneezed when in the privy . . .

'Cigony!'

His wife's sharp voice recalled him from the byways of alternative medicine. 'They are waiting for you in the hall.'

There was no budging the coroner. He'd had an unpleasant morning; he was frightened, disgusted and in no mood to be reasonable. 'Havloc's guilt is beyond question,' he insisted. 'He killed his master, stole the cup and fled. His ring was found by the corpse. This ring.' He produced it in evidence, a cheap silver band set with a bit of crystal. 'The lady and the priest at Devilstone identified it as his.'

The jury muttered to one another, but Straccan whispered something to the constable and Cigony asked, 'Where exactly was the ring found?'

The coroner looked peeved. 'As I said, close by the body. The murderer lost it in the struggle when he killed his master.'

Straccan prompted again and the constable asked, 'Who found it?'

From among the spectators a woman pushed forward. 'I did, my lord.'

'Who are you?' Cigony asked.

'Ceridwen of Devilstone.' The clerk of record hastily jotted it down. 'I washed my lord's body and dressed it for burial.'

'Where did you find the ring?'

'In his pocket,' she said.

There was some murmuring at this and Straccan said loudly, 'How did it get there? A man fighting for his life doesn't pick up his assailant's ring and stick it in his pocket. And if Havloc killed Drogo *he* wouldn't have put it there.'

'What difference does it make?' said Paulet crossly.

'Don't you see? The ring is no proof. Drogo could have picked it up anywhere, or someone else could have put it there. It proves nothing!'

'He's right,' said Cigony. 'The jury must ignore the ring.' He turned to them. 'D'you understand, you lot? Forget the bloody ring, it's not proof. Now, young woman,' to Alis, 'it's your turn. *A-a-a-cha!*' He wiped his nose on his shirtsleeve.

Overruled on the ring, the coroner stood firm against allowing Alis's evidence. He'd heard her story earlier that morning, at the constable's request, and didn't believe a word of it.

'She cannot be heard here. Women have no standing under the law,' he said loftily.

'She will bear witness on oath that she saw and talked to her father after Havloc had gone,' the constable offered.

'She is the accused's leman! Her oath would be meaningless.'

Cigony's lips tightened. 'She can take the oath on relics, can't she? I have a shoulder blade of Saint David and a fingernail of Saint Winifred. That ought to be good enough. If not, Father Ambrose can send to the church for some more.'

'Even on relics a woman's oath has no validity,' said Paulet in a tone that allowed no argument.

Straccan decided to argue anyway. 'I don't agree. A Christian woman's oath is as good as a man's.'

Sir Brian gave him an unfriendly look; his was a face made for unfriendly looks, closed, with shuttered eyes and a tight mouth that seemed reluctant to let words escape. He wasn't good at his job, he hadn't sought it, it wasn't possible to profit from the office and it even cost him his own money; the refund of his expenses was always overdue, every penny disputed. But he'd had no choice. The king appointed coroners. 'You, you, and you,' he said, and that was that.

'By law I can accept the oath of any *man*,' he said. 'Even, if he swears according to his custom, the oath of a Jew. But not a woman. It would be like accepting the oath of a dog!'

So there, thought Straccan wryly. He stood on the dais beside the constable's chair, with the coroner at the other side facing him and Alis standing below the dais, looking anxiously from one authoritarian face to the other.

A small crowd had followed them into the hall: a couple of priests there on business, a monk, some hopeful place-seekers, two of Cigony's squires, the captain of the castle guard and a man hoping to sell a horse. But word of this affair had got out and several townsfolk, lawyers and clerks with a professional interest, and others just plain curious had drifted in to listen.

They all found the business of absorbing interest. Havloc's predicament was well known, but whether he was guilty or not most folk felt sympathy for his pretty sweetheart. The story of her rescue from the bridge had spread from castle to town, losing nothing in the telling, and while no one wanted to see a murderer escape justice and a few would have been delighted to see *anybody* hang, Alis had many well-wishers.

Straccan tried again. 'If the king was to accept women's oaths, would that change your decision?'

The coroner sniffed. 'I am certain he would not. His highness has a profound interest in the administration of justice and the observances of law.' Then with a poisonous look at Straccan he sneered, 'But I hear you are a friend of the king. No doubt you know his opinions.'

'I wouldn't presume.' Straccan smiled. 'Nevertheless he *does* accept them.'

'Give me *one* precedent!'

'There are many. He accepts the oath of fealty, the most important oath of all, from anyone, man or woman.'

In the silence that followed the constable lifted his cup to hide his grin and said, 'You have the right sow by the ear, Sir Richard!' And to the coroner. 'There are your precedents, Paulet. There is no reason why you should not take this woman's oath. *Aratcha!*'

'Very clever,' said Paulet sourly. This would not have happened when William de Breos was lord here, but this upstart, this sneezing nobody, this *mercenary* had no respect for the law. 'You *may* be right,' he said grudgingly, 'but I have grave doubts. And in any case, your so-called *witness*,' he sneered, 'must produce pledges of good faith.'

There was a sudden noise at the foot of the steps outside the hall: a sharp challenge followed by shouts of anger, cries of indignation and, loud above the confusion a great hoarse voice booming, 'Who will lay hands on me? Who will dare?'

Attendants fell back, glaring and gabbling, and let the leper pass. With him came the reek and terror of his disease. People pressed back against one another, treading on toes, elbowing ribs as they tried to keep their distance from the leper. He stopped before the dais, leaning on his staff. Behind him the doorward hopped from foot to foot in a fever of anxiety.

'Sir! Me lord! I couldn't stop im!'

'It's all right,' said the constable, and to the leper, 'What do you want here?'

Before he could answer, the coroner, who had whipped the tail of his cloak over his nose and mouth for fear of contagion, shrilled, 'How dare you force your way in here! The law forbids it! I'll have you stoned out of the town gate!'

Cigony laid a hand on Paulet's wrist. 'Let us see what he wants.'

The leper was breathing hard. His cloak bore the marks of freshly flung mud and turds. When his eyes met Straccan's he bowed, an incongruously courtly gesture from such a figure. 'Sirs,' he rasped, 'forgive my intrusion.'

'What do you want?' asked the constable again.

'It is the matter of this young gentlewoman,' the leper grated.

'Get out of here!' Paulet trembled with anger and terror. 'You may not come among whole folk!'

The leper ignored him, shifting his grip on his staff and swaying as he stood. 'I know there will be objection to her as a witness, and her oath, unsupported, will not be acceptable.'

'What the devil do you know about it?' Paulet was beside himself with rage. 'My lord constable, have your men ring him with spears and get him out of here! This whole place must be fumigated!'

'Wait,' said Straccan. 'Hear him.'

'But if at least two men will stand as pledges for her reliability and good character,' the leper continued as if there had been no interruption, 'if two *men* can be found to vouch for her, that alters the case.'

Cigony nodded. 'True. Were you a man of law?'

'No. But *my* pledge, even as I am, should suffice for one of the two if another will also give *his* pledge.' He looked at Straccan, who nodded.

'Your word is nothing,' the coroner shouted. 'You *can't* give evidence! You're a dead man!'

'Not as dead as the one outside just now,' said Straccan. 'You were willing to hear him.'

There were shouts of 'Aye!' and 'Right enough!'

'Well said, Straccan!' Cigony was enjoying himself. He had even forgotten to sneeze. 'You can't deny that, Paulet.'

A crusted, rustling sound came from behind the leper's mask; he was laughing.

Paulet rounded on him. 'Damn you, who are you?'

'Do you still have the hound bitch puppy I gave you, Brian? Atropos, you called her.'

'God's mercy!' Paulet had gone a nasty colour. 'You! You *are* dead! They told me you had died!'

'Who is he?' asked Cigony. 'Who are you, sir?'

Tears washed the leper's sore eyes, blotting his mask. 'Before this affliction I was Bishop of Bordeville. My name was Garnier Paulet.'

'He has the same name as you,' the constable said to Paulet. 'Do you know him?'

'God have mercy,' said the coroner again. 'He is my brother.'

The hall emptied rapidly once the show was over, and Straccan looked sharply at Alis. She was very pale.

'I'll take you to Lady Margery. Shall we go into the pleasance first? Some fresh air will do you good.'

The pleasance was practical and plain, like the constable's lady. Shrubs and bushes stood in tubs spaced like soldiers in rows. Beds of herbs were outlined with river pebbles, arranged with a severe geometry. At the far end, the constable's wards, three little girls, played some complicated singing game. Seeing the grown-ups, they curtsied and giggled, but soon their game had them in thrall again and Straccan and Alis were ignored. There was a refreshing scent of rosemary. Alis picked a sprig and rolled it in her fingers, breathing in the fragrance. Some colour came back to her cheeks.

'Mistress Alis,' Straccan said gently, 'you trust me, I hope?' She nodded. 'Then tell me what happened at Devilstone. *Someone* murdered your father; if it wasn't Havloc, the killer must be found. I know you spoke with your father after Havloc had gone but you didn't tell the jury everything.' He felt her guilty start. 'How did that ring get into your father's pocket?'

Chapter 16

'Father sent me to his sister in Bristol,' Alis said. 'She was to find me a husband. I have no dower, you see. There are six of us girls at home and no portion for any of us. I was there three years.' She flushed. 'I became an embarrassment. Aunt Emma sent me home last Christmas.'

A poor homecoming she'd had; her father blamed her for the failure. 'You, is it?' He scowled. 'Back already?' Everything had changed: her mother was gone, consigned to a nunnery; there was a new step-mother, a timid girl younger than Alis herself. Of all her sisters only the next eldest, Petronella, was glad to see her. The manor was more run-down than she remembered and the old steward had died while she was gone. A new man, Havloc, had taken his place.

She didn't know when she'd found herself in love with him. For a time she refused to admit it, even to herself. Knights' daughters, however poor, could not marry commoners, especially moneyless commoners. She was afraid her guilty passion must be obvious to him but Havloc seemed rather to avoid her. He only spoke to her when necessary and never met her eyes.

Spring followed winter, and one day she heard Havloc asking Father Alkmund about the foreign towns where the old priest had travelled in his youth: Rome, Paris, Cologne. She knew with wretched certainty that he intended to leave.

That evening when everyone was at supper she waited in the stable until Havloc led his horse in, and stood forward in his way.

'Mistress Alis! What's the matter?'

He met her gaze. They stared at each other. His eyes were brown with golden flecks. She hadn't known.

'Havloc,' she said breathlessly. And because she had never spoken his name aloud and loved the sound of it, she said it again, 'Havloc,' and then, 'Please, don't leave!'

'I must,' he said hoarsely. 'I can't bear it!'

'What?'

'Being near you – the lord's daughter – seeing you every day, wanting you, knowing I can't—'

She went into his arms and silenced his mouth with hers.

They met when they could, desperately careful, for there were eyes everywhere. Their love had no future; sooner or later Alis's father would find a husband for her, some old dotard willing to dispense with a dowry in order to get a young virgin in his bed. She prayed the day would never come, but it came with new-widowed Sir William Redvers, sixty years old, fat, gouty, lecherous. No sooner was Lady Redvers coffined than Drogo invited him to Devilstone and dangled the pretty virginal bait before him.

He had judged his man well. Redvers stared at Alis, breathing hard, and made no protest about her dowerless state. He pinched her breasts in front of everybody and waylaid her in corners, kissing her as if he would eat her, thrusting his tongue into her shrinking mouth and his hard bruising hands up her skirts.

'A virgin, eh?' he'd said to her father in the crowded hall. 'You're sure? I'll have no man's leavings. If she's not I'll cut her nose off.'

He'd ridden away, but he'd be back.

Things happened very fast after that. Havloc had an errand for her father in Ludlow. The marriage contract would be sealed by the time he got back – unless Redvers backed out.

He wouldn't marry her if she wasn't a virgin.

That night she lay with Havloc in his narrow bed. He gave her his ring. It was loose; she had to close her fist to keep it on. In God's sight they were now husband and wife. When he came back they would run away to France. He gave her his savings to keep, enough for their passage and a start in life once there.

At first light they walked through the sleeping village, Havloc leading his horse. Where the highway began they kissed and clung together for a moment. He rode away.

On the outskirts of the village was an ancient shrine to the Blessed Virgin. She knelt there, turning Havloc's loose ring on her finger, putting it to her lips.

'Blessed Lady, guard Havloc my husband on his journey. Bring him safe back. Holy Mother, sweet lady, have pity on us poor lovers . . .'

Suddenly, as if he'd dropped from the sky, her father was in front of her. She shrieked. He swung his fist and knocked her down, half stunning her. Bending over her he tore the ring from her hand.

'Slut, whore! *Husband*, by God! *Lovers*, by Christ! I'll have his balls for this!' He thrust the ring inside his coat. 'If Redvers won't take you now I'll cut off your nose myself and you can join your damned mother in the nunnery!'

He drew his dagger. She scrambled up; he knocked her down again, aimed a kick that missed, lost his balance and fell. She tried to run but he grabbed her around the knees and pulled her down, seized her hair, twisting it round his hands and shaking her so violently that strands of her hair ripped from their roots. She screamed as he shifted his grip to the neck of her gown and ripped it to the waist.

'Father, please! Don't!'

She tried to get up; he pulled her down again. She crawled; he seized her foot, dragged her back, fell upon her, mouthing obscenities, aroused by her body, her terror, her helplessness. Sick with fear she realised what he meant to do.

'Lord Jesus! Holy Virgin! Help me!'

One of them – both perhaps – must have heard, for Talfryn the fowler came out of the trees and saw the couple on the ground, a woman struggling and crying, a man astride her.

'He didn't know it was my father, he only saw his back,' Alis said.

The fowler's great fist struck the rapist on the side of the head. He collapsed upon Alis who fought to get out from beneath the heavy body.

Only then did Talfryn see her face.

'Mistress Alis? Who ... Oh, *Iesu Crist*!' He pulled her up. At their feet Drogo groaned and moved. 'Run, mistress! Coming to, he is! *Run*!'

'So the fowler killed him,' Straccan said.

'No! Oh, no! He was so afraid! It's death for a man to strike his lord!'

What better reason to kill him? Straccan thought. *Then no one would know.*

'He ... We just ran,' Alis said.

The fowler had seized her hand and they fled into the forest, never looking back, with Drogo crashing after them. When legs and wind gave out deep among the ancient trees, Talfryn and his lord's daughter crawled into a gorse thicket and crouched, tearing air into their whistling lungs while the hammering of their hearts shook their bodies; listening in terror to the blundering sounds of pursuit coming closer.

But Drogo was no longer chasing them. Now, it seemed, someone or something was after him.

They knew what it was. Everyone knew the *Brenin Lwyd* was about, the Grey King who led the Wild Hunt. His hounds and horn were often heard at night; wise folk stuck their heads under the covers and prayed. Any daring to peep would be swept up with the Hunt and carried off, never to be seen again alive. In their extremity of fear Alis and the fowler heard the horn's weird shivering call and the hounds' unearthly baying at the heels of their prey. From their covert they saw Drogo stumbling through the trees, dagger in hand, bleeding where brambles had torn him, blowing like a hunted stag.

Close by their hide he turned to face what followed, slashing at empty air with his dagger. They heard a sound like the flight of an arrow and Drogo screamed, clapping his hands to his face, blood running through his fingers. Nothing visible followed his staggering desperate steps unless it was a chill shadow that passed then, like the shadow of a cloud.

Their thundering hearts quieted. Not far off Drogo screamed again, and they heard the horn's triumphant bray; then all was silence. Too frightened to move, not daring even to speak, they huddled there until the sun was fully up when Talfryn took Alis to Ceridwen's cott.

'She was kind. She cleaned me up, put something on my bruises, took my torn gown and gave me one of hers. She said not to be afraid, for my father was surely dead; no one ever escaped the *Brenin Lwyd*. She told me to go home and try to forget.'

And Ceridwen said nothing of this at the Hearing, Straccan thought. *She kept Alis's secret.*

'Father was dead, of course,' Alis said. 'Talfryn found him. It was a mantrap.'

Two days had passed before the fowler dared to retrace the path of their flight. Splashes of blackened blood led him to his lord's body, hanging head down, black, grossly swollen, terrible. Drogo's legs had been caught and jerked up among the leafy branches by the spring of the mantrap, and the broken end of a branch had pierced through his eye to the brain.

Talfryn got him down, removed all traces of the trap, found the fallen dagger and put it back in its sheath and carried the dreadful carcass to a distant clearing to await discovery. The crows soon flocked to their feasting.

Next day when the reeve found the corpse Talfryn had to help carry it back to the hall on a litter. Every step of the way he was afraid it would rise up and denounce him.

'Talfryn *didn't* kill him,' Alis declared.

'After he left you with Ceridwen he could have gone back and finished Drogo off.'

'No. Something else *was* chasing my father,' Alis said. 'We heard it; *I* heard it.' Despite the early afternoon warmth in Lady Margery's garden, remembering the horn, the baying of the hounds, she shivered.

Straccan put his cloak over her shoulders. 'We'd better go in.'

The little maids had stopped their singing game and were play-ing catch with a red cloth ball. The tallest of the three had the ball;

she tossed it up and caught it, laughing as she held it out of the others' reach. They jumped and stretched, the littlest one crying, 'Meg, give it to me!'

Passing, Straccan tweaked the ball from Meg's hand and threw it up. The smallest girl caught it and ran off, laughing, chased by the others. Their voices, clear and bright as birds', followed Straccan and Alis as they left the garden.

On the stairs he said, 'Why didn't you tell this to the coroner at Devilstone?'

'How could I? He'd blame Talfryn! But then, when he accused Havloc . . . I thought if I came here and told him about Father he'd let Havloc go.'

'Well, they're waiting for us. Let's get it over with,' said Straccan. 'Don't be afraid.' He had felt her flinch. 'I'll be with you.'

'What about Talfryn?'

The fowler had most likely killed Drogo but it was none of his business. 'Just tell them what happened. Your father attacked you, you ran, he followed, you hid in the greenwood until he'd gone. That much is true. No need for more.'

Havloc jumped up as his cell door swung open.

'They've agreed to drop the charge of murder but the coroner insists I take responsibility for you,' Straccan said. Paulet, forced to admit that he might have accused the wrong man, would never forgive him. 'There's still the charge of theft, and until that's cleared up you're in my custody. I've sworn to produce you on demand if necessary.'

He waved away Havloc's stuttered thanks. No need to remind him that he would still hang if the cup wasn't found. What he was to do with his unwanted charge he had no idea: another complication, as if he didn't have enough.

'The constable's signing your order of release now. Meanwhile they'll take the fetters off and Bane will bring you some clean things. By the time you're presentable we'll have the order.' He eyed the young man critically. 'You'd better shave as well. Bane will lend you a razor. Alis is waiting for you.'

*　*　*

'He's got manners, whatever he is,' said Lady Margery to her husband in the privacy of their chamber. 'Alis had better marry him as soon as it can be arranged. It would be nice to have the wedding here, but of course she may wish to be married at home with her sisters as maids of honour. Once he gets his memory back and this theft nonsense has been sorted out she'll probably do well enough with him, whatever his birth.'

'I suppose it's all right, them marrying,' Cigony said with a considering frown. 'She's no heiress so the king won't interfere— Ahem,' he coughed, shooting a quick glance at the door to make sure no one had heard that. 'I mean he won't *concern* himself with her marriage. All in all,' he mused, 'she's lucky to find a husband at all, even if he *is* just a steward. She may be pretty but she brings nothing with her.'

'I wouldn't say that, Cigony,' said his lady. 'She brought him his life.'

Chapter 17

Bane found Havloc in the hall breakfasting like a man who feared he might never have another chance, an attitude with which he wholly sympathised.

He sat down beside him. 'How d'you feel?'

'All right,' said Havloc, 'but I still can't remember. Not a damned thing! Not even Alis! I can't believe that we . . . that I . . . that she . . .' He pushed his trencher away impatiently.

'Believe it, you lucky dog. Don't you want that? Shove it over here, then.' And Bane finished Havloc's breakfast for him.

'Master Bane, what do you think? Suppose I offer a reward for the return of the cup. Alis brought my savings.' He pulled at a thong round his neck, drawing up a purse which clinked when shaken. 'Wouldn't a thief rather have money?'

Bane pursed his lips appraisingly. 'It's an idea. Might work, too, if he's still got it and if he's still around. You'll need to fee the town crier.'

'And Master Bane, I'd like to make a thank-offering to Saint Leonard.'

Bane nodded approval. 'Never hurts to say thank you. We'll go to the shrine. What do you have in mind?'

'A wax votive.'

'Right. Let's find a chandler.'

Overnight drizzle had left the cobbles slippery. Here and there along the street shopkeepers were forking straw out and spreading it over the treacherous surface, taking down their shutters and tipping the night's ordure into the broad kennel which steamed and stank in the middle of the road. A red kite alighted on the chandler's signboard, which creaked and swayed slightly. The kite gaped, stretched a wing, and took no notice of the hustle below as the chandler prepared for the day's business.

Early as it was there were customers ahead of them, one outside at the booth, another within, arguing with the master chandler himself. While one apprentice took the shutters inside another flicked his feather duster over the wax votives on display in the little booth projecting from the building's front and dealt with a well-dressed man in a quilted coat.

'How much for an arm?'

'Full size, sir, or a miniature?'

'Full size.'

'Sixpence.'

'Oh. What about just the elbow, then?'

'Lot of wax in an elbow. Fourpence.'

The would-be buyer stood undecided, gazing at the wares laid out on the booth: rows of hands and feet, arms and legs, breasts and heads, hearts and livers painted in crude colours, ears, eyes, tongues, teeth and genitals.

'Oh, go on, then,' said the customer eventually, carefully counting out his silver – two whole pennies, three halves and two ragged pie-piece quarters. He placed his waxen elbow tenderly in straw in his basket and departed, walking very carefully for fear of slipping.

Inside the chandler's shop a heated voice was raised. 'Sixpence is too much!'

'Up to you, master. Take it or leave it.'

'I'll give you threepence!'

'You'll not get work of this quality for threepence. There's the workman's time and the wax – that's dearer now, you know; there's an Interdict on. Everything costs more these days, master. And paint; you wanted them coloured. That costs extra, for artistry.'

'Artistry my arse! It's daylight robbery!'

'No one's forcing you, master. You can walk out of here with your silver still in your pouch. I didn't come to you and bother you to buy, did I? No, you came to *me*, and now you sit in my shop blackguarding me for my prices! Why, just last week you couldn't bear to sit down at all, and look at you now! There's a miracle, if you like. I'm happy for you, but now, master, excuse me, I must get on. There's a batch of moulds waiting to be filled and the wax about ready—'

'Fourpence!'

The chandler grinned and tapped his fingers on the counter.

'Oh, damn you, sixpence then! But wrap them up. I'm not carrying them through the streets like that!'

The chandler snapped his fingers for an apprentice, who carefully packed the curious luridly tinted wax mass in sheep's wool. The customer wrapped the tail of his cloak over it.

'You'll not see a finer set of emrods in the shrine, master,' said the chandler, pouching his six pennies. 'Have a good look while you're in there. There's some sorry-looking poor puny pale old emrods; I'd be ashamed if they was mine. You can be *proud* of *these* emrods!'

The apprentice in the booth saw the new customers waiting and gave them a cheerful smile.

'How can I help you, my masters?'

'We'll talk to the master chandler,' said Bane.

The boy nipped round from the back of the booth just in time to usher the first customer out, cradling his sixpenn'orth of waxen haemorrhoids as tenderly as a new-born child. The apprentice bowed the new clients into the inner shop where the master chandler popped up from behind his counter, radiating cheerfulness, as well he might, with such a good early start to the day.

'What d'ye lack, sirs?'

'A head,' said Havloc, nudged forward by Bane. 'I mean, how much for a head? Life-size.'

'Lot of wax in a head, sir.' The chandler eyed his customer's decent clothes and his companion's sword and good boots, and estimated their worth.

'How much?'

'Your basic head, fourpence. See? It takes all this to make one.' He delved under the counter again and brought up a pinkish-yellow ball, handing it to Havloc who hefted it nervously and gave it back.

'Have you got any finished?'

'Oh yes, sir, come round the back here, that's right.' He twitched aside a curtain and waved them ahead of him into a storeroom. At a table in the centre an apprentice was smoothing wax flash off a well modelled life-size foot. Several other anatomical pieces lay on the table awaiting attention – a forearm and hand, a heart, some teeth. At another table a boy surrounded by paint pots and brushes was colouring little male and female figurines. The chandler waved his hand expansively at the shelves which covered all four walls, filled with rows of wax creations. There were animals – hawks, horses, bulls, pigs, dogs – also miniature carts and boats and, pale and gleaming, human *disjecta membra*: feet, lower legs, legs entire, hands and arms, hearts and haemorrhoids, ears, noses, eyes – and heads, some with hair, others bald, some with painted blue eyes, others brown, all staring glassily.

Bane raised an eyebrow at them. 'That all?'

'If you don't see what you want, sirs, we'll make it especially for you. What sort of head are you after? Child? Lady?'

'Man,' said Havloc.

'Yourself, Sir?' And at Havloc's nod, 'What is the ailment? A wound? Headaches? Tumour?'

'I was hit on the head. Lost my memory.'

The apprentices looked up, interested, and the chandler pinched his lower lip thoughtfully between finger and thumb, pondering the problem. 'Can't make a votive *memory*,' he said, considering. 'Who knows what it looks like? It's just *in* there.' He tapped the side of his head and looked at Havloc as a collector looks at a rare specimen.

'Just a head,' said Havloc, but the artist had risen in the chandler, elbowing the mere businessman aside, and the intricacies of representing memory in wax had brought a creative gleam to his eye and seamed his brow with frowns.

'Ben,' he said to one of the boys, 'fetch ale and biscuits for these gentlemen. Sirs,' indicating a bench at the painter's table, 'do me the honour of sitting down in my poor shop and refresh yourselves while I think about this.'

'Just a head,' repeated Havloc, but Bane pushed him gently down and they sat watching a boy paint blue eyeballs, highlighting them with a touch of white so that they looked alive. It put Havloc off his biscuits, and Bane ate them.

'I've got it,' cried the chandler radiating triumph. 'Suppose we do a head, hollow, the usual, but put something *inside*. I mean, your head's empty *now*, isn't it, sir, meaning no offence, just that there's no memory in it. Now memory might be a sort of web, it catches and holds things after all . . . So, a web of wax, inside the head . . .'

The apprentices were nodding admiringly. The chandler looked smug. 'There you are then, sir. What about that?'

'How much?' asked Havloc.

They settled on sevenpence and promised to call back for the masterpiece in the morning.

Chapter 18

A pieman had stationed himself at the door of Saint Leonard's chapel in Corve Street and was doing a brisk trade. As yet not many candles had been lit; even so, there were a few people inside. Despite the early hour two young men were arguing prices with a whore while just inside the door, out of the wind, a pedlar was handing out pins and gauds and pouching coins while he kept up a sing-song chant praising his wares. Some folk had come to gossip, some to meet lovers; a few had even come to pray.

Someone was grovelling on hands and knees beneath a statue of the Blessed Virgin, with just his bare heels and black-gowned clerical bottom sticking out. Beside him on the floor a dustpan held curls of dust, a piece of bacon rind and two pennies. After hesitating for a few moments Havloc stooped and tapped the protruding bottom. The body jerked, there was a ringing thump and a muffled 'Ow!' and a young priest crawled out backwards and straightened up on his knees, rubbing his tonsure.

'Are you all right, father?' Bane asked.

'Just a bump,' said the priest cheerfully, dropping a third retrieved coin into his dustpan. 'Worth it for threepence.' He scrambled to his feet, brushing briskly at his dusty gown. 'Now, sirs, I'm Father Peter, chaplain here; what can I do for you? Depends what you want, of course. There *is* an Interdict, you know! Can't say Mass, can't give sacraments, can't even ring the bell! But there's no law says I can't pray for you. For everyone. Even the king,' he added with a mutinous scowl.

'Can you take offerings?' asked Havloc.

The chaplain beamed. 'Never more welcome! The Interdict paupers us and the king, God forgive him, bleeds us dry. What d'ye want to give?'

'I brought this for Saint Leonard.'

Havloc unwrapped the head, feeling a momentary twinge of disappointment. It looked smaller and less important than in the shop, he thought, but the chaplain examined it with admiration.

'A fine piece of work,' he said. 'I've never seen better. Come along and I'll show you where it goes.'

Havloc followed the chaplain, Bane wandered off towards the door and the pieman, while Straccan leaned against a tomb and watched the pilgrims shuffling in with their candles and coins.

One man, limping heavily, had brought a votive wax foot. A father carried his small sick daughter to be measured to the saint, and a deacon bustled up, meting out the cord to mark the girl's exact height so that her father could pay for a candle of that length. The man held his daughter to his chest, her head against his shoulder, her fair hair – just like Straccan's daughter Gilla's – falling over his arm.

Coins rattled in the collecting box. Some folk prayed, some wept, some moved on and others drifted in.

Straccan hoped Saint Leonard would be moved to grant Havloc's prayer and restore his memory. If he remembered what had happened to the cup, if it could be traced, he would be able to go home and marry his sweetheart and Straccan wouldn't be saddled with him.

Bane's voice said, 'Look what the cat dragged in.'

Straccan turned and saw Starling Larktwist.

Bane had the smaller man firmly by the arm and from the look on Larktwist's face the grip was none too gentle.

'What the devil are you doing here, Larktwist?' As if he didn't know! 'Spying again?'

'Ssshh! Please, Sir Richard, be careful what you say. There's ears everywhere! Matter o' fact I was looking for you. I *was!*' he squeaked as Bane's grip tightened.

'Let him go, Hawkan,' said Straccan.

Larktwist straightened his clothes, glowering at Bane. There was no love lost between them. Last summer, caught while following Straccan and Bane, Larktwist – one of the king's legion of paid informers – had been compelled to join them in their hunt for Straccan's daughter. He and Bane had never hit it off.

'What do you want?' Straccan asked.

Larktwist looked around carefully. 'I heard the crier. This cup you're after . . . I might be able to help.' He pulled his hood forward to shade his face. 'Not here. Too many eyes, too many ears. Be at the first milestone on the Shrewsbury Road around sext.' He slid away and was lost among the pilgrims.

'That's the last we'll see of him,' said Bane.

'I doubt it,' Straccan said. 'Where did you find him?'

'He was hanging round the door watching folk coming in. You're not going to meet him, are you?'

'He may know something about Havloc's cup.'

'He probably stole it.'

Havloc had finished his business with Saint Leonard and had paid a halfpenny to be shown a piece of a rib of the martyred Saint Thomas, which the chaplain was buying from Canterbury on an instalment plan. A fat puce-faced knight had also paid to view the relic; leaning on his arm was his equally fat but pale and wheezing sister. Apart from colour, they were as alike as peas in a pod. The knight had a hooded hawk on his other fist and greeted Straccan with enthusiasm.

'Here for a cure, sir? Wonderful, Saint Thomas, wonderful! I promised Ermengarde's weight in wax if she was cured.'

'Your sister, sir?' Straccan bowed to the lady.

'Eh? No, not her! My hawk, man! Splendid creature, ain't she? It would break your heart to see her as she was! Off her food, shed-din feathers, eyes all gummy, green droppins. Better now, eh, pet?' He kissed the gilt bauble on top of the bird's hood and it reciprocated with a copious creamy squirt all over his velvet sleeve. The knight beamed. 'There! See? Lovely!'

'Praise God,' said Straccan. 'I'm happy for you, sir.' He turned to Havloc. 'All done? Good. I have to meet someone.'

Outside the chapel several beggars had gathered to try their luck. People who came out in a good mood were often so generous that they more than made up for those who came out bad tempered and kicked a beggar down the steps. Below the steps where at least, if kicked or shoved, he hadn't far to fall, a pitiable creature caught Havloc's eye. The beggar, seeing himself observed, eyed the mark up and down, a wholly professional assessment: well fed, well clothed, well shod, good natured – above all gullible – and began his routine.

'Pity me, good sir, for the sake of Him who pitied all the world! Pity me, good sir, of your charity!'

Havloc froze and Bane, right behind him, nearly knocked him down the steps.

'God's teeth, man, look out! What's up?'

'That beggar! The voice! I heard it the night I was hurt! It was nearly dark, and . . . There was an angel!'

Bane looked at him sceptically. 'An angel?'

'I *saw* one,' Havloc insisted.

The beggar's practised whine cut in. 'Pity me, your honours, a poor cripple, one of God's poor, can't work, can't walk! Pity me.' He was well into his stride now, lying in his little wheeled cart displaying cruelly twisted limbs, dislocated hips and shoulders, feet pointing backwards, neck awry, a stained patch over one eye.

The knight with the hawk came down the steps followed by his unhealthy-looking sister.

'Poor soul,' said the fat man kindly, dropping a coin into the beggar's cup.

'God bless you, me lord!' The beggar reached along the edge of the bottom step, grasping it to pull his cart towards Havloc. 'Pity me, sir, for the sake of Him—'

Regardless of his good new breeches Havloc knelt beside the cart. 'Do you remember me?'

The beggar looked alarmed at this unexpected behaviour. The marks usually kept a healthy distance, pitching their coins from a few feet away; he'd become very skilled at catching them in his cup for if he wasn't quick enough some other poxy sod was sure to nip in and snatch the offering.

'You *must* remember,' cried Havloc wildly. 'It was near an inn, below the castle!'

'The Gabriel. I know it, your honour,' the beggar allowed cautiously. 'The better sort of folk stay there, good charitable folk like yourself. Pity me—'

'He doesn't remember,' Straccan said, reaching a hand to help Havloc up. 'Shame. It was worth a penny. Maybe two.'

The beggar's one bright eye stared up at them. 'What's worth tuppence?'

'This man saw you near the inn on the eve of Saint Audrey's Mass, just before he was beaten and robbed,' said Bane, stepping down to block the little cart's way.

The beggar squealed and put his hands over his face. 'Not by me, sirs! I'm just a poor cripple!' Through his fingers the poor cripple watched them warily.

'You were there when it happened,' Havloc said. 'You *must* have been; you can't move fast in this thing. You must have seen it all!'

'No I never,' the beggar whined. 'I never seen em, I mean *you*. Only got one eye, ain't I? it sees poorly.'

'He's lying. Let's wheel him along to the castle,' Bane suggested, getting hold of the cart. 'Crowner's men'll get the truth out of him.'

The beggar's muscles bunched, sliding under the skin with peculiar fluidity as his misshapen body rearranged itself, joints slipping smoothly into place. He scrambled from the cart, trying to duck away between their legs, but Bane had him by the neck of his shirt and yanked him back, twisting the fabric into a bunch to get a stranglehold on the beggar.

'What did you see?'

The man croaked and wriggled but Bane held on.

'I . . . can't . . . talk . . .' the beggar wheezed.

'Squeak, then,' Bane said. 'You might still get your tuppence. Or you can tell the crowner's men instead. They're not as gentle as me.'

'It was two men,' the beggar managed.

'That's better. Go on.'

'I was going home. It was late.' He jerked a thumb at Havloc. 'He came staggering up from the river, drunk, I thought. He fell in the midden. That's when they jumped him. They was behind the stairs, under the angel.'

'Angel?' said Straccan.

'The Gabriel's sign.'

'There!' said Havloc. 'I *told* you!'

'You knew they were there, didn't you,' said Bane, shaking him. 'You were in it with them.'

'I wasn't! I dint see em 'til they jumped him!'

'Who were they?'

'How the hell should I know?' He squawked as Bane shook him again. 'I don't know, honest! One was big and dressed like a monk; I never saw his face. The other was little, bald. Had a patchwork coat like a player wears.'

'Have you seen them since?'

'No.'

'Did you see what they took from me?' Havloc asked.

'Purse, shoes and something you had on a string round your neck,' the beggar said promptly. 'A little bag.' He made a fist to indicate size.

Straccan stooped, picked up the dropped cup and the coins that had spilled from it and handed it back, adding two pennies of his own. Relieved, the beggar relaxed, only to get a nasty surprise when Bane propelled him in the direction of the castle.

'Oi,' he protested, twisting and tugging in vain. 'You promised!'

'I promised you tuppence. There it is,' said Straccan. 'But you'll have to tell the coroner what you saw. You're a valuable witness. We can't risk anything happening to you.'

'But me lord,' wriggling desperately, 'they lock witnesses up!'

'So they do,' said Straccan, 'but I'll see you are fed, and when you've given your evidence to the justices you'll be a free man again. Havloc, fetch his cart along. It's his livelihood.'

Chapter 19

Without the ringing of church bells, forbidden under the Interdict, it was difficult to be accurate in the matter of timekeeping, but it was as near as Straccan could guess to the hour of sext when they reached the milestone. He saw no one waiting, but from the bushes at some distance from the road he heard the snort and jangle that betrayed a hidden horse and drew his sword.

'Come out!'

Larktwist appeared but Straccan did not sheathe his sword. 'Are you alone?'

'Course I am. I always work alone.'

'Ah,' said Straccan. 'So you *are* spying again.'

'Not at all, sir!' Larktwist looked injured. 'Matter of fact I'm sort of between jobs just now. Resting, you might say. It's been a busy year.' And indeed, the little spy looked more prosperous than when they had parted company after last summer's adventures. He had a horse for one thing, a plain but dependable-looking creature, and though the saddle and harness were old they were good. He wore a decent coat and adequate shoes and his cloak, thrown back, showed a long dagger ready to his hand. Larktwist had come up in the world.

Sheathing his sword Straccan dismounted, handing the reins to Bane, and crossed the road.

Over Straccan's shoulder Larktwist's bright knowing eyes examined Havloc. 'Doesn't look like a murderer, does he? Still, you never can tell. It's the quiet ones you have to watch.'

'I'm a busy man, spy. Are you going to spill what you know or do I have to squeeze every drop from your weasly throat?'

'There you go again,' said Larktwist, hurt. 'Spy's an unkind word, leads to misunderstandings. I prefer to call myself an agent; it sounds so much more professional. And is that any way to talk to an old friend?'

'Friend?'

'Journey-mate then. Be fair! You had no cause to complain of me last year.'

'True. But a man can't piss in a corner without you reporting the length of his cock!'

The spy grinned. 'It's my job, sir. If you want to piss go ahead. I won't look.'

'Get on with it, Larktwist!'

'You're looking for a stolen cup, or for the man that stole it. There's a reward, right?'

Straccan put a friendly-seeming hand on the spy's shoulder, but his fingers gripped like iron.

'Ow!'

'I don't have time to play patty-cake with you,' Straccan said, shaking him. 'If you know anything, spy, stop buggering about and tell me!'

'All right! All *right*!' Larktwist settled his dishevelled clothing and gave Straccan a reproachful look. 'Is it true about the reward?'

Straccan nodded.

Larktwist looked pleased. 'In that case . . . Have you met the abbot?'

'I've met lots of abbots. Which one?'

'The *beggars'* abbot, the *thieves'* abbot.' At Straccan's blank look Larktwist chuckled. 'There's one in every town. Beggars and thieves are all under him, like monks under an abbot, see? They give him part of their takings or whatever they've pinched and he finds a buyer and pays them a bit of what *he* gets. Every thief has to clear any plan with his abbot before doing anything – except for the opportunity of the moment, of course; that's understood. The abbot's their law and order.'

'That's monstrous,' said Straccan.

'No it ain't, it's sense,' protested Larktwist. 'Where would thieves be without law and order? How would they earn a decent living? Who could they trust to see fair play and keep knives in sheaths instead of in guts?'

'You're telling me thieves are organised?'

'It'd be sodding chaos if they weren't! Over the abbot there's a bishop – he's responsible for a whole area, a diocese, if you like – and all the abbots have to give him a rake-off.'

'Who's the bishop for this area?'

'No one knows that except the abbot.'

'Who's the abbot, then?'

'Ah, now there I might be able to help you.'

Ludlow's beggars and thieves had established a shanty settlement in a disused quarry outside the town. A few shelters were sturdily built of pilfered timber or driftwood lugged from the river but most were mere tents, and some folk simply tucked themselves into the narrow spaces between shacks, counting themselves lucky to be sheltered on two sides even though they lacked a roof.

The townsfolk had petitioned the bishop of Gloucester, who owned the land, to have the beggars driven out but the bishop had prudently fled to France, along with every other English bishop save one, and had more important matters to think about. The disgruntled people wanted the settlement pulled down and burned. They called it Beggartown, but the beggars called it Home.

This wasn't Sanctuary, where hard cases such as killers and rapists were protected for a time from the law's retribution; these were not Sanctuary-men but free people and proud of it. There was no thieving in Beggartown – the abbot had no mercy and no one got a second chance. Trussed and gagged, thieves were tossed in the Teme with only themselves to blame. They had all of Ludlow to steal from; Beggartown was sacrosanct.

'Where's the abbot, then?' Straccan asked.

'By the fire.'

Larktwist had met them as arranged, after dark, and brought them here by devious ways. He had abandoned his respectable garb for beggarly rags, and looked and smelled as repellent as the rest.

A big cloaked figure sat slumped on a barrel by the fire, leaning on a long cudgel. Wearing a spreading leather hat and with a patch over one eye he looked very like Wodan, lacking only the ravens. A small boy leaned against his knee.

The flames cast a festive light over the crowd of men, women and children, illuminating sunken cheeks and gummy grins, hare-lips and missing ears, bandages, crutches and the stumps of arms and legs. It lent skinny bodies in their tattered garb a theatrical gaudiness – here a flare of ragged scarlet, there the glint of soiled yellow silk in a patched kirtle.

They were a cheerful pack of vagabonds, for the day's work was over and it was time for supper. Clutching bowls and cups they queued at the fire. Savoury smells issued from a great pot on a tripod over the flames and a gaunt old woman ladled stew into the bowls held up to her. Nearby stood a thin man with a wax tablet which, as each dish was filled, he marked with a stylus.

'What's he doing?' Bane asked.

'Everyone pays,' Larktwist whispered. 'It's all reckoned up. We – they – settle accounts weekly.'

At the tail of the queue, hanging back at a considerate distance, were half a dozen men whose overpowering stink paled Larktwist's into insignificance.

Bane gagged. 'Christ! Who are they?'

Larktwist shrugged. 'Gong scourers.'

'Oh God!'

'Someone's got to do it,' said Larktwist defensively.

'Don't they ever wash?'

'Course they do,' said the spy indignantly. 'First thing they do is dip in the river, even when they have to break the ice. Makes no difference. It's soaked into them.'

The reeking band thoughtfully carried their suppers to the farthest reach of Beggartown, but the gusting wind brought their stink back.

'Introduce us to the abbot.' Straccan's hand on the spy's shoulder turned him about and pushed him towards the fire.

Abbots were elected. Beggartown and like establishments in every other large town had a shifting population with a small core of more or less permanent residents, and they believed in democracy. When the previous abbot had died they chose this one, Dimittis, to take his place. It was no light matter choosing their overlord. He must be a man whom all respected, and – within limits – trusted. A man able to keep bullies and thieves under control. One who would look out for the interests of the weaker among them, children and the genuinely crippled. Cunning and strong enough to enforce his rule, exact his tribute, and reliable enough to use a fair part of it for the benefit of all. Experienced in the wiles and tricks of his own kind and utterly ruthless in defence of their common good.

Years ago when Dimittis was a boy and his name was Edward, he had been a novice in a poor Cistercian convent. He'd had no vocation. He was that to-be-pitied creature, a younger son. A withered arm from birth prevented him from taking service with any lord or captain, although with his one good arm he was very useful with quarterstaff and axe, well able to look after himself at need. His older brother would inherit their holding, and his father gifted the Cistercians with an orchard on condition they took his worthless second son.

It was the convent, his father told him, or take to the roads and beg! And *that* would have been the better choice, he thought, when after six months of gruel, onion soup, black bread, hard labour and diarrhoea, he decided to run away.

Nunc dimittis, they were singing in Choir when he stuffed the bosom of his robe with stolen bread and hauled himself over the wall and away. *Lord, now lettest Thou Thy servant depart in peace.* He chuckled as he ran, hiding in hedges and ditches, sure of pursuit but certain that he would soon be too far away for any to find him.

He chopped wood for a woman who paid him with a good meal, the best he'd had for half a year.

'What's your name, lad?' she asked.

He chewed and swallowed. 'Dimittis,' he said.

He'd never gone hungry since then.

Now he sat on his barrel by the fire with his iron-bound cudgel under the armpit of his useless limb and watched as Straccan approached, followed by Bane and Havloc with Larktwist unhappily wedged between them. All eyes were on them. Greasy faces looked up from gnawing bones, food arrested on its way to open mouths; suspicious, resentful, hungry stares from men, women and children. The woman dishing out second helpings paused with ladle raised and the accountant glowered at them.

The abbot whispered something to his boy who scuttled off into the shadows rimming the firelit circle. After a moment or two he returned with a wooden bucket.

'Sit down, sir.' The abbot's voice was a deep rumble. Straccan sat on the upturned bucket; Larktwist shifted from foot to foot, uncomfortably the centre of attention.

'Master Bird,' said the abbot to Larktwist, and Straccan raised an eyebrow at the name. 'You have brought us guests. No doubt you had good reason.'

'The best of reasons,' said Straccan quickly. 'My knife at his liver.'

'Ah.' The abbot smiled. 'A universal persuader. Well, Master Bird, thank you. Have your supper in peace now while I talk with these gentlemen.'

Bane and Havloc let go. Larktwist, with a windy sigh of relief, pulled a wooden bowl from his rags and took his place last in the diminishing queue.

'It was you, sir,' rumbled the abbot to Straccan, 'if I am not mistaken, who caused Pity Me to be locked up.'

'The beggar? Is that his name? He's a witness. He'll be let out when he's given his evidence. Meanwhile I promise you he'll be well fed and none shall harm him.'

'That may be, but he is still in prison.'

'I'm sorry,' said Straccan. 'That's the way it is. Witnesses must be kept safely until they can say their piece. We dared not risk losing him.'

'And what was he unfortunate enough to see?'

'He saw two thieves attack and rob this man.' Straccan touched Havloc's arm. 'They stole his purse, his shoes, his belt and a small gold cup which was in a bag round his neck.'

'Why have you come to me?'

Havloc said, 'The thief may still have the cup. I will pay a reward to have it back.'

'How much?'

'Five shillings.'

'You have it with you?'

'Here? Not on your life!'

'At least your misfortune has taught you prudence.' Dimittis smiled.

'Have you heard anything of the cup?' Straccan asked.

'If one of my people took it he would have brought it to me. Believe me or not as you choose, but no one has done so. None here would keep such a thing from me. That would be treason and we have a way of dealing with traitors. Your thieves were not of my flock.'

'Pity Me said one was a big man in a monkish robe, the other small and bald and wearing a coat of patches,' said Havloc.

The abbot shook his head. 'I don't know them. You have come on a fruitless errand, gentlemen.'

'Will you at least question your people?' Straccan asked. 'Someone may have seen them; someone may know who they are.'

The abbot beckoned to the accountant. 'Mark, pass the word.'

The thin man gave the two strangers a searching stare before striding away to talk to the various groups and families. They heard exclamations of surprise, snorts and laughs, the hiss of whispered talk. The accountant reappeared in the ring of firelight and bent to mutter in the abbot's ear.

'I am sorry,' Dimittis said. 'No one has anything to tell you. You should leave now, sirs. I noticed some of my people slipping off, no doubt hoping to meet you as you go. I don't wish any guest of mine to come to harm. I will provide you with an escort back to safety.' He snapped his fingers and the small boy leaped out of the shadows to his side. The abbot murmured to him and the boy ran off past the row of shacks into the darkness beyond.

Presently half a dozen men padded back with him, grinning cheerfully and bringing an awesome stench. They were the gong scourers.

Chapter 20

At the Templars' Commandery, Straccan withdrew funds enough for his journey.

'Hang on a minute,' said the Master, rummaging among the piled deeds, documents and chirographs on his table. 'Got a letter for you – it's here somewhere – chap from your manor brought it while you were away. Ah, here it is.' The Master handed over a grubby packet wrapped in waxed cloth, sealed, and tied with string. Straccan couldn't make out the device on the smudged seal. He put it in his pocket.

'What tidings of the Irish campaign?' he asked.

'Sailed at last on Saints Mark-and-Marcellinus; landed on Saint Alban's,' said the Master promptly. 'Marched straight for Kilkenny, but the bird had flown.'

'Breos?'

'Missed him by a whisker. Got clean away. Not sure where to yet: toss-up between Philip of France and the prince of Gwynedd. Courier's held up by the floods somewhere, I suppose.'

'Are you a betting man?' Straccan asked.

The Master spread the fingers of one hand and rocked it from side to side. 'Given a certainty.'

'Put your money on Wales.'

In Prince Llywelyn's private chapel Lord William de Breos knelt in prayer.

He was a pious man.

Piety had never stayed his hand from the slaughter of innocents: hostages, guests, heralds, even women and children.

An infamous massacre had won him his nickname, the Butcher of Abergavenny. They said of him that after that infamy, he went red-handed to the Mass. It was his habit to hear Mass every day, and he never passed a wayside shrine without stopping to kneel and pray. He had always given generously to the Church, and expected God to see things his way, no matter what he did.

He had escaped from Ireland in a fishing boat a bare hour ahead of John's pursuing force, thanks to the woman Julitta in whose warnings and promises he now placed his trust. He still had friends; friends in Brittany had sent her to him. Heed her, they said. He had done so and was glad.

Lord William had landed at Aberffraw with just the clothes he was wearing and three attendants – his squire, his medicus and his witch – one of the greatest lords in the realm, reduced to seeking charity.

Hospitality was a sacred duty to the Welsh, so the prince of Gwynedd had taken them in, albeit coolly at first; Lord William would not soon forget that proud cold face and chilly greeting. But when his loyal knights and sworn men began arriving by ones and twos, then by fives and tens to join him, Llywelyn's welcome had grown warmer. This was no defeated rebel, no poor refugee on the run from King John's retribution; this was the leader of a small but formidable band of fighting men, a valuable piece on the chess-board where Welsh prince and English king strove always for the winning move.

In the clothes the prince had given him Breos still looked every inch the great man, but his confidence had taken a hard knock. The magnitude of his downfall had stunned him. In the nature of things royal favourites rose and were toppled. He'd seen others fall, helped tread them down, joined merrily in the scramble for their estates, never dreaming it could happen to him, the great William de Breos, lord of Brecknock, Abergavenny, Builth and Radnor, Hay and Gower and Kington; master of Glamorgan, Monmouth and Gwynllwyg, Whitecastle, Grosmont and Skenfrith; lord in Ireland of Limerick, and in England of much of Sussex and more besides. Answerable to none within his boundaries. Untouchable.

So he'd thought.

He hadn't been the only one to misjudge the king. Perhaps because John loved his comforts – good food and wine, rich clothes, jewels, especially jewels, his bath, his bed, his doxies, his wife – men compared him slightingly with his father, King Henry, who'd been admirably impervious to luxury; and with his brother King Richard, whose halo of crusader glory blinded men to the fact that he also had loved fine raiment, music, poetry, jewels and not only pretty women but pretty boys as well. At least no one ever said that about John! In battle he was as ferocious as his father or the Lionheart, and in enmity more thorough.

Lord William had never bothered to count the thousands of marks he owed the king, vast sums lightly promised for favours, castles, wardships and shrievalties, pledged in the comfortable certainty that he would never have to face a reckoning. For he was the right-hand man of the king, deep in his counsels, keeper of his secrets and of one secret in especial.

He who had been given much yet looked for more. All that he had was as nothing beside his burning desire for the comital rank. Lord of this, baron of that he might be, but the king alone could create an earl. John had done it for William Marshal, why not for William de Breos? It never occurred to him that the king would refuse, and in the disarray of his amazement, Lord William made a mistake: he dared to remind the king of something John preferred to forget.

That folly, that imprudence cost him everything: all his estates, fair manors and farms, great castles, rich abbeys, wealthy towns. Having seized the chance – he'd been praying for it – to drag down his ambitious and over-mighty vassal, John compounded Lord William's ruin by demanding payment of the staggering sums Breos owed him, and when Lord William protested that he had nothing left with which to pay, the king demanded his grandsons as hostages.

Greed had brought about the downfall of the house of Breos, but it was his wife's defiance that sealed their doom. When the king's marshal arrived to take the hostages, Lady Mahaut barred the gates and refused to hand them over. Her infamous words, hurled from the battlements, heard by all her household and dozens of others, were repeated in horrified whispers from one end of the country to the other, crossing the Channel to send shock waves rippling through Brittany and France.

'I'll never yield my grandsons to that monster,' she bawled down at the marshal. 'All the world knows he murdered his own brother's son!'

It was no more than all the world had *thought* for the past seven years, ever since the mysterious disappearance of the young Duke of Brittany, John's nephew, Arthur. But she *said* it. To the king's marshal. At the top of her voice. From that moment they were not only doomed, but damned.

But Lord William could not believe his cause was totally lost. John could not afford to have him as an enemy; he knew too much. Better to have him in the tent pissing out, than outside pissing in. Eventually there would have to be a reconciliation, with proud condescension on the king's part and grovelling gratitude on his own. William knew the routine; he'd seen it happen to others who slipped from royal favour and bought their way back. It would be humbling, it would cost him an enormous sum of money which he'd have to get somehow, but John would come round.

Of course, if he managed to track down this relic the Bretons set such store by, this banner of King Arthur, then John's pardon – and indeed the king himself – would no longer matter.

Chapter 21

The people of Shawl grieved for Dame Alienor. The steward's wife Sybilla had found her lady lying at the chamber door, blue in the face and unable to speak. A manservant lifted the dame's body, astonished at its lightness, and laid her on the bed.

Alienor's eyes sought Janiva. Obediently she swallowed the draught held to her mauve lips but it did no good. Propped on pillows she fought for breath all that night and the next day, and the following night, while her heart lurched and stumbled towards the end of its labours.

Father Osric, blinded by tears, gave her the last rites, his hands shaking as he anointed her with the oil. Janiva unhooked the shutter to let Alienor's soul fly unhindered to God. Her two elderly tire-women, poor cousins, resigned themselves to the inevitable cloister and began to cry.

Father Osric, clutching the chrysm of holy oil, looked helplessly at Janiva. 'What'll I do? I can't ring the bell for her. I did ought to ring the bell.' The Interdict had silenced all the church bells in England.

'It's not your fault,' said Janiva.

But he felt it was and stumbled wearily out of the death chamber. 'The bell did ought to be rung for her,' he muttered unhappily as he negotiated the worn steps down to the hall. 'How will Saint Peter know she's coming?'

Like icy water the news ran from the death chamber to the hall, to kitchen, stables, mews and bakehouse, and to the huts and cotts of the village. The people left their work to run to the hall, hoping it was a mistake, huddling in quiet grieving groups when they found it wasn't.

Father Osric wrote letters: one to Sir Roger in Ireland with the king, although God only knew when he'd get it, the other to Lady Richildis at her parents' manor at Shaxoe.

Janiva and Sybilla washed and dressed the body lovingly and laid it on the great bed, covered with a pall of black velvet. The pall was worn and thin in places. It had done duty for Sir Guy and his parents and grandparents. Dame Alienor's body scarcely mounded it, as though a child lay beneath the covering, yet while she lived no one had realised she was so small.

The manor's carpenter, his tears falling on her, measured his lady's body and sawed and sanded and hammered at her coffin, a temporary coffin to serve until the necessary lead one could be fashioned. The people of the dame's household took turns to keep the death watch in her chamber all that day, and the next.

At the bedhead Father Osric prayed. His soft mumble and the beads clicking as they slid through his fingers made a comforting homely sound. Janiva knelt at the other side of the bed, her tears falling on the black velvet. 'Lady,' she whispered, 'I shall miss you so much.'

She wept for both Sir Guy and his wife, remembering the years of affection, the warm heart and gentle capable hands of the woman who had been a second mother to her all her life. Remembering Sir Guy when young – strong, cheerful, generous, kindly – it seemed such a short while ago, yet the speeding years had changed him into an old man, breathless, tired, sick. His heart, like his wife's, had failed; his squire, hearing the hawks' clamour, had found him dead in the mews.

What made hearts wear out? Janiva wondered. Beating from birth through fifty or more years of life. How many beats? Thousands upon thousands. Yet there were older men whose hearts did not fail. Why?

All her griefs, great and small, overwhelmed Janiva and she wept for her father whom she could not remember, for her mother who had died young, for Guy and Alienor, for Richard who had not returned although he'd promised, and for her broken bowl.

Nothing had gone well since she broke the bowl.

Like the gleam of a fish in the river a fragment of memory flashed, dreamlike, and was gone. Green eyes, cold, pitiless, fixed on her own. A voice, remote as an echo in her soul: '*All that you love you shall lose.*' She tried to hold onto it, pin it down, but the candles flared in a sudden draught and there was a sound behind her.

She turned. Richildis stood in the doorway with Benet Finacre at her side. His eyes flicked from Janiva to Father Osric, and his over-full lips tightened.

'Lady Richildis,' said Janiva, standing.

The girl walked forward, one hand resting protectively on her belly, Finacre hovering solicitously. She drew back the pall and gazed at her mother-in-law's still face. Crossing herself, she knelt beside the bed, tugging a rosary from her pouch. Her fingers moved along the beads. Behind her, Finacre also knelt, bowing his head over his clasped hands.

Presently Richildis looked up, straight at Janiva.

'Get out,' she said.

'*To Richard Straccan, knight, at Stirrup near Dieulacresse, from Osric, priest at Shawl.*'

Straccan took the letter to the window. It was not easy to read. The writing was shaky and the writer had used an ill-cut splattery pen and poor home-made ink, grey and pale.

'*Know ye that Dame Alienor, widow of our good lord Guy died on Saint Hubert's Day, may God assoil her and receive her into eternal joy.*'

'Amen,' said Straccan, shocked and saddened, crossing himself.

'*Lord Roger being oversea with the king, his lady holds the domain in his absence. Take it not ill, I implore thee, that I write of Janiva, and fear not that she is sick, not so, yet are things ill with her here. If thou would stand her friend come, for she has need of thee.*'

He stared at the pale wavery lines. What did the old man mean? Why didn't he say what was wrong? She was not sick, no, but bereft . . . His heart ached for her grief but she had sent him away; what comfort could he give her?

He read it again. '*His lady holds the domain . . .*' Why write that? Sir Roger was in Ireland, possibly he didn't yet know of his mother's death, and in his absence his wife – he'd forgotten her name and Osric hadn't written it – would be lord in his place. That was custom. Why tell him?

Something was wrong. Janiva needed him; he must go to her. The floods were still high but there were boats, there were rafts . . .

There was Bane's voice at the door. 'Someone asking for you.'

Behind Bane, Straccan saw a little man with small hands and feet; tidy, clean-shaven, his greying hair lying in neat waves, his linen collar spotless, hose unwrinkled and the latches of his shoes shining like silver. He entered the room in a cloud of perfume. The king's clerk, what was his name? Mace? Race? Straccan's heart sank. What did John want now?

'Sir Richard! I was afraid you'd have left already, but of course, the floods . . . Dreadful. I had a terrible time getting here and they tell me me it's much worse to the south. Half the country is under water. You'll have heard that Breos is in Wales?'

'No.' *Wace*, that was it, and his shoe latches probably *were* silver; royal clerks were well paid. 'We've been cut off here since I got back.'

'About forty men have joined him. Some are his own knights but he has also welcomed outlaws and vile rybauds who fight for pay. They've razed a path across South Wales from Brecon to the Severn, plundering towns, priories, abbeys; they've even got a ship, a galley, to reive along the coast!' He sighed. 'It is a wicked thing when a great lord turns rebel.'

'I have never understood,' said Straccan, backing away from the cloying scent of violets, 'the quarrel between Breos and the king.'

'It's a long story; Lord William has committed many offences over the years. His grace lost patience in the end.' Wace looked embarrassed. 'And there was Lady Mahaut's, um, indiscretion.'

'I heard about that.'

'All Christendom has heard of it! A most unfortunate business. She refused to yield up her grandsons for the king to hold.' Wace looked down at his silver buckles, glanced up at Straccan and looked down again quickly. 'The king has many children in his care.'

Straccan wondered why the fool was maundering on in this fashion before he'd even taken his cloak off. Of course the king held daughters and sons of men whom he mistrusted hostage for their fathers' obedience. What had it to do with him?

Wace was still talking. 'They are well looked after, Sir Richard. Boys receive military training; the lord king frequently knights youngsters in his care. Maidens are protected, taught housewifely skills and the management of the great estates they will one day oversee. Good husbands are found for them, loyal men in the king's favour. They are not all hostages, of course. It is an honour for a man's son – or daughter – to be taken into the king's care. You, um, have a daughter, I believe.'

The shock struck through Straccan like a lance, a physical jolt below his heart that left him breathless. *Oh dear God, this is what the king does! This is how he manipulates men. Gilla! Oh God, Gilla!*

'How soon do you think we will be able to leave?' Wace's eyes slid about like jellyfish, missing no detail of the room, but if he saw murder in Straccan's eyes he gave no sign.

'What do you mean, "we"?'

'I am to go with you, of course, Sir Richard. The king believes you may find me, um, useful and I am to send reports to him at every opportunity.'

The urge to fling the little man aside, kill him if he got in the way, was nearly overwhelming but Straccan fought it down. 'Reports?'

'Certainly. Commending your diligence, I'm sure. The lord king wants to know every detail of your endeavours. He is concerned that no time be lost, and that you give this matter your *exclusive* attention. As you will, of course! Perhaps your man can find me a place to write my first report, assuring his grace that you will do his bidding in, um, *every* particular. Just a quiet corner somewhere . . .'

God damn John and his bloody Banner to hell, Straccan raged inwardly. *He'll not have my Gilla! Bane must take her to Janiva! No one will know she's there . . .* He became aware of Osric's forgotten letter still in his hand and closed his fist on it. *Christ, no. I don't know what's amiss; there's trouble there. If it wasn't for Havloc and his damned cup I'd have been gone before this scented slug came crawling in. God's holy face, is there no way out of this coil? What's wrong at Shawl?*

Chapter 22

The first Manor Court of the new lord's rule, held at Shawl in his absence by his lady, had dragged on through a long humid day and was at last over.

Richildis sat in her husband's chair on the dais, sipping mulled wine. She looked tired and unwell. Benet Finacre, acting as recorder, finished making notations in his book, rose, bowed and left the hall, while villeins with fines to pay queued at the board where Robert the steward sat with ledger, pens, ink and sand. The steward wrote a careful but slow hand, and the queue shuffled forward by inches, murmuring to one another and clutching their coins.

'Well, that weren't too bad,' the cowman's wife whispered to the shepherd's wife.

'Coulda bin worse.'

'She were a bit hard on old Avice, though.'

'It's her own fault.' And so it was. Age – she was nearly seventy – had not blunted the edge of Avice's tongue and she had been fined several times before for insolence. This time she had splashed the hem of Benet Finacre's fine wool robe with her slops; an accident, she said, but when he rounded on her she made it worse, far worse, by calling him a slimy little shit, an opinion with which the manor wholeheartedly agreed.

'Yes, well, like I say, coulda bin worse.'

No one had known what to expect from the new regime with Sir Roger away, and the new lady a stranger to Shawl and its ways. Now the ordeal was over and hadn't been as bad as they feared, the villeins grew chatty and expansive with relief, disposed to joke and nudge one another and even, as Lady Richildis got up to leave and the steward sanded his entries in the ledger and sharpened another quill, to joke with him.

Robert read from his book, 'Barnabas is fined tuppence,' and looked up expectantly at the next in line. Amid laughter, Barnabas pretended to tremble, turning his pouch inside out and patting his pockets. 'Shut up, you lot,' said the steward resignedly. They were always like this after the court. 'Get on with it, d'you want to be here all night? I don't!'

Barnabas found two pennies and slapped them in the steward's palm, rounding on his laughing mates who began shoving each other playfully as they turned towards the door where old Avice sat crying on the beggar's bench by the screens, waiting to be taken to the stocks.

Above the hubbub raised voices were heard outside the screens and everyone stopped dead as Janiva pushed in past the agitated doorward, who had orders to keep her out.

'Lady Richildis,' she cried.

'Court's over,' said the steward crossly. 'Oh! Mistress Janiva!' He got up and hurried across to her, flustered. 'You shouldn't be here.'

Richildis paused at the back of the dais, one hand holding the door-curtain aside. She didn't turn her head. 'My orders were not to admit that woman,' she said, clutching her belly protectively. She had dreamed last night again of Janiva; seen the slut lying in Roger's embrace and both of them laughing at her.

The dream came often and there were others. Sometimes Janiva smothered her with a pillow while Roger watched, smiling. Sometimes Richildis dreamed she lay in her open grave, unable to move, while Janiva and Roger together scattered handfuls of earth down on her; she felt small stones sting her face and in the morning when she woke there were small scratches, little scabs on her cheeks and brow. She knew it was witchery and Father Benet agreed, but there was no proof. Wait, Father Benet advised, give the witch enough rope to hang herself.

'Put her out!'

While the steward dithered, Janiva came to the foot of the dais and all around people moved back, not by very much, wanting to get out of the way of the new lady's wrath but willing to risk it for the chance to be in on a really good row.

Janiva said, 'Madame, I beg you, give me permission to care for the boy Alaric, who is sick.'

Richildis scowled at the steward. 'Alaric?'

'The blacksmith's son, my lady,' Robert said hurriedly. 'Four years old.'

'What ails him?'

'He has fits,' Janiva said. 'There are herbs in the still-room that will help him. Please, my lady, let me use them.'

'*No.*'

'You have good store of herbs and medicines there, my lady. Most of them I prepared myself. Dame Alienor gave them freely to any who needed them.'

'Herbs grow wild. The people are free to gather them for their own use.'

'But they don't have the knowledge.'

'You do, of course. That's your lore, isn't it? Potions, draughts, salves. Who knows what you put in them? Did you cause the boy's fits, that you might be praised and rewarded for curing them? What foul brew did you give my lord's mother before she died?'

The people were silent, listening avidly, but at this a murmur rippled through the crowd.

Shocked, Janiva stared at Richildis. 'You *can't* think . . .'

'Weren't you told to keep out of my house?'

'Yes, but my lady, the boy is so sick—'

'Children are always sick; often they die. It is as God wills. You are *not* to give him anything.' She dropped the door-curtain and came to the front of the dais. 'You people, listen! I forbid you, all of you, to take any medicine from this woman. That is my order. Anyone disobeying will be whipped. Pray for the boy, as I shall. If it is God's will, he'll get better.'

Dismayed looks were exchanged but no one dared protest. Richildis turned her back on them and raised the door-curtain again.

'My lady, in God's name, have pity! You carry a child yourself.'

Richildis went white. 'Are you threatening my child, witch?'

'*No*, my lady! No, before God!'

'Guard your tongue or I'll have it cut out! Keep away from my people and don't let me see your face again! Put her out!'

No one moved. Janiva walked through the appalled crowd to the door. On the dais Richildis suddenly gasped, an animal-like grunting *huff*, and clasped her belly with both hands.

'It hurts,' she said, her eyes wide with astonishment.

The steward's wife, Sybilla, ran up the steps of the dais and clapped her hands on the girl's belly, feeling the iron-hard muscles in spasm.

'It's started,' she said. 'It's too soon. You've a month to go yet.'

'It's her doing,' Richildis gasped through clenched teeth. 'Keep her away from me!'

Tugging back the door-curtain Sybilla bawled through to the chamber above, 'Mavis! Lilliana! Come help your lady! Quickly!'

Richildis' tire-women came pattering down the steps and with Sybilla's help carried their mistress to her bed.

Chapter 23

More than thirty hours had passed since Lady Richildis' labour started and it looked bad. Sybilla had put an old sword of Sir Guy's under the mattress to cut the pain and every knot, buckle and fastening in the chamber had been undone, the women even laying aside their girdles and loosening their shoes, but although from the beginning the contractions had been unusually strong the water had not broken. The girl screamed and bore down with each grinding pain but there was no progress.

The midwife had been there since being fetched from her cheese-making yesterday. She was tired and fearful that if the lady or the child, or both as seemed quite likely, died, she would be blamed. Between spasms Richildis slept briefly, exhausted, and whenever the girl's hoarse cries abated the midwife dozed too.

Held on the birthing-stool by her two women, Richildis hung like a sack from their grip. If they let go her arms she would fall to the floor.

'How much longer?' Sybilla asked.

'Er's gettin nowhere with it,' said the midwife crossly. 'Better break the water. Get us some lard, gal. Er'll never last. Er's buggered now.'

Sybilla flapped a hand at one of the hovering servants. 'Lard,' she hissed. The woman ran from the room, the sound of her feet slapping the steps echoing in the stairwell.

The midwife blotted her sweating face with her sleeve. 'Give over, let er lie down fer a bit. We'll ave another try presently, eh my duck?'

They dragged Richildis to the bed and laid her on it, a flaccid unresisting doll. Her closed eyes were sunk in patches of bruise-coloured flesh. Her vast belly stuck up like a white hill, making her arms and legs seem disproportionately small. Only the belly seemed alive as the child shifted, and then another contraction dragged Richildis back to consciousness to groan and struggle in vain.

The serving-woman hurried in with the lard. The midwife slathered her hands and pried the labouring girl's thighs apart. Richildis screamed hoarsely. There was a gush of bloody water and a foul smell. The midwife wiped her greasy hands on her filthy apron and shook her head.

'Ain't no good. It's lying wrong. That's its backbone I felt. Er could shove 'til Doomsday and get nowhere.'

'Can't you shift it?' Sybilla asked.

The midwife backed away, shaking her head. 'I dursn't.'

'She'll die if you don't.'

'Er'll die if I do, likely, and blame to me.'

Sybilla went to find Janiva.

'I *can't* help her,' Janiva said. 'She won't have me near her.'

'I know. But can't you tell us what to do?'

'I'm no midwife. A straightforward birthing maybe, but not this.'

'It's stuck fast crossways,' Sybilla said. 'Dear God, it happens to ewes but I've never known it happen to a woman.'

'Ewes,' said Janiva. 'Of course! Quick!' She began running, Sybilla panting after, past the huts and garden plots to a rail-fenced pen where a strong sheepy smell and a lot of bleating proclaimed that Tyrrel the shepherd was doing something, probably unpleasant, to a bunch of sheep.

He looked up from a clarty backside and waved his shears at the two women. 'What you want?' he asked rudely. 'I'm busy!'

As Janiva explained, Tyrrel became more and more uncooperative.

'It's lying crossways,' she said urgently. 'You can turn it!'

'Garn,' said the shepherd, spitting. 'I dunno nothin bout *ladies'* babies.' Nor did he. He assumed they appeared ready-made, clean and swaddled, on request.

'You've turned lambs inside their mothers,' said Janiva. 'And your own daughter last year, when that boy of hers wouldn't come.'

'Don't be daft, girl. They ain't the same.'

'Eh?' said Sybilla. 'What d'you mean?'

'*Them*, a course. *Ladies*. They ain't like *women*.'

The two women stared at him and at each other.

'Course they are, you old fool,' said Sybilla. 'How d'you think their kind get born, eh? They don't bloody lay eggs!'

'Never said they did. I ain't daft! But stands to reason. Ladies ain't like *real* folk. Birthin's mucky work, all blood and shit and screamin. Great folks'll ave a better way o' doin it.'

'Sweet Jesus give me patience,' hissed Sybilla. 'It's the same for all of us! I helped Dame Alienor at her birthings and I've had four of my own. Am I a lady?'

The shepherd snorted. 'Not bloody likely! I knew your dad.' He turned conversationally to Janiva. 'E were a right old— Oy!'

Sybilla had hold of his sleeve and jerked him to his feet. 'Get off your arse and come with me!'

Janiva watched her push and propel him to the house. As they reached the open door she called 'Sybilla! Make him wash!'

The baby was small and a bit floppy, but a boy and breathing, which was more than anyone expected. He lay swaddled and limp in the cradle that his father had shared with Janiva seventeen years before.

Richildis slept.

Thank God, thought Sybilla, *it worked*! She had lugged Tyrrel, reeking of sheep and almost speechless with indignation at having been made to wash, into the chamber. But his hands were as soft as a woman's, and once he stooped to the job he did it superbly. The lady, luckily, was too far gone to know what was happening and as soon as the baby slid into the cloth that the midwife held to receive it Sybilla hustled Tyrrel from the chamber before Richildis could see him.

'Ere,' he said truculently in the doorway. 'Don't I get a drink even?'

'God save you, Tyrrel, get out o' here, do! I'll see to you tomorrow.'

In the cradle the baby mewed feebly. *We'll be lucky if we raise this one*, Sybilla thought as she lifted him and took him to his mother.

'Wake up, my lady,' she said heartily. 'Your new little son is hungry!'

Chapter 24

The reek of burning carried on the wind for miles.

Llangrwys was – had been – a wool town, busy and prosperous, cupped like an egg in its nest in a hollow of the Monmouthshire hills and a fair sight yesterday for anyone looking down on its houses, shops and churches. Today it was a blackened ruin, deep in ash and smoking cinders.

The wool went up like, well, like wool; the torch barely touched it and flames were running like water, licking over the bales, pale in sunlight but fiercely hot. As the barns burned and their roofs fell in, the oily flames roared up, and now and then rags and tatters of flame would break loose and go flapping and cracking skywards.

The fire spread swiftly; soon the town was ablaze: houses, shops, inns and stables, storehouses, even churches. The noise of its destruction, the crash of falling stones, the screams of people and horses and the roar of burning could be heard far off.

Lord William had offered to let the churchmen go unharmed – providing they handed over their treasures, candlesticks, chalices, coins, anything of gold or silver – before the burning began, but the townsfolk, who had already given up their money and valuables in the hope that he would spare their town, were left to fend for themselves. Those who survived – and many died, foolishly resisting or trying to save their homes and families – must turn beggar now or face starvation.

Breos called his men to heel and rode on. If it was his town no more, no one else should have it.

Later in the day they came upon a small church set at a crossroads in the middle of nowhere, a place where travellers might thank God for their safe journey thus far and ask His protection for the miles that lay ahead. Priest's hut, pigsty and yard stood alongside, and the priest himself was milking his goat at the church door. Rising in terror when he saw the armed men and oversetting his bucket, he ran, tripped and fell sprawling before Lord William's horse.

Breos got down, pulled off his gauntlets and lifted the priest to his feet. 'Get up. I want you to say Mass for me.' Gripping the frightened man by an elbow he marched him into the church. His men waited outside and let their horses crop the priest's vegetable garden.

In the nave of the tiny church Lord William in his mail seemed three times the size of an ordinary man. The terrified priest who had at sword point and in violation of the Pope's ruling just said Mass for him shrank against the altar when he'd finished his Latin and trembled, but his son who served at Mass was hoping for a penny from the great lord, and smiled at him.

It was a long time since anyone had smiled at William de Breos. 'God be with you, son,' he said.

'God be with you too, my lord.'

It was the habit of a lifetime. Always he gave God's greeting to the young and innocent so that they would return the blessing to him. God heard the prayers of children. Both Lord William and Mahaut his wife scooped up such blessings like trawling seabirds. Every letter Lord William had ever sent ended with a prayer for God's grace – he tipped his scribes extra to be sure they would never omit it – and nearly every time he opened his mouth God's name fell out of it. 'If God wills . . .' 'In the name of God . . .' 'If it please God . . .' 'By the Grace of God . . .'

He'd got out of the habit lately, what with one thing and another, but now he felt more himself. Action had scoured melancholy and doubt from his mind. Reiving was filling his coffers and paying his men. The lady Julitta promised his restoration to power and, at last, in this Interdict-benighted land he'd managed to hear Mass, even such a bastard gabbled version as this uneducated illiterate fool of a priest was capable of. He'd confessed and been absolved, the child's blessing hallowed him and he had no doubt that the God he had honoured all his life, whose goodwill he had bought with churches and shrines and convents, whose man he was, would stand by him, just as he himself stood by the knights who served him. After all, that was a seigneur's duty.

He dropped a handful of silver before the altar and strode out of the church into the hot sunlight of the morning. Ahead, the thin mist not yet burned off them, rose a line of dark hills, with more hills, higher still, at their backs.

'Where are we going, my lord?' asked his squire.

'The abbey at Maesyronen,' said Lord William. The abbot there owed everything to him; he had supported the place for years. 'We'll stay there for the time being. Send four men back to escort the lady Julitta. Tell them if any harm comes to her, they will pay with their eyes and their hands.' Maesyronen had guested kings since Harold's day, before the Norman bastard reived the kingdom from its rightful lord. Queens had slept in the bed where Julitta de Beauris would lie tonight.

Abbot Hyacinth greeted Lord William with outward courtesy and inward despair. *Dear God in heaven, why did You let him come here? If I turn him away he will destroy us. If I give him shelter the king will destroy me!* But the king was far away in Ireland and Lord William, his knights behind him, was on the doorstep sword in hand.

The abbot privately commended his soul to God and with a smile like the rictus of a corpse welcomed his unwelcome guests. His long tempering in the fires of diplomacy even helped him conceal his dismay at having to welcome also Lord William's whore, but the guestmaster who showed Julitta to her chamber quivered with affronted modesty and made his disapproval all too clear. She thanked him prettily at the door and he had no idea how he came to stumble on the stairs on his way back to his cell, falling from top to bottom and snapping both ankles like dry sticks.

Julitta regarded her face in her silver mirror while waiting for Lord William's summons; not, as all his men believed, to lie with him, but to demand that she read the stars for him again, seeing past the veils that hid the future to tell him what lay ahead.

She was still beautiful. She laid the mirror down, satisfied, and chose a gown of cream silk with an overmantle of blue wool. With her golden tresses loose over her shoulders beneath a blue silk veil she looked like the Blessed Virgin herself, and knew it.

To her girdle she attached a chain from which hung an egg-shaped casket, cunningly wrought of black and silver metal strands, as closely woven as threads. By day this never left her body and at night she slept with it under her pillow. She had stolen it from the Breton sorcerer Benoic, court astrologer to the Duchess Alix; fortunately he had died before he could accuse her.

There was a knock at the door. A young monk gaped, dazzled, at the fair vision, stammering, 'M-my lady, Lord W-William requires your p-p-presence.'

She inclined her head. 'Lead on, brother.'

Once more she would pretend to read the future in the stars and tell the great fool what he wanted to hear, what he already believed. Some of it was even true. He *would* find the Banner, her demon had told her so; and when he did he would expect Brittany to show its gratitude.

She smiled. He was in for a shock there.

Chapter 25

It was that brief dark time between candlelight and daylight when Straccan and his unwanted companions led their horses up Ludlow's Broad Street. Bane had departed even earlier, by the town's other gate, on his way north to Shawl. So far Master Wace hadn't commented on his absence, but Straccan had no doubt it would go in his next report.

Yawning, Havloc wished he'd had time to break his fast and wondered if Alis was awake yet or still asleep, rosy and warm in her bed. She'd said they were lovers. My God, you'd think a man would remember that! He felt very lonely and sorry for himself, and Sir Richard, plodding morosely ahead, seemed to have a bad case of early morning ill temper. Ever since this man Wace had turned up Straccan had been unusually short-tempered.

A cock crowed, followed instantly by others from all directions, and a dog set up a steady, relentless, deep *wow-wow-wow*ing. Shutters squeaked open. Someone flung slops, splashing Zingiber's hind legs; the horse snorted steamily.

'Easy,' said Straccan softly.

From the mouth of an alley someone called, 'Sir!' It was Larktwist, still in his beggarly guise, towing another ragbag behind him.

'I hoped we'd catch you, sir, before you left.' He pulled the ragged bundle forward. 'This here's Arletta. The abbot's told her to talk to you.'

Arletta was stick-thin with big brown eyes and sunken cheeks. Her feet were bare and she wore two gowns, the stuff of each filling the holes in the other. Twenty years old, she looked fifty.

'Is there a cook-shop open?' Straccan asked.

'Ma Dumpling's always open, round the corner.' Larktwist led the way, keeping a firm hold on the woman's stick-like wrist.

Ma Dumpling, who had almost forgotten her real name, was a vastly fat woman perpetually presiding over a seething cauldron of soup and dumplings. She did a brisk trade from dawn 'til curfew and kept four daughters and a husband as fat as herself on the proceeds.

There was a bench for customers who chose to eat on the premises – many brought their bowls to be filled and bore them carefully away – and despite the early hour the pot was already simmering, the dumplings floating in a greyish glossy mass on top.

Arletta stared painfully at the pot until Larktwist pushed her gently down on the seat. Ma Dumpling, enormous breasts surging above a bulging belly, ladled soup and dumplings into a bowl and Straccan put it in Arletta's hands.

'And for yourselves, sirs?' Ma Dumpling asked, beaming, ladle at the ready.

Seeing Havloc's hungry look Straccan felt a twinge of conscience. He'd barely been civil to the poor sod since Wace arrived, blaming him, however unfairly, for his predicament. Come to think of it, he'd had no breakfast himself.

'Oh, all right. Two more.' Catching Wace's hopeful eye he added, 'If *you* want some you can buy your own.' Wace shrugged and handed over a coin.

It was surprisingly good. When Arletta's bowl was empty she licked it clean like a dog.

'Tell em what you told the abbot, girl,' said Larktwist. 'There's naught to fear.'

Her eyes skated from Straccan to the others and back to Straccan. 'You put my man in prison.'

'Your man?'

'She's Pity Me's woman,' explained Larktwist.

'E done nothin,' she said. In the steamy little room her nose began to run and she wiped it on her sleeves. Patches of colour flared and blotched her cheeks.

'He's a witness,' Havloc said. 'He saw the men who robbed me.'

'E ain't done nothin,' she whined. 'Men die in prison. What'll become of me?'

'Your husband won't die,' Straccan said. 'He'll be fed, I promise, and when the justices have heard him they'll let him go.'

'I'll starve!' Her filthy hands twisted together desperately.

'No,' said Straccan. 'You'll be fed too.' He looked at Ma Dumpling, wreathed in savoury steam, dropping fresh dough-balls into the cauldron. 'If you come here every day until your husband is let out, you will eat. I'll pay. That's if you've got something useful to tell me.'

'Every day?'

'Until Pity Me's released. And you can have another bowlful now and some bread.'

Arletta waited until she'd got it, just in case, before she said any more. 'Them fellers you're lookin for: the monk were took out of the Teme with is throat cut. Laid out in a cart by the castle gate, e were, but no one put a name to im.'

'What about the other man?' Havloc asked.

'Baldy little runt in a coat of patches. The monk called im Tom. I seen em together a couple times.'

'Did he kill the monk?'

Her gaze slid uneasily over everyone in the steamy room. 'Dunno. Could ave. Run off, dint e?'

'Do you know where he went?'

'Where they all go. The greenwood. Can I ave some more?'

Straccan beckoned Ma Dumpling and turned to Wace. 'Wait here. You too, Havloc. Cigony must hear this. I'll not be long.' It was a frail shoot of hope that would probably die a-borning but must be cherished, for until the missing cup was found he was saddled with Havloc, who didn't want to be here any more than he did.

Arletta hardly noticed him leave. She held out her hands for the refilled bowl, wondering how long they'd keep her provider in prison. At least a month, with any luck.

*   *   *

The land steamed under the hot sun and plagues of stinging flies hatched out of the mud, swooping, whining shrilly, upon men and beasts alike, so that the miry roads were filled with travellers afoot and ahorse who from a distance appeared to have gone mad, waving their arms and slapping at invisible tormentors. Many folk who had been kept in Ludlow by the floods left there that morning: pilgrims, merchants and clerks, couriers and soldiers, monks and nuns. Among them was the leper Garnier. The monks of the Maudleys – the lepers' refuge of Saint Mary Magdalene – besought him to remain with them, and when he would not outfitted him with new clothes and footwear and provisions for his journey. Best of all they had provided a guide: a leper like himself but young and still sturdy, a sinewy Welshman called Illtud, who knew the way to the Hidden Valley and carried a quarterstaff, hoping for nothing better than an opportunity to use it.

Chapter 26

Richildis' son was baptised Hugues, her father's name, and Shawl sulked because he'd not been named Guy and because Benet Finacre, whom they called 'Old Vinegar', baptised him and not Father Osric. The manor's people had been in bad fettle ever since Lady Richildis forbade them to have anything to do with Janiva. Nevertheless they welcomed their young lord's baby son and worried about his digestion, his colic, his vomiting, his stools, his night-crying and his eczema every bit as much as his mother did.

This was their old lord's grandson and, if God spared him, their future lord. It looked as if He might, for although the child was small and born too soon, after the first two anxious days he began to suck strongly. His mother being feverish by then a wet nurse was installed, and once again two babies lay in the old cradle, boys this time, one noble, pale and fretful, the other lowborn, ruddy with health and placid as a dormouse.

When the wet nurse burst into the steward's house before dawn, capless, barefoot and in her smock, and woke Robert and his wife from sleep with a wild story of witchcraft and murder, they thought she'd lost her wits.

'Keep her quiet, can't you?' Robert sat on the edge of the bed pulling his rumpled shirt and his breeches on, tying the flap of his codpiece while Bretta jabbered her nonsense. 'What's the silly bitch doing here? She oughter be up in the chamber with the babbies. Lady Richildis'll have her guts for garters if she wakes and finds her gone!'

Sybilla scowled at him over the silly bitch's head, holding the girl and patting her back comfortingly while Bretta wept and stuttered.

'Fore God, girl, what you on about? Who's been murdered? Jesus, Bretta, get hold of yourself! There, that's better. Now slowly, what's amiss?'

'Old Vinegar says Mistress Janiva m-murdered Dame Alienor and the old lord too, by sorcery, and tried to kill the lady *and* the b-babby!'

'Balls,' said the steward, dunking his face in a bowl of water and towelling it with his shirt.

'He's sent two of them Shaxoe b-bullies to f-fetch her to hall. Can't you do nothin, steward? She bin good to me, Mistress Janiva has.'

'Go and see what's happening,' Sybilla said, handing her husband his belt and jerkin. 'I'll be along as soon as I get my clothes on.'

Word had got about already, and by the time Sybilla had hurried into her gown and coif and arrived panting, a dozen or more horrified villagers were gathered in the hall. Benet Finacre stood beside Sir Roger's empty seat at the high board, and below the dais was Janiva, wearing only her shift, with her wrists bound together behind her back and one of the men from Shaxoe slouching at her side.

It was still dark in the hall. A couple of new-lit torches flared and sputtered in wall-cressets at the back of the dais, and the board was lit by a row of candles weeping wax all along its length. The candles cringed in a sudden draught as one of Richildis' women twitched aside the curtain at the back of the dais to let her mistress through. Yawning, Richildis sat in her husband's chair. Her protuberant blue eyes fixed, coldly, upon Janiva.

'I told that slut to stay out of my house.'

'You did, my lady,' said Finacre, 'but she must be brought before you to be charged.'

'Charged? With what?'

'Sorcery, my lady, and murder.'

The onlookers gasped and began to mutter among themselves.

'Silence!' cried Finacre. In the hush the thin wailing of the baby drifted down from the chamber above. Finacre turned to Richildis.

'God guided you in your dislike of her. She poisoned your husband's father, the lord of this place, who had done her no harm, and Dame Alienor, that good soul.' Despite his order the muttering continued and he raised his voice to be heard. 'She is a witch, a bedmate of Satan,' he said loudly. 'In malice she also sought to kill *you*, my lady, and your child, and when, because of your own virtue and with Our Lady's protection, you did not succumb, she wrought spells to cause your fever and dry up your milk.'

From the bosom of his tunic he drew something wrapped in a rag and threw it down on the board.

'There's proof.'

Richildis reached and picked it up. The rag fell away. Something dark, dry and shrivelled, something that seemed to have arms and legs and perhaps a head, like a small mummified monkey, rolled onto the board. 'Ugh,' she said, disgusted. 'There are nails in it.'

'Indeed there are. Note where they're placed, here, and here.' He touched himself lightly on breast and belly. 'I found it in her house, with other filthy devilish things. Bring her up here!'

Janiva was shoved roughly up the steps to stand across the board from the lady. In the brighter light her face showed bruised and swollen, and a gout of blood had dried below her lip where it had been cut against her teeth by a blow.

'Loose her hands,' the chaplain said, and to Janiva, 'pick it up.'

'It's a mandrake,' she said. 'A root that grows in the fields, that's all. It's used to ease pain. Any herbalist will tell you.' She turned it over in her hands. 'Who struck these nails through it?'

'It can also be used to kill,' said Finacre, addressing the growing crowd below. 'This manikin-root is wholly a thing of the devil! Does it not scream when pulled from the ground? A scream so fearful that any hearing it will drop dead! The witch who gathers it must stop her ears with clay from a new grave mixed with the fat of an unbaptised baby.'

There was a collective gasp of horror and disgust from the listeners. Richildis crossed herself and clutched the little reliquary which she wore round her neck.

'There were other things too,' Finacre said. 'Nasty powders and potions, made from weeds and toadstools. Charms of ill. Charms to rouse men's lust, to steal husbands from their wives' beds . . .' The murmuring in the hall grew louder. 'Charms to cause sickness and blind honest folks' eyes to her wickedness. I threw them on the fire. They gave off the reek of Hell.'

Richildis whimpered and drew back, crossing herself again, her mouth a dark O of fright. Gasps and cries came from the watchers. Those from Shaxoe crossed themselves and horned their fingers towards Janiva to ward off evil. Someone hissed, 'Witch,' and someone else shouted, 'Murderess!'

'Witch she is, beyond doubt,' Finacre cried. 'And she knows me for her enemy! Yestereven in the form of a hare she sprang up under my foot to try and bring me down, but I called upon Christ and Saint Anthony and she fled those holy names. I followed her to her house.'

'My lady,' Janiva appealed to Richildis. 'None of this is true. He is lying!'

'*This* is no lie,' the chaplain shouted, shaking the mandrake. 'With this, my lady, she tried to kill your child in the very womb! See!' He drew out a long nail from what might be thought the manikin's belly. Richildis gave a long moan as if it had been drawn from her own flesh. 'When that failed, in spite and jealousy she sought to dry your milk.' He displayed the other two nails.

Several women screamed. Richildis scrambled from her chair and backed to the curtained wall, her women supporting her on either side. Finacre thrust the mandrake at Janiva who tore it from his hand, flung it down and spat in his face. With all his strength he struck her, knocking her from the dais. Her head hit the stone floor hard and she lay still.

'Take her away,' he snarled. 'Lock her up!'

There was uproar in the hall.

Later that morning Lady Richildis took her son, with his wet nurse and her baby, home to Shaxoe, which pleased Shawl's people until they learned that she had left Benet Finacre in charge, with

Sir Roger's seal and four of her Shaxoe men to see his orders carried out.

'There's worse trouble coming, I know it, *you* know it. Rob, *must* you go now?' Sybilla was cutting bread and cheese for her husband to take on his journey. The steward had an errand for Father Finacre and would be away for a few days. He fidgeted as his wife straightened his jerkin, tucked the food into his satchel and spat on her finger to wipe a smut from his chin. 'Hurry back, Rob. There's no tellin what Old Vinegar'll do.'

He knew it, but what could he do? The chaplain had the seal, there was no arguing with that, and no sooner had Lady Richildis' cortege disappeared from view than Old Vinegar had demanded the manor's document chest and begun prying into all Shawl's business. After a while he sent for the steward and asked what service Janiva rendered to the manor and Robert, surprised, said none for she was free.

Finacre, deep in a litter of parchment rolls, raised a sceptical eyebrow. 'Was she born free?'

'No. Her mother was made free for fostering Sir Roger when Mistress Janiva was a baby.'

Finacre drummed his fingers on the table. 'So there should be a document proving her freedom.'

The steward hesitated. 'I suppose so. It was all before my time.'

'Very well. Go about your business.'

The chaplain was pleased with his day's work. The witch was trapped – and she *was* a witch, of course she was, how else could she visit him in dreams, filthy dreams intended to pollute him? Night after night ever since he first saw her she had troubled his sleep with images of lust and promises of pleasures unspeakable. And she was powerful! Even in God's own daylight she tormented him with loathsome desires, and although the hair shirt he wore to subdue his sinful flesh added to his physical misery, it failed altogether to stifle his obscene longings.

She was clever. The foolish people here thought much of her for easing the ailments she doubtless brought upon them in the first place. Thus had she won their trust. They must be made to see her as he did, to loathe and fear her. The mandrake had frightened them, he had done well there. The nails were a touch all his own.

The Devil must be fought with whatever weapons came to hand.

In the evening he sent for Robert again, saying there was nothing in the records to prove the freedom of the woman Audrey, widow of Adam, and her *sequelae*. When and where, and with what witnesses, he asked, had the grant been made?

Robert had no idea. Seventeen years ago he'd only been a child himself. 'Lord Roger'll know, of course, and he'll surely come as soon as he can leave the king. Come to think of it,' he said, his glum face brightening, 'Father Osric would've been a witness.'

'Ah yes,' said Finacre, pursing his lips thoughtfully. 'I shall speak to him, of course. Nevertheless there is no document.'

'But sir, everyone *knows* she's free!'

'Was her father free?'

'No.'

'There you are then. The child of an unfree father is unfree; that's the law. In the absence of any document or any living witness to a grant of freedom I must rule that the woman Janiva is unfree, the property of the manor like all other cattle.' The small skin roll granting Audrey's freedom and that of her new-born daughter was safely in the inner pocket of his robe and destined for the brazier in his chamber. 'As for the charges of murder and the attempted murder by sorcery of Lady Richildis and the child, if she won't confess she will be put to the ordeal.'

Robert stared, open-mouthed. 'Ordeal? There ain't been ordeals here in years!'

'If she is innocent,' Finacre said, 'fire will not hurt her. Or do you doubt God's justice?'

'No, sir, not me, no, never!'

Robert hadn't meant to tell his wife but she'd got it out of him anyway and now she followed him out to the stable and watched as he mounted.

'Somebody's got to do something,' she said.

'There's bugger all I can do about it,' the steward said. 'Old Vinegar's got the seal. He's the law here. He can do *anything*! Chop off hands, feet, ears, put out eyes for disobedience, like the bad old days.' He was trembling. 'You want that to happen here? If she's innocent she'll take no harm from the ordeal; that's what he said.'

'Ordeal, Jesus! What are things coming to? Rob, don't you know what happens? They'll heat a great heavy bar of iron until it's white hot and make her carry it!'

'Only for three paces,' the steward said. Seeing his wife's expression he added hastily, 'If she's innocent God won't let it hurt her!'

'Don't be a fool! This is *wicked*! God's my life, Rob, you don't believe all this shit about Janiva, do you?'

'Course not!' But he looked aside and wouldn't meet her eyes.

Sybilla shouted at his retreating back, '*Someone's* got to help her!'

Chapter 27

'Certainly I remember them, Sir Richard,' said the prioress. She could hardly deny it. 'We have never forgotten Lady Ragnhild and Hallgerd.'

Her eyes, the colour of dirty ice and as cold, met Straccan's like a clash of blades. Word of his arrival, in company with a royal clerk and sent by the king, had reached every part of the convent of the Penitent Sisters by the time he and Wace were shown into the prioress's parlour, and the nuns had closed ranks. Whatever they might be after, these spies of the king would learn nothing here. The nuns were accustomed to the lightning swoops of the bishop's regional inspectors, and everything they didn't want the strangers to see – pet dogs and birds, the charcoal brazier in the dormitory, private keepsakes and correspondence – was hidden with the swift efficiency of long practice. All questions met a wall of resistance concealed by a discreet curtain of good manners.

If she could manage it without getting herself arrested and her convent disbanded, Prioress Heloise de St Valéry was determined to obstruct the king's agents. It was the king, after all, who had brought down the full weight of papal wrath upon the kingdom, inflicting the Interdict upon the innocent and confiscating the priory's meagre revenues. And it was the king who had toppled Lord William de Breos, becoming thereby the author of all the priory's misfortunes, for Prioress Heloise was cousin to Lord William's wife.

That had been to their advantage when Lord William was high in royal favour; Lady Mahaut was generous, the priory flourished

137

and had plans. But since the downfall of the house of Breos the supply of gifts and legacies and well dowered novices had dried up; the new refectory remained half built, the masons were dunning for their money and the priory was hard put to make ends meet.

To make matters worse, these two snoops had arrived when the prioress was going over the accounts for the twentieth time trying to make economies, and had she not been a Religious she might have wished them to the devil for their interruption. Instead she told Sister Eglantine to serve wine, and hoped they wouldn't notice the cheap pewter cups or the darns in her sleeves, or the unmistakeable whiff of the piggery clinging to Sister Eglantine's patched boots.

The intruders would get nothing out of Mother Heloise. She tucked her hands into her sleeves and raised a formidable chin, ready for battle. She would not lie, of course, but she would meet their questions with vagueness, evasion and dissimulation. That they showed no interest in the priory's few remaining assets but asked only about the wreck of the Danish vessel ten years ago and the fate of the rescued girls was a relief, though puzzling, but the principle was the same: give the enemy nothing.

It seemed no one could remember who had brought the maidens to the priory door. Rough fellows, fishermen, but as for names ... After all this time? The prioress spread her hands in a gesture of futility and looked Straccan straight in the eye. He'd seen colder eyes, but seldom in the living.

'We just took the poor creatures from them, and put them straight to bed,' said Sister Eglantine, helpfully piling masses of useless trivia around the lack of solid facts. 'Poor things, they were soaked and shivering and exhausted. We took them straight to the infirmary and stripped them and put them in a warm bed with hot stones packed round. They slept for a day and a night. Dame Winifred or myself were always at their bedside. Hallgerd was very ill; we thought she'd die, but our Blessed Lady heard our prayers.'

'What happened to their things?'

'Their garments, you mean?' Sister Eglantine looked surprised at the question. 'They were ruined, of course. We made floor-cloths of them.'

'Did they have nothing with them? Pouches, purses or the like?'

'Lady Ragnhild had many rings,' Sister Eglantine recalled.

'So she did,' said the prioress. This was safe enough ground. 'She gave two of them to the priory upon her marriage.' They had been sold long since to keep the wolf from the door, along with the priory's silver chalice, its relics and vineyard, but in spite of all efforts the wolf was halfway across the floor by now and its breath hot on the prioress's back.

'But there must have been other things saved from the wreck,' said Straccan.

'There was her dower chest. She locked it when the ship struck and threw the key overboard. The river warden, Lord Maurice, took charge of it for the king.' The prioress's lips thinned for a moment in disapproval. She knew very well what Maurice de Lacy had been up to: spurring his poor horse so that the blood ran, back to the watchtower with the chest on his saddle-bow as if the devil was after him, and the locksmith sent for at once. The prioress saw a chance to start a hare that might lead these meddlers away from the priory, and a glorious opportunity to drop Lord Maurice in it at last. She seized it gladly.

'Five hundred marks of pure silver was in the chest, so Lady Ragnhild told me.' *That* should cook Lord Maurice's goose! 'All else was lost: her bride-clothes, her dogs, all the goods brought for her new home.' And soon after, she remembered sourly, Lord Maurice was poncing around (the prioress had four brothers and a fair command of their vocabulary) in new furs and silks, and riding a new Spanish stallion.

Straccan sighed. He was growing more certain by the moment that if the Banner *was* hidden here the nuns knew nothing of it. If they had it and knew what it was, they wouldn't be wearing mended habits and patched shoes; this backwater priory would be famous throughout Christendom. Skilfully managed, and he had no doubt of Prioress Heloise's managing skills, a relic such as the

Pendragon Banner could fairly take the wind out of Canterbury's sails.

He was wasting time here. Thoughts scuttled through his tired mind like ants. What was it the king had said? Ragnhild had taken the Banner from the chest and hung it round her neck. But supposing she didn't. Supposing it was still in the chest. Who had had the opportunity to ransack *that* before sending it on, ostensibly unopened, to the king?

Wace butted in. He'd had enough of all this feminine vagueness – the talk of floor-cloths and rings – although the matter of five hundred marks would be mentioned in his next report. It was time to remind these women who they were dealing with.

'Madame prioress, it would be to your advantage to help us. Obviously,' he stared pointedly at Sister Eglantine's patched apron and set his untasted cup on the table with the dull *clunk* of inferior metal, 'you are in want of, um, many things. His grace can be most generous . . .'

Straccan could have strangled him.

A dull flush suffused the prioress's cheeks and she pressed her lips together to hold back the retort that leapt to them. Then she smiled. It was like a hidden dagger suddenly drawn.

'Thank you, master clerk, for reminding us of the virtue of poverty,' she said with poisonous sweetness. 'How easy it is to be seduced by the pleasures and comforts of the world! It would ill become us to accept any favours from the lord king while throughout his realm the poor face starvation. If his grace is generous, then beg him in our name to bestow his gifts not upon us but upon God's poor outside these walls.'

Despite his frustration, Straccan felt like applauding her.

Impatiently Wace said, 'Is it possible, madame, that Lady Ragnhild might have had with her a relic of sorts – a flag – that had belonged to her father?'

The nuns exchanged mystified glances. 'There was no flag,' said the prioress firmly and Sister Eglantine shook her head.

No, Straccan thought, *that poor young creature was in no condition when she got here to find a cunning hiding place for her treasure. The nuns undressed the girls and watched by their bed. If there was a Banner, it never came here.*

Where did it go?

Was it in the chest? Or was it lost in the river? Or taken by the men who brought the girls from the wreck?

'Madame prioress,' he said. 'The fishermen who saved the girls, where did they come from?'

The prioress raised questioning eyebrows at Sister Eglantine who furrowed her own in apparent thought. 'One of the riverside villages, I suppose,' she said. 'But as to which one—'

'The priory keeps a chronicle, does it not, madame?' He knew damn well it did, for Wace had told him. Everything the nuns considered noteworthy would be recorded, from plagues and falling stars to the crowning of kings and the annual weight of the priory's wool-clip.

Prioress Heloise nodded. 'You are well informed, sir. There has been a chronicle kept here since old King Henry's time.'

'I should like to read the account of these events, if I may.'

She just *bet* he would, the literate nuisance, but she had anticipated this. 'Unfortunately our scriptorium was flooded during the recent storms,' she said smoothly. 'Most of our books have gone. I regret that the chronicle is no longer there.'

Deceive the enemy with truth, she thought, lowering her eyes to veil any giveaway glint of triumph. The scriptorium *had* been flooded and indeed most of the books were gone, sold to keep the little community fed and clothed. As for the chronicle, the prioress was sitting on it.

Wace, who loved books with a passion, was genuinely distressed. 'A great loss,' he murmured. 'I am sorry to hear it.'

'It appears you have had a wasted journey,' said the prioress. Now, please God, they would take themselves off and she could get back to her accounts. Her mind returned to its interrupted scrabble for solutions. Not only the nuns but also the poor and destitute must be fed. The beggars' dole must be there, at the gate, on demand, even if they went hungry themselves. It might be possible to save on candles. Rushlights could be used in the refectory. They sputtered a lot, smelled of mutton fat and the sisters would complain, but needs must. She took up her pen.

In the doorway Straccan turned back.

What now? Damn the man! Dear God, forgive me for swearing!

'Lord Maurice de Lacy, madame . . . Where will we find him?'

The prioress looked up from the page with weary politeness. 'There was report of pirates downriver this morning. I believe the warden went after them but they will tell you more at the tower.'

'What tower, madame?'

'The watchtower at Trevel. Five miles south, at the riverside.' She picked up her penknife and began to trim her quill. 'You can't miss it.'

They bowed and left. Prioress Heloise and Sister Eglantine exchanged satisfied nods.

'I wonder what they are *really* after,' said Sister Eglantine. 'Will they be back, mother?'

Prioress Heloise sighed deeply. It was one da— one *wretched* thing after another. 'I fear so. But tell the sisters not to worry; I will deal with them.'

Reassured, Sister Eglantine went back to her pigs, leaving her superior frowning at the columns of figures that, no matter how hard she tried, would not balance. Perhaps the sisters could be persuaded to wear wadmal this coming winter instead of wool; it was scratchy, but mortification of the flesh was good for the soul.

For the moment she pushed the ledger to one side and took up a fresh piece of vellum. In favour or disgrace, Lord William had been their patron; he was also her kin by marriage. It was her duty to tell him about this.

The rest of that day and the next, Straccan spent trying in vain to get answers from the folk of the three riverside settlements – 'village' was too grand a word for the diminishing clutches of huts that comprised Great, Less and Lesser Pinchel. The population of all three were playing awkward buggers, being as obstructive as possible without pushing it so far as to get themselves killed.

Storm? What storm? They were still clearing up after the last. Rare old storm, that. Not that one? Well, there was a bugger of a blow at the turn of the year. Half Less got washed away and . . . Not that one neither? *Ow* many years ago?

Noses were rubbed thoughtfully, lips pursed pessimistically.

'*Ten* years? You must be joking, mate!'

There were so many gales: spring gales, autumn gales, winter gales, not to mention freak summer buggers like the one they'd just had. As for wrecks, every big blow brought one or two.

Two young women?

Hands, mending nets, never paused; heads were shaken, shoulders shrugged.

'Can't elp you, squire!'

Straccan wished Bane was there. He'd have got this lot talking somehow, probably managing to get himself fed while he was at it . . . He should have reached Shawl by now, if nothing had hindered him on the way.

Straccan wrenched his thoughts away from Father Osric's letter, from Janiva and the threat to Gilla. Thinking about that could drive him to madness. He glared at Wace's unsuspecting back. How easy it would be to snap the clerk's weedy neck, slip his carcass in the river, abandon Havloc and ride hell for leather . . . *God and Jesus forgive me!* Like himself, Wace was only obeying the king; as everyone must or suffer the consequences.

Would John *really* take Gilla hostage? Straccan dared not risk it. The only way to make sure she was left in peace at Holystone priory was for him to obey the king and find this bloody Banner.

'What now?' Wace asked as they rode away from the third unrewarding village.

'Maurice de Lacy,' said Straccan, 'if he's back yet. We'll see if *he* knows who saved the Danish maidens.' *And if not*, he thought, *what then? Where do I begin? Take the nunnery apart stone by stone? John's got me by the balls! Holy saints, if you're listening, help me!*

The warden's watchtower had been built two hundred years before by an Irish pirate who came raiding, took a fancy to the place and stayed. One side was guarded by the river and a deep moat had been dug to carry the water all round. The present warden had enlarged the original simple tower by adding another storey and had it painted ox-blood red. It glowed in the sun like a gigantic boil. No wonder the prioress had said they couldn't miss it.

The drawbridge was up, and as they approached they saw cross-bows trained on them from the battlements. They halted and a voice from above demanded their names and business.

Wace urged his horse forward and shouted, 'I am Robert Wace, clerk to the lord king, with Sir Richard Straccan and his servant, to see Maurice de Lacy.'

'Throw down your weapons!'

The quarrels remained steady as the drawbridge squealed and juddered down, and a greasy kitchen lad, obviously expendable, darted out and picked up their swords, scuttling back inside with them tucked under his arm. The voice aloft shouted at them to go on in.

'What's going on?' Straccan asked, when the very young acting-captain of the guard came panting down the steps.

'Raiders. They've sacked the priory. The nuns' priest came last night for help but the warden had gone after pirates. He rode straight out again as soon as he got back, didn't stop for anything. You staying, sir?' he asked, eyeing the newcomers hope-fully. The clerk would be pretty useless but the servant looked a strong fellow and could surely pull a bow, and the knight *must* be experienced. The young captain, though immensely proud of his temporary status, had only five crossbowmen, none older than himself.

'Sorry, captain, I can't.' Straccan was buckling his sword-belt on again. 'When did it happen?'

'Yesterday, tween none and vespers.'

Chapter 28

Robert the steward came back to find Shawl's population scurrying about like chickens with their heads cut off, precious little work being done, the Shaxoe men throwing their weight about, Mistress Janiva still locked up like a criminal and the manor's parson dying.

Dear God, and he'd only been gone a few days!

Having shouted himself hoarse and given a couple of hard cases a right seeing-to, Robert went in search of his wife. In Father Osric's hut there was only Mag, a simple-minded girl – the old priest's nominal niece, actual daughter – trying to feed her unconscious father with soup. As he could not swallow, the stuff was running out as fast as she spooned it in and his ears were full of it.

'Christ, girl, don't do that, you'll choke the poor old man,' cried Robert, appalled.

'I be frighted,' she wailed. 'Da won't eat. E be gwinter die.'

So he was, thought Robert as he mopped up the mess, but someone would have to look after him until he did.

'What happened to him?'

''Twas when they locked Mistress Janiva up,' Mag snivvelled. 'Da were angry, e went to see that old Vinegar. "I'll ave un out with im," e said. They was shouten, an Da fell down and went funny like this.' She lifted her round, silly, tear-slimed face to Robert. 'I don't want Da to die.'

'Don't give him anything,' Robert said, 'not even water. Run and find Pog; tell him to send his wife here right away.'

Pog's wife Joan, a sensible soul, was installed in the parson's hut as nurse and the steward eventually found his own wife in the kitchen, chivvying the cook into getting some sort of meal ready. To his annoyance she rounded on him as if it was all his fault.

Men and women, routed by the steward's wrath, began to drift back to their homes. Presently smoke began to rise from thirty cooking fires.

'What happened to Parson?' Robert asked when at last he sat at his own table. He winced as Sybilla banged his bowl in front of him.

'They was arguin, him and Old Vinegar, about Janiva. Parson said ordeals ain't lawful and she was free anyway, not manor property. He got very het up, shoutin an all; then he fell, like someone'd hit him.'

'When he's dead that Vinegar'll probably get the living,' Robert said glumly.

His wife snatched his bowl away.

'Here, I haven't finished!' But Sybilla pretended not to hear.

When he tried to put an affectionate arm round her in bed that night she turned away. 'I've got a headache,' she said.

Next morning Sybilla stood at an upper window in the manor house wondering what to do. From there she could see the whole village, folk in the fields and with their beasts, in their gardens and going about as usual among the cotts. Everything looked as it always had but there was no laughter, no tuneless singing, no ribald calling back and forth as neighbours met, no whistling, no children shouting as they played, in fact no children in sight at all.

She could see the undercroft door, shut and locked and one of the Shaxoe men leaning against it picking his nose. He called out and made a rude gesture as Joan passed on her way to Father Osric's sagging hovel. Sir Guy had built a good sound little house for the old priest some years ago – hall and chamber, reed-thatched and snug – but Father Osric was used to his hut, it fitted him like a shell and the neat house still stood empty. Finacre would have his eye on that, Sybilla reckoned. Bad cess to him.

Joan was carrying clean blankets for the old priest's bed. To everyone's astonishment, after the stroke that had felled him last week, Father Osric was still alive. Well, still breathing. That was about all. But as long as his chest rose and fell they couldn't bury him.

Sir Guy and Lady Alienor couldn't be buried either, of course. Lapped in lead, the old lord's body lay beside his wife, but Dame Alienor was still in the temporary coffin awaiting the fashioning of a lead one. Both had been parked in the mew until they could be properly entombed in the church, when either the king or the Pope gave in. God knew when that would be! The Interdict, meant to bring King John to his knees in six months, had now been in force two years and folk had got used to it.

Alfred the falconer had draped sacks over the coffins but he knew they were there. He didn't like it; it wasn't proper and he reckoned it would bring bad luck. The birds weren't happy either, they were off their feed and starting to look poor, ruffled and dull of eye and feather. Alfred usually slept in the mew with his beloved hawks, but not since the coffins had been there. Not bloody likely. Sybilla saw him heading for the mew now, dragging his feet, hesitating before he opened the door and lingering in the doorway, reluctant to go inside.

There was Robert, coming out of the stable. She could tell by the way he walked, head down and thrust forward as if he was about to charge something like a bull, that he was angry and worried, and no wonder.

The manor's business carried on as usual, but sluggishly. Folk worked sullenly. There was a lot of muttering which didn't entirely die down when the steward came within earshot. They *wanted* him to know they were unhappy. He was unhappy too, smarting from the belt-end of his wife's temper. She kept nagging him. Robert thought it most unfair. It wasn't *his* fault that Janiva was locked up, the door guarded day and night. What the hell could he do about it? The chaplain had Sir Roger's seal, he was in charge, but Sybilla didn't seem to understand.

'Somebody's got to do *something*,' she had said last night in bed, pummelling his shoulders with her hard fists. It hurt. 'What will happen when Sir Roger comes home? D'you think for a moment he'd let that bloody chaplain hurt Janiva?'

'There's bugger all I can do,' Robert had muttered.

'There *is*! Send word to Sir Roger. Go to the sheriff. It ain't lawful, what he's doing! Manor courts can't do ordeals any more, Father Osric said so afore he was struck down. Sheriff'd put a stop to it.'

'I can't! Orders is orders.'

'Orders!' She grabbed his hands, staring into his worried face. 'Shame on you! When Edric stuck his hayfork through your foot and it went bad, Janiva poulticed it. You coulda lost that foot.'

'I *know*!' He wouldn't meet her eyes.

'When me and our Alice had the spotted fever and you thought we'd die, Janiva nursed us, day and night.'

'Sybbie, shut up!'

'We must help her! Get her away, before Old Vinegar sets up the ordeal.'

'We can't! We *daren't*!' He was trembling. 'If she's innocent she'll take no harm from it! The chaplain says God will be her witness.'

'Rob, please! Just send to the sheriff!'

'No man's to leave the manor,' Robert said, and seeing the mutinous set of his wife's mouth he added, 'nor woman neither! Them's his orders. You hear me? Don't you *dare*! You *do*, and we'll be right in the shit!'

His panic was ugly and understandable. Watching him now from above as he crossed the yard and disappeared below her into the house, his wife felt pity for his dilemma, but it didn't lessen her wrath.

A small boy ran from the kitchen door, nipping smartly out of sight between mews and stable as his mother followed, calling after him angrily. Peter, Clara's boy. He'd been tongue-tied, unable to speak properly and the butt of other brats' teasing until Janiva had cut the membrane that trapped his tongue.

Clara had given up on her son and gone back inside. Sybilla couldn't see Peter but she did see a gobbet of wet horse-dung whizz through the air and smack the Shaxoe guard on the ear. Peter at least was doing his bit to show solidarity with the prisoner.

Chapter 29

The priory had been utterly destroyed. Blackened sections of wall reared up starkly and pallid tongues of flame, almost invisible in the sunlight, still flickered along calcined roof-beams. Occasionally heaps of collapsed stone would shift and subside as fires still burning underneath ate through shattered timbers.

Every building – many had been built entirely of wood – had been systematically ransacked and then torched. The storehouse was gutted: bales of woollen cloth ripped and shredded, barrels of nails split open, hides and fleeces smoking and stinking. Even the kitchen had not been spared. Tubs of lard and oil had burned fiercely; spilled meal and oats, dried peas and beans were trodden underfoot, and there was an eye-watering reek of burnt vinegar.

The warden had come too late, to find the priory razed to the ground and the prioress dying. There was nothing he could do, so having sent to the nearest village for help he and his men went after the brigands. By the time Straccan got there, Heloise de St Valéry had died.

She lay on the bare ground, her head cradled in Sister Eglantine's lap, a mute *pietà*. Her face was the colour of wax and her lips ash grey but her pale eyes, reflecting the sky, looked warmer now than Straccan had seen them in life.

Straccan barely recognised the other nun, filthy with soot and ash, her face smeared with blood and tears. With shaking fingers Eglantine shut the dead woman's eyes and dashed the tears from her own.

'Where are the other nuns?' Straccan asked.

'They took them. They said if anyone followed, they would c-cut their throats. But the lord warden has gone after them all the same.'

Wace nudged Straccan and pointed to the convent priest, picking jackdaw-like through the cindered debris of his house, rescuing an odd collection of objects – a blackened candlestick, spoon, frying pan – carrying them in the lap of his gown. His blistered hands were wrapped in strips torn from his shirt. When Wace spoke to him and touched his shoulder, the priest took no notice, deep in shock.

All day, as word of the outrage spread, folk from the riverside and inland villages came trickling in to see if it was true and stayed when they found it was, although there was nothing they could do. Some of the women had brought food, and one tried to coax Sister Eglantine to eat.

'Got to keep your strength up, sister. There's things to be done. Mother Elweez wouldn't want you to give in, now would she?'

Straccan sent two men back to their village for a litter to carry the prioress's body to the castle.

'Havloc, get the cloak from my saddlebag; we'll wrap her in that. Sister, we'll take you to Trevel. You'll be safe there.' His eye caught sight of Father Petroc, distractedly clutching his lapful of salvage. 'Where's your mother house? You must send your priest to tell them what's happened.'

'Bristol,' the nun said. She fumbled with the pins that held her thick woollen oversleeves in place, pulling them off and folding them into a pad which she laid on the ground. Carefully she lifted the prioress's head from her lap and rested it on the makeshift pillow. Her skirt and the prioress's veil were dark with blood and the sleeves of her shift, falling back from her wrists, showed bruises on her arms.

'Are you wounded, sister?'

'No. It is *her* blood.'

Straccan reached to help her to her feet, but she struck his hand aside furiously.

'Don't touch me! You're to blame for this!'

'Me? How?'

'Mother was right. She said your coming here would bring harm to us. King's men, she said, no friends to our house! She sent word to Lord William.'

'To *Breos*? In God's name, why?'

For a moment Sister Eglantine's mouth worked uncontrollably, and she clenched her teeth to still it. Fresh tears tracked down her dirty face.

'He's her cousin. He has ever been good lord to us. She thought he should know. She thought he would help us, tell us what to do. God have mercy, she welcomed him! He pushed me out of her chamber and slammed the door. I tried to go back in but two of his brutes held me.' She rubbed her bruised arms. 'I could hear him shouting; there was a relic here, he said, something of great value. She told him we had nothing left of value, that if we had she would give it to him gladly, but he didn't believe her. He told his men to search. We tried to stop them but they brushed us off like flies.'

Her haunted eyes stared through Straccan, seeing all again in hideous memory: Lord William's dark face, swollen with anger, the prioress on her knees, begging him to stop the damage, clutching at his surcoat then at his legs, clinging to him as he strode about. Lord William setting his booted foot on her breast and thrusting her away brutally. His men grinning at that, laughing as they tore down hangings, broke open chests and cupboards, hacked at panelling and ripped up floorboards.

'Did they find anything?' Straccan asked.

'What could they find? What could we be hiding? We hadn't as much as a silver candlestick left! What did he want, what do *you* want? Oh, dear God in heaven, why did you have to come here? If you hadn't come . . .'

Havloc spread the cloak on the ground, and he and Straccan lifted the body onto it. With horror Straccan realised that only the prioress's coif held her shattered skull together.

'How did she die?' Wace asked.

'Those devils set fire to the stable with the horses still inside. We got them out but the roof fell; a beam struck her.' Eglantine hid her face in her hands. 'How could he do this? He must be mad!'

'No,' said Wace. 'This was always his way, raiding, burning. It wasn't very long ago he burned the town of Leominster to the ground. Runs in the family, his father was the same.'

'The warden was away,' the nun said dully. 'He came too late.'

'I think there was a false alarm to get him out of the way,' Straccan said.

The men had returned with the litter and the prioress was lifted onto it, wrapped in Straccan's cloak.

'Shall us go, then, sister?' said one.

'Yes.' She scrambled up and stumbled to the side of the litter.

'Wait, sister,' said Straccan urgently. 'Tell me who took those girls from the wreck! Who brought them here?'

'That again? What does it matter? It was ten years ago!'

'Breos asked about it too, didn't he? Sister, for God's sake and for the sake of your people, tell me who brought the maidens here! Who took them from the wreck?'

She shook her head. 'No.'

'If you had told me before, none of this would have happened.' That wasn't fair and he knew it, but he was past caring.

With a cry of despair she turned her back to him, her thin shoulders shaking with sobs.

'You know who they were. Take me to them!'

'I can't, I won't leave Mother Heloise! I'm going with her.'

'Sister, whoever they are they won't talk to me. You know that! Mother Heloise warned your villagers, didn't she, that I'd been sent by the king. She told them to keep their mouths shut.'

'She had no reason to love the king.'

'Neither have I,' said Straccan grimly. Let Wace put that in his fucking report if he wanted to, he didn't care. 'Neither has Lord William, and he won't stop here. Do you want the villages burned, too? He'll not stop until he finds what he's looking for, the relic, Ragnhild's flag. I *have* to find it before he does. Help me!'

'I must keep the dead-watch. There's no one else.'

Half a dozen village women were standing a little way off in respectful silence. Now they shifted and muttered together, and moved forward as one.

'We'll look after her, sister. Looked after all of us, Mother Elweez did.'

There were nods and murmurs of assent.

'Fed our kids and went hungry herself, dint she?'

'Found work for us . . .'

'Birthed our babbies . . .'

'Laid out our dead . . .'

'We'll take care of her, don't you fret. You go with him. We'll stay with her 'til you come back.'

Sister Eglantine looked at their dirty determined faces, took a shuddering breath and let it out again. 'Thank you,' she said. 'Thank you!'

She leaned over the prioress's body, tenderly turned the cloth back and touched the dead face with a gentle fingertip, a gesture poignant with love and sorrow.

Straccan nodded at the bearers. The litter moved slowly forward with the women walking alongside. He stared after it a moment, then cried, 'Wait!' Turning to the nun he said, 'He will pay for this, sister. I promise you. Will you let me take her ring?'

' "Vengeance is mine, sayeth the Lord. I will repay," ' murmured Eglantine. And who was she to say how He would do it? Might He not make use of this man's hands? She came of a martial family; her whole being resonated to the concept of vengeance. Let the knight have his gage. She bowed her head in assent and Straccan drew the plain silver band from the prioress's finger and cut a thin edge from her veil, knotting it through the ring.

Sister Eglantine watched the litter go. Then, with her chin up – just like the prioress – she said, 'Very well, Sir Richard. I'll do as you ask.'

Straccan sighed with relief. 'Thank you. Where are we going?'

'Less Pinchel.'

She rode Havloc's horse, he leading it, with Straccan and Wace on either side, and as they rode Sister Eglantine told them all she remembered about the Danish girls.

Ragnhild and her maidservant had been plucked from the wreck of their ship by two brothers, Stigan and Peter, who brought them to the priory. The porteress, called to the gate by the clamour of the bell, summoned help and the two girls – and a locked chest rescued with them – were carried straight to the infirmary.

Prioress Heloise sent word at once to the castle and Maurice de Lacy himself came to take charge of the chest. It was his duty to send it and all it contained to the king, but he'd have his locksmith at it first to see if he couldn't abstract a little something for his trouble.

Stigan and his brother got a silver penny each and life went on as before, until a year later in another gale Peter drowned, while Stigan was washed overboard and crushed between two hulls, one of his legs so fearfully mangled that a mere flap of skin held it in place.

The nuns couldn't save Stigan's leg but their careful nursing saved his life. That made him their responsibility, so he became the convent's odd-job man. He was no asset. He was surly and resentful, and incompetent as well, but he was a cross to be borne and they bore him with fortitude.

It was evening by the time they reached Less Pinchel, which Straccan had visited the previous day to no avail. This time however, seeing the nun, the inhabitants emerged from their hovels and surrounded the riders, each man casually holding some sort of implement – eel-fork, boathook, sailmaker's needle – which might come in handy; the women, Straccan saw, had furnished themselves with domestic items that could be put to similar lethal use.

'Oh, don't be silly,' Sister Eglantine said. 'It's all right! You can put those things down, all of you, and get back to work. Where's Stigan?'

'Greasin boats.' The headman prodded his small son and the child ran to a cluster of coracles lying upside down like huge black beetles. His excited piping was followed by an answering growl, and a man got up from behind one of the odd little boats and scowled at them.

'That's him.' Sister Eglantine beckoned. 'You, Stigan! Come here!'

The man hoisted himself along awkwardly on one good leg and one wooden. He was dark and burly, clarted with grease, and smelled overpoweringly of sheep. Wace's violets couldn't get a look-in.

'Where are your manners?' the nun snapped. 'Take your cap off! Sir Richard has questions to ask you. You're to answer him properly, understand? None of your cheek, mind.' She swung round on the villagers who clustered, agog, at her back. 'I thought I told you to get back to work.'

Reluctantly they shuffled back to their tasks, leaving hut doors propped open and snatching hide shutters from windows in case they should miss anything interesting.

'What's this about then?' Stigan demanded truculently.

Straccan dismounted, handing his reins to Havloc. 'Let's talk over there.' He pointed at the coracles, out of earshot of Stigan's wondering neighbours. Wace slid from the saddle and followed. For a moment Stigan looked about to bolt, but a glance back at the erect figure of Sister Eglantine changed his mind.

'Is it true bout Mother Elweez?' he asked.

'I'm afraid so.'

Stigan spat and crossed himself. 'Cess to em, the buggers,' he muttered.

Straccan said, 'Stigan, a ship was wrecked here ten years ago. You and your brother brought two women to safety. Do you remember them?'

Stigan grunted in surprise. That wreck? Those girls? The memory reeled through his mind in those few moments after Straccan spoke: a series of images, brighter and more vivid than they had been in reality. The stranger, the knight, what was his name? Sir Something, was watching him, waiting.

He said, 'It was my brother found them.'

Chapter 30

They had set out on the river as usual, he and Peter, for the hermitage; a weekly duty, to take the saint his provisions, ask his prayers for anyone who needed them, and on that particular morning to make sure he was all right after last night's storm.

Four miles downriver they found the wreck.

Only the stern showed above water, surrounded by a floating tangle of broken mast and yard, shredded sail and snapped sweeps. The next tide would take it for sure.

The saint would have to wait a bit; he wouldn't mind. Hoping to salvage something, anything they could use or sell, the brothers scrambled onto the wreck, and just as Stigan happened upon a small locked chest that looked promising, so his brother Peter, peering into the shattered cabin, cried, 'Praise God! Brother, here is a woman alive!'

Alive!

What Peter never knew, what no one ever knew save Stigan and his confessor and what he remembered for ever after with bitter shame, was that in that moment the woman's life tilted in the balance. That his first thought on hearing his brother's glad cry had been, *Shit! Just my luck!*

Alive! Now they'd have to take her to safety and bang went all hope of keeping the chest! It was heavy. Perhaps there was money in it. It could be the chance of a lifetime . . .

For a perilous soul-lurching instant Stigan considered murder. *Slip the bloody woman into the water, let the tide take her.* The weight of the chest tugged at his muscles, dragged at his hopes. He'd never get another chance like this. But the weight of mortal sin was heavier and with a hot surge of shame he set the chest down, crossed himself and splashed to where Peter, on his knees, was trying to unbuckle the belt bound round the bodies of two young women.

Breast to breast they lay clasped together, their hair, dark and fair, floating like feathery seaweed in the water pooled around them.

'One's dead,' said Peter, turning tear-bright eyes on his brother. Soft-hearted Peter, always in tears over things hurt or dead.

Stigan looked down at the two still bodies. 'Just maids,' he said in pity and wonder. 'You sure one's alive?' But he could see for himself the rise and fall of the dark one's breath. Drawing his knife he leaned over and slit the tough leather. 'Take her,' he said. 'I'll bring the dead un.'

They put them in the boat and Stigan splashed back for the chest. Beneath his feet the shattered deckboards gave way and he dropped into the sucking well beneath, saved only by his outflung arms.

God was merciful, rebuking him for his wicked intention but allowing him to save himself that he might repent of it. There was no need to tell these nosey sods about *that*, however.

'We took em to the nuns,' he finished. 'We thought one was dead, at first, but she come round.'

'What condition were they in?'

Stigan blinked. 'Eh?'

'Could they walk?' Straccan asked patiently.

'No. A couple of lay sisters come to the gate and carried them in on shutters.'

'What else was salvaged?'

'What?'

'Did you fetch anything else off the ship?'

'Oh, the chest.' He had never forgotten the chest, nor the penance it had cost him. 'Lord Maurice had that.'

'Was there anything else? A satchel, perhaps, or a bag?'

Stigan shook his head.

'Nothing?'

'The fair one had rings. Nothing else that I saw. And if you think me or my brother took anything from them,' he said truculently, 'you're barking up the wrong tree!'

'No, I don't think that.' And he didn't. The maidens had lived. If anything had been stolen from them, especially the relic, they'd have complained of it as soon as they realised.

He was beginning to believe he'd been right from the first. The Pendragon Banner was nothing more than a fantasy born of delirium.

Chapter 31

The river warden returned to Trevel that night, tired, hungry and smarting at his failure to catch the raiders, but with eight nuns by way of a consolation prize.

'Bastards took em a few miles, then left em,' he said, pulling off his helmet and lobbing it at his squire, who fielded it neatly and perched it atop the armour pole. The eye-slits left two stripes of dirt across Maurice de Lacy's sweaty scarlet face, and his small, angry red-rimmed eyes peered out like those of a boar at bay. He unbuckled his sword belt, tossed it after the helm and stretched, yawning hugely, while his squire unlaced his mail and draped it on the pole, leaving Lord Maurice in damp, rust-stained gambeson and braes. The liberated smell of several days' concentrated sweat could have felled a horse.

The warden scratched himself ferociously. 'God's nails, that's good! Been dyin to do that for hours.'

'Are the sisters ... um ... you know, all *right*?' Wace asked delicately.

'The Blessed Virgin protected em, they say. The wife's organisin em now; baths, clothes, beds, all that sort of thing. Someone get me a drink!' He flung himself into his chair and thrust out a hand for a cup of ale, downed it in three swallows and held it out for a refill. The warden was turning a normal colour again under the dust. He scowled at Wace. 'Who the devil are you?'

'He's with me,' Straccan said, stepping forward before Wace could reply.

Surprise wiped away Lord Maurice's scowl and replaced it with a grin.

'Straccan? God's blood, what are *you* doin here? Found any good bones lately? God's eyeballs, I've not seen you since the tourney at . . . Where was it?'

'Rouen,' said Straccan.

'That's right!' Lord Maurice chuckled. 'You lost.'

'I won. You still owe me a horse and mail.'

'God's lights, is that what you've come for?'

'If I thought there was a beast worth having in your stables, yes, but a sorrier bunch of old screws I've seldom seen. Mine's the only decent animal in there. Was there no sign of Breos and his cut-throats?'

The warden snorted. 'Fat chance! Long gone by the time we got there. Clean away, vanished into thin air! Found the nuns at the forest edge, marchin along like troopers, singin psalms, would you believe? Brave ladies! Only they were goin the wrong way.'

'That will gladden Sister Eglantine.'

'Ah, was it you brought her here? Bad business, *bad* business! God's cods, I never did like that whoreson Breos! Burnin nunneries, killin nuns—'

'He didn't kill the prioress,' Straccan said. 'A falling beam smashed her skull. But he was responsible for her death all the same.'

'I've sent word to their mother house at Bristol,' de Lacy said. He paused, sniffed the air for a moment, shrugged and continued. 'Meanwhile I'm lumbered with a parcel of nuns! Still, company for the wife, I spose. She don't get many females to gossip with. Nuns *are* females of a sort, ain't they?' He sniffed again, suspiciously. 'What's that blasted stink? Ain't me, is it?' He raised an arm and sniffed. 'No, that ain't it.' His accusing gaze traversed Straccan and bore down on Wace. 'It's *you*!' And to Straccan, 'God's eyeballs! What the devil is it?'

'Violets, I think,' said Straccan.

'*Violets*? God's teeth! I thought he'd trodden in something.'

'His grace the king gave me this perfume,' Wace said indignantly.

'Oh?' De Lacy arched his eyebrows. 'He likes his joke, does John.' He turned to Straccan. 'Well, what *are* you doing here?'

'Wondering if you'll ever offer me supper.'

The warden burst out laughing. 'God's whiskers! Sit down! You and that smelly fellow with you. You, sir! What's your name?'

'I am Robert Wace,' said the affronted official, drawing himself up to his full five feet two inches. 'Confidential clerk to his grace King John.'

Lord Maurice snorted. 'Just sit at the *other* end of the board, will you? There's a good chap.' He raised his voice to a bellow that rang back off the stone walls. 'How about some food here? God's belly, I'm starved!' Then, settling back in his chair, he said cheerfully, 'When you've stuffed yourself, Straccan, you can tell me what you've really come for. Last I heard, you were muckin about in Scotland. Is it true the king gave you a horse?'

De Lacy was cagey at first ('Chest? What chest? Oh, *that* chest!') but eventually in a cautiously roundabout fashion he admitted that well, yes, he had *happened* to look inside the chest 'just to make sure I wasn't sendin the king a box of old boots, you know' and there had been coin-silver to the value of two hundred marks. At the mention of this sum Wace's head swung up like a questing blood-hound's but the warden didn't notice. 'There was nothing else. Just all those dear little bags of coin.'

'D'you think de Lacy took it?' Wace asked, when he and Straccan had retired to the room and bed they must perforce share.

'I wouldn't put it past him,' said Straccan, 'yet . . .'

'What?'

'When the ship foundered, Ragnhild hung the relic round her neck, didn't she?' Wace nodded. 'She tied herself and her servant together and trusted to it to save them both. So she had it, she *must* have had it, when Stigan and his brother found them, but she *hadn't* got it by the time they reached the priory.'

'The brothers took it.'

'Ragnhild would've spoken up if they'd robbed her. No, if there's any truth in the tale at all, she hid it somewhere. Where? What happened in between?'

'Between what?'

'Between the wreck and the convent. There's something missing. We'll have to talk to Stigan again in the morning. I'm going up to the battlements. I think better in the fresh air.'

An hour or two later Wace was shaken awake none too gently to find Straccan leaning over him, candle in hand. 'Here,' said the clerk, annoyed. 'It's still dark! What's the time?'

'Time for you to talk, Master Wace.'

'Eh?'

'You know more than you've told me. I've got questions and I want answers. I asked the king how he found out about the Banner. Remember? He wouldn't say. He started speculating about my Breton forbears instead. I didn't like that. And then *you* turned up, threatening my daughter.' He ignored Wace's splutter of protest. 'The king commanded me to find this Banner, *if it exists*. If it doesn't, I'm wasting my time and I have better things to do. So unless you tell me the rest of it, every last detail, I'm going home, Master Wace, to take care of my daughter, and you can put that in your report and stick your report up your arse for all I care.'

'Sir Richard, there's no need—'

'How *did* the king find out about the Banner?'

'Really, I don't . . .'

Straccan rested his hand on the hilt of his dagger.

Wace's prominent Adam's apple bobbed as he swallowed. He shivered and pulled the blanket up round his meagre chest. 'It was a letter,' he said sullenly.

'Go on.'

'A letter from the Hidden Valley, from Sulien.'

'Sulien wrote to the king?'

'Um, not exactly . . .'

'*What*, exactly?'

'Sir Richard, I *am* the king's confidential clerk, you know; I must keep his secrets.'

'Not this one,' said Straccan, toying negligently with the hilt of his weapon.

Wace took a deep breath. 'Sulien wrote to a man called Michael Scot. The letter, um . . . happened to come into the king's hands.'

'I see. Go on.'

'Lady Ragnhild – Hallgerd I mean – told Sulien about the Banner before she died. In fact, she *gave* it to him; or rather she *would* have, if she'd had it.'

'You're not making sense.'

'She didn't know where the real Ragnhild had put it, but she wanted Sulien to find it so that he could keep his hospital.'

Straccan drew his dagger, ignoring Wace's start and squeak of dismay, and began cleaning his nails with its fine point. 'Keep his hospital?'

'The Hidden Valley belonged to William de Breos,' Wace said hastily. 'He gave it to Sulien seven years ago, to found the hospital. He also provided stone and timber, masons, carpenters, and every year after the hospital was built Lord William sent money, and gifts of food, wine, cloth . . . He was a good lord to them, but—'

'Of course, there *would* be a "but".'

'He never got round to putting anything in writing; there was no deed of gift. And now that all the Breos lands have been seized back and given to others, I'm afraid the new lord of Cwm Cuddfan wants his valley back, or its price.'

'And the Banner would buy the valley.'

'The valley? The true Pendragon Banner would buy half a kingdom! Michael Scot serves King Frederick of Sicily, and King Frederick would pay more than you can imagine for it.'

'So King John wants his cut.'

'Yes, but there's more. Somehow – I don't know how but the king isn't the only one with spies – the Bretons got to hear of this. It would *never* do for them to get their hands on the banner. They hate the king. They believe he murdered their duke, Prince Arthur, and they think Arthur was the rightful king of England. With England under Interdict and the king likely to be excommunicated—' He stopped, aghast at his slip. 'You must forget I said that, Sir Richard! But don't you see, it's what the king's enemies have been praying for! If John is excommunicated, his barons are absolved from their oaths of fealty; they will turn on him. He'll have France and Brittany *and* his own lords at his throat!'

'Why does Brittany want the Banner?'

'Well, there are two factions. One says the Princess Eleanor, Duke Arthur's sister, should be queen of England and duchess of Brittany. John keeps her under guard; she's been his, um, guest for seven years. The other faction's loyal to Duchess Alix. Both sides want the Banner. Whoever has that has God on their side. Who would dare to take up arms against the blood of Christ?'

'So it's true about Breton plots.'

'Of course! And there are French plots, and Scottish and Irish and Welsh plots, not to mention those of the English barons. But Brittany's behind Breos's search for the relic. They've promised to restore his estates, of course, and that witch, what's her name . . .'

'Julitta de Beauris.'

'Yes. Lady Julitta. Brittany's a dangerous place, riddled with spellcraft and enchantments; Duchess Alix even has her own sorcerer! Of course they don't call him that, he's officially the court astrologer, but it's all one. Julitta made quite an impression at the Breton court. They think highly of her, um, abilities and she's very beautiful, I'm told. Anyway, they sent her to make sure of the Banner.'

'And the king wouldn't tell me about this because my forbears came from Brittany, and he thinks my sympathies might lie with Eleanor or Alix.'

Wace shrugged. 'It is hard to be sure where any man's loyalties lie.'

'I'll tell you where mine lie, master confidential clerk: with my daughter. I'll storm Hell itself if she's in danger, and believe me,' he slipped his dagger back into its sheath with a sharp *snick* that made Wace jump, '*believe* me, I'll kill anyone, *anyone* who threatens her. What else was in Sulien's letter?'

'Nothing important. He wrote of the lady's death and what she'd said about the Banner. Michael Scot is a famous scholar; Sulien asked what he knew about the relic.'

'I presume the king also "happened" to see Scot's reply?'

'Um, yes, but it didn't help. Master Scot sent copies of everything in King Frederick's library to do with the Banner – Gildas, Nennius, Beda – but I had already studied their writings. There *was* one detail, though . . .'

'What?'

'A letter written by Saint Kentigern. He said Queen Guinevere herself embroidered the pennant, and that for gold thread she used her own golden hair. The true Banner would be known by that, and of course by the precious relic, the bloodstained cloth, which is stitched between the two pieces of silk.'

'Was it the king's own idea to send for me?'

'Oh yes. But first he sent me to see what else Sulien knew.'

'You've talked to Sulien?'

'Well, I, um, told him of the king's interest. He was anxious to help.'

'I'll bet.'

'But he knew nothing about the Banner. The lady was already crazed with fever when she was brought to the hospital. Her mind was wandering. Sometimes she thought she was on the wrecked ship and sometimes with her dying companion, lost in the snow with wolves howling all around. Her mind cleared briefly when she told him of the relic. She begged him to search for it, and if he found it, sell it to buy the valley and save the hospital. Then there was just nonsense: she raved about King Arthur and Guinevere. At the end, Sulien told me, she kept saying, "Tell him, you must tell him, Guinevere." Over and over. And he asked her, "Tell who? Tell him what?" But she did not speak again.'

Pale and remote, the almost-full moon gazed at the world incuriously as it turned beneath her single opalescent eye. Along the road to Talgarth her light was bright enough to cast shadows of the two lepers who chose to travel by night, when neither dogs nor good Christians were likely to take exception to their passing.

At Shawl she looked down on the sleeping village but could not see Janiva, for the door of the undercroft where she was imprisoned was locked and there was no window. Awake, alone, afraid,

Janiva lay staring into darkness. She did not know how many days had passed, for in the undercroft day and night were the same. She did not know that Benet Finacre had ordered her cottage burned to the ground, but the moon lingered, briefly, to touch the deep ash with silver.

At Ludlow her pale beam caressed the face of Alis, asleep and dreaming on her pallet among Lady Marjory's women.

Moonlight threw a pale path across the flagged floor at Holystone for Gilla to tread, barefoot and silent, to the Blessed Virgin's shrine. There she knelt – as she did every night when the other girls slept – to pray for her father's safe return from wherever he might be. The votive lamp burned with a steady flame and, if she stared into its golden heart and willed to see him, the flame would open like a door, letting her look through to where her father was. It opened now. She saw him clearly but without colour, in shades of grey. He knelt before a crucifix, praying.

She breathed a soft sigh of relief. He was well, he was safe – but then he raised his face to the candlelit Christ and she saw the tears on his face.

Through the chapel window at Trevel the moon's indifferent eye watched, for a time, a man kneeling before the altar. Unable to sleep or endure Wace's wuffling snores, Straccan had crept down to the chapel, a tiny curtained closet in the thickness of the wall. No one was there, thank God. There was a faint sweet scent of honey from the candles burning on the altar before the veiled cross. He stared at the shrouded shape of the life-sized Christ, marking where the bowed head and bulges of ribs and knees moulded the linen covering. Presently he reached up and gently tugged the heavy samite away.

Candlelight cast a shifting glow upwards, illuminating the tormented face, the jutting nose and staring eyes of Christ. A great iron spike transpierced the feet of the image with shocking realism.

Not daring to touch the carved feet Straccan grasped the nail instead and prayed as he had never prayed before: that Gilla be unharmed, that Janiva be safe and that – if it was God's will – he should find the Pendragon Banner and end this nightmare of uncertainty and fear. How long he clung to the nail, like a drowning man clutching at a rope, he didn't know, but when at last he tried to let go his fingers were stiff and cold, and left blood on the spike.

He sank to his knees on the altar step and wept, great tearing sobs that tore at his chest and throat. When at last he was quiet the moon had slipped away uncaring and the candle had burned well down. It must be long past midnight but he had no wish to return to the perfumed room above. Shivering, he wrapped himself in the pall from the crucifix. Huddled, exhausted, on the floor before the altar he even slept briefly, with fleeting dreams of shipwrecks, of a treasure chest guarded by a dragon, of children playing with a ball and of a dying woman whispering, 'Tell him, Guinevere.'

Waking, cramped and chilled through, he thought, *Tell who, tell him what?* Something so urgent that with her last few breaths a dying woman had striven to pass it on.

'*Tell him, you must tell him, Guinevere.*' He stayed there, praying, until dawn.

Chapter 32

Waking to darkness, for a disorienting moment Janiva had no idea where she was until the smell of sheep brought her to reality. She was in the old undercroft lying on bales of unwashed wool. Gingerly she touched the side of her head where dried blood matted her hair. The scabbed lump was still tender but didn't feel as large as it had been, and the blinding headache and swooping dizziness, intensified by the darkness, that had followed her fall seemed at last to have gone.

The key rattled in the lock, the door squealed open and a flood of daylight dazzled her. She squeezed her eyes shut against it as a stab of pain knifed through her head, and heard the now familiar sounds as her guard set down a jug of water and a platter of broken bread, and picked up yesterday's empty jug and dish.

With her eyes watering and half closed against the blinding light, she could only see the man's black tear-blurred shape in the doorway. 'What day is it?' she called, but without a word he slammed the door, and the darkness enveloped her again.

It was a fine dry day with a warm breeze, a perfect day to air the bedding and clean the great chamber, burning the old rushes, and sweeping and scrubbing the floor before bringing in armloads of fresh sweet rushes and strewing-herbs, with plenty of fleabane. All morning Sybilla had been overseeing the serving-women as they stripped the beds, took sheets to the wash house, spread blankets and coverlids on the hedges, and dragged mattresses and pillows downstairs to beat, and air in the sun. She had laid on food and ale for everyone, and when the heavy work was finally done the field workers came to share the meal, and they all sat in the meadow eating and drinking. It was an annual event, always lively with talk and laughter, while the children made daisy chains, young girls danced barefoot in the grass and older women gossiped and complained. But this year there was no dancing; the children played as usual but the grown-ups' voices were subdued, their eyes anxious, all aware of Father Osric's illness and the prisoner in the undercroft.

It was Bane's habit – it had saved his life more than once – to spy out the land before riding openly into any place. Finding the burned remains of Janiva's cottage he had retreated and sought a vantage point from which to observe the village. It seemed normal enough, field work going on as usual and the house servants busy with blankets and mattresses and bundles of rushes in an orgy of cleaning. When at last everyone stopped work to rest and eat in the meadow, Bane slipped past the deserted cottages, through the orchard and round behind the hall to the mew. The door was open and the falconer absent, the premises occupied only by seedy moulting birds and two coffins, one lead, the other wooden. The wooden coffin was much smaller than the other. Bane's throat tightened with sudden fear. *Please, God, not Janiva!*

Someone was crossing the yard. Bane melted back into the shadows of the shuttered mew.

On her way to the brewhouse to refill the jugs, Sybilla nearly dropped them when she heard her name called. The voice came from the mew, which should be deserted this afternoon; she had seen Alfred the falconer with the others in the meadow.

'Mistress Sybilla!'

The door stood ajar; she could see the dark shape of someone just inside. She set the jugs down carefully and loosened her eating knife in its sheath at her belt.

'Who's there?'

'Mistress Sybilla, do you remember me? I'm Hawkan Bane.'

Chapter 33

As luck would have it, while Havloc was saddling their horses in the morning to ride to Stigan's village, the man himself arrived unsummoned at the watchtower, crutching along in a cloud of homely stink behind a dozen solid bristly pigs.

'Fine beasts,' said Havloc, flattening himself out of harm's way against the stable wall.

'They was Sister Eg's.' Stigan lunged smartly with his crutch to foil a porky escapist's break for freedom. 'No you don't, you bugger! These're all that's left. They run off in the raid,' he explained. 'Them devils speared the others, just for the fun of it, and they're still lyin there.'

Fresh pork, no matter the method of its dispatch, was valuable, and as soon as the cook heard about it a cart was readied and two hefty fellows assigned to fetch the carcasses to the garrison kitchen.

Emerging from the kitchen, frowning over a few fourthings in his palm, Stigan found Straccan and Wace waiting. He stopped, scowling. *Them again. What now?* 'I got things to do,' he said.

'Oh? Well, never mind. I can see you're a wealthy man this morning. A whole silver penny won't interest you.' Straccan turned away.

'I dint say that, did I?' said Stigan indignantly. 'A penny? What for?'

'Pay him, Master Wace.' With a *tsk* of annoyance Wace dug into his purse. 'Where did you find the wreck? Can you see the place from here?'

Below them the wide mud-brown river seemed sluggish and harmless. Two small boys were squabbling on the bank; one had a toy boat, a hollowed piece of wood, and the other was trying to take it. His cry of 'Give it to me!' caught Straccan's attention for a moment, reminding him of something he couldn't quite remember.

'Twas five, six mile from here,' Stigan was saying. 'Down by the saint's island.'

'Saint? What saint?' Wace asked.

Stigan looked surprised at their ignorance. '*Our* saint, our holy man. Everyone knows about *him*.'

'A hermit?'

Stigan nodded. 'Always been a holy man on Saint Winnoc's island. Used to be an old watchtower long ago. He's snug enough; when it floods he just moves up to the top. We look after him, turnabout; take food and stuff. That's why we was down there, me an brother, that morning when we found the wreck.'

Wace started to say something but Straccan's sudden painful grip on his arm stopped him.

'We was all soaked through,' Stigan remembered with a faraway look. 'He give us soup.'

Straccan's heart slammed against his ribs. 'You went to the island *before* you took the girls to the priory?'

Stigan nodded again.

'What happened? You *must* remember!'

Of course he did! Memory swamped him afresh as he stared down at the river, not seeing it, seeing instead the broken-backed ship, the chest, the girls, gulls diving and screaming around them; hearing even the sobs of the dark-haired girl weeping over the body of her dead companion.

He had jumped ashore to make the boat fast and turned back to pick up the sack with the hermit's supplies.

'I'll tell the saint,' he said, but God had already done that for the old man came clambering over the high bank of seaweed as nimbly as a boy.

'Bring em in,' he gasped as he reached them. 'I've soup on the fire and there's dry blankets to wrap em up in.'

'This one's dead,' mourned Peter.

The old man leaned over to look and touched the fair-haired girl's blue-white icy cheek. 'No she ain't,' he said.

The dead girl — and she *was* dead, Stigan had pulled enough drowned bodies from the river in his time to know dead from barely living — coughed up a lot of water and opened her eyes.

He remembered all right. You didn't forget something like that.

'Where can I borrow a boat?' Straccan asked.

'I'll row you,' offered Stigan. He wouldn't miss this for a month of Sundays, but in case his sudden helpfulness made them suspicious, he added 'It'll cost you, mind!'

The islet, a seaweedy carbuncle surrounded by low-tide mud, lay closer to the Welsh shore than the English and was very small, barely an acre of ground. Gulls strutted over the seaweed, stabbing their cruel beaks into the smelly fly-swarming masses in search of shellfish. Here and there along the banks of weed Straccan could see the remains of a stone wall which must at one time have encircled the islet. The only sounds were the slap of water and the non-stop screaming of the seabirds, and there was an all-pervading reek of decaying fish. Straccan could not imagine a more wretched place. Anyone who chose to dwell alone here, in order to feel closer to God, must indeed be a holy man.

The receding tide had exposed a rotting wooden jetty and several posts. Stigan tossed the mooring rope over one.

A louder screech from the bank above startled the gulls to noisy flight. There atop the bank was a wild hairy vision, a shapeless bundle of sackcloth and tatters atop two skinny legs, very like a ragged stork.

'How nice! The saint has come to greet us,' said Wace. Raising his voice he called, 'Good morrow to you, hermit! God be with you.'

'Piss off!'

Chapter 34

Ludlow, small though it was and young as towns go, was a flour-ishing borough. The castle, built by a forgotten de Lacy more than a century before, loomed protectively over the town, backed by meadows and orchards and warded by a broad stretch of the River Teme. The wide streets were kept in good repair, and all around the town the sheep-dotted hills were richly green.

There was prosperity: busy shops and stalls, and a lively market that brought buyers from far afield. Although the burgesses resented, on principle, the imposition of the mercenary captain Cigony as constable instead of William de Breos – better the devil you know – they could not in truth complain that he interfered with their liberties or squeezed more in taxes, fines and fees out of them than they could manage to pay. In fact, as he was a foreigner and a stranger to their ways, they were sometimes able to put one over on him. Lord William might yet make his peace with the king and return but in the meantime the folk of Ludlow cheerfully took advantage of every opportunity to swindle the new lord.

To his credit, Cigony had certainly tackled the outlaw problem with enthusiasm: never a week went by without a clutch of outlaws dangling from the town's gallows. Ludlow folk were pleased. It was relatively safe to travel the roads again, as long as one kept out of Wales, and that brought more business to the town. Whenever Cigony and his troop rode down Castle Street people waved, and when the hunters returned with a few more wretched prisoners, cheered. Things could be a lot worse.

Shadows were long in the Shropshire greenwood by the time Cigony blew his horn to call the stragglers in. The prey had run well, but out of breath and out of luck had gone to ground at last in a blackthorn thicket where, with nothing to lose, they defended themselves with knives, killing two of the harriers to the fury and grief of their handlers. Now the dogs were held back and someone would have to go in and flush the buggers out.

Panting and red with exertion, Cigony waited. A tremor shook his body as he tried to suppress a sneeze, and failed. *Aratcha!* As one, the hounds' heads swung round to eye him reproachfully.

Protected by their stout leathers the dog-handlers thrust their way through tangles of savage barbs and dragged the prey out: two breathless, bleeding, shuddering creatures. Two men.

Men. Well, yes, technically they *were*, but nobody thought of them as men. These were outlaws, rybauds, wolf-heads. Thieves, rapists, killers or all three, and as good as dead anyway; most when caught were strung up there and then from the nearest strong branch. Indeed Alun the verderer was already unhooking the coil of rope from his saddle and had his eye on a suitable tree. But a few would be taken back to Ludlow alive for the townsfolk's entertainment and satisfaction at watching them kicking at a rope's end on the morrow.

The hunters jeered.

'That all there was?'

'Not worth stuffin!'

'Throw em back!'

From his commanding height on horseback Cigony looked down on the repulsive creatures lying where the berners had flung them. One had met justice before, and more than once, for he lacked both his ears as well as a hand and had been branded between the eyes.

'Not a lot of him left to hang,' the constable observed cheerfully. 'Never mind.' He sneezed again, less explosively, and wiped his eyes on his sleeve. 'String him up.' He glanced at the other wolf-head, small, bald, and bloody where thorns had torn his flesh. About to condemn him too, Cigony paused and looked again, harder.

Pallid dirty flesh showed through rents in his shirt, but his padded sleeveless coat, though torn and filthy, had – surely . . . yes! – a touch of blue, a touch of red, a touch of yellow.

'Patches!' said the constable with satisfaction. 'As I live and breathe, a coat of patches! Strip him!'

The outlaw squealed as coat and shirt were torn from his scrawny carcass. On a thong round his neck hung a soiled doeskin pouch no bigger than a child's fist. Cigony nodded to a squire who drew his dagger and leaned from the saddle. The prisoner, arms pinioned behind him by one of the berners, uttered a whistly shriek of terror, shut his eyes, dropped to his knees – nearly pulling his captor off balance – and began to pray.

With a grin the squire cut the thong and handed the pouch to his master.

'Well, well, well.' Something small, gleaming and unmistakeably gold slid onto Cigony's broad palm. 'What have we here?'

'Looks like a cup, my lord,' the squire said helpfully.

'Bit small,' said Cigony. He turned it about, tracing the crude lettering with a calloused forefinger. 'Not much more than a mouthful in that, eh?' He put it back in the pouch and put that in his saddlebag. 'Right. Take him back with the rest. Hang them, but put him in the thieves' hole. I don't want him hanged yet.' *Aratcha!*

Two oxen drew the cart, a plain farm wagon with a strong iron cage big enough for a dozen wolf-heads bolted to the floor and sides. All in together, the living and the hanged, they jolted the seven or eight miles back to Ludlow. There the castle's accommodating dungeon swallowed the live ones until tomorrow's gallows and the dead were identified – enriching Cigony by a shilling apiece – ticked off the 'Wanted' list and shovelled without ceremony into the town ditch.

The bald thief was slung into the thieves' hole, a nasty pit with a grating over the top and about four inches of indescribable sludge at the bottom. Past caring, Tom hunkered down in one corner, perfectly capable of sleep in such a place and attitude. At least he wasn't getting rained on and perhaps, now they'd taken his cup, that bloody ghost would leave him alone at last.

Chapter 35

With one foot in the mud and the other still in the boat, Straccan stood dumbstruck, staring at the apparition on the bank above. The biblical scarecrow clutched a long knotty staff in both hands and looked as if he knew how to use it and was itching for the chance.

'You can't land here! Bugger off!'

Straccan heard a muffled snort of mirth from Stigan and swore to himself. *Another dead end! The old man's mad.*

Wace got to his feet, making the little boat rock. 'You give a sorry welcome, for a holy man,' he shouted.

'Nothing holy about me. I scratch and fart like any other man. Clear off!'

'We've come a long way. Won't you give us your blessing?'

'Fat lot of good that'd do you. I'm a sinner like you.'

'Then welcome us as fellow-sinners,' Wace called. 'Give us *your* sinner's blessing, and we'll give you ours.' He smiled slyly. 'After all, you may be entertaining angels unawares. D'you want to risk it?'

The hermit spat, turned his back and started descending the bank on the far side, disappearing from their sight. His cracked voice floated back. 'Are you coming, or what?'

'Oh, well done!' Straccan thumped Wace on the back, making him stagger, then scrambled up after the hermit, stopping halfway to reach down and lend a hand to Wace and give Stigan a look that promised a later reckoning. 'You stay here,' he said. Still grinning, Stigan settled himself in the boat to wait.

With some difficulty they climbed up and slid down the far side of the bank of seaweed which, on its base of stone, must have been more than twelve feet high. Within this enclosure they saw the fragmentary remains of ancient buildings – humps in the ground and the outlines of storerooms – and in the centre what had probably originally been a Roman watchtower and was now the saint's habitation.

Only the stone stump of the tower remained, the ground and first floors; the upper wooden storeys having decayed long ago. At ground level it had been extended in a haphazard fashion with a miscellany of driftwood, bits of canvas, broken baskets, barrels and salvaged ships' timbers. The door of this jackdaw-like nest stood open and, following the saint inside, they found it furnished with bench, table and narrow box-bed, all home-made from salvaged flotsam. A high-walled well occupied one corner, covered with a wooden lid, and a crackling fire of driftwood burned with blue and green and yellow flames in a central hearth; an impressive stack outside showed how some of the saint's time was spent. A string of fish hanging to dry in the smoke showed another side of his industry.

Against the back wall was a row of basketwork cages, some empty, some occupied by damaged birds in various stages of convalescence. The largest cage was half covered with a piece of sacking. A grating *c-r-rawk* came from its darkest corner.

'Now then, Mickey,' the saint said. He lifted the sacking to reveal the occupant, a big strong-smelling cormorant with a splinted wing. Mickey fixed the strangers with an unfriendly emerald eye and gnashed at them.

'Manners,' said the saint reprovingly. The bird yawned fishily, closed its eyes, turned its head until the wicked beak lay along its back and took no further notice of company.

'Well, what do you want?' the old man asked, glaring at them from under tangled white eyebrows. 'I'm a busy man, and if you're angels, I'm the Pope's uncle!'

'Ten years ago a ship was wrecked near here,' Straccan said, wasting no time on preliminary courtesies. 'Two young women were saved. Stigan and his brother brought them here.'

The old man scratched his bottom meditatively. 'There's been lots of wrecks.'

'It was a Danish ship. All aboard perished save those two. The lady's name was Ragnhild. You gave them soup and she spoke privately with you.'

'My memory's not what it was.' The whites of the hermit's eyes showed all around the dark irises. He looked like a mad owl.

'I believe she asked you to take care of something for her.'

'She did, did she? What was it?'

'A flag,' Wace said, butting in eagerly. 'A swallow-tailed pennant.'

The saint stared from one to the other as if expecting something more. When neither of them added anything he lost interest and turned away to open the cormorant's cage, lifting the piratical occupant out and cradling it carefully against his chest. 'I can't help you,' he said over his shoulder. 'Go away.'

Straccan clenched his fists, fighting the urge to take the saint by the throat and shake the truth out of him. Rage rose within him. The Banner had to be here; it *was* here, he knew it, he could *feel* it, and this mad old man knew perfectly well what he'd come for. The search for the Banner had been all of a piece throughout, baulked and obstructed at every turn, at the nunnery and then at the riverside villages. Even Wace, who was there to make sure he got the relic, knew more than he'd let on.

The saint was stripping the splint from the cormorant's wing. When he'd finished he put the bird back in the cage and carried it outside to a low moss-covered wall some distance from his door. The bird gnashed its beak excitedly, scenting freedom. The saint lifted it out, held it for a moment whispering to it, his eyes perilously near the savage beak, then tossed it into the air where it hung for a moment, great wings spread, before flapping away with a harsh cry.

From the far side of the bank came another cry. Stigan's voice, urgent and alarmed.

'Raiders!'

The saint ran up the bank like a gawky heron, Straccan at his heels. There, rounding the bend of the river, was a raiding galley, slim and deadly, sail already furled, oars driving it swiftly towards the jetty.

'Too late,' the saint said. 'You should've gone when I told you, fool!'

There were five oars a side, twelve men with the steersman and their captain in the prow, a wide-shouldered man in the full mail of a knight, with a plain surcoat over all. Although Straccan had only seen him once before and at a distance, he knew Lord William de Breos.

'We can't stop them landing. Stigan,' he shouted. 'Come up here! Back to the tower!' At least there he would have a stone wall behind him. The saint was hopping up and down yelling and waving his fists, and Straccan, who saw Breos reach for a spear, grasped a handful of rags and tatters and swung the old curmudgeon off his feet like a child, down behind the bank's brief shelter, half carrying, half dragging him – wriggling like a pilchard – back to the house.

'Put me down, you whoreson!'

Straccan shook him. 'If you've anywhere to hide yourself, in God's name get to it!' He looked back for Stigan but he hadn't followed. From behind the bank came the noise of men bellowing, the rattle as the oars were put up, and shrilling eerily over all the weird wavering howl of a bullroarer.

They must have got Stigan, Straccan thought with remorse. The blame was his. *God, have mercy on his soul! Christ, receive him into your kingdom!*

The saint settled his ruffled tatters about his skinny frame with affronted pride. 'I won't hide from the Evil One. If God wills, He'll safeguard me. You too,' he added as an afterthought.

'Get down on your prayer-bones, then, and pray for that man's soul,' said Straccan roughly.

'Did they get Stigan?' But the old man had no time for shock and grief for now the first raider was over the ridge, swinging the bullroarer. To Straccan's astonishment a stone flung with startling accuracy by the saint struck the man on the temple. The bullroarer flew from his hand as he teetered, mouth open, then toppled backwards out of sight. The saint bounced up and down with glee.

'Here they come,' he cried, shaking his fist.

Why had they come? Straccan wondered. What was there in this poor place, this wind-scoured desolate dot of land with nothing but a ruin and a mad old man on it? Only one thing, and how had Breos learned where that was hidden?

Atop the ridge heads sprouted like fungus, some shaggy, some helmed; and in a howling mass the raiders came down upon them.

Wace appeared in the doorway, his pale face crumpled with fright. Straccan just had time to shove him back inside and fling the old man in after him, shouting 'Bar the door!' before turning to catch the first raider's sword on his own, stabbing upwards left-handed with his long dagger, twisting the blade to loosen the grip of the dead flesh and shoving the body back with a thrust of his knee. A man with axe upraised fell over the carcass and spitted himself on Straccan's sword.

The saint, who had no bar to his door anyway, heard the *thrumm* of Straccan's whirling sword and the grunts and curses of the raiders and popped out again to see Straccan jump a low sweeping slash and dodge an axe that would have cleft him from neck to chine. But a blade had opened Straccan's forearm, and the blood on his hand loosened his grip on the dagger.

They were all round him now, a struggling mass of men, and his sword was struck from his hand by a numbing blow with an axe. He switched the dagger to his sword hand and shoved it up under someone's chin, but the blade stuck fast and he couldn't get it out again. Powerful arms seized him, pinioning his own. An ill-looking man with but one ear crouched at his feet, dagger ready to hamstring him, but Straccan kicked him in the throat and he fell over, rolling helplessly, retching and whooping for air.

Lord William stepped in front of him. His mail coif framed a heavy-browed face with yellow eyes and a moustached upper lip that lifted in a triumphant smile with a missing front tooth. He was strong, thick-legged, with heavy shoulders and a neck like a bull.

'There's nothing for you here,' Straccan panted. 'No nuns to kill!'

The smile turned to a snarl. 'Five men you've cost me, Straccan, if that's who you are. Where's the Banner?'

'*What* banner?'

Breos struck him in the face with one of his mailed gauntlets. Straccan's cheek split; he felt the icy burn of air on raw flesh.

'Don't play the fool. The king sent you to get it. Where is it?'

The one-eared outlaw, recovered from Straccan's kick but looking the worse for it, grabbed the saint by his long white hair and hauled him to his feet. 'Cat got your tongue, grandad?' he husked.

'Whoreson,' the saint said, his eyes watering. 'God is watching you.'

'Let's give im somefing to laugh at, then.' The outlaw hit the old man in the mouth with a sound like rotten wood breaking.

'Careful,' said Breos, with mock concern. 'He won't be able to talk if you break his jaw. Where's the Banner, old man?'

The saint spat blood and teeth. 'Someone's bin havin you on, you and these other pusbuckets.'

'I don't think so.' Breos slipped a little knife, a skinning knife, from his belt and tossed it to the one-eared man. 'Peel the old fool until he talks.'

'No!' Straccan plunged and struggled uselessly against the hands that held him.

Breos pushed back his mail coif and wiped his sweaty forehead. '*You* tell me where it is, then.'

'I don't know what you're talking about . . . *Oof!*' He sagged, gasping, as Breos's fist thudded into his belly.

'So why are *you* here? You were at the priory, asking questions about a *flag*; my loyal cousin the prioress told me so. You found nothing *there*, and now you're *here*. I owe you thanks. You led me right to it.'

There was a reedy scream from the saint.

Straccan lurched forward, dragging his captors off balance, but only for a moment. Breos's dagger was under his chin.

'Let him go,' Straccan yelled. 'There's nothing here! We came for his blessing, that's all!'

The old man screamed again and Breos laughed.

'Coward!' Straccan shouted. 'Killer of nuns and old men!'

Breos set the point of his dagger delicately just inside Straccan's right nostril, and with a jerk of his hand slit the flesh right through, wiping the blade on Straccan's sleeve. Blood – a considerable amount for so small a wound – and involuntary tears ran down Straccan's face. He shook his head like a dog, spattering blood-drops.

Breos bent over the one-eared man, now squatting by the saint's body. 'Losing your touch, Brun? He's very quiet.'

'E died, dint e,' complained Brun. 'I'd hardly started and he just died!'

'Clumsy fool!' With a growl Breos slashed his dagger across the one-eared man's throat, sidestepping the jetting blood. The outlaw fell across the body of the saint.

Breos turned back to Straccan. 'So there's only you after all. Lucky I didn't cut your insolent tongue out. Now, where's the Banner?' He jerked his chin towards the saint's tower. 'In there? Of course, where else?'

Straccan could hear the raiders crashing about inside. Someone threw a stool from an upper window. Breos stamped into the ransacked chamber and Straccan's captors followed, dragging him. The meagre furnishings had been smashed to splinters, the cages crushed, their occupants with them, and the hermit's scanty provisions trampled: a mess of flour, grain, blood, feathers and dried peas.

'Here's another one, me lord.'

Breos stopped as one of his men shoved Wace forwards with his arms wrenched up painfully behind his back.

'What have we here?' Breos looked intently at the clerk. 'I know you, don't I? Yes! You're one of John's damned scribblers. Let him go, he's only a pettifogging clerk.' He beckoned Wace forward, took him by the shoulder and pushed him outside, pointing at the bloody bodies and brandishing his dagger under Wace's nose. 'See that, scribbler? That's what'll happen to you unless you tell me where the Banner is.'

Wace gave a cry of dismay. 'You've killed the hermit!' His face was mask-like, rigid with fear. He clutched at his own throat, as if to shield it from the slice of the knife. Then, so quickly Breos never saw it coming, the clerk pulled a stiletto on a cord from under his shirt and flung himself bodily on the rebel lord. Breos was taken by surprise, and although Wace's blade skidded harmlessly off the links of his mail, he stumbled backwards over the bodies and fell, with Wace on top, screeching and jabbing at his unprotected face.

Breos roared, heaved and flung the small man off. Blood streamed down his face. Wace's stiletto had just missed his eye, glancing off the cheekbone and scoring a long jagged gash down his cheek. He dabbed at it, staring at his bloodied hand incredulously.

Two men seized Wace, each grasping an arm. Breos got to his feet, red with blood and fury, and drove his dagger into Wace's belly. With a soft 'Oh!' the clerk convulsed and hung limply from his captors' grip. They dropped him. He fell to his knees, clutching his belly, blood running between his fingers; then toppled onto his side and lay with legs drawn up, moaning.

Raging, blood running down onto his hauberk, Breos made for the tower again. Behind him he heard an odd sound and paused, glancing back. The clerk's eyes were fixed on him and, unbelievably, he was grinning.

'You bloody fool,' he gasped, barely above a whisper. 'You killed him. Serves you right. Now you'll never find it!'

'What?' Breos glared at the clerk who now lay still, whether already dead or just near death made no difference; he was past speech. Breos stormed into the tower room to confront Straccan.

'It's here, isn't it? That old fool hid it here somewhere.'

'Christ, I don't know,' Straccan said thickly. His face and nose, still bleeding, felt like red-hot brands, and he spat as blood ran into his mouth. 'He never told us. And now he can't!'

A horn blared – the galley's lookout. One of the outlaws ran up the bank to see.

'A ship!' he yelled. 'The warden!'

'To hell with him. How'd he get wind of us?' Breos kicked at the embers of the saint's fire, scattering them across the floor. The debris began to smoulder.

'What about him?' asked one of the men holding Straccan.

Breos's gaze came to rest on the well. At his gesture two men heaved the lid aside. The well gaped like a horrid mouth, breathing out cold sour air.

'He's no damned use to me. Pitch him down and put the cover back. Let's go. We'll come back later and take this tower apart.'

De Lacy's cumbersome vessel had no chance of catching the reivers' galley; it would be clear away and tucked out of sight in a pill in no more time than it took to say a *Pater Noster*. Safe hidden, Breos and his raiders could outwait the warden and come back to search the island when all was clear.

Straccan twisted and lunged desperately but had no chance. He was dragged to the well, pressed back against it, upended and tipped in.

Chapter 36

The lady Julitta bolted the door of her chamber, unlocked the iron and silver casket on a chain at her waist and took out a cloudy grey crystal, the size and shape of a hen's egg.

Holding the stone in her left hand, she traced on it the runes of summoning and command. For a moment the crystal itself appeared to be encased in a darkly glowing fine-meshed net, then the interwoven strands faded and were gone. Within the stone a dark shadow shifted and settled, waiting.

Julitta spoke the name of the demon imprisoned in the stone. 'Agarel . . .'

Despite the fire, the room grew chill enough to show her breath. The shadowy heart of the crystal cleared and a reptilian face looked sulkily out at her, human in shape but lipless and scaly-skinned like the feet of a hen. The slanting eyes, all yellow without white or pupil, gleamed with malice.

'Agarel, I command you!' The yellow eyes took on a misty reddish tinge, and although there was no sound she knew he hissed with rage, hating her and her power over him. He was her prisoner and while confined in the stone must do her bidding.

'Show me Duke Gaillard,' she said huskily.

The crystal clouded, cleared. She saw, small but distinct, a man kneeling beside a bed, a woman lying in it, bright and still as a wall-painting. The woman's lips moved and the man took her hand, turned it palm up and tenderly kissed it. Light caught in the tears slipping from his eyes.

Julitta smiled. Duchess Urraca still lived. Soon, though . . . soon . . . And then the duke must take another wife; no matter how greatly he loved Urraca he *must* take another for he had no heir. His counsellors would have a new wife picked out already for the duchess had been long dying, but they would be disappointed of their choice. The duke would marry again; his people would be dismayed, would say he was bewitched.

They'd be right.

She passed her hand over the crystal again. 'Show me the great Lord William.' *Great fool, great brute* . . . but he would serve his purpose; through him she would gain the Banner. There he was, in the prow of his galley, face and surcoat bloody. She could sense rage and disappointment boiling off him like steam.

Mist dulled the stone, then cleared to show Agarel grinning impudently, chewing and slavering over some nasty leggy thing. Julitta sketched the rune of pain, of punishment, and watched dispassionately as he writhed and jerked, fanged mouth gaping in a soundless scream. Benoic, the Breton sorcerer, had taught her how to summon and trap such lesser demons, among other useful skills. The hellspawn must be kept confined. If Agarel got free from his cage he could turn on his captor, rip away her mind and all her powers, leaving her helpless. But she had no fear of that. Benoic had thought himself her master, he who was as wax in her hands. Much had she learned from him, and much that he had not intended her to learn, before she poisoned him.

She released the silently shrieking demon from his agony. 'Show me Mahaut de Breos.'

The stone showed a wild landscape, mountains rising beyond mountains, rain falling in sheets, and a man and woman in a cart. On either side of the cart rode a file of armed men. The cart lurched and bounced – there was no road at all – and its occupants were thrown against each other or to the floor, scrambling up with difficulty, clinging to the cart's sides. They wore the common brown wadmal of pilgrims, torn and sodden; the woman's long grey hair hung wet around her shoulders and both were heavily shackled.

These were no pilgrims. Bruised, bloody, defeated, afraid, these were Lord William's wife and eldest son.

Julitta bit her lip. How long could this be kept from Lord William? How long before his wife's capture became common knowledge? And yet . . . It might be she could use this to advantage, for if Breos loved anyone, he loved his wife; he would do anything to save her.

The demon's squamous face reappeared, sneering. She slashed the pain rune in the air again, and Agarel twisted. In her mind she could feel the strange soundless pressure of his howls. 'Worm!' Furiously she slammed the stone back into the iron and silver case, leaving the demon in torment until she called him again.

As he fell, Straccan's head struck the shaft wall, stunning him. Some tiny part of his mind clung to consciousness; he fought against the tide of darkness that threatened to swamp him, but to no avail. He was going to die in this horrid hole.

Faint, far away he seemed to hear a woman's voice repeating, 'Tell him, tell him, Guinevere,' and then, strangely, he heard children laughing: the small boys by the river, the little girls in the pleasance at Ludlow, high sweet voices crying, 'Give it to me!'

He could smell smoke. Was this Hell? His cheek and nose throbbed with pain. He opened his eyes and found himself, to his astonishment, alive.

Chapter 37

When they had bread or meat to be baked, Shawl folk must use the lord's ovens. For this compulsory privilege they had to pay, so of course they made do instead with flat griddle-bread, soups and stews, or anything that could be cooked in pot or frying pan at home. This morning, though, the communal ovens offered the only meeting place where neither the chaplain nor any other man was likely to come poking his nose in, and at Sybilla's urging a group of village women had gathered, ostensibly to enjoy a good grumble.

The manor's baker counted loaves, three, counted heads, eight, and raised a sceptical eyebrow; but it was nothing to do with him and he promptly came down with a diplomatic bellyache and took himself to bed. If there was Something Going On he wanted no part of it.

As soon as he'd gone Sybilla got down to business; she had picked her team carefully. When she had explained her plan she waited for them to start arguing. They didn't.

Hawkan Bane had promised to help, had gone to fetch his master, but the knight had not come. In times of trouble, she thought with grim satisfaction, you had to know who you could rely on. In times of trouble, you couldn't rely on men.

The rats were hard to bear. Janiva could hear them scratching and scrabbling somewhere behind the bales and involuntarily drew her feet up off the floor, hugging her knees and shivering. The scratching went on. Odd; there was a strange regularity to it. She listened. *Scratch-scratch, scratch-scratch.* A pause. *Scratch-scratch, scratch-scratch.* That wasn't a rat.

The noise came from the wall opposite the door. Janiva clambered over the stacked bales to get closer. The undercroft was used nowadays to store the wool-clip because it was too small and inconveniently old-fashioned to house the manor's provisions and stores. Dame Alienor had had a new storeroom built backing on to the kitchen.

There were *two* doors in the undercroft.

The bulging bales were too big to get her arms round and tied so tightly that Janiva couldn't work her fingers between the cord and the sackcloth wrappings to get a grip. Her fingernails tore to the quick as she struggled to move the great rough hairy bundles, lugging them aside to make a passage to the back wall, to the door. With desperate eagerness she toiled on.

After what seemed a long time, *was* a long time, her palms first blistered then flayed raw, the soft skin of her forearms sandpapered by the coarse sacking, she had managed to shift enough to get at the top half of the low door. Crawling over the bales she knelt and leaned her hot face against the thick oak.

Scratch-scratch. Scratch-scratch.

She made a fist, wincing, and banged on the door. The scratching stopped and she heard a voice, muffled by more than two inches of solid oak. She thumped again. The voice said something else. It was no good, she couldn't make it out.

Eagerly she resumed shifting bales. At last there was a space in front of the door. She thumped it again. Clearer now, the voice – a woman's – seemed to be coming from somewhere down by her waist. Of course, the keyhole. She felt down the door until she found it and crouched.

'Janiva! It's me, Sybilla. Are you all right?'

'Yes! Can you let me out?'

'There's no key! This door ain't been used in years.'

Janiva's hopes plunged. But Sybilla was still talking.

'Old Vinegar won't let anyone in to see you and there's always a guard at the main door, but listen, tonight, when you hear the supper horn, be ready! We'll get you out then.'

'How?'

'Never mind. Just you be ready; we'll have to move quick. You *sure* you're all right?'

'Sybilla . . .'

'What? I got to go.'

'Don't risk yourself to help me.'

'Just do your bit. We'll be fine!'

Sybilla hurried back to her waiting troops. There was risk, but with any luck, if their plan worked, no blame could be pinned to any one person, certainly not to any man or woman of Shawl.

When the supper horn sounded and Father Finacre stood to say grace in the hall, Joan gave her daughter Ellen a leg-up through one of the stable windows. Ellen nipped up the ladder into the hayloft and crouched, striking steel on flint and nursing the sparks until a wisp of smoke rose from the loose hay. She blew gently and a small yellow flame licked up towards her face. She then ran to the far end of the loft where she slipped out through the hoist-hole, lowering herself by her hands until it was safe to let go and drop.

Flames were roaring already, the stable boys shouting, leading out the horses then running to and from the rain-butts with leather buckets and flinging water over the flames and one another.

In the hall a serving-woman stumbled over a dog and fell, dropping her tray of roasted eggs. Catching at the high table's great linen cloth she dragged it with her, bringing a cascade of trenchers, knives, spoons, roasted ducks and pigeons, baked fish, beakers of ale and wine, sauces, napkins, finger bowls and curses down around herself. The steward, red with shame and spouting apologies, pulled the grizzling woman to her feet and gave her a ringing slap, while the dog seized the opportunity and a pigeon and slunk under the table.

Diners leapt up, swearing and mopping at their laps. Servers got in one another's way as they retrieved napkins and dabbed at the diners' soiled clothes, picked up utensils, cleared away the debris, fetched clean tablecloths and salvaged what was still edible: a quick wipe and most of it went back on the board.

At the undercroft door Janiva's guard heard the distant rumpus, smelled the smoke from the stable and wondered what was going on. His belly gurgled; his dinner was late coming tonight and he wondered who'd bring it. That juicy little tease Ellen, maybe. Or the one with the tits, what was her name, Clara. He fancied her something rotten. She was playing hard to get but he knew what *she* needed, and he'd bloody well give it to her first chance he got.

And by God it looked like this was his chance for here came Clara with his dinner.

He took it. 'Ta. What's goin on?'

'Hayloft took fire.'

But he wasn't interested in the fire. A fire within him had begun to take hold and he wasn't even interested in his dinner any more either, for Clara's admirable bosom was within reach. He leered and reached. She slapped his hand but he wasn't put off; that was only Step One.

His forgotten dinner steamed on the doorstep as he carefully took Step Two.

'Not ere,' said Clara breathlessly, in the middle of Step Three.

It was his lucky day. Night. 'Where, then?'

She jerked a thumb towards Father Osric's garden shed, clinging like a wart to the side of his hovel. Entwined, they lurched towards it. Inside was a spade, a heap of trugs and – oddly – a straw pallet. By now his brains were entirely below his belt and the curiously convenient mattress rang no warning bells. They fell on it. Step Three progressed to Four.

Perhaps he heard the door creak behind them but Sybilla had grabbed the spade and brought it down on his thick skull with a reassuringly solid thump that laid him out before he could look round.

Clara wriggled out from under. 'Ere, that was a bit close!'

Sybilla dropped the spade. 'You'd've managed.'

The two women rolled the heavy body over.

'You've killed im!'

'No such luck; his head's too thick. Get the key.'

Clara rummaged at his belt and unlatched the key.

'You sure that's it?'

'It's the only one e's got.'

'Come on, then.'

When Janiva had slipped through the half open door Sybilla shut and locked it again and gave the key to Clara.

'Put it back, quick. Then go help in the kitchen.'

The guard would come round and dash back to the undercroft door, relieved to find the key still on his belt, the door still locked. He'd curse himself for a fool and Clara for a slut, but when Janiva's escape was discovered he would never admit to leaving his post. Finacre believed she was a witch; let him think she got out by spellcraft.

Sybilla handed Janiva a packed satchel. 'Food. Come on.'

They crept behind the storehouses and kitchen, round behind the mew, where the ground sloped to a stream. On the other side of the water was the apple orchard and beyond that the forest. In the orchard a dark figure bulked, moving forward with a practised silence that had caught many a poacher napping.

'Tostig! What are you doing here?'

Janiva grasped the forester's hands, wincing as he squeezed hers. He took the satchel and slung it over his shoulder.

'That boy Peter came to fetch me; Sybilla sent him. And your knight's man, Bane, he had a word wi me before he left. Come on. We must hurry!'

Janiva turned to Sybilla. 'Bane was here?'

'He said he'd bring his master but we dint dare wait. God go with you, Janiva!' They clung together for a moment, and Sybilla felt Janiva's tears against her cheek. 'Don't cry, love. You'll be well out of Vinegar's reach. He'll come to a sticky end, mark my words.' And to Tostig, 'Look after her.'

'Didn't she save my life when I was bad hurt? I'd give mine for her. I'll see her safe.'

'Where you taking her?'

'Better you don't know. When they find she's gone there'll be questions. If they ask, you can swear you don't know. I'll tell her knight when he comes.' He led Janiva into the trees. 'It's on foot for a while. Stick close to me. I've a horse waiting at Willowford.'

'Where *are* we going?'

'To the anchoress at Pouncey. No one'll look for you there, lass. It ain't Sir Roger's domain.'

The great granite ridge of Pouncey Edge ran from east to west for nearly five miles, and above Pouncey village it shelved in three great steps – the lower two well wooded – and was watered by narrow falls that leaped from step to step to the river below. In the cliff face near the top weathering had exposed a broad vein of milky quartz, visible from afar. Pouncey folk held it to be lucky and believed their cattle did well under its guardianship, and who can say they were not right?

It was an easy climb from the village to the first level, but after that it became more difficult; only the agile or the desperate could make it to the third level where Osyth, the anchoress, had lived for seventeen years in her chosen solitude.

A cleft in the rock had provided her shelter when she first came; the previous anchoress had dwelt in a sod hut, now much decayed, but the folk of Pouncey had with great labour carried wood and stones up and built a chamber around the fissure for the new lady and a low stone wall enclosing the tiny house and its garth. They provided her with food and necessities, and in return she prayed for them and did such doctoring as she could. If her prayers were not always orthodox so much the better. The villagers reckoned they had the best of the bargain.

No one knew where she had come from or how old she was, but her hair had been white when she came to Pouncey. In the early years she used to roam the woods that clothed the lower levels of the Edge, gathering herbs and mushrooms, berries and nuts – she never ate meat – but seventeen winters had bitten into her bones and now she hobbled with a stick and never left her anchor-hold.

Since the house had been built no one else had stepped across its threshold and now, with two guests – greeted as if she knew of their coming as mayhap she did – the little chamber was crowded.

They had come a long way these two, four days' journey, and Osyth made them welcome, fetching water for them to wash and setting bread, cheese and little sweet wrinkled apples from her store before them. She built up her fire – the fissure made a natural chimney – for it was cold here in the stone heart of the Edge, and although Osyth was used to it she saw the young woman, Janiva, shiver. Not entirely from the cold, the anchoress realised; that pallor and the haunted eyes indicated shock, or grief, or both, and there was the ghost of a great bruise on one side of her face.

'Go warily,' Osyth told the forester as he prepared to leave.

'I'll be all right.'

'There's danger in the forest.'

'Wolves?'

'Two-legged wolves.'

'You take care of my lady,' Tostig said. 'I'll take care of myself.'

After the forester had gone Osyth put Janiva to bed and when night came lay down beside her. She was aware of the shadow shrouding the girl and knew it for something other than grief. Something dark, old and evil had this good child in thrall.

Chapter 38

The well had been dry for a century and a long succession of saints had chucked their rubbish down it rather than plod up the bank to consign it to the river. So instead of drowning Straccan had landed on a deep mass of fishbones, feathers, rotting skins and other smelly debris. A long way above, impossibly remote, was a small lunette of murky daylight where the cover rested slightly askew.

Time still passed at its normal rate, but the violent events of the day seemed to have occurred with extraordinary rapidity, in moments, not hours. He had experienced the same distortion in battle. Straccan swayed as he got first to his hands and knees, and then gingerly to his feet. The debris shifted under his weight, foul water surged over his feet and he lurched against the wall, feeling nauseous. His nose and cheek had stopped bleeding but burned like fresh brands, and his head throbbed sickeningly.

Nothing seemed to be broken but his mind wasn't working properly. The details of the raid and the fight were a blur, but Stigan and Wace and the saint were dead, that much he remembered. He couldn't have saved them, he knew that, yet felt he should have. As he muttered a prayer for their souls, dizziness and nausea overwhelmed him and he fell to his knees and vomited.

After that he felt a bit better, and gingerly got to his feet again. High up beneath the cover, hanging like cobwebs, was a thin smoky haze, but if the saint's den above was burning he was at least safe from the flames down here. He reached out to feel the shaft wall. It seemed to be made of thin rough bricks. Groping upwards, his hand encountered a brick jutting out a bit and closed on it. He felt around with his other hand for another hold.

Yes! There!

Now, if he could pull up on *this* one and get a foot on *that* one, it would be a start. Grunting as pain lanced through his head, he began.

As he put his weight on it the brick crumbled, precipitating him back into the refuse. He throttled back despair. If he didn't get out of here he'd never see Gilla again, nor Janiva. *Lord Christ, help me now!*

As he got to one knee, then up again, something pressed hard against his calf. His sword and dagger were gone but they hadn't bothered to search him, and sheathed inside his boot was what Bane called 'insurance', a short broad-bladed knife for use in emergencies.

This certainly qualified.

Thank you, Lord!

His jerkin would only hamper his efforts; he stripped it off with his shirt. Then he tackled the crumbly brick with his knife, gouging a shallow hole and feeling around the wall for other rotten bricks. After a while, he had hand- and foot-holds to start his ascent, and began creeping slowly and painfully up the shaft.

When he couldn't find any more decaying bricks, he clenched the knife between his teeth and stretched his body across the well shaft. With his feet pushing against the wall at one side and his back and elbows scraped raw against the other, he slowly inched his way up, stopping often to prod around with the knife for soft bricks.

The tremendous effort and the strain on the muscles of his shoulders and chest soon exhausted him, weakened as he was by the blow to his head.

Christ, in your mercy, don't let me lose my senses and fall.

Clawing his way up inch by painful inch, he thought of his daughter and prayed that he might hold her in his arms again; and of Janiva, that he would return to her. And then it seemed to him, hanging spreadeagled halfway up the well shaft, that he could hear again the voices of the boys he had seen by the riverside that morning and the little girls at Ludlow, laughing, crying, 'Give it to me!'

Why did that keep coming back to him?

A memory stirred, took shape. Himself as a small boy, his nurse teasing him, holding something, a toy or an orange, out of his reach.

'Give it to me!'

'Now then, Master Richard, what's the magic word?'

Oh God! Oh Jesus! The magic word!

Too late!

His sudden short, bitter laugh – for what use was the knowledge now? – nearly made him fall, but somehow he clung on and kept going. He closed his eyes and thrust again with both feet, scraping his flayed back another inch or two up the wall. His legs were cramping.

It was no good; he wasn't going to make it. His back was slippery with blood, his shoulder muscles on fire. Another inch. Another. It was getting smoky.

Straccan coughed and opened his eyes – he didn't remember closing them – and to his surprise the top was very near, four or five feet, no more. But he could gain no more height and he was light-headed now for he could hear voices again. This time they were calling his name.

Bracing his back and splaying his palms against the wall, ramming his feet against the other side, he kept himself from falling. The muscles of his legs quivered and burned like hot wires inside his flesh. Blood from his back had soaked his breeches.

I'm not going to fall, I'm not going to die, and when I catch up with that whoreson Breos I'll poke his eyes out with a short stick!

'Straccan!'

'Sir Richard!'

He was still hearing voices. It would be heavenly choirs next. Any minute now.

Into Thy hands, Lord God . . .

'Sir Richard!'

'God's lights, what's the use? He's dead, he must be. We might as well push off.'

'No! He's not among the bodies. He's alive, he must be here somewhere!'

Havloc? That was Havloc's voice, loud and desperate. And the other voice had been Maurice de Lacy's.

Bastard! Anything to welsh on a debt . . .

'Here!' But instead of a shout only a feeble croak came from his throat. He tried licking his dry lips but his tongue was dry as well. He sank his teeth into his split lip, moistened his mouth with blood and tried again.

'Havloc! Havloc, here! The well!'

'Come on, man, we're wasting time. Let's collect the corpses and go.' De Lacy's voice was further away now.

They hadn't heard him! They were leaving!

'Havloc!' The smoke was thick now and made him cough; he felt himself slipping and knew he had reached the end of his strength.

There was a noise overhead and a great burst of light as the cover was dragged off. 'Wait! Here! In the well!'

Convulsively Straccan braced his body once more and looked up to see the black shapes of heads and shoulders no more than a foot or two above him.

Chapter 39

Chilled to the bone, Straccan opened his eyes and saw the faces of Havloc and the river warden bending over him. Behind them the stone walls of the hermit's tower stood striped with soot and wreathed in smoke. He shivered.

'What . . .' he began huskily, and then again, louder, 'what happened?'

'You fainted,' said de Lacy. 'We got you out. You folded up on us. No wonder!'

Havloc slipped an arm round Straccan's shoulders to help him sit up and the warden peered at his damaged face.

'Nasty! They've spoiled your beauty for you, I'm afraid. How you got up that sodding well I'll never know! God's feet, I'd've bet a hundred marks it couldn't be done!'

Straccan looked around. The mast and yard of the warden's ship swayed gently, moored beyond the bank, and de Lacy's men were going methodically about the business of stripping the raiders' bodies.

'The hermit . . .'

'Over there.' De Lacy pointed. 'Amazing thing! Tough old bird.'

'He's *alive*?'

'Don't ask me how!'

Getting to his feet, wondering which bit of him hurt the most, dizzy and disoriented and with the nagging feeling that there was *something* he should remember but couldn't, Straccan saw the saint, a bloody scarecrow tottering from corpse to corpse, falling on his knees beside each one, tears pouring down his face.

'What's he doing?'

'Praying for the bastards.' The saint's cracked voice rose and fell in passionate pleading for God to spare the souls of these wretches. 'Don't bother, I told him,' muttered de Lacy, 'but he just told me to sod off.'

Straccan counted six bodies, five he had accounted for and the one-eared outlaw that Breos had slain himself.

'Where's Wace?'

The warden looked grim. 'We carried him over there, out of the wind.' He waved a hand towards the low broken wall where the saint had freed the cormorant.

'Dead?'

'Not yet. Won't last long though, belly wound. No chance. I'll send word to the king.'

Straccan stumbled over to Wace. The clerk was laid out as if dead already, neat and straight and covered with the lord warden's own splendid scarlet cloak, his body mounding it no more than a child's. His face was parchment-pale, eyes sunk in brownish hollows.

Straccan knelt beside him. 'Master Wace . . . Robert.' The moth-wing eyelids fluttered open, the pallid lips moved.

'Sorry . . .'

'Christ, man, what for?'

'Didn't . . . kill him.'

'You had a bloody good try! He'll carry your mark.'

To his astonishment Wace's lips twitched in a weak smile. 'Not bad . . . for a . . . pettifogging clerk.'

Under the cloak his hand moved. Straccan took it, damp and cold as a fish, and clasped it between his own. 'It was a brave thing.'

'In his grace's service one must . . . be prepared for anything. A pity . . .'

'What?'

'We didn't find . . . the Banner.'

The Banner! *Now* he remembered! Gently Straccan laid the clerk's hand down and tucked the cloak over it again. 'Hold on, Robert,' he said. 'I'll be back.'

The hermit was still kneeling by the dead but either his frenzied prayers were finished or he was waiting for his second wind. Straccan squatted stiffly at his side until the mad faded eyes swivelled to focus upon him.

'You still here?'

'As you see.'

The saint cackled suddenly. 'Me too! In spite of that whore's get! What was all this dying for, eh? What did he want? Tell me that!'

'The same thing I came for: the lady Ragnhild's banner.'

A shifty look crossed the old man's face. 'I told you, my memory's poor.'

'I've a word that may remind it,' Straccan said. The saint was waiting, watching him with a curious intentness. He hesitated, then plunged. 'Guinevere.'

In the silence that followed he could hear gulls crying overhead, the suck and slap of the river on the far side of the bank, and his own heart thumping.

'Help me up, then,' said the saint.

Straccan put his arm round the old man's waist and lifted him – withered and light as a bundle of sticks – to his feet. Fresh blood gouted from the flayed patches on his meagre slat-ribbed chest, where Brun's knife had started work, but he ignored it.

'Ten years,' he said disgustedly. 'You took your time! Is Lady Ragnhild well?'

'She died.'

The saint crossed himself, mumbled a prayer and set off briskly towards the mossy wall where Wace lay. What was he doing now? Did he mean to give the dying man the last rites? No. He stepped straight over him to the empty cage, opened it, slid aside a panel at the back and took out a long flat leather satchel.

'There,' he said ungraciously, pushing it into Straccan's hands. 'Take it and clear off.'

Without knowing it, Straccan had been holding his breath. Now he let it out. 'Do you know what it is?'

'No.'

'You never looked?'

'No.' And without another word the old man returned to the dead, signing each body with the cross as the warden's men began carrying them, one by one, to the ship.

The leather was salt-caked, dry and cracked, and its brittle ties crumbled as Straccan touched them. Inside was a softish roll wrapped in oilskin tied round with thongs. These too were dry and stiff, and he had to wet them with spit and work them with his fingers before he could undo the knots.

He looked around. No one was watching. De Lacy and his men were on the far side of the bank, Havloc with them; he could hear them grumbling as they dumped the bodies on the ship.

Carefully he slid the oilskin wrappings off.

The pennant was of stiff heavy sendal, once white but soiled and darkened with age. His hands shook as he unrolled it.

The dragon's head blazed up at him, vivid as new-shed blood, its eyes stitched with garnets, its flaming mane and lolling tongue with gold thread, and the terrible jaws set with slips of ivory for teeth. The doubled silk had been slashed to show, stitched between the layers, another fabric, finely woven linen, brown with age and darkly stained.

Stained, possibly, with blood. Allegedly, with the blood of Christ.

His hammering heart shook his whole body as he knelt beside Wace. The flesh of the little clerk's face had collapsed to show the skull beneath. He was still breathing but the end could not be long. Straccan touched his cheek gently. 'Robert, look. We have it: the Pendragon Banner.'

The sunken eyes opened. Straccan held the half-opened pennant up so that the dying man could see it, and then touched the stained cloth gently to the clerk's lips. Almost soundlessly, Wace whispered, 'Is it in truth?'

Looking closely at the goldwork, Straccan saw among the metallic threads some strands that were indeed human hair of a rare deep golden shade.

'Yes, it is. See!'

'Guinevere!' A smile of childlike wonder transfigured the clerk's face. 'It was true . . . after all.'

There was a tremendous rumbling noise. Straccan turned. Stones were falling from the wall of the tower. As he stared the whole thing collapsed, belching up a great cloud of dust and smoke.

Chapter 40

The new leper-master visited each of his charges every day. With himself and Illtud, who had come with him from Ludlow, there were thirteen lepers at Cwm Cuddfan that summer: seven other men and four women. No children, thank God.

Here in the Hidden Valley they had an island to themselves, Ynys Gwydion, lying like a green gem in the lake called Llyn Gwydion. The lake, by some freak of chemistry, was an astonishing blue, and from the cliffs above the valley the jade island in its lapis setting was fair to see.

Sometimes, followed by Illtud who had appointed himself his guardian, Garnier climbed the difficult path to the shrine of Saint Nonna to pray, think and gaze upon the beauty below, marvelling that God should trouble to create such perfection of shape and colour and wondering if He, too, eyed it from far above and took pleasure in it. The shrine was a tiny shelter perched on a ledge of rock where the saint had fled from her father's wrath. A fire was kept burning, said never to have gone out since the saint dwelt there. It was a daily task to carry up the wood, eagerly undertaken even squabbled over by penitents and pilgrims.

From this window-hole the saint had seen the sun rise as Garnier did now. From this perilous place she had threatened to leap to her death after her son was born, unless her furious father gave up his intention of dragging her back to another marriage, when she – now widowed – wished only to answer God's call and become a nun.

From here Garnier could contemplate his new domain in its entirety, a miniature landscape spread beneath him. Most leper hospices housed the occupants in dormitories, men and women strictly segregated and often overseen with harshness, for was not leprosy God's punishment for hidden sin? But on Ynys Gwydion the two married pairs had huts to themselves, the two unmarried women shared a hut and four of the single men shared another. The fifth, the silent man whose name in the register was Geoffrey, dwelt apart and alone.

He had always kept to himself; no one had ever heard him speak and now, in the last stages of the disease, he was too ill to leave his bed. Garnier always left the Silent Man until last so that if he should choose to speak, to make his confession, to ask for something or just to complain about the food, the weather or his fate, the master would have the rest of the day to listen. But the Silent Man never spoke. Perhaps he no longer could. No one knew anything about him, Sulien no more than the rest.

'Is he dumb?' Garnier had asked soon after his arrival.

'I don't know,' Sulien said. 'I talk to him but he says nothing. He can write, though. He sends me notes from time to time, writ in courtly French.'

'Does he?' Garnier was intrigued. 'What about?'

'Requests. More charcoal, another blanket; once he asked for perfume.'

'Perfume!'

'He said he wanted to smell something other than death.'

'How old is he?'

'He was quite young when he came here. He can't be more than twenty-five now.'

He'd been there seven years, the first leper to come to the valley; a Breos protégé, brought by Breos retainers and with Breos silver paying for his keep and extra comforts.

Lord William was Cwm Cuddfan's founder and patron. 'A young lad of my household,' he had said, and his orders were clear: Geoffrey was to have what food he fancied, not just the hospital ration; he must have fuel for his fire and not need to share any other man's fire; and instead of the coarse wadmal the others wore, fine linen and good woollen cloth were provided for him.

He had a silver cup and plate, a fur coverlid, a cloak lined with otter skins, fur-lined slippers, even books! In life he must have been a rich young man with family, friends, a sweetheart or even a wife, yet no one came to see him. Once a year a Breos clerk came to enquire if he still lived and hand over a purse of silver for his needs. There was far more money than the Silent Man could ever use and Sulien said so. No matter, he was told. Do as you please with it so long as he lacks nothing.

The Silent Man must be one of the numerous Breos tribe, shut away when his disease became apparent. That was the usual thing. A leper, an unmistakeable sign of God's displeasure, was an embarrassment to his kin. This Breos cast-off was the fount and origin of Lord William's patronage.

The hospital here was unique in being run not by any religious order but by a physician, Sulien. At first no more than a wattle and daub hut, it had grown in the eight years since he had somehow talked Lord William de Breos into giving him the valley. Men and women were now nursed separately in two large airy halls, each with twelve beds and capable of holding two dozen patients at two to a bed; three, if push came to shove. In addition to the sick halls there were one-room cotts where patients could be cared for by their families if they wished, with the help of Sulien's students. For the well-born there were two modest hall-houses where they and their own household servants could stay as long as necessary.

The students, men and women both, came from all parts of the kingdom to study the healing arts here, where foundlings were cared for, lepers made welcome, the sick and injured found help and the bereaved were comforted.

And now, without Lord William's money, without a wealthy patron, without a *miracle*, this refuge in the Hidden Valley would be no more.

Chapter 41

Two dusty figures, considerably the worse for wear, limped painfully across the outer bailey of Ludlow castle to the gatehouse of the keep. Challenged, the taller and older of the two croaked his name from a dust-dry throat and waited for the guard to step aside.

Looking him up and down, the man laughed. 'Pull the other one,' he said. 'Get out of here!'

The younger man moved forward angrily, but the other held him back and addressed the guard again. 'I *am* Straccan,' he said, 'and if you don't want to cool your heels in your own guardhouse you'll either let me in or send to tell Lord Engelard I'm here!'

With a disbelieving sneer the man-at-arms called to a passing servant. 'Find the steward and tell him there's a fellow here wants to see the constable. Says his name's Straccan.'

Straccan leaned back against the wall and looked despondently at his boots. He wasn't used to walking and these boots had never been meant for it. The sole of one was hanging off; he had tied it in place with the thong that once laced his shirt. The other boot was so worn and down at heel that even a beggar would have rejected it. Havloc's shoes had suffered worse and been abandoned five miles short of Ludlow.

Aratcha! The stone arch of the gatehouse rang with the echo.

'My lord,' said Straccan. He was surprised that the constable should appear in person but Cigony had obviously just come from his beloved hawks; there was a small barred feather in his hair and birdshit on his boots. He loosed another violent sneeze, wiped his eyes and stared at Straccan.

'God's teeth, it *is* you,' he said. 'What happened? Where are your horses?'

'We were set upon,' said Straccan, following him into the damp dim coolness of the keep, with Havloc trailing in their wake.

'Outlaws, was it?' The constable led the way to the stairs.

'Breos's men. A foraging party in the forest, ten miles back. They took everything,' he said bitterly. He'd *never* forgive himself for that.

Cigony stopped and looked back at him in some surprise. 'Why didn't they kill you?'

Straccan shrugged. 'Luck, I suppose.' Luck! That was a joke. His luck had played Judas. Nevertheless he *was* alive; he could do something about it. 'Is my man Bane here?'

'I've not seen him.'

As they crossed the hall, followed by curious stares, nudges and whispered comments, Alis came running down the stairs and flung herself into Havloc's arms. The two stood in a tight embrace, oblivious to all else, as Straccan followed Cigony up to the constable's private room.

Impatiently Cigony waved him to a stool. 'Sit down, man. You've had a long walk by the look of it.' He poured ale and handed Straccan a cup. 'So, what happened?'

'We stopped at a ford, to water the horses. Yesterday evening, it was . . .'

As the thirsty beasts dipped their heads, Havloc had said hesitantly, 'What'll happen to me, sir, when we get to Ludlow?'

With a pang of shame Straccan realised that not since the burning of the priory had he given any thought to Havloc or the missing cup that could still put a noose round his neck. What *was* going to happen to him? Short of a miracle it was unlikely that the thief or cup would ever be found, and the coroner's animosity could make things difficult.

'Don't worry. I'll take care of it,' he said. And he would. Of course. Somehow. If it had been left to Maurice de Lacy he'd still be in the bloody well on the saint's island. It was Havloc who'd found him, Havloc he hadn't wanted along. 'Havloc—' he began.

The horses' heads swung up, dripping, ears cocked forward alertly. Havloc was staring past him, shocked pale, and whatever Straccan had been going to say died a-borning.

It was his fault. He'd been off guard. His exhaustion, the dizziness that still plagued him were no excuse. He had been *criminally* stupid, and if anyone under his command had been caught napping like that he'd have had the fool flogged.

There were half a dozen crossbowmen, bolts aimed at their hearts. How the devil had they appeared, surrounding them, without a sound? Two more materialised silently from the shadows under the trees and relieved them of their weapons and horses. It was quick, efficient and wholly professional.

No need for quiet now. Branches shook and rustled as two more men brought the troop's horses out of hiding, several heavily laden with sacks and barrels. A foraging party. Too well accoutred to be outlaws; these were Breos's men, of course. Straccan groaned. He should have been prepared; He should have *expected* something like this.

Two at a time the crossbowmen mounted up while the rest kept their bolts trained on Straccan and Havloc. The whole business took perhaps ten minutes, not a word uttered until the captain of the band swung himself up into Straccan's own saddle and bowed curtly, saying, 'We need your horses, sir. I regret the inconvenience to you.'

'Like hell you do! You're no better than outlaws. Like master, like men.'

The last man afoot tensed. 'Shall I kill them?'

'Let them go,' said the captain. Straccan would never forget the old disillusioned eyes in that young face. 'We've got the horses.'

They had the horses and everything on them: saddlebags, cloaks, bedrolls, water bottles, provisions, weapons and the satchel that held the Banner.

* * *

'Hmpff,' grunted the constable when Straccan fell silent. 'And Master Wace?'

'Dead.' Straccan told him how. Cigony twirled his cup in his hands, staring into it as if he saw something nasty at the bottom. 'The king won't like it.'

'*I* don't like it either,' Straccan snarled. 'Robert Wace was a brave man.'

'A cock-up all round,' said the constable grimly. 'The priory burned, the prioress dead, a royal clerk dead, *and* the local holy man—'

'No,' Straccan interrupted, recalling his astonished disbelief at finding that bloody scarecrow still alive. 'He's all right.'

'Is he?' Cigony crossed himself. 'He must be a truly holy man.'

Straccan would never forget the truly holy man's wicked accuracy with a stone, his glee when he scored a hit, the sulphurous abuse he heaped on his tormentors, nor the fervent passion of his prayers for the slain raiders, tears pouring down his face as he begged God His mercy, Christ His mercy, and the intercession of every saint he could name for their souls' salvation.

'A bad business altogether,' Cigony was saying. 'I suppose poor old Maurice de Lacy will get the blame for it.' He paused, blinking, grimacing in anticipation of a sneeze, but none came. 'Does your heart good though, don't it, to hear of another Lacy in the shit! Too many Lacys, if you ask me, and their fingers in too many pies. I can't turn round for bloody Lacys! The king's sent *Roger* de Lacy after Breos now, not a day too soon. D'Athée's been recalled. Useless. We kept running into his patrols. I *told* him he was looking in the wrong bloody place but he didn't want to know.'

'Have you heard where Breos is now?'

'Eh? Oh, that's no secret.'

'Isn't it?' Straccan's eyes glinted dangerously. 'Where is he?'

'Holed up in the Hidden Valley, and not even the king's men can get him there.'

'Why not?'

'It's Sanctuary, didn't you know? Some old Welsh shrine. He's untouchable for forty days. Poor old Roger will have to siege the place and nab him when he comes out.'

'Are you sure he's there?'

'No doubt of it. We had a pedlar wailing they'd robbed him when he stopped there. Lucky chap! Anywhere else but the Hidden Valley and he'd be a dead pedlar. I'm up to my arse in claims for compensation. I've got the burgesses of Leominster *and* Hereford petitioning for troops to guard the towns. Even the *outlaws* are wetting their drawers, or would be if they had any. That reminds me.' Cigony unlocked a chest in the corner and took out a grubby pouch. He tossed it to Straccan. 'Your man's stolen cup,' he said, looking smug.

Holding his breath, Straccan opened the pouch and shook out a very small shallow cup with two lug-handles and a band of irregularly stamped letters around the rim. He ran his thumb over them. '*Cymbium Vulstani sum*,' he read.

'Belongs by rights to Drogo's daughters now, of course,' Cigony said. 'That girl Alis asked me to look after it until she goes home.'

Straccan sighed. At least *something* was turning out right; Havloc was out of danger, a free man. He and Alis could go home, marry, live happy ever after if God willed. Straccan hoped He did.

He slid the cup back in the pouch. 'How did you find it?'

'Got the thief,' said Cigony, cheering up at the memory. 'Spotted his coat of patches, like you said. Mad as a March hare! Goes on and on about the cup being haunted!'

'You haven't hanged him yet?'

'No, no! Kept him for you. He's in the pit.'

'Can I talk to him? Havloc still remembers nothing about the theft. If this man will tell us what happened it might help.'

'The coroner will have to be there, I suppose,' grumbled Cigony. 'He *still* thinks your fellow got off too easily. Ha!' He grinned at the memory of the trial and Paulet's discomfiture, then cast a regretful look at the sunshine outside his window. 'I *did* hope to get out for a while this afternoon. Still,' he brightened, 'if he *does* confess we can hang him right away.'

Chapter 42

Tom was hauled up from the pit and a couple of buckets of water tossed over him to sluice off the worst of the muck. He stood between two disgusted guards who had better things to do, stinking, shivering and dripping dismally in his own puddle.

'He'll talk more readily if he's warmed up a bit,' Straccan said. 'Can't we take him to the guardroom fire and sling a blanket or something round him? I can hear his teeth chattering from here!'

At a nod from the constable it was done, and a man sent scurrying for a cup of hot ale. The audience waited impatiently until the wretched object had swallowed it all and his convulsive shivering abated somewhat.

'That's better. Get him some bread and meat and another drink,' Straccan said, eyeing Tom critically. 'He's still a bit blue.'

The heat from the guards' brazier, the food, the unaccustomed ale and even more unaccustomed kindness started Tom snivelling, but he wiped his eyes and nose on his sleeves and the backs of his hands and needed no urging to launch into his tale.

He and his mate Paul had snugged up for the night under the outside stairs of the Gabriel Inn. It was past curfew, the streets were empty and they were just settling down to kip when the man, the mark, came stumbling up from the river.

Paul flung himself on the man, who fell with a startled yelp, Paul atop him, fists pounding. Eager to help, Tom joined in, kicking the prone body with enthusiasm. He tugged off the man's boots, unbuckled and pulled off his belt, while Paul cut the man's purse-strings and groped in the breast of his coat, finding another purse on a string round his neck.

They heard hooves, two riders coming, and fled.

'Gold, is it?' Tom asked, staring at the little footless cup in the early morning light.

'Na,' said Paul. 'Brass, that, but we'll get a few pence for it.'

A day or two later Tom remembered it. 'You got rid of that brass cup?'

'Not yet. I've took a fancy to it.'

After that Tom forgot the cup, until one night Paul said, 'Got to meet someone. E might buy that cup. But I don't trust im. Ere it is,' handing Tom the stolen pouch with the cup inside. 'Keep old of it and stay out of sight 'til I see if e's got the bunce.'

Crouched behind a water-butt Tom waited. He heard Paul and the stranger start arguing. Then Paul said, 'No,' sharply and turned away. The man snatched at his sleeve. Paul's hand dropped to his dagger but the other man moved faster. Paul folded slowly at the knees and fell, making a horrible whistling, bubbling noise, like a pig at the butcher's.

Flattened behind the barrel Tom watched as the murderer rummaged through Paul's clothes, failed to find anything and kicked the body viciously several times before running away.

Tom began to cry. He tried to stand but his trembling legs wouldn't obey so he crawled past the huddled shape that had been his friend and hid behind a rubbish dump until dawn. He begged a ride out of town in a dung cart and eventually, as most outcasts did, made his way into the greenwood. It was not long after that that the spook first appeared.

('See?' hissed Cigony, jabbing Straccan painfully in the ribs. 'What did I tell you? Moon-mad!')

Unaware of the interruption, Tom continued.

The ghost looked just like one of the painted saints on church walls: surrounded by a nimbus of light, tall, stiff, one hand raised, equally ready to bless or smite. But the apparition talked like an ordinary man and thereafter gave Tom no peace, turning up night after night as soon as he dozed off, whingeing on and *on* about its bleeding cup!

('A dream,' the coroner said scathingly and the constable nodded. A dream, of course. What else could it be?)

After several of these nocturnal visitations Tom was afraid to close his eyes but too tired to help it. He even put pebbles under his bum to keep himself awake but it was no use; the spook appeared just the same. He pretended not to see it but that was worse because it jabbed him in the ribs with an all-too-corporeal bony knuckle to secure his attention. What kind of dream was *that?*

'I was a reasonable man,' the ghost told Tom. 'I'm a reasonable saint. Even a thief must live. Our Saviour had a soft spot for one at the end. Still, that's by the by. About my cup . . .'

Tom pulled his coat up over his head and shut his eyes tightly. He screwed himself into a foetal ball and rocked miserably back and forth, moaning.

'I can see you're not in the mood,' the ghost said kindly, 'so I'll leave you to think about it. We'll talk again another time.' And it winked out like the spark in a candlewick.

Tom attached himself to a bunch of outlaws, half a dozen assorted killers, thieves and rapists on the run from that bastard constable's patrols and almost as wretched as he. For several nights the spook didn't bother him. Then came that last night before they were caught.

He lay sandwiched between two outlaws: one had lost a foot to justice and the other grinned like a skull even in sleep, having had his lips sliced off for uttering blasphemies. Sharing their lice and blanket but shivering all the same, Tom thought longingly of the town, where well fed people lay cosy in their beds. Fat useless sods, all lying snug, while he, Tom, who owned a gold cup, lay starved with cold.

'Come off it!' The spook's voice was right in his ear. 'You don't own it. It's mine; it's got my name on it.'

Tom howled and leaped to his feet, tripping over his bedmates, lurching and stumbling among the trees until he ran right into a low branch with shocking force and collapsed half stunned.

'You'll have a nasty bruise there,' said the spook compassionately. 'I'd put some liniment on it if I was you. Now, about my cup.' It settled down with crossed legs beside Tom. 'This is your last chance. Take my advice: go back to town, find a priest, tell him all about it and give him the cup. You'll be safe then; well for a while, at least. If you don't, I can't stop what's coming to you.'

Whimpering, Tom jammed his hands over his ears but the spook had a penetrating voice and he could still hear it. He was going mad! Loonies saw things, heard voices too. He'd seen a whole bunch of loonies at York a few years ago, all tied with ropes to the belt of a weedy little monk. He'd thought they were funny then; how he'd laughed when folk threw turds at them and made them cry! But now he was a loony himself he couldn't see anything funny in it.

'I never wanted a *gold* cup,' the spook was saying crossly. 'Pretentious vanity. Common clay was good enough for Christ and His disciples. It was good enough for God to make Man. But it was a gift from the king and I didn't like to hurt his feelings. You have no *idea* how touchy Harold Godwinsson could be! I never used the wretched thing. My servant *would* pack it when we travelled, and then the fool lost it.'

'Go away!'

'Don't say I didn't warn you,' said the spook, but its voice seemed distant and surely its image was getting misty at the edges? 'You can't say I haven't tried. You weren't much, in my opinion, but it's not mine that matters and you're precious to God. *He's* not fussy. He'll roll up whatever's worthwhile in you, to use again.'

'Eh?'

But, like breath in freezing air, the shape hung a moment longer and then was truly gone.

Just after dawn they heard the braying of the hunting horns and started the long futile run for their lives.

* * *

'They goin to ang me now?' Tom asked when he'd finished his story. Straccan nodded. 'Can I ave a priest, then, to shrive me? I don't want to go to Ell like them poor buggers me lord anged in the greenwood, with no priest or nothin, and ave that spook naggin at me for ever.'

Straccan waited and watched Tom hang. Thief or no, it seemed an ill thing to let the man die utterly alone, jeered and mocked by the crowd of honest – or at least not yet rumbled – tradespeople and burgesses who found such spectacles gratifying. A friendly face, if only one, might help. Luckily for Tom his neck snapped clean, with no struggling or strangling. When he was cut down Straccan promised the chaplain a shilling to ensure the thief's body wasn't slung in the town ditch with the rest of the castle's refuse at the end of the day.

He drew funds from the Templars, paid the chaplain and arranged for the beggar Pity Me's release and reward. Then he returned to the keep to ask the constable's permission to stay the night. Tomorrow he'd outfit himself again and get another horse. Where had Bane got to? He should have been back by now. What was happening at Shawl? Was Janiva all right? Was Gilla safe?

Straccan still couldn't go to Shawl; he had to go to the Hidden Valley. The young captain who'd stolen his horse hadn't known what Zingiber was carrying. It was just possible that he still didn't know, and that Breos had no idea the Banner was in the Hidden Valley.

All these matters jostled for his attention, and all the while the words on the cup were running through his head like a repetitive tune.

Cymbium Vulstani sum, I am Wulstan's cup.

What had the thief's spook said? '*It's got my name on it.*'

It couldn't be! And yet it was certain that Tom couldn't read and had no idea what the inscription meant. What else had he said? '*It was a gift from the king,*' and then something about Harold Godwinsson.

Could it be *Saint* Wulstan's cup?

As Straccan climbed the winding stair he heard feet on the steps behind him, and his name called. He looked back. 'Captain von Koln.'

The young German's unsmiling eyes looked up at him. 'Sir Richard, you vill come vith me.'

'Not just now.'

'*Ja*. Now.' The captain's sword was in his hand and its point at Straccan's belly. 'Chust go on up the steps to the constable's chamber. Don't try anything or I'll run you through.'

'What the hell is this?' Straccan demanded, continuing up the steps. 'What do you want?' He entered the room, von Koln at his heels. Cigony was there, looking grim.

The captain shut the door. 'Vere is Master Vace?'

'Dead.'

'How did he die?'

'Breos murdered him.'

'Did you find the Banner?'

'Yes, but—'

'Vere is it?'

'I haven't got it. I was ambushed on the way here. Breos's men took it.' It sounded worse every time and the German looked as if he didn't believe a word of it.

'His grace vill be displeased.'

'You don't see me laughing, do you? God's name, man, put that sword away!'

'I haf my orders, Sir Richard, you understand. You are under arrest.'

'What? Why?'

'You haf betrayed the king's trust. You are hand in mouth with Breos.'

'Glove,' said Straccan automatically.

'Vat?'

'Hand in *glove*. And I'm *not*.'

The German brushed aside the correction. 'You vanted Master Vace out of the vay so you could gif the relic to Breos. He had to be killed. And the so-called ambush vas arranged too, so you vould haf a vitness, the man Hafloc.'

Straccan looked at the constable. Cigony's usually cheerful face was resolute and cold.

'My lord—'

'I can't help you, Straccan. You know conspiracy's a capital offence.' Cigony turned away and looked out of the window.

The iron-bound door slammed behind Straccan with an echoing crash. In the foul-smelling darkness he fell down a short flight of narrow stone steps onto something soft.

'Ow!'

'Sorry . . .'

'Geroff!'

The body beneath him heaved and threw him sideways. Before he could scramble up there was a rattle of chain and the other prisoner was on him, bony knees on his chest to pin him down and hands gripping a length of chain pressed across his throat, all in impenetrable blackness.

'Who are you?' his assailant growled, and just in time, about to burst the other's eardrums, Straccan stayed his hands.

'Bane!'

They sat on the bottom step, companionably side by side in the stinking darkness.

'Where the hell have you been? Did you see Janiva?'

When Bane didn't answer Straccan felt his heart turn into a lump of lead behind his ribs. 'What is it? What's wrong?'

Bane sighed. 'There's a new priest at Shawl; he's accused her of sorcery and she's locked up in the undercroft. There's talk of putting her to the Ordeal.'

'Oh Christ!' Straccan scrambled up the steps and hammered on the door. 'Von Koln! Let me out!'

'Don't bother,' said Bane. 'The guardroom's a long way up; no one'll hear. Listen, that woman Sybilla had something in mind and I had a word with Tostig. He promised to help.'

But Straccan slumped, defeated, on the top step, his head bowed on his knees. The dense blackness enfolded him, suffocated him, crushed him. He felt helpless and dreadfully afraid. The horror threatening Janiva was more than he could bear and there was nothing he could do to help her. He longed for a sword in his hand and an enemy at the business end of it. Tears of impotent frustration seeped out under his eyelids.

Bane thrust something into Straccan's clenched fist, a soft sticky pellet. 'What's that?'

'Raisins,' said Bane. 'I had some in my pocket. I been rationing em. Suck em, they'll last longer.'

'Thanks.' He pulled himself together, ashamed. 'Why did they put you down here?'

'Buggered if I know. I came looking for you, thought you'd be back, and before I could turn round that bloody German stuffed me down here. I never liked him.'

'How long have you been here?'

Bane thought a bit. 'It was Saint Ethelwold's day.'

'This is the eve of Saint Sixtus.' Straccan reckoned back on his fingers. 'Five days. Did they hurt you?'

'Not much. What's going on?'

'Von Koln thinks I killed the king's clerk.'

'Wace? What happened to him?'

'Breos.'

They sat silent for a while, and presently soft whuffling sounds told Straccan that Bane had fallen asleep. He wished *he* could sleep; at least there'd be some brief oblivion. He wished there was a window but this cell must be deep underground. How long would von Koln leave them here?

He'd been a prisoner before, a galley slave of the Moors. Things had seemed pretty hopeless, chained at the rowers' bench under the overseer's lash, but he hadn't lost hope then. Under the killing sun, as his comrades died in their chains at his side, he had believed passionately that somehow, some day, he would see his home again and hold his daughter in his arms.

Gilla . . . He took a deep breath and raised his head. He'd get out of here, of course he would. They had to open the door some time and he wasn't chained. But then what? If he escaped and went to Janiva, Gilla would be taken hostage. She was only twelve years old but youth and innocence would not save her if the king believed him a traitor in league with rebels. A capital offence meant a traitor's death. Traitors' property was seized by the Crown. His daughter would be penniless, ostracised, welcomed nowhere, a traitor's brat.

He groaned. As a slave, the shackles had been only on his wrists and ankles – he still had the scars – but the invisible chain that held him fast now was stronger than any iron links: his love and fear for Gilla.

Chapter 43

In Carrickfergus castle upon the morning of Saint Samson's day, the king sat at chess with the bishop of Winchester, while a blind harper played for their pleasure.

John was in high good humour. The campaign had achieved all he wished, and more. He had marched on Ulster and frightened the life out of it, taken the county of Meath from its rebel lord and stormed triumphantly across the country accepting surrenders and homage everywhere. He had seized the castle at Carlingford, bridging Carlingford Lough – which everyone said would be sure to stop him – with boats to get his army across.

Anglo-Irish lords with wavering loyalties, finding the king's host beneath their castle walls, capitulated and grovelled with gratifying speed, paying fines and handing over hostages with jittery alacrity. John was now ready to go home, leaving this bothersome country subdued and in better order than anyone, even his mighty father, had ever been able to achieve.

The bishop's hand hovered over a piece, hesitated and moved another instead. The king chuckled.

'Not your day, Peter. Checkmate in two moves. There, look, and there. Didn't you see it? You need more practice.' He picked up one of the pieces and turned it over in his hand, admiring the small ivory face.

Below, in the bailey, guards challenged a rider and the man answered, reining in his foam-streaked horse and sliding stiffly from the saddle. He came clattering up the steps two at a time and burst into the hall, smelling powerfully of sweat, horse and garlic, and so caked in dust that he looked as if he'd been dipped in flour.

'My lord,' he panted, 'Mahaut de Breos is taken!'

The king crashed his fist onto the chessboard, sending pieces flying and rolling about the floor.

'She alone? What of Hugh de Lacy?'

'The earl got away, sire. So did Breos's son, Bishop Reginald, but the other one, the eldest, William, was taken prisoner along with his mother.'

John let out a long hissing breath of satisfaction. 'Where are they?'

'On their way here, sire. They fled to Scotland but King William has sent them back to you. They'll be here by nightfall.'

John smiled. Bishop Peter, glancing sideways at him, looked hastily away again. It was a nasty smile. The king crooked a finger, beckoning the seneschal from the group in attendance. 'Prepare a welcome.'

The seneschal looked worried. 'Where do you wish them housed, my lord?'

'William may reflect on the consequences of rebellion in one of the dungeons; do be sure to make him uncomfortable. As for Mahaut' – he grated the name through his teeth like an obscenity – 'chain her and keep her under close guard in a *very* small chamber. Have her watched closely. I don't want her left alone for a moment, day or night, until I've heard what she has to say.'

At the thought of what Mahaut de Breos had already said, fury began to heat his blood; John could feel it pulsing in his head, swelling until it seemed he must burst with the effort to suppress it.

'Leave us!' And as they all began moving hastily to the door, 'The harper may stay.'

Music alone, he had learned, could help him when this mindless rage overwhelmed him. It was as well the harper was blind, for when everyone else had gone the king stood staring in his direction, teeth bared like an animal, face dark, swollen and distorted by the ungovernable Angevin fury that had been his father's legacy to all his sons. Silently, to the accompaniment of the harp's liquid notes, John fought and throttled it. He was used to these battles.

Never, never would he let that insane rage get the better of him again, as it had done that time at Rouen.

Rouen . . . Strange that he could remember everything that happened before, and every selfsick guilt-ridden moment that bludgeoned him afterwards, but still had no memory of killing Arthur.

He'd never meant to do it.

Traitor, oath-breaker, taken in armed rebellion against his liege lord, the young duke of Brittany had been John's prisoner. No one would have batted an eyelid if he had been executed, or at the very least blinded and castrated, as was customary to remove any focus around which the infection of treason could gather. The Pope himself had urged that Arthur be executed for the good of the realm and the peace of Christendom. But John had imprisoned his nephew in the castle of Rouen, a valuable hostage for the troublesome Bretons' good behaviour.

When Arthur learned that the king his uncle had come to Rouen and was in the castle, he threw a classic Angevin fit of fury, smashing the furniture in his cell, ripping up his bedding, tearing his own clothes until they hung in rags, flinging the contents of his chamber pot at the unfortunate guard and attacking the poor man with a bed leg; biting Hubert de Burgh, punching William de Breos and screaming abuse when they tried to restrain him until his raw throat could only croak.

'You'd better not see him, sire,' said Hubert de Burgh, who held the office of keeper of the castle. Behind John's back he gave William de Breos a warning look. 'He's a bit upset.'

But John had supped well. The food was excellent and there had been expensive burnt wine, a novelty. He'd drunk a lot of it; it made him feel magnanimous, even sentimental, and he decided to see his nephew.

'I've been thinking. I might let him join his sister if he promises to behave.'

The princess Eleanor, known as the Pearl of Brittany, was in England in the gentlest of captivity. John was generous. She had clothes to suit her rank, waiting-women, hawks, horses with gilded saddles, lute and cittern to play the mournful songs of Brittany. John sent occasional gifts: jewellery for her birthday and at Christmas, game when he was hunting nearby. Bored, lonely and well fed, the Pearl of Brittany was growing fat.

'Behave?' said Breos before Hubert could speak. 'Arthur? God's teeth, you should have seen him earlier!'

'Quietened down now, has he?'

'Not really,' said Hubert, glaring and kicking Breos's leg under the table. 'Actually we've had to put him in chains to move him while they clean up his room.'

'Where is he now?'

'In the Pocket,' said Breos, glaring back at the keeper.

John grimaced. It was one of the less salubrious apartments for prisoners, a filthy little cell that overhung the river.

'I'll have a word with him. He's probery . . . proll . . . *probly* sorry by now.'

'Leave him be, my lord,' said Hubert de Burgh unwisely. 'It's late and we're all tired.'

'I'm not,' said the king.

He had come round by himself in a cold damp little room he'd never seen before. He remembered lying on his own cloak on the bare stone floor, being sick, lying down again.

And William de Breos came in.

Last night's unaccustomed brandy had given John the worst headache he'd ever had. 'Wha matter?' he asked feebly, wishing the walls would stop revolving around him.

Breos helped the king to his feet, steadying him. They were both trembling, John with weakness, Breos with the tension of excitement.

'In God's name, my lord, don't you remember?'

'Remember what? Get me some wine. Jesus, my mouth's like a gong!'

'My lord, get hold of yourself now . . . You're not going to like this.'

'What?' John coughed, wished he hadn't, clasped his riven head with both hands and groaned. 'Oh, Christ! God's feet!' Was sick again. Felt better. 'Get me a drink, I said!'

'In a minute, my lord.'

'Now, damn you!' He could handle the headache. What he needed was something to wash the dreadful taste out of his mouth, then a bath and a change of clothes; these were fouled. His sleeve was damp and sticky. He touched it. Was that blood?

While the king stared, puzzled, at his reddened tacky fingers, Breos said urgently, 'My lord, listen. The duke is dead, God assoil him.'

'Dead?'

He didn't believe it until he saw the body: a dirty bundle of rags in a dark corner of the stinking cell, one outflung stiffened hand wearing the ruby ring of Brittany, a boy's hand, nicked and scarred, with bitten dirty nails. The head hung forward on the breast. Steeling himself, John grasped the greasy fair hair to lift it, but rigor held the body fast; he couldn't budge it to see the face. Crouching, all he could see was a livid swollen cheek and blood caked on the fluffy chin.

He stood up, cold, shaking, sober. 'He looks smaller.' What an idiotic thing to say. 'What happened?'

'God's teeth, my lord, don't you remember? You throttled him! You tried to talk to him but he wouldn't listen. He swung his chains at you, leapt on you. You knocked him down. He cursed you, insulted the queen your mother, called her a whore and you a bastard. My lord, I couldn't stop you! *Four* men couldn't have stopped you! You went mad, just like your father. You strangled him with his chains. I couldn't get you off him. You pulled your dagger and kept stabbing him. He was already dead before the knife went in.'

John pressed the heels of his hands against his eyes and moaned. It was no nightmare. Arthur was really dead. He'd killed him, *murdered* the arrogant, vicious, treacherous, oathbreaking little bastard. Only Arthur *wasn't* a bastard; no problem if he had been.

He was the duke of Brittany, the legitimate and only son of John's deceased older brother Geoffrey, and if it hadn't been for William the Marshal's support when the Lionheart died, Arthur would have been crowned king of England, not John.

Just for a moment reason shoved horror aside. 'I didn't need him dead; he was worth much more alive, a hostage to keep the Bretons off my back. Why should I kill him? You're lying!' His hand went to his dagger but it wasn't there.

Breos groped at the slumped body and with a grunt of distaste tugged a knife out. Wordlessly he held it out to the king. It was his. John was trembling violently. 'Christ, William, what shall I do?'

Breos took the king's arm. 'Come away, my lord, back to your chamber. I'll get you cleaned up.' He hesitated, then went on, 'If we're careful, if we tell the same story, no one need ever know what happened here.'

'But . . .' John gestured at the corpse.

'I'll see to it, my lord king. Don't worry. I'll tell no one, I swear! In God's name, trust me.'

John came back to the present sweet late July day chilled and sick. Outside, men were shouting and horses stamping and snorting. A hesitant voice at the door said, 'My lord, if it please you, the prisoners are here.'

'Good. I've always wanted to see Mahaut de Breos in chains.'

He opened his hands. One was bloody where the sharp edge of the little queen's broken neck had cut his palm.

Chapter 44

Straccan had never enjoyed a bath so much in his life. The sybaritic pleasure was so intense it was no wonder, he thought, the Church thundered against bathing. He revelled in the comfort and the soaped cleanliness of his body. His bruises were fading and the flayed skin of his back healing quickly, surprisingly without any suppuration. Even the wounds to his nose and cheek had closed cleanly, though he would carry those scars to his grave.

In another steaming barrel alongside, only Bane's head and the island tops of his bony knees showed above water. His eyes were closed and he looked asleep, though Straccan wouldn't have bet on it. Two guards lunged at the bath-house door, leaning against the wall, looking thick-witted and careless; he wouldn't have bet on that, either.

Captain von Koln had made him a proposition. He had agreed and given his parole. He had no choice. Offered the alternative of that black hole under the guardroom with no way out except the gallows, what choice was there?

'Let's get this straight,' he'd said to the German when that young man eventually appeared at the door of their cell holding a flaming torch and prudently backed by four men-at-arms. 'I am to go after Breos and get the Banner back?'

'Chust so.'

That suited him; it was what he'd intended anyway. 'And there'll be no more talk of treason?'

Von Koln nodded. 'I must ride vith you, of course.'

'Oh, of course!'

'I am taking a risk, you understand. Ven you get the Banner ve vill take it to the king. He is on his vay back now from Ireland.'

'Then what?'

'As long as his grace gets the Banner that vill be the end of the matter, Sir Richard.'

'All right, I'll do it. But first I want a bath.' In the darkness behind him, where the captain's torchlight did not penetrate, Bane coughed. '*Bane* wants a bath, and clean clothes for us both.' Bane coughed again. 'And a bloody good dinner,' Straccan added.

He'd also demanded their weapons, and been refused. His sword, which he'd recovered from the mud on the saint's island, had been taken along with the horses, the Banner, and everything else. But on the morrow he and Bane, escorted by Bruno von Koln and twelve men-at-arms, would set out for the Hidden Valley, and he would have his chance to get the Banner back, and perhaps his horse and sword as well.

As Devilstone lay on their road, Havloc and Alis were to ride part of the way with them, glad of the protection on their way home. Murderers' Country, the Marches were called, and one murderer Straccan hoped to run into again. Once on the way, he would contrive to get a sword, although a dagger would do just as well, or even his bare hands, providing he could lock them round the throat of William de Breos.

The leper-master let the hide door of the Silent Man's dark hut fall shut behind him and stood in the soft Welsh rain, shocked and shaken to his very soul. Could it be true? It was wicked, infamous; could any man's mind, however corrupt, devise so devilish a scheme? No, it *couldn't* be true. And yet . . .

The Silent Man had spoken at last, and the halting, bitter story he told was unimaginable. Or would be, but for the ring.

Garnier opened his gloved fist. In it lay a heavy gold ring of antique design, set with a great ruby. He'd recognised it as soon as the Silent Man showed it to him. He'd seen it before, twenty-five years ago in the camp at the tourney field in Paris. A young priest then he'd been among the onlookers, just there for the entertainment, and instead had been called upon to give a dying man the last rites. He'd been there in the tent when the king of France, weeping, drew the ring of Brittany from Duke Geoffrey's thumb and gave it to the new-made widow, the dry-eyed Duchess Constance. This was the same ring, of that he had no doubt.

Like his namesake piece on a chessboard Garnier had been moved by the marvellous hand of God to this place and now he knew why. If the Silent Man spoke truth – and why should he lie? He was dying – a monstrous wrong had been done, and he, Garnier, must bring it to light and the wrongdoer to justice.

Chapter 45

The first thing Lord William saw when the foraging party rode in at dusk was the cinnamon-coloured stallion that made the rest of the bunch they'd picked up look like donkeys. What a beauty!

'Where'd you get that, Thibaut?'

'On the Ludlow road, my lord, in the forest.' He was pale and had a bandage on one hand. 'Two men, there were, with this stallion and the brown gelding over there.'

Breos frowned at the muzzle and the tight martingale which stopped the animal from raising its head. 'Is that necessary?'

'Better safe than sorry, my lord.' After taking the animal Thibaut had tried to mount it, only to be flung like a bundle of washing into a holly bush. His men had laughed themselves silly, the fools, and laughed still more when he tried again and the beast bit him. All attempts to get on its back met with the grunting, striking, snapping repertoire of a horse trained to fight. A huge iron fore-hoof smashed the shoulder of one of his arbalists, and another was crushed against a wall, breaking his ribs. He began coughing blood and was dead by nightfall. It took every man in the troop hanging onto the animal to get it muzzled and the martingale on. Sulien was seeing to the injured now and had salved and bound up Thibaut's hand.

'What have you done to your hand?'

'Oh, nothing, my lord.' He'd hoped Lord William wouldn't notice. 'Just a scratch.' He'd been lucky not to lose his thumb, and – more painful than his damaged pride – the bite had turned septic, throbbing with every pulse-beat; a red streak was spreading up his forearm from the base of his thumb and the evil-smelling stuff Sulien had smeared on it drew painfully at the wound.

Breos ran his hand down the stallion's flank; it twitched its skin and rolled its long-lashed eyes. Thibaut tensed, ready for any trick, but restricted as it was, that was all the horse could do.

'Fine saddle, too,' Lord William was saying. 'What manner of man was it?'

'A knight with his servant; we took their weapons. Hi! Girard! Bring the sword we took from the man in the forest.'

Breos fingered the plain worn leather scabbard and drew the blade, looking closely at pommel and hilt. 'Old-fashioned,' he muttered, 'but good steel . . . Hey, what's this?' Just below the crossguard, inlaid in the blade, was a silver cross within a circle, and beneath that some words in Latin, *Advocato Sancti Sepulchri*.

'What does it say, my lord?'

' "I defend the Holy Sepulchre." ' Lord William ran his thumb over the silver letters. 'An old crusader's sword, by God! Who was he?'

Thibaut shook his head. He hadn't been ordered to demand names from those he was sent to rob, but he knew better than to say so.

Breos snapped the blade back in its sheath. His own bore the legend *Homo Dei*, in which he saw no incongruity. 'You should have left him his sword. An old crusader . . . Still, you weren't to know. I'll keep this. What else did you bring in?' Pillaging supplied most of his band's needs, but any deficiencies could be made good from Cwm Cuddfan's stores. Having provided the hospital with many of its necessities for seven years, Lord William felt no compunction now in taking what he needed.

'A good haul, my lord: flour, wine, cheeses, blankets, five other horses and the personal baggage, of course. We haven't sorted through that yet.'

'Put the provisions in store and share out the rest.' Tucking the sword under his arm, Breos went back inside. How much longer would he have to skulk here? By now his wife should have joined him but although each day he looked for news of her, none came.

* * *

The road began easily, winding through low hills and skirting dark woods. Now and then they caught glimpses of ragged figures melting into the trees, but outlaws had no wish to tackle armed men and Bruno von Koln's company had nothing to fear. The second day took them into wild foothill country, far from the March patrols and what passed in Wales for towns. That night they came to the small *pentref* of Maeselyn, where they hoped for a night's shelter for Alis, only to find that William de Breos had been there before them. The huts still stood, charred and roofless but saved by rain. The rain couldn't save the villagers, however; they'd been slaughtered like sheep.

So had those of Llantali, which they entered at noon the next day, and by the time they reached the little town of Tresaint that evening they knew from the stink what to expect. Crows and ravens rose with noisy protests; rats and dogs ran away at their approach.

The little church, being stone, still stood. Pinned to its door by several crossbow bolts was the brutalised naked corpse of an old man, by his tonsure priest of this place; and from the yew in the churchyard hung three bloated bodies, gutted like herrings, turning slowly at their ropes' ends, heads on one side as if puzzled by this turn of events.

'Why?' Havloc wondered. 'These were his people, his villages. He was their lord.'

'*Was*,' said Straccan. 'He'll lay all waste sooner than let another have it.'

When they reached the crossroads where Havloc and Alis were to strike off for Devilstone, Havloc came to Straccan with a suggestion.

'You know Breos will be on the lookout,' he said. 'His men will be watching all who come, for fear of trickery. They'll take note of a man alone, or two men, but they won't look twice at a sick man with his wife.'

'Wife?'

'Me,' said Alis.

Lord William's medicus had just bled him and was packing up his lancet and dishes when Thibaut came in.

'My lord, Sulien asks to see you.'

Lord William had been feeling pleasantly languorous but at this he jumped up eagerly, almost knocking over his restorative wine. His sleeve still hung loose and he held out his arm for Thibaut to fasten the cuff.

'He must have news! Send him in!' He stood watching the door to see the man's face as he entered, but Sulien looked sombre, not like a man with glad tidings. Lord William's heart sank.

'What is it?' he asked, in dread to hear.

'My lord, I have to tell you that your kinsman is dying.'

'Kinsman?' Not Mahaut? Not his son? Relief took him at the knees and he sat down with a thump. '*What* kinsman?'

'The young man you sent here seven years ago, my lord. Geoffrey.'

'Geoffrey?' For a moment Lord William looked baffled, then awareness and something else – it looked surprisingly like fear – wiped the puzzlement from his face. He sat up straight, knocking his wine cup to the floor where it clanged and rolled. Thibaut dived for it anxiously; the cup was gold, if it should be dented Lord William would blame him.

'Dying? Are you sure?'

'It is a merciful release,' Sulien said. 'My lord, the man who cares for him has asked to speak with you. Will you see him?'

Lord William was very still but a nerve jumped in his cheek, and jumped again, and would not stop. 'Bring him in.'

'He can't come in; he is a leper. Will you hear him, my lord? He waits by the path to the lake.'

From under the willows that grew densely right down to the shore of Llyn Gwydion a shape moved into Lord William's path, a darker shadow among shadows.

Lord William rested his hand on the hilt of his sword. 'What do you want with me?'

The tinny clank of a bell answered him and the shadow raised its hooded head. Although he had known the man was a leper, grue gripped the lord de Breos. Of all horrors, since childhood he had loathed lepers most. Some men feared spiders, others snakes, but for him the gut-dissolving terror of nightmare had always been lepers.

'Keep back,' he said loudly. 'Keep off!'

'God save you, my lord.' Two black triangular eyeholes faced him with no gleam of life but the mask puffed in and out with breath as the leper spoke; a rasping, rusted husk of a voice, and to Breos's surprise that of a well-born man speaking the polished Langue d'Oc, just as King Richard had done. It was seldom heard since the Lionheart's death, for his brother favoured Poitevins above the men of Aquitaine.

Lord William's eye caught movement further back under the trees. Christ, was that another? It stepped forward, big, burly, leaning on a quarterstaff. The lord's hand clenched on his sword hilt, drawing an inch or two of steel.

'One step nearer and I'll cut you down!'

The first leper laid a gloved hand on the other's arm. 'Wait by the boat, Illtud.' And to Breos, 'I am no threat to you, my lord. See?' And he stooped to lay his own staff on the ground.

Sweating, Lord William threw his purse at the creature's feet. 'There! For my kinsman's burial.'

The leper ignored it. 'That's not why I am here, my lord. There is something I must ask you.'

'In God's name, ask and be gone!'

'Who is he, my lord, the young man you sent here seven years ago?'

The question hit Lord William like a blow from the quintain. He blinked and rocked on his heels. 'Poor Geoffrey? One of my godsons.'

'You have not visited your . . . *godson*,' Lord William tensed at the emphasis, 'or even sent word to him since you came here.'

'God's name, what's that to you?'

'He is my charge and he is dying.'

It was true then. Breos crossed himself and murmured a prayer, partly for the dying man's soul and partly in thanks because he *was* dying at last. God knew it had taken long enough.

The leper's dreadful voice went on and on. 'I have sat with him these last few nights lest he die alone, although he did not ask it. He has not uttered a word in all his wretched years here. Did you know that, my lord? He kept himself apart even from us, his comrades in misery. Seven years ago he came here, silent as an image, and silent he's been ever since. None of us knew he *could* talk: but at last he has, and I have listened.'

Breos breathed deeply. The notion of murder surged and ebbed, and Garnier saw it in the tensing of the muscles and in the eyes.

'Go ahead,' he invited. 'What is one more among so many souls that cry out to God against you.' His ruined voice had a terrible authority. 'His holy name which you use so freely is fouled in your mouth.'

'How dare you!' Lord William's affronted pride swelled. To be rated so, by such a creature! 'You go too far, by God! A stinking leper! Who do you think you are?'

'As I stink in your nostrils,' Garnier said, 'your soul stinks in God's. Look, my lord de Breos, see yourself as God sees you!' He pulled off his hood and stepped out of the shadows.

Lord William gave a cry of loathing. There in the sunlight was his fear made flesh: featureless, suppurating, rotting, like a man long drowned. He turned aside just in time to vomit in the bushes instead of over his own feet.

'No,' he whimpered, falling to his knees and heaving until his stomach had nothing left to cast up. 'God help me! No!'

'Who is Geoffrey?' the leper persisted.

Wiping his mouth, Breos mumbled something.

'What was that, my lord?'

'His name is Arthur!' He tried to get to his feet but found it easier to stay on one knee, at least for now. It was the bleeding, of course, the fool medicus had taken more than he should. He'd have him whipped for it.

'The prince?' the leper asked. 'The duke of Brittany?'

'What has he told you? Name of God, does he want to see me? I won't . . . I can't—'

'He couldn't see you if he would. He has been blind these past two years.'

'No one told me,' Breos whispered, wiping his nose on his sleeve.

'I knew his mother, Duchess Constance,' Garnier said. 'I served in her household after her husband died. When Arthur was a child I knew him well but here, now, until he spoke, I had no idea who he was. All Christendom believes his uncle King John murdered the prince at Rouen; your own wife accused him. Did the king send him here?'

Breos shook his head.

'Then how did he come here? What really happened at Rouen?'

Painfully at first, as if every word was physically scraped from him, Lord William began to talk, but once he got into his stride he couldn't stop and frequently a note of self-pity, and sometimes of brag, crept in.

It had been his wife's idea, clever, ambitious Mahaut de Breos, who after a restless night dug her sharp elbow in her lord's side and told him her audacious plan.

'Get on the right side of him,' she said.

He was still half asleep. 'Who?'

'Arthur.'

The prince was John's prisoner. Powerless, useless. Why waste time sucking up to him?

'Arthur? What on earth for?'

She explained. Win the boy's confidence, befriend him and help him escape.

'*What?*'

'Be quiet and listen!'

It was terrible; it was treason. Overthrow the king and proclaim Arthur the rightful ruler. John was unpopular. France and Brittany would rally to the cause. Then, with the crown set on his head by the might of the house of Breos, the young king would refuse them nothing. With Arthur married to a Breos daughter and his sister Eleanor married to a Breos son . . .

'You see?' Mahaut had whispered, right into his ear so that neither the page at the bed foot nor her women on their pallets might hear. 'One day, a grandson of ours could wear the crown of England.'

'It'll never work,' he'd protested but, 'Trust me,' she'd said, and he always had.

He'd been nurturing the seeds and first frail shoots of Mahaut's plan, winning the boy's trust, sympathising, listening to him rage against his uncle the king and flattering him – he couldn't get enough of that, there never was so vain a creature – while he tried to think of a way to get him out of the castle. And then John came to Rouen . . .

Lord William's voice droned on and the leper's featureless mask stared. Arthur's fury, John's maudlin insistence on seeing him, the stinking cell, the screaming boy, the king's drunken collapse, the huddled corpse with John's dagger in it . . .

'Who was the dead boy?'

'No one. A thief from the pit, the right age, fair like the prince. A bit smaller but John hadn't seen Arthur for some time.' That was Mahaut's idea too. He'd never have thought of it.

'Take Arthur out in your retinue,' she'd said. 'No one will be looking for him now, he's supposed to be dead. Get him out of France. We'll keep him hidden until we've brought John down.'

'What did you do?' Garnier prompted.

'Brought him to Wales, to my stronghold at Grosmont.' Lord William scowled, remembering. 'He wasn't the least bit grateful! I'd saved him from being murdered by his uncle – well, he *thought* I had – you'd think he'd show a bit of gratitude, but no! I offered him my daughter in marriage. He refused! The arrogant little prick *sneered* at me, at *me!*' His voice rose. 'Said he intended to marry a daughter of the king of France. I could have killed him myself!

'He must already have been ill but I didn't think there was anything *really* wrong with him. You don't expect it, do you? Leprosy? Not princes.'

'His mother died of it.'

It was Lord William's turn to stare. 'Constance? Did she? Kept *that* quiet, didn't they? So that's where he got it! I always wondered. I didn't realise what it was at first. He got spotty; boys do. You don't think every spot on a boy's face is leprosy. He wouldn't leave his room; he'd always been vain, he couldn't bear anyone to see him like that. I told him he'd grow out of it but it got worse. I *still* didn't think . . .

'He was shooting up fast, thin, weedy, and he *coughed* a lot, I remember; couldn't shake it off. He whined a lot too. His *legs* ached. I told him it was growing pains. His fingers and thumbs felt *prickly*, he was always *tired*, his *feet* hurt, his *skin* felt like fire, his *eyes* were sore! Whingeing little sod. He made *me* sick too, sick of him!

'When my household moved to Whitecastle he wouldn't budge. Short of trussing him up and carrying him, what could I do? I left half a dozen people to look after him, and God knows I was glad to leave him there! One day his barber saw the rash. Flung down dish and razor and *ran*! Left Arthur bleeding where the razor'd cut him, screaming with fury and fright, slapping and kicking the servants and demanding the barber be brought back and flogged.

'He locked the door, wouldn't let the servants in. They sent for me. I could hear him in there, breaking things, banging himself against the walls, howling. I sent everyone away and fetched a doctor. We had to smash the door down.

'It was a shock,' Breos said plaintively. 'I hadn't seen him for weeks. His face . . . There were lumps all over it. He was crying and shaking his hands about as if he was trying to get rid of them. The room was filthy, he'd torn the tapestries down, ripped up the bedding; there was blood and skin on the stones where he'd beaten his hands on the wall.

'Leprosy, the doctor said. I paid him and let him go. He didn't know who his patient was but I couldn't risk it so I sent a man after him, one I could trust, and I saw to the barber and the servants myself.

'I didn't know what to *do* with him. I couldn't keep him there or at any of my castles. He begged me to hide him. He was mad with fear lest anyone should see him so foul; I told you he was vain.

"Don't drive me out," he begged. As if I would, as if I *could*! "I'll *kill* myself if anyone sees me," he said, and he meant it. I didn't want his blood on my hands.'

'What difference would it make?' Garnier asked. 'With so much on them already.'

Lost in recollection Lord William didn't hear. 'I promised to find a safe place where no one would see him. Sulien had just come here – a godsend. I gave him the valley, gave him stone and wood to build his hospital. I sent everything he needed: food, wine, cloth, chattels. I had Arthur brought here.

'Stop staring, damn you!' Lord William turned away from those accusing black holes. 'It's what he wanted. He was grateful. Oh yes, I had his gratitude *then*, for all the good it was! When I told him about this place he vowed to pray for my soul every day that he lived, so long as no one ever found him.'

'He kept his word,' the leper-master said softly. 'Every day he has prayed for your damnation; so he told me.'

Lord William didn't hear that either.

'I told Sulien he was one of my household. He said, "What's his name?" I nearly said "Arthur", just stopped myself in time, said "Geoffrey". It was his father's name.'

Chapter 46

On the Edge at night the anchorhold hung suspended between earth and heaven. So many the stars, so bright, so close, it seemed Osyth had only to reach up to touch them. Far below, soft lights shone in the squat dark cotts, and threads of bluish smoke, clearly seen in the moonlight, rose straight for a long way before vagrant air currents teased them apart.

The anchoress had spread a wolf skin on the ground, and sat on it with her arms around her knees. She had asked for guidance and waited to receive it. Nearby a nightjar chirred, answered by another farther off and interrupted by the distant calls of owls.

Osyth breathed evenly and thought of the task ahead. She must help Janiva fight the evil that was destroying everything and every one dear to her before it succeeded in destroying the girl herself. Was Janiva the one whose coming she awaited, the one who would – in time, and not so long now – take her place? There was no doubt of her power; the glow of her spirit haloed her flesh and would shine clear and golden but for the shadow of ill that stained it.

An urchin snuffled along the foot of the garth wall, and somewhere nearby its babies, hidden but anxious, whistled plaintively. The urchin paused to crunch a beetle, then saw Osyth's still shape and scampered away, showing surprisingly long legs as if it held up its skirts the better to run.

Deep in meditation, Osyth felt her spirit withdraw gently from her flesh and rise to walk among the stars.

The approach of the sun was lightening the eastern sky when, in the north-west, stars fell. The anchoress counted four, one after another, and presently three more, and lastly two. Nine, the sacred number. She got up stiffly. Each time she fared forth from her body it was harder to return and put on again the painful limitations of aching flesh and bones. But, as she hobbled to the house, she was satisfied. She had sat out for a sign. The Mother had given her one.

'What do you see?'

Janiva jumped guiltily. She'd been staring into the rock pool beside the narrow waterfall and the noise of the falling water had covered Osyth's footsteps. For all her bulk the anchoress – a big woman, with bare earthy feet and hands stained with the juices of herbs and berries – moved quietly.

'Be easy, lass. There's naught to fear.' Osyth knelt, grunting as arthritic knees took her weight. She peered into the pool, then stirred it with her finger. 'Don't believe all it shows you,' she said. 'Water can only show what *may* be, and that ain't always what *will* be.'

From her belt pouch she took a piece of green stone, a rough half sphere; the curved surface knobby, puckered, the flat side smooth as glass.

'This'll serve you better'n water,' she said, putting it in Janiva's hand.

Janiva held it to the sun, which struck points of green from its depths. 'What is it?'

'There's a place where these things litter the ground. Folk say they're bits of a star that fell to earth.'

'Oh,' Janiva exclaimed, delighted. 'A shooting star!'

'That's what they say. Now, tell me what you saw in the water.'

Janiva clenched her hand around the stone. 'Flames,' she said reluctantly. 'Myself, standing in fire, my hair and my hands burning.'

The anchoress nodded. 'Don't fear it. It ain't what it seems. Help me up.' She struggled to her feet with difficulty and turned towards the house. 'I must see to the fire. Come.'

Janiva followed her inside. 'You aren't what you seem either,' she said, watching as Osyth made up the fire. 'Why did Tostig bring me here?'

Bent over the fire Osyth glanced sideways at her. 'Pouncey folk're good Christians,' she said. 'They go to church an keep the feasts, but this is a place of the Mother first of all, and we are all her servants here.'

She saw Janiva's eyes widen with sudden comprehension. This was a shrine of the Mother Goddess, worshipped in this land before monks brought their Christ-teachings from over the sea. A few hundred years of compulsory Christianity had skimmed over many such small enclaves where the Old Faith remained, secret and strong.

The anchoress stood up. 'We listen for her voice and do her bidding. Tostig was born here, didn't he tell you? The Mother bade him bring you, so we can break this curse that's on you.'

'Curse?' But . . . That was it! Of course! Why hadn't she recognised it? Grief upon grief, loss after loss, all that she had, all that she loved stripped from her. What else *could* it be? Understanding lanced through her, leaving her cold with shock. 'I've been a fool! I should have *known*!'

'Don't blame yourself. That's how it works: it blinds your sight. You'd 'ave seen it soon enough if it wasn't yourself.' The anchoress sat down and leaned her elbows on the table. 'Who did it?'

'I don't know.'

'You must. Think! Who hates you?'

Who hated her that much? Richildis? No. The girl was all jealousy and spite but there was no power in her. Benet Finacre, that pallid bundle of malice and ambition? No, not him. Who, then?

Green glints, like glossy wet leaves, like broken glass. Green eyes . . .

Eyes she had seen before but where? When? Green eyes that held her own, hard and malevolent, and a voice she heard inside her head, '*All that you have, all that you love, all that you are you shall lose . . .*'

She tried to grasp the memory but it slid away like water. She shut her eyes and struggled to pin it down. Osyth's hands, cool and strong, closed over hers.

Green eyes and the lour of foul magic . . . cruel laughter . . . a mind filled with malice . . .

A woman's mind, selfish, contemptuous, greedy and gloating. And she knew it, knew it by the taint she had met before. The woman who had bespelled Richard, sending the bane of an incubus to drive him to madness and destruction; who had kidnapped and abused his daughter and sought to murder her to buy greater power with her blood.

Rainard de Soulis' creature, Julitta de Beauris!

Bright, hot, a core of anger began to glow within her. 'I know her! What shall I do?'

'Turn it back, a course.'

Of course. Her mother had told her the same thing. There was only one way to be rid of a curse: turn it back upon the sender. And to do that she must fight her face to face.

Chapter 47

'You're lying, by God!' Lord William had picked up a jug of ale, but at his squire's words he slammed it down, smashing the jug. Ale ran over the table and dripped on the floor.

Thibaut swallowed. 'As God sees me, my lord, it's truth! Sulien has it from the prior of Abergavenny; the messenger is still here, you can question him yourself. Lady Mahaut is captured, and William your son. They fled to Scotland but the Scottish king sent them back to King John, in chains.'

There was an ugly sound: Lord William grinding his teeth. 'What of Hugh de Lacy? She was in his care!'

'He got away. No one knows where he is.'

'The Devil snatch him up for a false traitor!' Lord William chewed his lip until blood and foam speckled his chin, but even more shockingly, tears started from his eyes, running unheeded down his cheeks. His embarrassed squire didn't know where to look.

'Sir,' he began, then yipped in pain as his lord clutched his sore arm in a bruising grip.

'My wife, my lady,' Breos groaned, 'in chains! Lord God, she has honoured You all her life! How could You let this happen?' His voice rose hysterically. 'John's prisoner! He'll kill her, he hates her; you know what she said of him, that he slew his nephew. He'll never forgive that, never . . .' He let go of Thibaut, who staggered and nearly fell. 'God in heaven! In *chains*!'

He couldn't bear it. His wife, his Moll, so proud, in chains! The little room was closing in, the walls crushing him. He must get outside in the open air or suffocate! Thrusting Thibaut roughly aside Lord William lurched out of the chamber like a drunkard, through the main room where his knights, at their supper, sat transfixed, and out under the sky, where he clenched his fists, threw back his head and *screamed*, a shocking noise that went on and on until his voice cracked and broke on it. Spittle ran down his chin and dripped onto his shirt, the cords of his neck stood out like drawn ropes and his face darkened to the colour of sloes.

It's an apoplexy, Thibaut thought, panicky and shaky from the poison circulating in his bloodstream. His lord would fall like a cut oak any moment now.

But he didn't. Breos staggered, then steadied; slowly his dark empurpled colour paled to a death-like grey, except for the inflamed slash down his cheek where that murderous little scribbler had gone for his eye. At his howl, just as Thibaut had feared, folk came running to see what was going on: Breos's own men, hospital attendants, pilgrims and even a couple of lepers. They watched, anxious to miss nothing. Lord William took no notice of them. Through clenched teeth he mumbled something indistinct.

Thibaut shivered. 'My lord?'

'God,' whispered Lord William. 'God has broken faith with me. I will be His man no more!' He tore off his necklace of relics and holy medals and threw it down. '*That* for God,' he snarled, and spat on it. 'And for the saints, the useless bastards!' He trod on the bright tangle at his feet and ground it into the earth. 'How could they? After all I've done for them!'

The onlookers murmured, edging back a bit, still able to see and hear but out of harm's way if God's thunderbolt should strike the blasphemer.

'All my life I've honoured the Lord God and His Son! I've poured out gold to glorify them. When did I ever stint? I've built churches, convents; I gave one of my sons to the Church; I fought for God in the Holy Land . . . For what? For *this*? Is this my reward? I'd've done better to serve the Devil! Satan,' he howled, tilting his face skywards as if addressing God, then remembering that the Devil dwelt otherwhere and stamping furiously on the ground instead to get the Lord of Hell's attention.

'Satan, hear me! Save my lady and I vow, I swear before God, I'll be your man!'

The crowd and Thibaut gasped as one. The squire looked at their avid faces and wondered how in God's name he could shut his lord up.

'The king is always short of money,' he offered hesitantly. 'He will surely accept ransom for Lady Mahaut. You've taken much treasure these past weeks—'

Lord William uttered a mirthless bark. He looked dreadful; new lines chiselled his face and the grey flesh cleaved to the bone of his skull like a dead man's.

'Don't be a damned fool. Do you think there's treasure enough in the world to buy off John's vengeance on my lady? Shut your damned mouth if you've nothing worth saying. Get me wine, damn your eyes! And bring the lady Julitta to me.'

Escorting Julitta, close enough to be aware of her scent and the warmth of her body, Thibaut closed his good hand over the holy relic in the pommel of his dagger and bit his tongue to still the unwelcome twinge of desire her presence always roused. Despite her beauty she made him uneasy, and he knew he wasn't the only one. Bevis de Rennes, the most senior of Lord William's knights, swore she sent evil dreams to torment him, and Thibaut, who'd had a few disturbing dreams himself but kept quiet about them, believed it.

At the door a woman was waiting with a baby in her arms. At their approach she held out her hand for alms with the whine of a professional beggar.

'Penny, me lord, me lady? Ha'penny? I've no milk for the little un. Just born yestiddy, e was. A fourthing, me beautiful lady—'

'Go to the hostel kitchen,' Thibaut said. 'No one starves here. They will feed you and give you milk for the child.'

But with an angelic smile Julitta dropped a coin in the outstretched palm and the woman mouthed her thanks, flashing Thibaut a 'So there!' smirk as she scuttled off.

He didn't look at Julitta, but as he held the door of Lord William's small side-chamber open for her to pass in he felt the mocking gaze of her green eyes, palpable as a kiss.

In the main room of the storehouse they'd taken over as their quarters, helping themselves to the bales and barrels, Lord William's knights paused in their talk and tasks to cross themselves and make the forked sign against the Evil Eye as the door closed behind her.

'Have you heard? John has them, my wife and son!' Before Julitta could answer Lord William seized her by the arm and dragged her to the table, pushing her into his own chair. 'What shall I do? What *can* I do? He'll kill her! You know he will; you know his vengeance!' She knew it, none better, whose husband had been put to death on John's orders, the gold he'd taken to betray his king melted and poured down his throat.

'What do you want of me, my lord?' She got up from the chair and laid a gentle hand on his shoulder. 'Sit down, you are shaking; you were let blood, and then this shock—'

'Yes, yes,' he muttered, sinking into the chair. 'I was bled . . . That fool of a medicus.' He glowered; the man had run off before he could be flogged. Nor was he the only one; four of his knights had deserted too. Only Bevis de Rennes and Ralph de Morwenni were still with him, and Thibaut, of course.

'Let me pour you wine, my lord. Mayhap there is something we can do.'

She picked up his cup – it was dented, he must have been too upset to notice – and went over to the aumbrey for wine. Keeping her back to him she slid a small bottle from her sleeve, cracked the wax seal with her nail and let three drops fall into the cup.

'There, my lord. Drink, it will ease your mind, and we will see what may be done.'

He looked up eagerly. 'There is something, then? Something you can do?' His hands shook as he took the cup and it rattled against his teeth. He held it out for more. She smiled, turning away to refill it. When he had drained that she looked sharply at his eyes, and judged him ready.

'There *may* be a way to set your lady free,' she said, but hesitantly. 'It is not easy.'

'Anything,' he said eagerly. 'Whatever you need, whatever you want . . .'

'I want nothing from you, Lord William. Duchess Alix will reward us both when we put the Banner in her hands.'

'I haven't got the bloody thing,' he cried in despair. 'And Alix of Brittany can't give me back my wife!'

'You *will* have it, my lord. I promise you, you will.'

'Is that what the stars tell you?' he asked thickly, wishing to believe.

'The stars, of course.' Agarel had told her but no matter how much she hurt the demon he could not – or would not – say how this was to come about. However, as her captive he could not lie to her. Lord William *would* find the Banner and when he did Julitta meant to have it, not for Brittany, but for herself.

Breos stared at her, his pupils mere dots, his mouth slack, looking twenty years older than he had this morning. 'You're a w-witch,' he said, stuttering on the word. 'That's why they sent you to me, isn't it?' Forgetting his new allegiance he crossed himself.

'So they say,' Julitta murmured. 'Listen, my lord. There is a spell . . . But no, no, what am I saying? You are a God-fearing man; you cannot put your hand to sorcery, not even to set your wife free.'

'God has not used me well,' Lord William said sullenly. 'How do I know the one *you* serve will keep faith with me?'

'He is the lord of this world and knows how to reward a good servant. He doesn't want your silver, you don't have to build cathedrals to his glory, nor does he hand out penance and punishment, only the Church does that. But consider well, my lord: if you set your feet on his path you must follow it to the end.'

'As for that—' he began, then stopped abruptly, the words 'It's never too late to buy absolution' left unsaid on the tip of his tongue. He got up and paced the small room, pondering what she had said and finding it good. But he had already offered his allegiance to Julitta's lord, and *that* had cost him four good men.

'I must have a token of his good faith.' An odd thing to ask of the Devil, but those were his terms.

'It is not too late to draw back,' she said with a shrug. 'You have done much for your God. Perhaps he will move the king to mercy.'

She sat down and took an apple and began to peel it, as if she had lost interest in the matter. He became agitated then and sought to persuade her, shouting and sobbing by turns. Soothingly she spoke, seeming all the while to dissuade him, until he was on fire to do that which she counselled against. And all the while she watched him, noting the fine tremor of his hands and smelling his sweat.

There was a sheathed sword lying on the table. Her glance had passed over it at first, but now it came back and fixed on the weapon.

'Where did you get this?'

'Eh? Oh, that. The crusader's sword. Thibaut brought it in.'

She touched the leather scabbard gingerly, as if it might burn, and snatched her fingers away with a cry as if it had.

'You told me Straccan was dead!'

'What?' Lord William stopped pacing. 'Straccan? He is.'

'Did you *see* him dead, when you went back there? Did you fetch up his body to be sure of him?'

'There was no need. The tower fell in and buried him. There's no way he could've got out.' *Was there?* Sudden doubt tightened his throat uncomfortably. He'd gone back to the abandoned hermitage next day, to take the tower apart stone by stone if he must and rake the islet from one end to the other, and found no more than a pile of rubble. A search of the rest of that smelly mud hole yielded nothing but broken walls and an empty birdcage.

'It's his sword,' Julitta said. She ran her fingers along the scabbard and took hold of the hilt, closing her eyes the better to see the images that crowded upon her inner sight. She saw him clearly – Richard Straccan, that cursed bone-pedlar – the cause of all her misfortunes: her husband's death, the failure of their plot to kill the king and her own exile. Hatred scalded her belly like acid.

'He was man alive when your squire took this from him. I see it.' She frowned, eyes closed. 'Straccan, and another with him, a servant. Their horses were drinking, your men took them by surprise.'

'*Merde*!' Breos picked up a footstool and hurled it at the door. 'He had it! He knew where it was all the time and he got away with it!' The stool struck the door frame and a leg fell off. The door was flung open and Thibaut rushed in, sword drawn, ready for anything that threatened his lord.

'The man who had this sword, was he marked?' Breos touched his own scabbed cheek where Wace's mark scorched afresh.

Seeing no danger in the room Thibaut lowered his blade and thought back to the encounter at the ford. 'His face yes, and here,' tapping the side of his nose.

'God's name, God's mother, it *was* him! I should have cut his throat!' Breos looked around for something, anything, to destroy, and stabbed the table furiously with his dagger.

Julitta touched Thibaut's sleeve and the squire jumped as if scalded. 'What else did you take from him?'

'The horses and everything on them,' Thibaut avoided her eyes, addressing his lord instead, 'bedrolls, provisions, weapons, baggage. I set a guard over it when the others left. Nothing's been touched yet.'

'Bring it all here,' Julitta snapped. 'My lord, Straccan had it with him. He had the Banner!'

Breos slammed his dagger back in its sheath. 'Do as she says,' he ordered his squire. 'All of it, every last scrip and bundle! If anything's missing I'll have you whipped. *Move*, damn you!'

At the door, feeling a sudden chill at his nape, Thibaut glanced back. Lord William's witch had taken a glassy egg-shaped stone from the case at her girdle and was gazing into it. The hairs rose at the back of his neck and he shivered.

'I should have killed him,' Breos said again.

'You may yet,' Thibaut heard her say with a throaty laugh. 'You asked for a token of faith, my lord. You have it! Straccan's on his way here.'

Chapter 48

Lord William's chamber reeked of stale smoke and incense. Thibaut set the hot-water jug down and flung back the shutters to let in the clean morning air. What had they been doing in here all night, his lord and the witch, after they found the Banner?

After all their searching for it, clear across Wales, over the Severn and back again, the Banner had come to Lord William's hands as if by magic. It had been there among the jumble of weapons, boxes, barrels and bales, saddlebags and bundles, the miscellaneous property of many luckless travellers: an old satchel, shabby and stained.

They came to it late, after turning over and pawing through dozens of bags and bundles, flinging their contents aside. It was Thibaut who took up the satchel, but before he could open it Julitta had snatched it from him with a triumphant cry. He had the briefest glimpse as she unrolled it of the dragon's gaping jaws and eyes like rubies – as perhaps they were – before his lord thrust him roughly out of the chamber, locking himself in with his witch. Thibaut had wrapped himself in a blanket on his pallet in the hall, but he hadn't slept.

Around midnight the witch went out, wrapped in her mantle, stepping silently across the hall lest she wake the sleeping men. She returned soon after, and Thibaut heard the key turn again. After that there were bumps and thuds and a thin mewing like that of a kitten or some other small animal. Thibaut heard the witch chanting what sounded like prayers and his lord giving the responses, but the language wasn't Latin. A haze of smoke seeped under the door, and the stink of burning. And there were other sounds, but perhaps he had briefly slept and only dreamed them.

She had gone yawning to her own chamber before dawn. The usual racket of his men getting up hadn't woken Lord William. He was still fully clad, asleep at the table with his arms folded over the satchel that held the Banner.

'My lord.'

Lord William opened bloodshot eyes and waited until the two wavering images of his squire had merged into one. 'What?'

'It is morning, my lord. It is late.'

'Eh?' Intelligence struggled through the fumes of drugged wine and smoke and sought to make connections. 'Jesus! Get me water to wash. Here,' he held out the satchel, 'lock this in the chest and give me the key.'

Thibaut was shocked at his lord's appearance. With grizzled stubble, matted hair and ravaged face, he looked like a church door beggar.

'My lord, are you ill?'

'Ill? No. Too much wine! Doesn't help. He's got my wife, you know. The king. He's got her in chains.'

'I know, my lord. I'm sorry.'

'The devil you are.' Breos knuckled his eyes, then stared at his hands, turning them over and spreading the fingers.

'Is something wrong?'

'No!' Breos put his hands behind his back like a child hiding something. For a moment Thibaut thought he looked desperately afraid.

When his lord had gone out, alone – to the old shrine, he said, the little cell perched on a rock ledge where Saint Nonna had hidden from her cruel father and borne her holy son – Thibaut started setting the small chamber to rights. All the rejected flotsam from last night's search he carried into the hall, where the sergeants fell upon it, each grabbing what he fancied as his share.

Thibaut found the dented cup on the floor and rinsed it, wondering what Lord William had been drinking for the sticky dregs had a queer unpleasant smell. The candles had burned right down and he scraped the holders clean of wax. That, too, was strange: grey, greasy, and ill-smelling.

The brazier was quite cold. He picked it up to empty ash and cinders outside and stopped, for a moment unsure, and then all *too* sure of what lay half hidden in the curls of ash. Bones. Little delicate charred bones, broken and crushed.

His unwilling mind rejected what his eyes recognised. They were the bones of some small animal, of course; what else?

It was a steep climb to the shrine. Lord William was wet with sweat and hard out of breath by the time he reached it. A woven wicker shelter had been built over the ledge where the saint had dwelt and inside it was a carved wooden figure, life-size, that might have been Nonna and her infant son, or equally the Blessed Virgin and hers.

A wood fire burned there, never allowed to go out; outside the shrine stood a great stack of firewood. No one climbed the path without an armful of wood. Perhaps the fact that Lord William had brought no wood accounted for the saint's faintly reproachful expression. There was neither bench nor stool. Pilgrims did not climb all this way to sit in comfort; they came to implore or give thanks, and they did it humbly, standing, kneeling or lying face down on the bare rock floor. Some even mortified their sinful flesh further by putting pebbles in their shoes before trudging up the path; a barrel-full stood at the foot of the path for those who chose that penance and there was a great heap in the shrine itself, left there by petitioners.

From up here Lord William could see all the valley. Its beauty did not move him; beauty never had. There was some activity at the gate, tents struck, men riding away – had the siege been lifted? No, some other company was setting up camp. Fat Oliver had been relieved. A nuisance, but the new commander would prob-ably be just as accommodating.

What shall I do?

Who was he asking? Who heard? The God he had bribed and bargained with all his life, or the one Julitta called Lord of this

World? How could Satan be more powerful than the God who had cast him out of heaven?

The memory of last night swilled nauseatingly around his mind. He wasn't squeamish, but the way that monster, whatever it was, that *thing* had fed and glutted, the gross sounds, the livid eyes . . . On the way up here he'd tried to believe that it was all a nightmare but there had been blood under his fingernails this morning.

God, what have I done? I didn't mean it! I was mad!

Mad. Of course! He turned the word over in his mind and felt a vast sense of relief. He had been mad, and the mad were not held accountable for their actions. Fear for Mahaut and his son had unseated his reason, and in his madness that witch had sought to trap his soul with her promises to free his wife and son.

I was bewitched!

Bewitched, ensorcelled, led astray like Adam.

The woman tempted me.

She had lied and deceived him. It was not her dark lord who'd brought the Banner to him. That was God's doing.

And God had answered him! He knew what to do now. He didn't need the Bretons, that misbegotten pack of enchanters and warlocks, and he didn't need the witch. He would get rid of her and her hellish familiar, and offer the Banner to John for the release of his wife and son. The king would not refuse. It was God's will.

Leaning from the window he gave an exultant shout which echoed back from the opposite cliff, and rang again and again, diminishing until it died away. '*Deus vult!*'

But the old leper had been right. His soul *was* an abomination, but God would forgive him. Whatever the cost – and it would be high – he would make his peace with God. Do penance, go to Rome wearing a sack, barefoot if he had to, and if the Pope ordered him on crusade to purge his sin, well, he'd done it before, he could do it again.

And the leper . . . There must be no risk that he might tell his tale to anyone else.

* * *

'I'll take your word for it,' Oliver le Gros had told Sulien. 'If you tell me each morning that the bugger's still in there, I'll believe you.' A week had passed, seven of Lord William's forty days, and the bugger was still in there.

Roger de Lacy had left his fat son-in-law in command and hurried back to his domain in case anyone was making hay in the sunshine of his absence. The siege of Cwm Cuddfan had settled down at the entrance to the valley. It was the only way out. The cliff sides were too high, too steep and far too unstable to climb, so if Breos made a break for it he must come this way. They couldn't go in and drag him out, for by virtue of the shrine the whole valley was Sanctuary, and by the laws of Sanctuary a fugitive had forty days' grace during which not even the king's men might enter. But if after forty days he had not yielded, they would come in after him.

Meanwhile the host and its plump commander were very much at ease. It was like a holiday, for no one shot at them and the besieged obligingly sold the besiegers fresh supplies – eggs, milk, meat and vegetables – every day, and for a price even undertook to do their laundry.

Pilgrims and the sick were let in as usual, but the arrival of one of the king's captains with a dozen men-at-arms and a handful of civilians in tow brought Oliver himself from his noon meal to see what they wanted. Von Koln took a letter from his pouch and offered it 'in the king's name'.

Oliver looked angrily at the royal seal, and grew angrier on learning he was to be relieved of this comfortable sinecure and, worse still, of the backhanders William de Breos had been paying to send and receive letters.

'So you're Straccan,' he said nastily. 'Heard of you. Traffic in old bones, don't you? Pah!' With that he swung on his heel, bawling, 'Break camp!' and marched back to his tent, resentment showing in every line of his body, a resentment presently echoed profanely by his men, done out of their cushy billet.

Bruno's company set up their camp as a sick man, veiled and supported by his pretty, tearful young wife and with two menservants fussing around him, passed almost unnoticed through the gate into the valley. Just another leper, poor sod.

Cwm Cuddfan was a deep gorge, a cul-de-sac, narrow at the entrance, broad in the middle where the lake and the lepers' island lay, narrowing again at the blind end where a cataract cascaded down the rock face. The valley bottom was heavily wooded and the hospital buildings stood in small clearings amid the trees.

The new patient and his wife sat down to wait while the servants arranged for their master's admittance and treatment.

With some hundred or so people living and working in the valley, not counting patients and pilgrims who frequently brought their families as well, there were bound to be accidents and injuries, and the bench where Straccan and Alis waited offered a good view of the open-sided tent where Sulien's assistants dealt with casualties. Patients lay or sat, groaning or stoically silent according to temperament, while the attendants – Alis was surprised to see that some were women – dealt with their injuries.

Today there were two men slashed or pierced with daggers, a woman who'd been stabbed with a pack-needle in an argument with a friend, a man bitten by a dog, another bitten by his wife and one of the hospital's cooks, splashed with boiling fat, together with his apprentice – the splasher – whose jaw he'd broken by way of return.

'The guest house is rather full, I'm afraid,' said the almoner when Bane and Havloc found him. 'Your lot'll have to double up in the beds, ladies belowstairs, men above. If your master's not leprous he can go in the men's hall, but it's two to a bed in there just now as well.'

'My master wants to see Sulien,' Bane said.

'Everyone wants to see Sulien. I'll tell him. You'll have a long wait.'

It was late afternoon when they were taken at last to Sulien's hut. As Straccan's shadow fell across his table Sulien – a young man, barely thirty, with untidy curls and friendly eyes – looked up from his writing. Beside his feet in a basket a battered-looking cat curled protectively around a single ginger kitten. Sulien laid down his stylus, took a jug and dish from the shelf behind him and poured milk, which he set beside the basket. The cat rose stiffly and began to lap.

'I fished her out of the river, in a sack,' Sulien said, as if carrying on a conversation. 'There's just the one kitling left now.' He picked up the tubby ginger mite, which opened a bright pink mouth and emitted a surprisingly loud mew. The mother sprang onto the table, pawing anxiously upwards.

'There, puss, forgive me.' Sulien set the kitten down again. 'Saint Gregory had a cat, you know,' he went on, 'in his retirement. Jacobus Diaconus wrote that the saint would carry his cat in the bosom of his robe, petting it, his sole companion. Please, sit down. I'm sorry you've had such a long wait. If you will lay aside your veil, Master' – glancing at his notes – 'Richard of Nottingham?' He smiled reassuringly at Alis. 'Don't worry, mistress. I shan't hurt your husband but I must examine him. There are other conditions that may be mistaken for leprosy. We must be sure.'

'There's nothing wrong with me,' Straccan said, unwinding the stained fabric from his head and neck to reveal a hideously pustulant countenance. 'This is just paint and glue; it'll wash off. Forgive the deception, Sulien. I'm Richard Straccan; this will explain why I'm here.' He handed Sulien the letter Bruno von Koln had shown Oliver le Gros.

Sulien read it. He looked at Straccan unbelievingly and read it again. 'The Pendragon Banner . . . You *found* it? It's *real*?'

'I found it, yes, and William de Breos stole it. The king has commanded me to get it back.'

'But you've seen it,' Sulien said excitedly. 'You've held it in your hands! How in God's name did you find it? Oh, if only Lady Hallgerd could know!'

He sat entranced as Straccan told him from the beginning when the king had sent for him to the bloody debacle on the saint's island and the ambush at the ford.

'God's mercy, is it true? Lord William has it *here*?'

'It came here, I'm sure of that.'

'How I wish I could see it!'

'You shall, if I get it back.'

Sulien's face clouded. 'How . . . Sir Richard, this is Sanctuary; you mustn't challenge him here. William de Breos has been our good lord.'

'Not everyone's been so lucky. I followed his bloody track here from Maeselyn,' said Straccan grimly, 'and Llantali, and Tresaint. And before that,' he added, anger rising and hard held in check, 'from the convent of the Penitent Sisters where Mother Heloise died, and Saint Winnoc's island, where your good lord murdered Robert Wace. And that's just a small part of his handiwork. Don't tell me you've heard nothing of this!'

Sulien's face was taut with grief. 'No matter what he has done, you can't take him from here until his forty days are done.'

'I don't intend to.' Nor did he. He intended to challenge and kill him, and get the Banner back, God alone knew how.

'This letter commands me to give you any help you need,' Sulien said. 'What shall I do?'

'Where is he housed, and how many men has he got?'

'They've commandeered one of the hall-houses, next to the stable. Some of his men have deserted and some he's dismissed but he has – let me see – two knights of his own household, five sergeants and his squire.'

'We need a hut to ourselves.' Sulien nodded. 'And I want a gown such as your lepers wear, so that I can scout around without anyone else knowing I'm here.'

'The leper-master must be told,' Sulien said.

'Why?'

'He will hardly fail to notice the addition to his flock.'

Chapter 49

From the coast at Fishguard on the morning of Saint Ninian's day, a watchman saw the sail of the royal galley, *Esnecca*, tautly pregnant with the wind from the west and the royal standard flying at the mast, and blew his horn to alert everyone to the imminent arrival of the king.

John had good reason to be pleased. Even his father, great Henry fitzEmpress, had never managed to bring Ireland to heel as *he* had; and to crown his satisfaction Mahaut de Breos was his prisoner, together with her eldest son, below deck. Standing in the prow with the bishop of Winchester, watching the Welsh coast getting clearer and nearer, John whistled a cheerful tune – to the dismay of the crew, who reckoned whistling might raise a contrary wind even now, at the very last moment.

The galley's captain, acutely conscious of the crew's reproachful looks and wholly sharing their anxiety, tactfully suggested that king and bishop might enjoy a cup of good Anjou wine in the deck-cabin to toast their swift and easy passage. In high good humour, John agreed, and the dangerous whistling stopped: none too soon, the captain reckoned. Those on board could now see the crowd gathered at the quayside, and smoke rising from kitchen fires.

John drank and set down his cup. Ireland had been very rewarding, very submissive, very *green*, but it was good to get home. There were pleasures in store. The Irish ladies had been more than welcoming and John was not the man to disappoint them, but he was fond of his wife and eager to see his young son. But before he was reunited with them at Windsor, he would have the satisfaction of seeing William de Breos on his knees, pleading for his wife's freedom and offering in exchange the enormous amount of plunder he'd gathered during the past few weeks.

John smiled. That would *really* come in handy! He'd need every penny for the show of force necessary to put the wind up those barons and lords who had grown complacent in his absence, up to all their old tricks, hatching plots and making trouble. The king laughed.

'I'll teach 'em,' he said.

Bishop Peter des Roches looked puzzled. 'Sire?'

'My lords temporal,' said John, his mouth twisting as though the good wine tasted sour. 'They'll have got cocky while I've been away. What other king was ever cursed with such subjects?'

'Indeed, my lord,' agreed the bishop. He'd been miserably seasick all the way across and wasn't really thinking, which was never safe with John. 'You are afflicted even as Job was.'

'Don't mention Job to me. He only had boils; I've got barons.' John looked slyly at des Roches. 'Worried, Peter? Do you see my throne crumbling? *Do you?*' His voice cracked like a whip and the bishop jumped. 'The campaign was a great success and we're almost home.' He cocked his head as a wobbly '*Huzza!*' came from the shore. 'Ah, they're cheering! How nice! Or is that the sound of my realm groaning under the papal fist? Be honest, Peter. *Do my people hate me?*'

Des Roches blinked. The king's moods changed so suddenly, and he really didn't feel well at all. 'Um, no, my lord king,' he said, 'they don't.'

'They don't, do they?' said the king smugly. 'That's because they hate foreigners and foreign meddling and Romish interference more than anything else.' He put a companionable arm round the bishop's shoulders, which didn't reassure the prelate one bit.

'That's the secret, you see,' John confided. 'They look on themselves, *and* me, as victims of a busy-fingered avaricious leech in a funny hat hundreds of miles away in Rome. What business is England – and my archbishop – of his? Shoving Rome's nose up our arses! Determined to terrorise us until we give in! Well, *I* won't and they won't, and that's what keeps em sweet, Peter.'

He waved to the crowd, close enough now to see their faces. 'My English,' he said fondly. 'They're a funny lot. No one has ever understood em like I do. Father never did, God rest his soul, and brave brother Lionheart wouldn't have pissed on England if it caught fire! But I understand them, they understand me, and *they're on my side.*'

So they were, for the most part, the bishop thought: the common folk, the country gentry and especially townspeople, for John had been liberal in the matter of charters and privileges. The towns knew which side their bread was buttered and Rome never buttered it. But the common folk had neither silver nor levies, and most of the lords – who had – were *not* on the king's side.

A ragged cheer rose as the gangplank went down. The king snapped his fingers and a page darted into the cabin and came out again with a purse. John flung a handful of coins into the crowd, the sun gilding the silver pennies to a shower of gold as they spun. The cheering redoubled.

A messenger in royal livery waited on the jetty with letters. A clerk seized them and trotted close behind the king, breaking seals and reading aloud. A name caught the king's ear.

'What was that?'

'From the constable at Ludlow, sire. He writes that Wace has been killed and that Straccan has returned without the Banner, saying he'd been robbed by Breos's men.'

The king looked hurt. 'Straccan,' he said. 'Well, well. And there was a man I almost thought I could trust.'

Chapter 50

With her thumb Osyth traced on Janiva's brow and breast the runes of guard and warding, murmuring the spells that would draw power from the rock of the Edge, its trees and waterfalls, and from the new-waxing moon, to protect her.

'Drink this; it'll make it easier to leave your body,' Osyth said. The drink smelled musty and tasted of rot. Janiva swallowed obediently and almost gagged on the thick lumpy brew, 'You must keep it down!' She managed to, though it was touch and go for a minute.

During these past few days, waiting out the waning moon, they had talked for hours. 'She's a dark heart, that one,' Osyth said when Janiva spoke of Julitta, of the kidnapping of Straccan's daughter and the innocent child the sorcerer Rainard de Soulis had murdered to feed his demon. 'Dark through and through. We're born with power in our blood, in our bones, and it ain't good nor bad; it's what we *do* with it. She'll fight you with fear and despair. She'll use illusions to trick you and break your will. Don't believe em. They'll be lies.'

The fire in the rock cleft blazed up higher than Janiva's head. She took a deep breath, balled her hands into fists and walked into it.

Flames were all around her, beneath her feet, licking her legs; her skin was lit by fire. For a moment she quailed and felt the heat, smelled her hair singeing . . . then she breathed out, stepped forward, trod the flames underfoot and stood among them. They were cool, whispering silkily over her skin. She was herself a being of flame, burning but unconsumed, her hair a torch, her breath fire, fingers blazing like candles. She stood a moment more, then parted the flames with her hands and passed unscathed to the cave behind the fire.

The runes Osyth had marked felt cold on her skin, as if drawn with ice. The only sound was her breathing. Lit by the distant flickering fire, the cave was full of shifting shadows.

These last days as the moon waned, her courage had waned with it. She knew fear. Julitta's curse had so damaged and diminished her that she might not have the strength, even with Osyth's help, to defeat her enemy. But now, the night of the new moon, fear had gone; she felt a fierce eagerness. Perhaps the drink had lent her courage.

The two women had made and brought here a pallet of boughs and leaves: oak for courage and strength and rowan for protection against spellcraft. Lying down, Janiva slowed her breathing, aware of the pulse of her blood slowing too. The words of the Summoning still rang in her ears and seemed to echo from the walls of the cave, as if many voices repeated it, until the whole cave rang like the resonant aftertone of a bell.

There was the scent of herbs – vervain for strength, woodruff for courage – and of wood-smoke from the fire which hid and guarded the entrance to this secret, sacred place. *Cranna ca mar*, Osyth called it, the Womb of the Mother; the women's place, this cave in the rock where supplicants of the Goddess in long years past had come to seek answers to their questions in dreams.

How many, Janiva wondered, over how many hundreds of years? And although she was still awake, the grip of her body was loosening and her inner sight glimpsed them: many faces, one blurring into another; many women, young, old, grieving, joyous; numberless as the stars, clad in skins or in linen, wool, or silk. Here she must sleep and leave her body, to find her enemy in the world most folk remembered only dimly from dreams while Osyth tended the Mother's fire, a beacon to guide her back if she should lose the way.

The Summoning would draw Julitta from her sleeping body. 'She won't expect it,' Osyth said. 'Catch her nappin, you will. By now she reckons you're destroyed, but you were stronger'n she thought.'

'What if she won't come?'

'She'll come,' said Osyth. 'She *must*.'

Asleep in Cwm Cuddfan Julitta moved restlessly, her hand groping under her pillow until it closed on the oval casket. Beneath their closed lids her eyes moved rapidly, flicking from side to side, and she muttered in her sleep. Under her hand the casket grew warm.

No one answered Sulien's knock and after a few moments he pushed the door open and called softly, 'Sir Richard!' He could see the pallets on the floor, each mounded by a sleeping body, but there were no snores, no sighs or murmurs. He nudged the nearest sleeper with his foot. No response. Puzzled, he stooped to shake the sleeper's shoulder and found nothing under the blanket but rustling straw.

The voice at his back made him jump. 'Shouldn't you be in bed?'

Sulien turned to see Straccan in the open doorway. 'I might say the same for you, Sir Richard. Couldn't you sleep? Where are your companions?'

'It's the best time to reconnoitre,' Straccan said. 'The new moon's bright enough and there's no cloud. We've been having a quiet look round while everyone else is in bed.' At his low whistle two more figures Sulien recognised as his servants appeared behind him. 'We were going to bed now, unless you have something else in mind.'

'I do. Will you come with me, Sir Richard? It won't take long, I promise, but you must come alone.'

'Where?'

'To the island. To Ynys Gwydion.'

Straccan followed Sulien through a dense belt of willows, emerging at the lakeside, where three coracles lay upside down on the sand. The water was black in the moonlight and utterly still. Moon and stars were reflected in it, like the sky of some other world beneath the lake, where water elves might dwell.

'Why are we going there?' Straccan demanded.

'There is something you must see, something you must know before you fight Lord William.'

'I didn't say I was going to fight him.'

'But that is why you're here.'

Sulien flipped one of the boats over and got in, Straccan after him.

'You're right. If you're trying to warn me off, don't waste your breath, Sulien. I mean to challenge him.'

'Even though this is Sanctuary? You know the consequences.'

Of course he did. To violate Sanctuary was sacrilege. By fighting, shedding blood in the holy precincts, he invited excommunication.

'If this was God's antechamber I would still challenge him,' he said relentlessly. 'Don't try to stop me.'

The craft had a most peculiar motion, Sulien seeming to stir the water rather than paddle, but it made its erratic way across the lake with admirable speed. As they neared the shore a light flared and Straccan saw a dark figure bulk out of the shadows, holding a lantern.

Sulien beached the coracle, and the man with the lantern came closer. He wore the gown and hood of a leper. 'Go with him,' Sulien said. 'I'll wait here for you.'

'God save you, Sir Richard.'

Straccan stood still. Surely he knew that painful rasp, all that remained of a man's voice?

'Garnier? What are you doing here?'

'I am master of the lepers on the island.'

'I never thought to see you again.'

'Nor I you,' Garnier said. 'But God, it seems, had other plans.'

'Why did Sulien bring me here?'

'Will you come with me? I have something to show you.'

'Something to do with Breos?'

'Come and see.'

They passed a few huts with doors and windows fast shut against the dangers of night, elves and whatever else folk feared in this part of the country. The rise and fall of the ground now hid the lake and it was dark here, with trees crowding close. An owl ghosted into the branches and not far off a vixen yelped.

'Where are we going?'

'We are here.' It was another hut, somewhat larger than the others and set well apart from them. 'You need not come in,' the leper said. 'You will see well enough from the door.' Pushing open the door he went in.

Straccan could see a bed and on it a body. Garnier held up the lantern. The corpse was small and thin, the uncovered face, framed in limp white hair, so horribly disfigured by the nodules of leprosy that it was impossible to say whether this was man or woman.

'Look well,' Garnier said.

'Why? Who's that?'

Garnier came out and closed the door. 'What do you know of Prince Arthur?'

Surprised by this change of subject Straccan said, 'The duke of Brittany? He's dead.'

'So all the world believes. He died at Rouen eight years ago, murdered by his wicked uncle the king, so they say.'

The lake came into view again, and it was with relief that Straccan saw the coracle at the water's edge and Sulien in it.

'I've heard the tale,' he said, wondering where this mystery was going and how much longer it would be getting there.

'That's what it is, a tale, a tragic story such as minstrels sing.' The leper coughed rustily. 'A convincing story, isn't it? It must be; even the king believes it.'

'What?' said Straccan, who in common with the rest of Christendom thought that King John had killed the duke, and had no trouble believing it.

'He has carried that blood-guilt all these years,' Garnier said, 'but it isn't true, my friend. John didn't kill Arthur.'

'How do you know? And what's it got to do with that old man . . . Was it a man?'

They had reached the boat. 'Have you told him?' Sulien asked the leper.

'Not all, not yet. If you'll be patient a little longer, Sir Richard, I'll tell you what happened, as the lord de Breos told it to me.'

With mounting disbelief Straccan listened as Garnier recounted the events at Rouen eight years before. 'Breos deceived them both,' the leper finished. 'John thinks himself murderer and kin-slayer, and believes Breos got rid of the duke's corpse so no one would be able to prove what everyone suspected. To Arthur, Breos was – at first – his saviour, who not only rescued him from his uncle's drunken rage but spirited him out of prison and promised to make him king.'

'I never thought Breos was that clever,' said Straccan.

'Nor he is. The plan was all his wife's, the lady Mahaut.'

'It would never have worked.'

'No? Kings have been overthrown before, and many held Arthur's to be the better right. And of course, if Breos made Arthur king—'

'He'd be the mightiest lord in the realm,' said Straccan, beginning to find this believable after all. 'The power behind the throne.'

'That's not all,' Garnier husked, coughing again, unused to so much talking. 'With a Breos daughter married to the young King Arthur, a Breos son to the Princess Eleanor—'

'A Breos dynasty, by God!' He believed it altogether now, and it was frightening.

'That was Lady Mahaut's plan.'

'But nothing came of it! Why didn't Breos play his king?'

'Don't you understand?' Sulien said. 'You've just seen him.'

'What? That was an old man!'

'He was just fifteen when John took him prisoner at Mirebeau,' Garnier said, 'and only twenty-three when he died today. He has been hidden here for more than seven years.'

'God forgive me,' Sulien said. 'I had no idea!'

'Sir Richard, I have a charge for you, if you will undertake it,' Garnier said.

'What is it?'

'To take a letter to King John – Sulien will write it – and tell him what you have seen here.'

'I saw a dead man. How do I know it's Arthur?'

Garnier took a purse from his pocket and upended it, spilling something small and bright into his gloved hand. A man's ring.

'Look.' It lay in his palm, a great carved ruby set in gold. He held it close to the lantern. The design cut in the stone was the seal of Brittany.

Straccan looked at the ring, and then back in the direction of the lonely hut with its dreadful secret. He crossed himself.

Garnier put the ring back in the purse. 'Lord William *had* no king to play.'

'Ask someone else,' Straccan said harshly. 'I'm in trouble enough with the king.'

'I believe God means this task for you. Why else would he bring us together again, here, now?'

'Not for this! Choose another messenger.'

'I trust you, Sir Richard. And you have the king's ear.'

Straccan laughed. 'Whatever gave you that idea?'

'My brother said so, at Ludlow.'

'Paulet? He was wrong.'

'The king gave you a horse, he said.'

'That was a whim! Kings have em. And since then I've "incurred his displeasure", as they say.'

'But you can approach him.'

'Anyone can!'

'I can't.'

'Well, no.' Straccan paused, that unarguable truth pushing past his resistance to sink home. 'He'll never believe it.'

'It's the truth. He *will* believe it.'

'What good will it do after all this time?'

'It will lift the burden of guilt from his conscience.'

'They say he doesn't have one.' There was a strange crackle from inside the leper's hood. 'Garnier, are you laughing at me?'

'No, Sir Richard. I'm laughing at God, but He's used to it. Will you undertake to do this?'

Straccan sighed heavily. 'If I *live* to speak to the king again, all right, I'll tell him.'

'What do you mean, if you live?' Sulien broke in. 'You're not going to fight Breos now, surely?'

'Oh yes I am. Why should this make any difference?'

'He must face the king's justice! This was high treason and I don't know what else! You can't fight him! If you kill him the king will have *you* put to death!'

'He's right, Sir Richard,' Garnier said. 'This is too high a matter for you to take into your own hands. Kill him, and the king's wrath will consume you.'

Chapter 51

In the Womb of the Mother the firelight woke a million quartz points to silver glinting, so that the cave seemed full of stars. The jewelled points sparkling from the rock, red and gold, green and purple, started to spin around Janiva, slowly to begin with, then faster, until she lay at the heart of a whirlpool of diamond fire.

The aftertaste of the drink still clung to her tongue and throat but no longer seemed foul; now it warmed her from head to foot and filled her with energy. Suddenly alert, she raised her head, listening. What was that?

She heard a woman's laugh, and smelled perfume: cinnamon and heady roses. The scent was drenchingly sweet but beneath it was a taint of rot, of putrid meat, of cesspit and the gases that bubble up from marsh mud.

With no warning an avalanche of hatred and venom rushed upon Janiva, but even as it threatened to sweep her away she found strength, here in the Womb of the Mother, to withstand it; and the first surge of her enemy's rage broke against the rock of Janiva's will, its force dissipated. She braced herself for the next onslaught.

It came in images of death and ruin to those she loved: images of pain and horror, of rape and torture and burning, blood and desolation. Richard lying lifeless, arrows in his body – Gilla violated – Sybilla imprisoned, starving – Osyth a twisted bundle of agony – Roger fallen to an enemy's blade, crows picking at his eyes . . .

There was a prickling sensation at her ankle; she brushed at it. There was another on her calf and on the back of her hand, and suddenly the itch was unbearable. With loathing Janiva saw her feet and arms black with ant-like crawling things. They swarmed up her legs, her thighs and belly, all over her body. Writhing, she slapped at them but she they were smothering her, filling her eyes and nostrils, slipping between her clamped lips.

Julitta was stronger. She had braved the flames for nothing . . . Yet she *had* braved them; she remembered that fiery exaltation as the flames sprang from her fingertips. She coughed, choking on the bugs, tasting their foulness.

'No!' They were . . . What had Osyth called them? *Illusion.* That was a weapon Janiva could also use. Fire erupted from her mouth; she breathed out flames like a dragon in a wall painting, scorching and shrivelling the crawling horrors. Flame poured from her fingers; she washed her hands in fire, drawing the flames around her like an enveloping cloak. Bugs cracked and hissed, popped and fell, blazing sparks, and were gone, leaving no ash.

Clean and whole, she stood, ablaze from head to toe, and heard her enemy's frustrated cry.

Next came a whining buzz, like angry bees, louder and closer until the ugly sound filled the cave and a host of flying, stinging things, not wasps or any creatures of true Creation but black and yellow streaks of poisoned malice, fell upon her like needles. She felt their venom thicken her blood so that every pulse-beat was agony.

Maggots and bugs, she thought, *these are her weapons.* And fire was the answer to these, too. She became a creature of fire with a core of flaming bone, and blood like molten metal coursed through her fiery flesh. The stinging tormentors flared and vanished.

Now there was only darkness, silence and numbing cold.

'Show yourself,' she cried.

From the shadows came a thick throaty giggle that made her skin crawl. Something was forming there, taking shape, human shape . . . but it was not human. Whatever had made her think Julitta would fight fair, face to face? The demon took on the witch's form but its skin was scaly as a lizard's, its eyes the colour of pus, and it had teeth and claws like a wolverine. Springing on

Janiva it sank its teeth into her shoulder and raked her back with talons an inch long.

She cried out and fell to her knees under the demon's weight. Her dream-body had no substance in the real world, but here it felt pain, and its wounds, deep and ugly, bled. Her hands scrabbled weakly at the demon's arms, feebly trying to pull away the cruel claws and the teeth grating on her bone.

She was so cold. Her strength was draining away, she could no longer summon fire and she had no weapon that could injure this spawn of Hell. If she lost consciousness now, in this world, she would never wake again in her own.

Oh, Richard, she thought, too late, *I love you.*

The demon picked the thought from her mind and shrieked with laughter, mimicking her voice in a mocking echo. 'Oh Richard . . . I love you . . . I lo-o-o-ve you . . .'

Who loves you, you black-hearted bitch? I am loved. Richard loves me, and Gilla. My mother loved me . . . Dame Alienor and Sir Guy . . . the folk at home . . .

She called to mind their faces, the people she had grown up with at Shawl. Their love for her, and hers for them, was a reservoir from which she could draw power: Father Osric, Roger, Tostig, Sybilla, the boy Peter, and the baby she had not been allowed to see but loved because he was Roger's son.

Strength filled her. The demon whined – she had it by the throat, tearing its claws from her flesh, its teeth from her shoulder – it twisted, squealing as she tightened her grip. Changing shape it became a great snake, its throat as thick as her thigh, coils flailing to encircle her. *Illusion*, she told herself, *lies*, as it transformed again, this time to something beaked and feathered, stinking of garbage on a hot day, slashing at her legs with taloned feet. *Lies, all lies . . .*

'Janiva! Don't!' It was Gilla's voice. Her hands were crushing the child's throat; the slight body struggled feebly against her, hands clutching at her wrists. 'Janiva, you're hurting me!'

'Gilla!' She could not help herself; she let go and clasped the child in her arms. Gilla nestled close, sobbing softly against her breast. As Janiva stroked the soft fair hair the girl raised her tear-wet face to Janiva and smiled . . . and bit her in the breast.

Fool! Tricks, lies! Pain transfixed her as the demon, a lizard-like thing with leathery wings, hung from her breast, grunting as it gnawed her flesh, seeking her heart while its small clawed hands kneaded obscenely at her, like a baby's.

On her brow the rune Osyth had marked, Eihwaz the yew-rune of magical defence, grew burning hot, and on her breast the rune Nauthiz, whose virtue was to disempower adversaries, scorched like a brand. She clutched at the neck of the squamous horror greedying on her flesh, but the creature's knife-edged ruff of scales cut her fingers, sliced her palms.

She felt the drag of her sleeping body, a desperate need to wake. If she abandoned the fight now she would never wake; Julitta and her demon would have won. 'Christ help me!' she gasped aloud. 'Mother of God, Mother of all, help me now!'

Her hands closed around the demon's narrow skull and squeezed. The creature squirmed, chewing at her. She clamped her bleeding fingers together and dug her thumbs into its eyes, fighting to keep her grip as her blood, like oil, made the scaly head as slippery as a peeled egg.

It seemed then that many voices, many faces, all the servants of the Mother who had dwelt in this sacred place, echoed her prayer. The cave rang with their shouting and her own as with a great cry she wrenched the demon's teeth from her flesh and squeezed with the very last of her strength. Its skull shattered. She heard the bones crack, felt them break between her hands. The creature squealed like a pig, then, horribly, whimpered like a mortally hurt child and hung lifeless, twitching, in the grip she could not slacken.

She heard far off a furious screaming, cry after cry that finally died in a despairing wail.

Tearing her locked fingers apart was like breaking the grip of a clump of ancient roots, but at last she shook off the shrivelling leathery carcass, now no bigger than a dead hen and its flesh – or whatever clothed its skeleton – fallen and dry, parchmenty skin over the disturbingly childlike bones.

'There were noises, my lord, and she cried out. She may be ill or hurt. The door's barred.'

Thibaut had fetched Breos from his bed, and the tentative light of dawn showed Lord William unbarbered and unwashed. For the first time Thibaut noticed streaks of white in his lord's grey hair.

'And my lord, that's not all. There's a man outside swears that the wi— that Lady Julitta has stolen his baby son.'

Lord William unclipped his purse. 'Give him this. Shut him up. Get rid of him.' He hammered on Julitta's door with his closed fist.

Just risen from their pallets, half awake, half dressed, his men – all but Bevis de Rennes, who wanted nothing to do with it and snored determinedly – avoided his eyes. Any one of them could have broken the door down, but not after what they'd heard. They had fought in battles and skirmishes uncounted – give them an enemy and these were happy men – but the sounds from the lady Julitta's room had put the fear of God into them.

Lord William kicked the door in.

Craning over his shoulder Thibaut saw Julitta's body sprawled across the bed. Dead, he thought, but no, she was breathing. Her shift was ripped and her throat purpled with the bruises of manual strangulation. Lord William had seen, had inflicted, marks like that and knew she hadn't done that to herself. There was no one else in the room. No one could have got out, unless he could pass through the slit-window, and only a kitten could squeeze through that.

'Who was in here?' Breos demanded.

'No one, my lord,' said Thibaut. 'We were just getting up when she started screaming; we all heard her.'

Lord William's foot knocked against something on the floor: Julitta's iron and silver box. The nerve in his jaw began jumping again. He heeled the door shut in Thibaut's face and stamped on the casket. There was a gush of cold foetid air and, he thought, a thick gloating chuckle that lifted the hair on his head.

He raised his foot. The crystal had cracked in halves and, as he looked, dissolved into dust.

Julitta coughed feebly and opened her eyes. Something was wrong. Her limbs felt leaden, her head ached violently and her throat hurt. She had been dreaming; a frightening dream full of confused images – flames, crawling things, voices echoing in a cave – and Agarel had been there.

Agarel . . .

It was an effort even to slide her hand under the bolster, groping for the reassuring solidity of the casket. It wasn't there. She sat up, gasping at the pain in her head, and pushed the bolster aside. It had gone. The floor . . .

She slid from the bed, her legs giving way under her weight. What was wrong? A sickness? She'd never been ill in her life. Crouching beside the bed she stared underneath, and her reaching hand grasped curls of dust, a crust of ancient bread, and nothing else.

'Are you looking for this?'

Lord William stood in the doorway, dangling the casket on its chain. Broken. Crushed.

'The stone . . .' She clutched her throat, croaking like an old woman. 'What have you *done* with it?' Grabbing the bedpost she pulled herself up, swaying on her feet.

'It broke. Some kind of stink came out of it and it turned to dust.'

Her eyes were shocked pools of darkness, face and lips bloodless. Shivering, she pulled one of the sheets off the bed and wrapped it round herself like a mantle.

'What have you *done*?'

'What have *you* done, bitch, you and your devil in a cage? Used me to get the Banner, promised to save my wife, and all the while driving me mad with your filthy spells and potions in my wine! God rot all sorcerers! There's talk against you out there. A baby missing,' he said, 'and a man who'll swear you stole it. Can you produce it, my lady, alive?'

'What do you mean? You were there, you know what we did!'

'I know what *you* did.'

'For you! At your command! I'll tell—'

'Who will believe you? You're already condemned to death, remember? The king was displeased with you for practising your devils' arts on *him*.' He stepped forward, and she backed away.

'Don't touch me! I swear I'll—'

'You'll what?' he jeered. 'Strike me blind? I don't think you can. I think you've lost your powers.' He looked at the smashed casket with disgust and tossed it on the bed.

Julitta began to panic, trying frantically to remember even the simplest of spells to stop this nightmare, but her thoughts moved sluggishly as if through glue, and all the while at the back of her mind a voice murmured, '*All that you are, all that you have, all that you love you shall lose.*' It sounded like her own voice.

Lord William ripped a length of linen from the sheet and pushed her onto the bed, flipping her onto her belly to bind her hands at her back. With another strip he stopped her mouth, cramming material in until he could force no more between her teeth, and winding the tail end of the strip tightly over her mouth, knotting it hard.

'I was going to give you to my men,' he said. 'But you're too rank for their taste and I've got a better idea.'

He hauled her outside, his men watching silently from the doorway. No one protested or followed as he dragged her into the willows in the direction of the lake. Sir Bevis, who'd got up at last, said, 'Good riddance,' spat, crossed himself and went back inside to his breakfast, and presently the others did the same.

A coracle carrying two hooded figures was making its erratic way across the water from Ynys Gwydion for the day's supplies. As it neared the shore Julitta began to struggle, a dreadful awareness in her eyes. The lepers jumped out and beached their craft.

'Good morrow,' said Lord William. They bowed awkwardly, and one grunted by way of response.

'Poor fellows,' Breos continued, smiling. 'Such a lonely life. No family, no friends, no women.' To Julitta he added casually, 'That's the thing about lepers. As long as they still have men's parts they have men's desires. You do, don't you?' he asked the silent pair. 'And to add to their misery their desires are stronger, oh, much

much stronger than those of living men. They cannot be satisfied, I'm told.'

He picked her up like a child. Over the gag her frantic eyes implored him. She thrashed in his arms like a great landed fish and he nearly dropped her, but staggered to the coracle and threw her in.

'There,' he said to the lepers. 'You fancy her? She's yours. I'm sure you know some quiet and private place where you won't be disturbed. She's fair, I promise you, under the gag. You might want to leave that on, by the way, if you don't want her screaming for help.'

The hooded heads nodded eagerly. Their errand forgotten, they shoved the boat back into the water and scrambled in. One of them thrust the woman down with his feet to hold her still, and the other wielded the paddle furiously, but instead of returning to Ynys Gwydion he steered the little craft around the western end of the island. Squinting against the sun, Breos watched until it was out of sight.

Bevis de Rennes was waiting with news. 'Word has come from Fishguard. The king has returned. He's on his way to Bristol.'

'What will become of her?' Janiva asked, warming her cold hands on the cup Osyth gave her. She sniffed the hot brew. 'What's in this?'

'Rosemary and gentian to comfort your heart, valerian to ease your mind, and honey: that's good for everything. You had a hard struggle. As for *her*, if she lives she'll be powerless. She's broke; the curse she put on you is broke, and every other curse she wrought.'

And indeed, in the distant mountains of Razes bells were ringing for the miraculous recovery of the Duchess Urraca, new-woken from her deathly sleep; and the ill fortune and ill health of many folk, men and women both, wherever Julitta de Beauris had dwelt, mended from that hour.

Janiva sipped her drink. She was utterly exhausted and longed only to sleep. The marks of the demon's teeth and claws had almost disappeared, fading from her flesh as if they had never been. The drink coursed through her body, warming and strengthening her.

'It is all your doing.' She set the cup down and took Osyth's worn old hand, its skin like pleated silk, and kissed it. 'How can I ever thank you enough?'

'You did your own fightin, once you knew the way of it. Now you can go back to your home and your lover.'

'He's not my lover.'

'Ain't he? Well then, the man who loves you, and you *don't* love.'

'You're right. I do love him.'

'Wants to marry you, don't he? How long are you goin to keep sendin him away, tearin your own heart like that nasty imp of hers tore at you, eh? You're young. You should be wife and mother, teachin the old ways to your own daughters while you grow in your power.'

'There's so much I want to learn!'

Osyth snorted. 'Call down rain when fields lie dry, hold off storms to save the harvest? Bring the sick to wholeness, take pain from the world?'

'Yes!' Janiva longed to do all that: to turn the wind, to drive the clouds, to shape-shift and run through the fields as a hare or soar above the trees on hawks' wings. She could almost feel it, that power, tingling in her hands and so nearly hers, hers for the asking and for the price. There was always a price. The sudden hunger shook her body and soul, and in that moment she understood Julitta de Beauris and the greed for power that didn't care what the price was or who paid it.

'I can't have both,' she said. 'Love and power.'

'Can't you?' Osyth asked. 'Is your heart so small?'

Chapter 52

'Pack!' said Lord William.

His men looked up eagerly. 'Where are we going, my lord?'

'I ride to Bristol,' Breos said. 'I take the Pendragon Banner to the king.'

'The king? But my lord . . .'

'His quarrel's with me, not you. Your first loyalty was to me, your lord, and you've been staunch. No blame now if you think best to seek your fortunes with another lord. Go with my blessing. Who rides with me?'

They looked at one another and at him. 'I will.' 'And I.' 'Me too.' 'And me.'

There were tears in Lord William's eyes; he had always wept easily. He knuckled them away. 'Then we'll make our dash tonight, they won't expect anything after dark. What are you waiting for?' This to Thibaut, who had made no move. 'You heard me! Pack!' Lord William slapped the young man's cheek, not hard but it stung.

Thibaut had been the youngest of the half-dozen well born squires in Lord William's service. The rest had been removed by their fathers at the first whispers of Breos's impending disgrace and only Thibaut, whose stepfather was glad to be rid of him, stayed on, having nowhere else to go.

From the age of seven he had unthinkingly taken his lord's side. Graduating from page to esquire, he fought against Lord William's enemies, for his friends, and single-mindedly served his interests. More recently he had shared his disgrace and poverty, and at his command had burned villages, raided towns, sacked churches and hanged men.

The sack of the Penitent Sisters' priory had started him thinking, as a midwife's slap will jolt a sluggish newborn into squalling life. Robbing travellers, some of them pilgrims, like any common thief, filled him with shame, and the torture and killing of the old priest at Tresaint, too terrified to say a Mass, sickened him to his soul. The murder of the baby was the last straw.

When everything was packed into panniers he laid Lord William's sword on the table next to the other one, the crusader's sword in its shabby sheath. There remained only the great chest to empty but Lord William had the key of that.

His brooding had come to a gloomy conclusion: he would not go with Lord William. And that led to a second and even gloomier conclusion: no one else would take him on.

It was different for the knights. They could take service under another lord without so much as a raised eyebrow. Not so a squire. No one would employ a squire who had deserted his lord. It would make no difference that his lord was a traitor, rebel, murderer, and had vowed himself to the Devil in the hearing of at least a dozen witnesses. Thibaut would be outcast. He'd never be knighted, never make his fortune, never win a lady's heart or a king's gratitude. His future had suddenly become an endless desert of nevers.

'Thibaut de Sens?' men would say. 'Oh, him. The one who abandoned his lord.' No one would speak for him.

Unless . . .

His gaze returned to the shabby sheath. Lord William's voice echoed in his mind. *'You should have left him his sword.'*

'Shove over,' said Bane. 'There's scrambled egg and bacon at the kitchen, if you hurry.'

Havloc took his bowl and joined the queue. Someone tacked on behind him. Up at the front a voice shouted, 'Next!' and the line moved forward a pace.

'Don't do anything silly,' a voice breathed hotly against Havloc's ear. Something – it must be a knife – prodded his back at kidney level.

Havloc stiffened. 'I've no money!'

'I don't want your money. I want to talk to your master.' They moved forward again.

'Who are you?'

'Just don't yell or try some stupid trick. I'm Thibaut de Sens, squire to William de Breos. It was me took your horses in the greenwood.'

'You?' Havloc spun round regardless of the knife and saw that all Thibaut had in his hand was a comb. 'I ought to punch your head,' he said furiously. 'You're no better than a bloody outlaw! A thief, that's what you are!'

'All right, don't tell the world,' hissed Thibaut. 'I *have* to talk to your master.'

'Next!' The woman in front of Havloc held up her bowl to be filled.

'Get your dinner,' Thibaut said. 'Go back to your hut; I'll come there. Tell Sir Richard I mean no harm.' He gave Havloc a shove and walked off in the opposite direction.

'Next!'

Staring at Thibaut's retreating back, Havloc didn't hear.

'Next!' bellowed the cook again. 'Oy, cloth ears,' waving his ladle and spattering Havloc with bits of egg, 'there's plenty poor sods want it if you don't!'

'I remember you,' said Straccan, looking intently at the young captain of thieves. 'How did you know I was here?'

Thibaut had brought a long bundle, loosely wrapped in his cloak, which he laid on the bench. 'I recognised him,' jerking his chin at Havloc, 'and my lord's witch said you'd be coming.'

'Witch? Ah, yes. Where *is* the lady Julitta? I've not seen her.'

'My lord took her away this morning and came back alone. He killed her, I think.'

'She's not easy to kill.'

'She bespelled him,' Thibaut said. 'She put stuff in his wine. He was always harsh, but now he has done things—' He broke off abruptly and occupied his shaking hands with the bundle. Letting the cloak fall he offered the crusader's sword to Straccan. 'Sir, this is yours.'

Surprised, Straccan drew and hefted his sword, relieved and gladdened by its familiar weight and balance. 'Good,' he said, sheathing it again, his fingers caressing the leather. 'You stole our horses as well, and everything they carried.'

'Your horses are here, and the Banner.'

Straccan's hand stilled on the scabbard. 'Where is it?'

'Locked in the chest in my lord's chamber and the key on a cord round his neck.'

'Tricky,' observed Bane.

Straccan held up the sword. 'Why give me this?'

Thibaut clasped his hands together, white-knuckled. 'I can't serve Lord William any more.'

'Doubtless you have your reasons.'

'Yes.' There were things he couldn't speak of, the dead baby for one, and the dreams. Would they stop if the witch was dead? He hoped so. 'Sir Richard, I beg a favour.'

'What is it?'

'W-will you speak for me, to any friend of yours, to give me some place in his household? Not as squire, of course – I know I can never be a knight now – but any honest employment.'

'For a squire who has deserted his lord?'

Thibaut flushed, then paled as his hopes died. 'No,' he said, look-ing at the floor. 'Of course not. I shouldn't have asked. I'm sorry.'

'Will you stand with me when I challenge him?'

Thibaut looked even more miserable. 'No, sir. I can't take up arms against him.'

'Not even for a place?'

Thibaut shook his head. 'When I entered my lord's service I took an oath never to raise my hand against him.'

'Then you should keep it. If he has the Banner, why's he still here?'

'We— He leaves tonight.'

Straccan swore. Bruno von Koln and his troop would probably be a match for Breos and his, but if it came to a battle there were no certainties. Breos could still escape. He had a galley waiting somewhere; if he got to it only God could stop him from taking the Banner to Brittany, and with God there were no certainties either.

'Where's my horse?'

'In the stable behind our hall.' That too was guarded, always a man at the door. 'The fourth stall on the right. He's muzzled and hobbled.'

Despite his anger, Straccan grinned at that. 'Gave you a bit of trouble, did he? Good for him.'

'We thought he'd kick the stable wall out. He killed one of my men and hurt four others badly. The grooms are terrified of him.'

Straccan nodded, unsurprised, 'Well, boy, he'll be wondering where you've got to. You'd better go back now and carry on as usual.' As Thibaut turned miserably away Straccan added, 'If I get out of here alive I'll speak for you, I promise.' Thibaut began stammering his thanks but Straccan raised a hand to stop his flow. 'You spared our lives at the ford. I'll not be in your debt.'

'Locked in a chest,' Bane mused when Thibaut had gone. 'And nothing round the back but slit-windows. How do we get in?'

'We can't. We'll have to winkle him out, him and the Banner. I've a thought . . . I'll need grease – drippings from the kitchen – a bucketful. Havloc, will you get that?' As Havloc left he called after him, 'Better make it two!'

'Will you challenge him now?' Bane asked.

'It's now or never.' Damned if he'd let the bastard walk away. It was too much to ask!

'What about his men?'

'If I can draw him onto the path that leads up to the shrine they won't be much help to him. One man could hold off an army there. And thanks to that wretched boy I have my sword back.'

Raising it to his lips he kissed the crossguard. Sulien's warning flickered in his mind again, to be doused by his rising rage. 'That murdering cur did his damnedest to kill me. He's had his bloody hands on my sword and his fat arse on my horse, and if they think

I'll stand meekly by and let him get away with my relic, they can think again!'

'What?' said Bane. 'Who?'

'Oh, nothing.'

When he'd killed Breos he would ride straight to Holystone and get his daughter, and to Shawl for Janiva, and take them to safety. Where? Blaise d'Etranger would give them refuge, and in Scotland they'd be out of John's reach. After the business with Rainard de Soulis last year the Scottish king had offered him an estate near Coldinghame. He'd take him up on it. As for the Banner, Bruno could take that to the king.

Havloc set the buckets down carefully.

'What now?' said Bane.

'Eh?' No, it would never work; John's reach was too long. Hadn't he plucked Mahaut de Breos from King William's weak hands? There was no way out.

He scowled. 'I need rags. This'll do.' Pulling the voluminous leper-gown over his head he ripped the seams apart and started tearing the material into long strips. 'Havloc, will you do this? Roll them into balls, about *this* big, not too tight. Leave an end sticking out.' He demonstrated. 'Like this. That's it. When you've done, leave em round the back of Breos's hall, with the grease.' He had come to a decision. He would challenge Breos and if the rebel lord fought fairly, one of them would die. It had better not be *him*. But as it wasn't like Breos to do anything fairly, he needed a fall-back plan. 'I need your help, Hawkan. Can you find a hurdle? I've got an idea, something you can help me set up before I get Zingiber out of there. You'll have to get the guard's attention when I slip into the stable.'

Bane nodded. 'Right. Then what?'

'Keep it while I set the place on fire.'

'I know two *sure* ways to get a crowd,' said Bane when he returned, grubby and sweating, two hours later. 'One's a pair of copulating dogs, the other's a fight. And I don't see any dogs.' He eyed Havloc up and down, assessing his height and strength. 'How about a bit of wrestling?'

'*Me?*'

'Don't worry, I'll try not to hurt you.'

Havloc frowned at a vagrant memory. 'I can fight, I think. With sticks.'

'Quarterstaves? That's an idea. The lepers use ash poles, there'll be spares around somewhere. Hang around near the stable. I'll be right back.'

He returned with a couple of sturdy poles, each about eight feet long.

'Here. Bit of friendly sport, all right? Just do your best,' Bane said cheerfully. 'I'll make it look good.'

He grasped his stave in both hands and feinted at Havloc who, with his head tilted as if listening to a voice only he could hear, appeared hopelessly unready. But at Bane's lunge he sprang back instinctively, dodging the blow and twirling his stave like a mere straw, to meet Bane's with an almighty crack. Bored and fidgety, Breos's guard outside the stable perked up and began offering encouragement.

Bane staggered back, and before he could recover Havloc had thrust the pole between his ankles, bringing him down. He fell heavily, winded and astonished. Laughing, Havloc tossed his stave high overhead and caught it one-handed.

As they edged along the side wall of the stable, staves revolving, the guard followed, loud in criticism. The rattle and crack of the staves attracted others as well, and soon ten or a dozen were cheering, jeering and offering advice.

'Where'd you learn to use a stick?' Bane panted.

'My brother taught me,' Havloc gasped without thinking. A startled expression crossed his face. 'My brother! I've got a brother! Alaric! I *remember*!'

Taking advantage of his distraction Bane shoved his stave under Havloc's arm, twisting it to jerk him off balance, following that up with a thrust that sent him reeling into the applauding crowd, who received him with yells of derision, and launched him back, Havloc laughing like a lunatic.

'Master Bane! I remember!'

Bane feinted left and struck right, a tactic that usually brought results, but Havloc was ready for it. Bane found himself sitting in the dust with his opponent grinning at him like a village idiot.

'What d'you remember?'

'All of it! My mother, my brother, old Drogo, Alis . . . Get hold of this.'

Bane grasped the end of Havloc's stave, kindly proffered to help him up. Another mistake. The stick was thrust forward with Havloc's powerful muscles behind it, and to his disgust Bane found himself on his arse again.

'You're good at this.'

'I know.'

Jabbing, flailing, jumping in to attack and skipping aside to evade, they worked their way round to the front of Breos's hall, where the guard at the door called to his comrades inside to come and watch the fun.

'What about the cup? Ooof!' A hard poke in the belly took Bane's breath away.

'Ugil dug it up in his onion patch.'

Bane managed to get in a couple of whacks but this was a fight he wasn't likely to win. Just as well it was friendly. His ribs would be black and blue.

'Drogo sent me to Ludlow to sell it,' Havloc panted, as the staves whirled and cracked. 'I took it to a goldsmith.'

Marvelling, he remembered every shining detail, the goldsmith's sly eyes . . . *'Gold? Never. Brass. Threepence, take it or leave it.'* When Havloc said no the man got nasty. *'Stolen, ain't it? I'll take it off your hands — a favour — shilling. It's better than the gallows.'* When Havloc got up angrily to go the man began cringing. *'I meant no offence. Times are hard. Stay, have a cup of wine with me, show there's no hard feelings.'*

When he'd left the room to fetch wine Havloc took up a pen and a scrap of parchment and copied the words on the cup.

'I thought I'd show them to a priest, to find out what they meant.' He sidestepped Bane's stave and fetched him a painful crack on the shoulder that numbed his arm. 'I slipped out but he sent his bullies after me, two hefty sods. Ow!' Bane grinned; he'd got one in.

'I hid along the river,' Havloc gasped. 'The bank gave way and I fell in. I can't swim.' Stave spinning like a windmill he advanced on Bane. 'I nearly drowned, but I got out somehow . . . ' *Whack! Crack!* 'And ran into those thieving bastards on my way back to the inn.'

Pilgrims and guests from the hospice had come to swell the crowd, along with some of the students and sick-hall attendants, Alis among them, heart in mouth for her sweetheart.

Even inside the stable with its thick stone walls Straccan could hear the shouting and the sharp crack of wood on wood. The horses twitched their ears and shifted their feet nervously as he stepped quietly along behind them to the fourth stall. Zingiber whickered softly and blew a snuffle of greeting as Straccan unbuckled the muzzle, fondling the velvety nose and whispering into the stiff forward-cocked ear.

'Did you miss me, pilgrim?' As he cast off the hobble Zingiber snorted and tossed his head, pleased to be rid of the tiresome thing. 'Hush, now,' whispered Straccan. 'Let's go.'

He led the stallion to the door, unhooking the lanthorn that hung there – a bit of luck, that – and stuck his head out cautiously. No one was in sight but there were fifty yards of open ground between the stable and the nearest trees. Anyone might come along, or glance out of a window in Lord William's quarters at just the wrong moment. With a quick prayer, *Lord, keep them busy!* he trotted Zingiber into the shelter of the willows, expecting all the time to hear a yell behind him, or feel the impact of an arrow between his shoulder blades.

The crowd had grown to more than forty vociferous spectators, whooping and making wagers. Even the great Lord William had come out, with his squire, irritated at first by the noise but hooked like all the rest by the action.

Behind the hall Straccan dunked the balls of rag in grease and held the trailing ends to the flame of the lanthorn. As each one caught he dropped it through the slit-windows. They fizzed and sizzled in the dry rushes, smelling strongly of bacon. No shout of alarm was raised. Spearing a couple of spitting fireballs on his sword he stretched up as high as he could reach to jam them firmly into the reed thatch. It was dry and brittle, and after only a few moments flames were rippling along the roof, pale in the afternoon sunlight, crackling hungrily as they licked their way up to the ridge.

On the far side Havloc saw smoke rise above the roof and come rolling down like a wave, while out of the thatch with a tremendous squeaking poured a torrent of rats, racing ahead of the smoke and leaping off when they reached the edge of the roof. Smoke billowed suddenly from the door, and someone yelled, 'Fire!'

The crowd's attention switched abruptly to the fire, and to the escaping rats fleeting between their feet. In the press of screaming women and stamping men Bane and Havloc leaned on their staves, out of puff and sweating. Lord William plunged for the door, evading his knights who tried to stop him, and was swallowed by the smoke. His men hesitated, but leapt back as part of the roof fell in and a choking gust of smoke and blazing reeds belched from the doorway.

Sulien came running, shouting, 'Is anyone in there?'

'Lord William,' cried Thibaut.

Coughing, cursing, eyes streaming and face and tunic black with soot, Lord William came stumbling out, clasping a leather satchel. With an almighty *whumpf!* the rest of the roof fell in, and flames leaped up to engulf what was left.

Chapter 53

'William de Breos!'

Where the path to the shrine began its tortuous climb a man stood, with a sheathed sword in his hand.

Breos coughed sootily and spat. 'Straccan!' Then he grinned, teeth shining in his blackened face. 'Julitta said you'd come.'

'Is she dead?'

'Dead?' He laughed. 'Worse than that – in hell. What do you want?'

'To challenge you!'

Sulien cried 'Sir Richard! No!'

'Get the horses,' Breos ordered. His men ran to obey.

'Let all bear witness,' Straccan shouted. 'I name you thief, desecrator, murderer, and I challenge you to single combat, here, now!' In the stunned silence he cast down his gage: a strip of rusty black woollen cloth, knotted around two rings.

Breos glowered at it. 'What's that?'

'One ring I took from Prioress Heloise's dead hand.'

'I didn't kill her!'

'As good as. The other belonged to Robert Wace, and him you *did* kill! I see you still carry his brand,' he sneered. 'A pettifogging clerk!' Steel rang as he drew his sword, letting the scabbard fall. 'What say you? Will you fight or cry craven?'

Breos recognised the sword and ground his teeth with rage. Whoever had played Judas would die for it as soon as he'd killed this meddling nobody who by rights should be dead already. His men rounded the far end of the hall in a tight bunch, their horses' hooves raising clouds of ash, and Bevis de Rennes spurred to his lord's side, scattering the crowd, leading Breos's own stallion.

'Stand and fight!' Straccan yelled furiously, as Lord William swung into the saddle and hooked the rescued satchel over the pommel. 'Will you ride off, coward, butcher of nuns and priests?'

'Let me take him, my lord,' begged Bevis, but Lord William's blood was up.

'No! He's mine!'

Standing in his stirrups he shouted his battle cry, *'Homo Dei!'* Veins bulged at his temples – the medicus would have reached for his lancet had he been there – and his face was the colour of damsons. He raked spurs along his stallion's sides so that the beast squealed and reared, dancing on its hind legs while its rider clung like a burr. Then, like a battering ram, he charged at Straccan, drawing his sword with an echoing whine and tossing the sheath away.

As the great horse rushed upon him Straccan backed up the narrow path. Its steepness barely checked the stallion's way, but the barrel of penitential pebbles Straccan kicked over did. The horse slipped and slid, pebbles rolling under its steel-shod hooves. Scrabbling for purchase, it went down hard on its side.

For a heavy man, Breos was quick. Kicking his feet free of the stirrups he jumped away from the heavy horse and its thrashing legs. The stallion rolled right over before it could get up again, shaking itself and looking embarrassed.

'Foul!' Breos bellowed. 'A foul trick!'

Straccan was several feet above him on the path. Blowing like a bellows Breos rushed at him, wielding his sword two-handed, like an axe, in a tremendous blow that would have cleft his enemy from shoulder to waist had Straccan not caught the blade on his own. Edge screeched along edge and slid away unblooded.

'My lord! Sir Richard!' Sulien shouted. 'You must stop this!' He went unheeded as a moth.

The might of Breos's blow – he was the heavier man – jarred Straccan's wrists and forced him back, but turning, he brought his sword round and up to deflect the next blow, driven back once more by the weight behind it.

The turn of the path took them out of sight of the watchers below. Grunts and gasps and the clang of steel on steel could be heard, growing fainter as they fought their way up the narrow track. Bevis dismounted and beckoned to two of his archers; sword in hand, with the men following, he started up the path after his lord.

Straccan had drawn first blood, a long shallow cut across his opponent's ribs that would have done for him had he not jerked back. The gash bled freely but not enough to slow him down. Breos's point had pierced Straccan's thigh, but the wound hadn't bled much. They'd done taunting each other, saving their breath instead.

Straccan had killed enemies in many battles and skirmishes, and fought for his life on dozens of other occasions, beating off the murderous attacks of outlaws, pirates and even cannibals, but seldom had he felt such loathing for a foe. The tortured corpse of Tresaint's old priest, the cracked shell of Mother Heloise's skull and the still face of the king's clerk kept rising to his mind's eye; he could not be rid of them. This butcher had killed them, he must pay. He parried another great killing stroke, and backed away uphill again. Breos came on.

Feet were pounding up the path, not yet in sight. Breos's men were coming, and would not hold off while Straccan and their lord fought. This was what Straccan had expected, and his contingency plan was ready. Head down, he cannoned into Breos, bringing them both down and knocking Breos's sword from his grip. Lord William lunged for it, but Straccan reached it at the same instant. Breos elbowed him in the face and snatched up his sword. Scooping up a handful of grit Straccan flung it in Breos's face. Blinded, he lost his footing and fell on his arse.

As he struggled up, cursing, he saw Straccan disappearing round the next turn. They couldn't be far from the shrine. He had him now! There was nowhere for the bastard to run; he'd finish him there. Suddenly there was a rumbling, rushing noise that reminded

Lord William of a battle-charge, thundering hooves and the roaring of men about to kill or die. Under his feet the ground quivered and up ahead someone – Straccan, who else? – cried out in alarm. Breos charged round the last twist in the path, where the shrine had stood for six hundred years.

It wasn't there.

The rock ledge was scoured bare. Not a fragment remained of the wicker shelter, the statue of the saint or the perpetual fire. All had gone, swept with the landslide from above into the gorge. And Straccan with them.

'God's name,' he gasped, breathless and astonished, as Bevis de Rennes and his archers came panting up behind him.

'What happened, my lord?'

'A rockfall . . .' Thank God it hadn't happened when he was here just a few hours ago. Another sign that God had not cast him off.

'Did he go down with it?' Bevis asked.

'Must have.'

They inched to the edge and peered down. Far below the debris of the rockfall looked insignificant.

'Can you see him?'

'Aye, there! Lying to the left of the stone.'

'Where? I don't see him.'

'There, me lord!'

Something pale moved down there. A sheep? No, too long: a man.

'Shoot!' Breos cried.

They strung their bows, sighted, drew and let go. The pale shape jerked as the arrows struck. Its legs kicked. It lay still.

'Did you hit him?'

'Bleeding, lord,' said one archer, seeing a spreading stain.

'Christ, you've got good eyes,' said Breos, glaring down. 'Shoot again.'

Two more shafts whipped down, and this time the body didn't move.

Chapter 54

Bane reached the site of the shrine out of breath and with a ferocious stitch in his side. He paused momentarily on the rock ledge, bending, hands on knees to ease the stitch, eyeing the devastation with pleased surprise. He'd never thought it would work.

As soon as he had breath for it he whistled two clear notes. An answer came from further up and apparently out of the ground.

Straccan's wounded leg had stiffened, and other cuts he hadn't even noticed at the time had begun to burn and throb. He was huddled in a cramped hollow among wiry roots, concealed by a curtain of overhanging heather. Earth coated him, stuck to the blood on his shirt and breeches, and he crawled stiffly from his hiding place like a resurrected corpse at Judgement Day.

Bane helped him stand. 'Are you all right?'

'I'll mend. Help me down. He's gone?'

'Gone, yes.'

Something in his voice made Straccan stop. 'What?' And again, as Bane hesitated. '*What?*'

'He's taken Alis.'

Straccan lurched and would have fallen but for Bane's bony shoulder.

'God's blood! How?'

'Easy does it. Lean on me or you'll have us both arse over tit.'

'Damn it, Hawkan, what *happened?*'

'That German challenged him.' Bane panted the story as they descended the path, remembering as he told it Bruno on his horse in the gateway, a solitary plug in the bottleneck, in full mail and with lance couched. 'Breos snatched her up in front of him, said to let him pass or he'd cut her throat, and he'd kill her if they followed. Havloc tried to stop him – fetched him a hell of a crack with his stave – but they rode him down.' He could still see that, too: Havloc's body tumbling under the horses' hooves like a broken scarecrow.

'Is he dead?'

'No, bruised but . . . Well, you'll see. Slow down a bit, it's steep here.'

'I must go after him, get her back.' All this contrivance and mummery had been for nothing; he needn't have bothered. He was going to have to kill Breos after all.

'Mind these bloody pebbles!'

They were at the foot of the path. Many more people had swelled the crowd, staring and pointing at Straccan, and there was Havloc, arguing with Bruno von Koln, gesticulating and looking angry.

'We heard the fall,' Sulien said. 'Lord William said you went down with it.'

'That was a trick, something Bane and I set up. It all depended on whether I could get get Breos up there.'

'But they saw your body. They shot you. And you're hurt . . . Your leg.'

'I'm all right. That was a dummy, Garnier saw to it. Havloc!'

Havloc's face was bruised, his clothes were thick with dust and there was blood in his hair, but he seemed otherwise unhurt and shouldered through the crowd, ignoring the people who reached out to touch him, hoping a bit of his luck might rub off on them.

'Sir Richard, he's got Alis!'

'We'll get her back.'

'He'll kill her!'

'She got him through the gate. After that she'll only slow him down. He'll drop her off after a couple of miles.' He hoped to God he was right. 'Hawkan, get the horses. Zingiber's down by the lake, near the boats. I'm sorry, Sulien. I did my best, but it looks like I'm going to have to kill him after all.'

Sulien held out a wallet. 'For the king,' he said. 'The ring and the letter.'

Straccan took it. 'I burned one of your halls, wrecked your shrine and broke the laws of this Sanctuary. I ask your pardon, Sulien. If I can, I'll make amends.'

'You did what you had to, Sir Richard. And for all of it, except breaking Sanctuary, you had royal licence. As for burning the hall, it hardly matters.' He looked around bleakly, saying, 'All this will be gone soon,' and walked away.

Straccan saw the leper-master at the edge of the crowd. 'Garnier, you did well.'

'It wants neither brains nor brawn to pull a few cords and twitch a mannikin's limbs,' Garnier said. 'And the statue of the saint is undamaged. When it's back in the shrine pilgrims will have another miracle to marvel at. You are going after the girl?'

'I hope to find her unharmed. He has no reason to carry her far, still less to kill her.'

Garnier's eyes regarded him sceptically through the holes in his hood. 'I pray you're right, Sir Richard.'

The crowd parted again to let Bane through, bringing the horses. Straccan took a small parchment packet from inside his belt. 'Garnier, will you give this to Sulien? It may be he can use it to save this place.'

'What is it?'

'A thread from a napkin stained with the blood of Christ. It came from the Pendragon Banner.'

After all, between leaving the saint's island and encountering Thibaut at the ford he'd had the Banner in his possession for two nights and a day and he wasn't a man to ignore opportunity. With no apparent damage to the relic he'd managed to abstract half a dozen precious threads.

'Why didn't you give it to him yourself?' Garnier put the little packet in his purse,

'He's a bit annoyed with me.'

'God go with you, Sir Richard. I will pray for Mistress Alis, and for you.' Garnier bowed and walked away.

At Straccan's back Bruno von Koln murmured, 'The poor devil. That is a living hell.'

Hell indeed, thought Straccan. *What could be worse?* But a monstrous suspicion began shaping as he watched the big cloaked figure limping away. What had Breos said about Julitta? '*Worse than dead – in hell.*'

'Oh my God!' He knew what Lord William had done; he knew where Julitta was. Straccan opened his mouth to call Garnier back and tell him, and shut it again.

Justice had been served.

They rode hard for the first two miles, across open heath where nothing could be hidden, but after that sapling trees and thick underbrush closed in upon the road. Alis could be hurt or dead, and lying only a few feet away and no one would see her.

They slowed and Straccan began calling. 'Alis! Hoy, Alis!' The others took it up, stopping frequently to listen for an answering cry.

'Alis!'

'Hoy-hoy-hoy! Alis!'

Again and again Havloc spurred his horse into the scrub, urging it through brambles that left bloody scratches on its legs and belly.

'Alis!'

Straccan began to despair.

Three miles from the Hidden Valley Havloc found a man and mule lurking unsuccessfully behind a clump of hazels and dragged him out, goggle-eyed with terror. Yes, he'd seen Lord William and his men. He'd prudently left the track and hidden and he'd been trying to hide again in case this lot were no better.

'Was there a girl with him?' Havloc demanded. 'A young woman in a blue gown?'

'I saw no woman.'

They rode on, calling, listening.

Lord Christ, Holy Virgin, Straccan prayed. *Let her be safe!* But his heart felt cold and shrunken with dread.

Bruno saw it first – something blue, hanging from a branch up ahead – and called out, pointing. With a cry Havloc plunged towards it. By the time the others came up with him he'd got it down and was rocking back and forth in grief, Alis's blue surcote crushed against his breast. There was blood on his hands and on the gown.

Tears poured down his face as he looked up at Straccan. 'He's killed her! Alis, oh God, Alis!' He pressed the gown to his face, sobbing.

'Let me see.' Straccan drew it gently from Havloc's grasp. Blood had soaked the hem of the surcote but he could find no rent from knife or sword. 'It's whole,' he said, 'and look.' He indicated two bloody smudges. 'See here, she was kneeling; she knelt in the blood. Alis!' He shouted, reining Zingiber about. 'It's not her blood.' He shouted again, 'Alis!'

Off to their right they heard an answering cry.

Following a track they found her sitting on the ground, cradling Thibaut's head in her lap. His right arm was swathed in blood-stained fabric torn from the hem of her kirtle. He looked dead but he breathed.

'Oh God, thank God!' Havloc flung himself down and clasped her in his arms. 'Are you all right?'

She nodded. 'I knew you'd come.'

Bruno knelt by the squire. 'His arm . . . Vat happened?'

'Lord William cut his hand off. I tied my girdle round it. I took off my surcote and tied it to a branch where you'd see it. Will he die?'

'Not if we can get him back to Sulien,' Havloc said. 'It's less than five miles. Captain Bruno, Alis and I will take him back if you'll lend two of your men to help.'

'Ralph, Villiam, go vith them. Take care of him.'

Thibaut opened his eyes and stared at Straccan. 'My lord said . . . dead.'

'A mistake he's made before,' Straccan said.

'Not easy to kill,' Thibaut whispered, and his pallid lips managed a smile.

'What happened?'

298

'His horse . . . lame. He ordered me down, took mine. "Judas",
he said.' Thibaut paused, gathering strength. 'He drew . . . sword. I
threw my hands up. Funny, didn't feel it, just saw . . . blood.'

'They rode on,' Alis said. 'Lord William's horse is here
somewhere.'

'Vere are they going?' Bruno asked.

'His galley,' Thibaut said. 'Somewhere on the Usk . . . beyond
Abergavenny.'

'Vunce he gets aboard ve vill haf lost him. Ve cannot follow him
to Brittany.'

'No,' said Thibaut. 'Bristol.'

'Bristol? Why?' Straccan asked.

'He's taking the Banner to the king.'

'Are you sure?'

'Yes . . . In exchange for Lady Mahaut and his son.'

'Ready to go, sir.' Bruno's men, capable in that as in all else, had
contrived a litter from saplings and slung it between their horses.
Now they lifted Thibaut onto it.

'Where shall we rejoin, sir?'

Straccan butted in. 'If we ride hard, Bruno, we can get to Bristol
before he does.'

'He still has the Banner,' the German objected.

'Yes, he's doing our job for us. We'll be there to greet him.'

Bruno thought for a moment. 'Bristol, then.'

Havloc and Alis were talking, and as Straccan mounted they
came hand in hand to his side.

'We're going back to Devilstone when we've seen Thibaut to
safety,' Havloc said. 'Sir Richard, I remember everything: I didn't
kill Alis's father. I was afraid; I didn't know if I had. Even after the
Hearing I was still afraid. But I didn't kill Sir Drogo.'

'I never thought you did.'

Alis took the gold cup from her purse. 'Sir Richard, will you take
this and sell it for me? Whatever you get for it I'll share with my
sisters.'

Straccan took the cup. 'I'll do that, Mistress Alis. Tell Thibaut I'll
not forget my promise. God go with you both.'

Chapter 55

As they rode in through the castle gate they had to huddle up side-ways to make room for a group of riders spurring towards them, half a dozen knights led by a square heavy man on a black stallion who rode head-down as if charging an enemy force. The riders thundered past, causing shrieks of alarm as people scrambled out of the way. Straccan, seeing their pennants in the flaring torchlight, said, 'That was the Earl of Derby. Breos's nephew.'

'I vonder vy he's here.'

They soon found out. The castle was buzzing with the news. The earl had brought a letter from Lord William, what it said no one knew, and the king had agreed to meet Breos on the morrow.

'I must see the king at once,' Straccan demanded. But the king had gone to bed, they were told, and short of a French in-vasion *nothing* would wrench him from his bedmate's arms until morning.

Castle and town were crowded. Earls and barons back from Ireland had the best beds and lesser lights were forced to sleep on the rushes like mere esquires, who in turn were banished to draughty corridors and chilly stairs where other folk stepped over them all night.

Straccan slept badly and dreamed worse.

'Vake up!'

Straccan cursed the hand that shook him, none too gently, and opened his eyes upon Bruno's clean-shaven, freshly washed countenance.

'God, is it morning already?'

'*Ja*. Come. You must report to the king.'

Straccan sluiced his face and hands in last night's scummy washing water; he had slept in his clothes and felt scruffy. Bruno was enviously clean and smelled of soap.

'Are you ready?'

'Can you lend me a razor?'

'No time. You vill haf to tell the king your cock and hen story chust as you are.'

'Bull.'

'Vat?'

'Cock and bull. And what do you mean by that?' he asked indignantly. 'You were there.'

The German looked at him suspiciously. 'Bull? That is stupid. Vat has bull to do vith cock?'

'Oh, never mind!'

It was five in the morning and the king was still in his bedchamber, for none dared intrude upon him until the lady had left. A guard stood at each side of the door, pike in hand, and from time to time the king's valet, Petit, pressed an ear to the door and the knights of the bedchamber, waiting with the king's clothes in their arms, tensed expectantly only to slump again when Petit shook his head. A gaggle of sleepy-eyed pageboys, unnaturally silent under the grim eye of the chamberlain, waited to begin their morning duties and two clerks, writing desks hung round their necks, passed the time in sharpening their quills. On a charcoal stove in a corner a jug of water steamed gently, ready for the king's ablutions.

Outside the ante-room, in the passage and on the stairs, the morning's petitioners had been waiting since before dawn. Unlike the knights and pages, they at least could sit on the floor, and although subdued by their surroundings and the intimidating nearness of the king, they gossiped quietly and shared what food they'd brought.

Petit applied his ear to the door again and raised a warning finger. The knights poised to move and a ripple of excitement ran from the bedroom door through the waiting room to the passage and stairs beyond, where folk stuffed the last of their breakfasts in their mouths or back in their scrips, gathered their arguments and began to edge forward.

The door opened and the lucky lady of the night, wrapped in a furred silk mantle and blushing becomingly, slipped shyly through the gap, snatching the purse Petit proffered, before scampering away to boast of her night's adventure.

The valet entered first, the knights surging after him, followed by the clerks and pages, one bearing the king's hot water. Straccan brought up the rear and waited for the king to notice him.

The September day promised fine and the king was in good spirits as his knights washed and dressed him. While his drawers and tunic, surcote, belt and shoes were put on, the king fed titbits to his dogs and dictated letters, using Latin and French with equal ease. The two clerks wrote as one, and as fast as each letter was finished the king started on another.

'Ah! Straccan.' He interrupted his dictation. 'Why have you come before us empty-handed?'

'I haven't, sire.' All eyes followed Straccan as he crossed the room and knelt before the king. 'My lord, will you read this?' He held out Sulien's wallet.

The king ignored it and turned away, leaving Straccan on his knees while he greeted the petitioners. The first half-dozen were dealt with and dismissed, and the rest turned away and told to try again tomorrow. As they departed disappointed, the Bishop of Winchester came striding in, abrim with news.

'God save your grace!' He fell to one knee, kissed the ringed hand and bounced up again. 'My lord, William de Breos is in the bailey with the earl of Derby.'

'There's two dogs that run together.' John scowled. 'Put them both under guard.' He turned back to Straccan, still on his knees. 'We wonder that you dare show your face here, having failed in all we asked of you. Where is our Banner?'

'I haven't got it, my lord.'

'Really? What a surprise. You were told to find it and you did, but instead of bringing it to me you let Breos have it!'

'Not willingly, sire.'

'No? We shall see. He has come to make his peace with me. I had a letter from him.' He snapped his fingers and a clerk produced the letter from his desk. The king unrolled it and began to read aloud. ' "William de Breos to his liege lord John, king of England, greeting." ' The king looked up, bright-eyed. 'Isn't that nice? He begs to see me, sues for mercy, promises to pay his debts, blah blah blah, and offers to give me the Pendragon Banner.' He let the letter roll up with a snap and pointed it at Straccan like a dagger. 'Has he got it?'

'Yes, sire.'

'Explain!'

'I challenged him, my lord; we fought. I would have killed him, but . . . he was too clever for me.' He held up Sulien's wallet again. 'My lord, don't see him before you've read this.'

Again the king ignored it. 'Where is Captain von Koln?'

'Here, sire.'

'You were there. What happened?'

'Breos took a hostage, my lord, a young gentlewoman; he threatened to cut her throat. We had to let him pass.' He recounted the chase, the finding of Alis and Thibaut, and learning that Breos was bound not for Brittany after all but for Bristol and the king.

'So you let him go.'

'We let him come to you, my lord, to face your justice. Please, sire, read this!' Straccan offered the wallet again.

John snatched it impatiently. 'Get up, man, do. What is it?' He cut the ties and tipped the ring into his palm.

For a moment he just looked at it. Under its tan his face paled. 'Body of God! Where did you get this?'

'Sulien's letter tells all,' Straccan said.

'Leave us, all of you,' said the king, and as everyone trooped to the door, 'you stay, Straccan; you too, bishop.'

John took the letter to the window and broke the seal with trembling hands. When he'd read it he was quiet for what seemed like a long time, staring unseeing out of the window. When at last he turned back to them Straccan didn't like the feverish glitter in his eyes nor the bone-white knuckles of the hand that crushed Sulien's letter.

'You know what's written here?'

'Yes, sire.'

'You saw him? His b-body?' He cursed himself for stuttering.

'Yes, my lord.'

'Traitors!' John slammed his clenched fist against the stone wall, breaking the skin. 'The worst that ever were! It beggars belief! God's feet, God's body! Read that, bishop!' He threw the crumpled letter at des Roches. 'That bitch wife of his; it was all her idea?'

'Yes, my lord,' said Straccan, wishing he was anywhere but here.

The bishop looked up from the letter. 'Oh my God. Is this true?'

John's voice had a hysterical edge. 'God's feet, I might have known. God's holy body, I *should* have known! They made a fool of me, those two. They were laughing behind my back while I stuffed their purses with my silver. Never was there such treachery, not since Judas kissed the Lord Christ!'

Straccan saw the king's face darkening with congested blood, the veins in his forehead swelling like worms and the whites of his eyes reddening. John began to bang his head against the wall, hard, making sounds like a dog in pain.

'Go,' said the bishop urgently to Straccan. 'I can deal with this. Go!' He gave Straccan a shove. 'Now! Wait outside.'

Closing the door he turned back to the king. John stood as if turned to stone. The flush had left his face, he was clay-coloured, grey as a corpse. Blood trickled down his brow and he didn't even seem to be breathing.

'My lord . . . John . . .'

John sucked in a shuddering breath and threw up his arms like a man drowning. 'God! Lord God!' Colour came back to his face patchily and he trembled.

Des Roches reached out a tentative hand. 'My lord king,' he began, and stopped, then tried again. 'John,' he said gently. 'Come, sit down, you are much shaken.'

John stared at him as if he was a stranger. So softly that the bishop could barely hear he muttered, 'I didn't do it! God's feet, all these years I believed . . .' Another deep breath. His face hardened. 'Laughing at me . . . all these years . . . I'll kill them with my own hands, I swear I will. They made me the fool of Christendom! So drunk, so stupid, so easily deceived. God's face, if this gets out!' He stopped ranting and looked at the door through which Straccan had gone. 'And what do I do about him? *He* knows!'

Des Roches sighed. 'For that matter, so do I.'

'Ah, but you're my bishop, Peter, the only one loyal to me. If you vow before God and His Son to keep silent, I might even believe you.'

The bishop smiled wryly. 'Sire, my enemies call me a worldly man. I don't deny it. I was a poor knight; when I turned to God I became a poor cleric. You raised me, gave me Winchester, made me a power in the realm. I've nothing I don't owe to you. Believe me or not, my lord. I'll stick to you through thick and thin, come hell or high water. And I'm not the only one.'

'You're the only bloody bishop.' John grinned crookedly. He seemed calmer now. 'Don't you feel conspicuous, Peter? All the rest have run off like rats. There's just you left, sticking your mitre up over the parapet.'

'No one will gain by shooting me down.'

'That you're my friend is reason enough. God's body,' he growled through his teeth. 'What punishment is fit for such treachery?' The veins in his forehead and neck darkened and swelled again as the Angevin rage threatened to overwhelm him, but he controlled it. Des Roches wasn't encouraged. John in a rage was one thing, but John holding himself in check and planning something nasty was quite another. 'I sent Mahaut de Breos to Windsor,' the king said thoughtfully. 'Gerard d'Athée commands there. Tell him . . . No, never mind, I'll write to him myself.'

'My lord king.'

'Careful, Peter.' John held up a warning hand. 'I don't want to hear their names from your lips again.'

'You'll sleep no better for my silence, John.'

'Maybe not. Can I trust it?'

'Will you eye me with doubt for the rest of your life?'

John shot him a hard look. 'Well, we both know, don't we, bishop, that no promise to an excommunicate need be kept?'

'John,' said des Roches impatiently, 'I can promise you silence 'til I'm blue in the face and you still won't trust me. Nevertheless you *have* my promise, not as bishop to excommunicate but as friend to friend. And as your friend I must remind you, "*Vengeance is mine, sayeth the Lord. I will repay.*"'

John regarded him with bleak, unforgiving eyes. 'I warn you, don't plead for them, bishop.'

Des Roches bowed. 'As you command, sire.'

'I'll see Breos in the hall. Tell them to bring him up, but keep him outside until I'm ready and don't let him see Straccan.' He laughed; it almost sounded natural. 'I've a few surprises for him.'

Lord William had insisted that witnesses be present at the meeting, one of them another William, his nephew the earl of Derby. 'Don't leave my side, Will,' he ordered. 'Stick to me like shit to a blanket and I might just come out of this with my head still on.' Of course, if the king ordered his arrest and had the guards drag him down to a dungeon there was nothing he could do about it, but at least the witnesses would know he was there, that he had come in peace seeking reconciliation, and what had happened to him. He wouldn't simply disappear, like Arthur.

There were high-ranking witnesses aplenty. Besides his nephew he saw the earls of Chester and Salisbury, and the Justiciar, Geoffrey fitzPeter, in the throng that packed the hall to gloat at his humiliation. He didn't notice the shocked buzz, swiftly hushed, when the crowd saw the once-great Lord William so changed – an old man, white-haired and haggard with a habit of darting nervous glances over his shoulder all the time, as if there was someone at his heels.

The king lounged on his cushions with one of his dogs in his lap, a cup of wine in his hand and a bishop at his elbow. Breos was glad to see Peter des Roches; he was, within reason, known for a godly man.

John kept him waiting on his knees long enough to get uncomfortable before looking up with a smile, which wasn't necessarily reassuring.

'Well, William. It's a sorry thing when friends fall out.'

'No one regrets it more than I, your grace.' Lord William shuffled his knees a bit.

'You've been busy while I was away.'

Here we go, thought Breos. He knew the routine. 'My lord, I humbly ask your pardon for all my offences, I beg to be restored to your favour and I offer full payment of all my debts to the Crown.' There.

'How much is it now? I've lost count.'

'Twenty thousand marks, my lord.'

'Indeed?' John arched his eyebrows and gave a small whistle of surprise. 'Do you have so much?'

'In coinsilver and in precious goods, sire, yes.' That and more. With luck he might manage to keep the rest, a foundation on which the house of Breos could rise again.

'How nice. Where?'

'In a place of safety, my lord. It can be brought to you at once. I have only to send the password and my seal.'

'Send, then. But not twenty, William. Forty thousand.'

Breos turned pale. At his side his nephew twitched. That was it almost to the penny. How did the king know? He swallowed. 'My lord, do I have your forgiveness?'

'You're asking a lot. What value do you set upon the town of Leominster, which you burned? And what about all the damage you've done this summer? You've offended a lot of people. I've had complaints from every county. Brigandage, arson, murder—'

'I've murdered no one, my lord!' He shot a look behind him as once again the tail of his eye caught some movement, some small scuttling thing . . . But there was nothing there.

'Come off it. Don't tell me your hands are clean.' The king beckoned to a clerk, a small pale man clutching a sheaf of documents.

'See these? They're claims for damage, pleas for restitution, complaints against your men and you.' The king took the documents. 'Thank you, Robert. You remember Robert Wace, don't you, William? My clerk. You left your knife in his belly.'

'Sire—' Sweat stood in blisters on his forehead.

'By some miracle he lived to tell the tale. Well, where's the hoard? It's mine anyway, not yours; you reived it from *my* towns, *my* abbeys, *my* merchants and citizens, and you'll give it back, every penny, before we talk of pardon. Captain von Koln! William will tell you where my treasure is. Go and get it.' John leaned back in his chair and stroked his dog's head. The bishop bent down and whispered at his ear; the king laughed and nodded, and waved to someone in the throng as if he'd forgotten the man on his knees before him,

As Bruno bore down on him Breos looked desperately around and seeing no friendly face hissed at his nephew, 'Speak for me. What d'you think you're here for?' But the earl, having come this far, was not willing to go the extra mile and kept his mouth shut. Sullenly Breos told the king's captain where the hoard lay and grudgingly handed over his seal. Surely the king would let him get up now? His knees hurt so much he was afraid when he *did* try to get up he wouldn't be able to, and *that* would give them all something to laugh at.

'You still here? Was there anything else?' asked the king.

Breos ground his teeth. John was playing with him; he should have expected it, he'd seen it done a hundred times and smirked at the victims' discomfort. 'The pardon, my lord?'

'I'll think about it.'

'Sire, my wife.'

'Lady Mahaut? What about her?'

'Will you release her, my lord? And my son? I beg—'

'Why should I?'

'Sire, I can ransom them. I have the Pendragon Banner.'

'So you wrote in your letter. I don't believe it. He didn't find it on the island, did he, Robert?' The clerk shook his head. 'A knight in my service, what's his name, Straccan, *he* found it.'

'My squire took it from him, my lord. I have it.'

'A fake.'

'No, sire!'

'Show it to my clerk, then. He'll know true from false. The true one saved his life, he says. A miracle.'

'Sire, take the Banner, please, and let them go!'

'Where is it?'

'I have it here, sire, under my mantle. May I get up?'

'No. My lord of Derby, divest your uncle of the Banner, will you?'

Stone-faced, the earl stripped Breos of his mantle and took the satchel from his back.

'Robert?' said John gently. Wace took the bag, opened it, and drew out a long deerskin-wrapped coil. With unsteady hands he undid the ties and shook off the wrappings. There was a collective gasp of admiration and wonder as the Banner unrolled and the red dragon rippled as if alive. Garnets glittered, goldwork glittered, the king's eyes glittered.

'Is it the real thing?'

Wace's eyes brimmed with tears; they ran over and down his cheeks. 'Oh yes, my lord. This is the true Pendragon Banner.'

'Sire,' cried Breos, toppling forward on both hands to ease the agony in his knees. 'Take it, and let my wife go! My son—'

'They remain in our custody, at our pleasure,' John said, getting up briskly and setting the dog down on the floor. It trotted over to the man grovelling on hands and knees, and pissed against his boot. 'But I will be merciful to you, William, for old times' sake. You may go, unharmed.'

'My liege, please, does all my past loyal service count for nothing? You were glad of it once!'

'You speak of loyalty? *You*? No fouler traitor breathes! I know what you've done, you and that sow you married.' He held out his hand. Those near enough saw the great ruby ring and wondered at it.

Breos hid his face in his hands and wept.

'You have two weeks to take yourself out of our realm of England. Set foot in it again and I'll have you disembowelled. Guards! Get this traitor out of my sight!'

After supper the king played with his dogs in the castle garden, with just a handful of attendants, and sent for Straccan.

'There you are, Sir Richard! You remember Master Wace?'

Straccan couldn't believe his eyes. 'My God, you're alive!' He grasped the little clerk's hand.

Wace coloured with pleasure. 'Thanks to you, Sir Richard, and the Banner.'

'What d'you mean?'

'You touched it to my lips, remember? I was dying. It was a miracle.'

'Robert has told me all about it,' the king said, taking Straccan's arm and walking through the rose beds out of his attendants' hearing. A small four-legged mop, something like a hairy ferret, darted across the grass at high speed, making the king change feet smartly so as not to fall over it.

'Damn thing,' he said, glaring at the corner round which the animal had prudently vanished. 'Some sort of German dog. My nephew Otto gave it to me. It pisses everywhere. And I always thought he liked me. Well, Straccan, I have the Banner, and from what Wace and Captain von Koln have told me it seems I may have judged you too hastily.'

Coming from the king that amounted to a handsome apology, and Straccan wisely bowed and said nothing.

'So, what do you want?'

'Want?' Straccan asked, taken aback. 'Nothing, my lord.'

'Nothing?' The king looked amused. 'You're a widower, aren't you? What about an heiress, young and pretty and with a manor near . . . Where is it you live? Near Dieulacresse? Or a grant of lands to march with your own?'

While the king spoke Straccan had done some swift thinking. 'Not for myself; I have all I need. But there is something—'

'Ha! I knew it! What?'

'Sulien's hospital, my lord. Breos gave him the valley but never confirmed the gift. The new lord of Brecknock wants it back. Sire, your generosity to lepers and the sick is known throughout the realm; will you give Sulien his valley?' He held his breath, awaiting the answer.

None came. As the king walked on between the flower beds an elderly wolfhound rose stiffly from its sunny patch and padded gravely at his side.

'I like dogs,' said John. '*People* you can't be sure about, but you know where you are with dogs. This is Nazar.' He pulled gently on the hound's soft ears. 'My father had a bear, once. Took it everywhere with him. Really loved it. It bit him, I remember. Most things he loved bit him, sooner or later, people especially. What happened to Julitta de Beauris? Let her go, did you?'

Straccan exhaled. At least he'd tried. 'No, my lord, but she is beyond your vengeance, or mine.'

'Dead? How?'

'Not dead. In worse case.'

The green eyes glinted dangerously. 'Don't speak in riddles to me! Where is she?'

Straccan told him. As he left the garden the king's laughter followed him through the roses.

Straccan and Bane left Bristol an hour later, heading for Worcester, where Bane would turn north-east towards Derby and the convent of Holystone, to get Gilla and take her home, while Straccan made for Shawl. It was a hundred and fifty miles, more or less. If he rode hard he could be there in three days.

Watching them leave from his solar window, John beckoned the bishop of Winchester to his side. 'What do you think, Peter? Will he keep his mouth shut?'

'He'd be a damned fool not to, and he doesn't strike me as any sort of fool.'

'He interests me,' mused John. 'They all want something. They jump and yap like a pack of hounds. Not him. He's content with his small estate. I offered him a rich wife and he didn't want her. As for money, he has enough.'

'A happy man,' said des Roches.

'There's an old story I had from Hodierna, my nurse, about a king who was bowed down with troubles. Probably had barons! Anyway, he was in despair when a wise man told him there was only one cure for his misery. He must sleep one night in the shirt of a happy man. Heard it, have you?'

'No, sire. Did the king recover?'

'He turned the realm upside down to find a happy man. Sent riders the length and breadth of his kingdom. At last – and *years* had gone by, mind – his searchers brought a man to him.'

'Was he happy?'

'Oh yes. Not a care in the world. Sang. Whistled. Danced.' John performed a small caper.

The bishop nodded. 'So the king got his shirt, and they all lived happily ever after.'

'Not quite. You see, the man was a beggar. He didn't have a shirt.'

Des Riches coughed. 'My lord, about the lady Mahaut—'

The king bent his head over the wolfhound. His hand sliced up, palm out, cutting off the bishop's words. 'He's picked up a tick again, look!' He tackled it with his thumbnail. 'There, that's better.' He smiled.

Des Roches dared try once more. 'Sire, the lady and her son—'

The hand slashed down again. The smile was still there but the eyes were cold as ice. 'Take care, bishop. No more on this matter. It is forgotten!'

Chapter 56

There was no need to spur Zingiber, the great horse responded to the slightest pressure of its rider's heels, but no matter how fast the miles fleeted by they went too slowly. What would he find when he got to Shawl? Dreadful possibilities crowded Straccan's imagination but dwelling on them was useless; he clamped his mind shut against them and worried about Gilla instead.

She was safe, thank God, but it had shaken him to the marrow to realise how vulnerable they were. The king could take Gilla as a hostage whenever he chose, to force her father's hand. It might never happen again but the bare threat would be enough. Unless . . .

Unless she was married.

He'd known it would happen one day. For knights' daughters there were only two destinies, marriage or Religion. Gilla was certainly old enough to be married; she'd be twelve on Saint Brice's day. Most girls of her age were betrothed, many already wed. When the king married his beautiful queen, Isabelle of Angouleme, she was no more than twelve years old.

Straccan was a rich man. His daughter's dowry might tempt those who would normally look to the higher ranks for their brides, and she was already beautiful. But she also had a liability – her father.

He'd overheard the comments when his peers discussed the unmarried and widowed with an eye to matchmaking.

'*Who's that?*'

'*Straccan. Sir Richard Straccan.*'

'*Oh*, him.'

'*Why? What's the matter with him?*'

'*The feller's in* trade, *dear boy!*'

'*You don't say!*'

'*Got money, though, and a manor. His wife's dead.*'

'*Yes, but would you let* your *daughter marry him?*'

He must do something, and soon. But dawn of the third morning was colouring the sky with a gaudy brush when he reached the edge of Shawl village and turned Zingiber towards Janiva's cottage, still having made no decision.

Sir Roger of Shawl, safely and expensively confirmed in possession of the manor by the king, arrived home in the dark hour before dawn, weary from his long ride and – if truth be told – relieved to find his wife not there, although he'd been looking forward to seeing his new son.

Dogs barked as Roger's servant – he didn't yet run to a squire – hurried ahead to wake the household. Duty and affection took Roger first to the church, to pray for his parents, and he was astonished and angry not to find the coffins there. He stamped into his hall in a bad temper, flung himself down in the great chair at the high table and demanded something to eat.

The steward roused the cook and chivvied him into producing bread and meat, which he bore, with a jug of ale, to the hall and set before Roger.

'Ah, Robert. Where's my wife?'

'At Shaxoe, sir.'

'Send and tell her I'm home. Bid her come to Shawl at once and bring the boy.'

Robert bowed. 'I'll tell Father Finacre, sir.'

'Finacre? What's he doing here?'

'He's in charge when Lady Richildis is away.'

'Why, where's Father Osric?'

'Sick abed, sir, all summer.'

Roger ate and drank, questioning the steward between mouthfuls. 'My parents' coffins, where are they?'

'In the mews, sir.'

'*What?*'

'Father Finacre said—'

'Get him. And get them *out* of there. Now!'

'Shall we put them in the ditch then, sir?'

'What?'

'The Interdict—'

'Bugger the Interdict! No, they're not going in any bloody ditch! I want them in the church where they belong. It's all right, there'll be no lawbreaking, no Mass, but at least they will lie in peace until this bloody Interdict's over.'

'That cannot be, Sir Roger.' The chaplain came forward into the torchlight and bowed. Roger looked at him with distaste; he'd never understood his wife's liking for the fellow.

'What's that you said?' Roger had changed, Finacre saw. The boyish, rather plump and cheerful face had hardened and he'd started a beard, perhaps to cover the new scar, still red and bright, along his jawline.

'Your noble mother and father *cannot* rest in peace, my lord, until their murderer is brought to justice.'

'Murderer?'

Sir Roger's shout rang back from the walls as he sprang to his feet, toppling the heavy chair with an echoing bang. The empty ale jug tipped over, rolled, fell to the floor and smashed.

'I grieve to give you such tidings, Sir Roger. Your wife and child nearly lost their lives and Dame Alienor was poisoned!'

'God's breath, poison? Who did it?'

'The woman Janiva, my lord.'

Roger was too shocked to speak. His mouth opened but no sound came out. The hard-faced young veteran was suddenly transformed back into an uncertain eighteen-year-old boy. He looked around helplessly. 'This is madness. Where *is* Janiva?'

'That's what I want to know.' No one had seen Straccan come in. He stood by the beggars' bench, a tall man in a travel-stained cloak under which the jutting line of the sword proclaimed him a knight.

Roger's hand settled on his sword hilt. He straightened. 'Who are you, sir? What do you want here?'

'Straccan's my name. I've come for Janiva.'

Roger bristled. 'What's she to you?'

'My wife to be.' There was a general gasp of astonishment, not least from Roger. 'I've come from her house; it's gone. Burned. Nothing left. Where is she?'

Events were moving too fast for Roger; he floundered, fumbling for a grip on any fixed fact.

'How burned? God's mercy, is she dead?'

'I ordered it done,' Finacre said boldly. 'The woman was a witch. She lay with demons, she brewed poisons and all manner of evil. Sir Roger, she cast spells to bring on your lady's labour too soon, to kill your unborn son!'

A voice rose in protest from amid the throng. 'Cods! E wouldna bin born at all but for er!'

'Who said that?' Roger demanded. 'Tyrrel, is it? Come here!' The shepherd shuffled forward. 'Speak up!'

Tyrrel sucked his teeth, an essential preliminary to speech, and almost spat on the floor but remembered where he was just in time.

'Come an got me, dint she,' he said. 'Tole me to turn the brat inside his dam. I said I couldn't, but she *would* ave it. An I did,' he finished with a snort of triumph. 'I did an all! E'd never ave breathed else!'

'Where is she, Finacre?' Roger snapped.

'The devil spirited her away,' the chaplain said. 'She was locked in the undercroft until the Ordeal—'

'Ordeal?' Roger stared. 'God's breath and bones, what's been going on here?'

A dozen or more voices tried to tell him at once, but Finacre shouted them down.

'She knew I had smelt her out; she sent evil dreams to frighten me off. There were devilish things in her house: a mandrake, that devil's root, all pierced with wicked nails, a mannikin of your *wife*, Sir Roger.'

'Mind your tongue or I'll have it out, priest or no! Where's my sister?'

'The Devil himself carried her off! There's no other way she could have got out. The door was locked, the man on guard saw nothing—'

'Twasn't no Devil, my lord!' Sybilla pushed forward to stand beside her husband. 'Twas me.' She felt a tremor shake Robert's body and reached for his hand, clasping it so hard that he winced. 'I got her out of there and Tostig Forester took her away. Robert here knowed nothing about it, nobody did, just me and Tostig.'

A wave of astonished babbble surged across the hall.

'Send for Tostig,' Roger ordered. 'Sir Richard, come up here. We'll get to the bottom of this.'

'Mistress Sybilla,' Straccan said, weak with relief, 'I thank you with all my heart for your courage and kindness to my lady. Where did Tostig take her?'

Sybilla gazed wretchedly at him, tears gathering to roll down her cheeks. 'He wouldn't tell me. Said it was safer that way. Said he'd tell you when you came for her. But, oh sir, something must've happened to him. He never came back!'

'Get off my manor before I have you flogged,' Roger ordered when he'd heard what everyone had to say – a long job that took the rest of the morning, with accusations flying, all pointing to Finacre who not only didn't deny them but seemed to think he deserved reward. 'And if I hear of you creeping about any of my manors,' said Roger viciously, 'I'll have your lying tongue out of your head, understand? Keep off my lands and keep away from my wife and son. Get out!'

By the time he'd packed his bag the news of the chaplain's dismissal had reached workers in the farthest fields and they had all come running to see if it was true and, if it was, to give him a suitable send-off.

He saw them waiting at the end of the village and hefted the bag on his shoulder. In it were his spare gown, and wrapped in that his chalice and paten and several small articles of silver which he was pretty sure wouldn't be missed before he was well away from Shawl.

'Let me pass,' he cried. 'Anyone who lays hands on a priest of God will burn in Hell! Remember Becket!' Despite himself his voice quavered.

'Ain't gonna lay a hand on you,' someone called.

'Wouldn't touch im with a ten-foot pole,' said another, amid laughter.

For a few more steps he thought they were going to let him pass unhurt, but then the first stone hit him. He squealed, dropped his bag and ran.

'Cur!'

'Liar!'

The next stone hit his ear, numbing it instantly, although he felt the heat of his blood running down his neck and the scalding urine on his thighs.

'No, don't! You can't! You mustn't! No, please!' This couldn't be happening, not to *him*. He screamed like a rabbit when the fox's teeth close on it.

The third stone smashed his lips, breaking teeth, and his mouth filled with blood. After that stones flew thick and fast and couldn't be counted. Then he was past them and out of the village; they weren't following. Sobbing, praying, cursing, he stumbled on, blood splotching his trail. The road rose and dipped, taking the village out of sight behind him. He staggered on, unaware of the thunder of hooves behind him until dust choked him as the knight from the hall, Straccan, swept by.

The villagers shunned the crossroads, they said it was haunted, but no ghost bothered Benet Finacre as he sank down by the spring to splash his ruined face. Blood stained the water and he spat out bits of teeth, whining at the pain.

This was all the witch's doing. She had got away but he would track her down. He would write to the bishop; even in exile in France, the bishop would take notice of such an accusation and stir up the Church authorities in England to act. Wherever she was, they would find her.

But now, where could he go? Which road should he take? *That* one, he knew, led to Shaxoe. If he followed it, sooner or later he would meet Lady Richildis on her way to Shawl. She would give him some money and he was certain he could persuade her to recommend him to some other household. Whimpering, bleeding, he stumbled on.

Chapter 57

The morning sun was hot, but the first frosts had already bitten Pouncey Edge and autumn promised a wealth of nuts and berries. Sitting idle for a few moments, lost in thought, her spindle in her lap, Janiva looked up with a smile when she heard Osyth's footfalls.

'Tobias the potter will be off on his rounds in a day or two,' Osyth said. 'Before the rains come. He'll take a message for you to your knight, if you want.'

Janiva shook her head. 'No, it's too late. I sent him away. He said he'd come back, but he didn't.' She had refused him then, how could she turn to him now? It would be shameful to creep to the shelter of his arms, the protection of his name, now that she was bereft of all else.

'Ah well, if your cott and goats mattered so much to him,' said Osyth, with her disconcerting habit of answering thoughts rather than words, 'and if your pride matters so much to you . . .'

'It's not pride,' said Janiva quickly.

'Ain't it?' Osyth gazed into the cloudless distance. After a while she said, 'You can always stay here, you know. I've a year or two left in me. Want to take my place?'

Janiva let the spindle drop and twirl at the end of its woollen thread. 'I don't know, Osyth. I don't know *what* to do.'

'Ask the Mother.'

'*How*, when I don't know what to ask?'

'Put yourself in her hands,' the anchoress said, 'and trust her.'

The shrine at Cwm Cuddfan had been rebuilt. A bright new shelter of woven willow boughs shielded the statue of Saint Nonna from wind and rain, and once again the fire burned high above the valley.

Garnier climbed to the shrine every day. The death of the Silent Man and all that followed would always trouble him, but now he had other matters on his mind. There was the tragic death of two of his flock, Meurig and David. They had been friends and – despite their affliction – young enough to laugh at times and young enough in both years and affliction to hope . . . They *all* hoped, for the first few years.

The two had disappeared about the time of the battle between Breos and Straccan; at least no one recalled seeing them after that. Meurig's corpse, bruised, battered and stabbed with his own knife, had been found beside his beached coracle on the far side of the island, a rocky shore where no one ever landed. A few days later searchers with dogs found David, beaten to death with fists and a stone in a cave behind the cataract. The remains of a fire and fish bones showed the two men had spent some time there; the sandy floor was a palimpsest of their footprints and the traces of their fight.

It seemed they had quarrelled and fought: Meurig had killed David and fled, only to die of his own injuries. Not unusual. Tempers flared easily and men, whole or leprous, frequently killed one another. A tragedy, but no mystery.

Except for one thing: the single imprint of a bare foot among the many in the cave, a *perfect* foot, small and narrow. That they had fought over a woman, Garnier was sure, but whoever she was she had fled.

The other matter was a mystery of a different kind. In the palm of his right hand, in the very spot where Straccan had placed the thread from the Pendragon Banner, he had felt for some time a sensation of warmth, a tingling thrill that this morning had spread to his thumb and three remaining fingers. He stripped off his mitten but kept the hand clenched and pressed to his chest, not daring to look. When at last he did, the shock ran through his whole body.

In the centre of the palm was a patch of pink firm healthy skin, twice as big as a penny. Yesterday it had been only half that size.

He was trembling from head to foot, stunned, afraid to believe what he saw. But there it was. Tentatively he touched it with his other gloved hand, and he could *feel* it, could feel the coarse fabric and the pressure of his touch.

' "Oh Lord my God, I cried unto thee and thou hast healed me. O Lord, thou hast brought up my soul from the grave. Thou hast turned for me my mourning into dancing, thou hast put off my sackcloth, and girded me with gladness . . ." ' The words of the psalm echoed back from the other side of the valley, sending a flock of birds soaring and wheeling above his head.

'Master Sulien.'

It was the German captain who had brought Straccan to the valley at summer's end. Sulien frowned. What could one of the king's captains want with him? The man carried a document case. Sulien's heart sank; it must be the order to leave the valley.

'I am to give you this.' Bruno opened the case and handed Sulien a letter-roll, from which hung a very large black wax seal. Sulien looked at the seal, a depiction of the king enthroned, wielding the Sword of Justice. On the other side was the king on horseback, wielding the Sword of War.

'From the king,' Bruno prompted unnecessarily. 'Aren't you going to open it?' He looked almost gleeful, Sulien thought wretchedly. Probably the man would relish the job of driving them all out.

He unrolled the parchment and read aloud. ' "We, John, by the Grace of God King of England, Lord of Ireland, Duke of Normandy, Aquitaine and Count of Anjou do hereby grant . . ." ' His voice failed him there and he read to the end silently. Then he went back to the beginning and read it again, slowly and carefully, to make sure there was no mistake.

'God in heaven! It's a grant of land! The king has given us the valley!' His legs failed him and he sat down on the stool. He looked at the beaming Bruno. 'I must write at once, and thank His Grace . . . such generosity. How did he know? Someone must have spoken to him for us. Of course, my lord de Breos.'

'Straccan,' said Bruno.

'What?'

'Sir Richard Straccan. For finding that Banner the king offered to him a rich vife. He asked for this instead.'

Lord William trudged the pebbled beach from one boat to the next, pausing briefly at each. The skippers eyed him warily, a grizzled old man, fierce and gaunt. The stuff of his cloak was good, the purse at his belt was heavy, but one after another they shook their heads and turned him away, spitting and forking their fingers at his back to ward off the Evil Eye.

He looked unlucky. Seafaring men need all the luck they can get. They weren't willing to risk theirs for a Jonah, no matter how much he offered for passage to Normandy. A man would have to be desperate to take *him*.

There was such a man eventually, of course; there always is.

Lord William watched the Sussex coast sink below the horizon with tears running down his cheeks and tried to pray for his wife.

She was to be forgotten.

She had always had a terror of confined spaces but of course John had found that out. After the first night and day Mahaut de Breos knew she would never see her husband nor her children again. This cold, narrow cell, which held only a verminous straw mattress and herself, was to be her tomb.

No food was brought to her. Soon she understood that none would be.

Where had they put her son? Was he here at Windsor, or at Corfe? Perhaps John had let him go. The offence, after all, was hers. She prayed for him, for all her children and for her husband, pleading with God for their lives. She had nothing to bargain with now, nothing to offer in exchange. She would build no more churches, endow no more shrines, feed no more beggars in the hope of keeping God's goodwill. With no priest between them she must speak to Him directly, admitting her sins and beseeching his mercy not for herself but for her family.

The cell was set in the thickness of the castle wall. A shaft of light came through a slit-window far above her head. She could tell night from day and so count the hours of her dying.

Hunger was uncomfortable but thirst was worse. Thirst was torment unspeakable as her tongue thickened in her parched mouth, and she bit at the veins in her hands to moisten her lips with her own blood.

There was an iron grille in the floor, too small to let a body through, covering the mouth of an old well shaft. When the sun was high a beam of light shone down and she could see the oily gleam of foul water far below. On the third day she discovered a rusty iron ring fixed to the grille and a chain dangling from it. When she drew it up, a small battered iron cup was on the end.

The chain was too short to reach the water.

Chapter 58

Straccan's manor of Stirrup lay halfway between Dieulacresse and Nottingham, and the domestic quarters followed the plan of the Roman villa that had once been there: a square of buildings around a central space. The main entrance was guarded by a modern watchtower with an old cracked bell to give warning of anyone approaching. Various doors opened off the yard into stables, mews, storerooms, kitchen, bath house, bakery, brewery and living quarters.

Separated from this complex by a stream and an orchard were the farmworkers' cotts and farm buildings. The surrounding fields, apart from pasture and hay, yielded wheat and barley. It was a small manor but well run and – unusually – there were no villeins. The farmworkers and their families and all the manor servants were free.

Straccan could have bought more land but he was content with Stirrup. It didn't do to be too obviously rich. Rich men attracted notice and notice meant trouble, and he'd managed to avoid both until the events of last summer, which had first brought him to the king's notice.

When the tinny clank of the bell announced his arrival his daughter gathered up her skirts and ran to meet him and be scooped up in his arms. His housekeeper and steward, his clerk Peter and Bane, gathered at the gate to greet him.

'Where's Janiva?' Gilla asked. 'You said you'd bring her home.'

'She wasn't there, sweetheart. I don't know where she is. I don't know where to begin but I won't stop looking until I find her.'

Later, in the room that served as their office, his clerk picked up the small gold cup and frowned at the inscription. ' "*Cymbium Wulstani sum*" – what's this?'

'Lock it up, Peter. That's Saint Wulfstan's chalice, given him by King Harold. Write on the morrow to all our agents and tell them it's for sale. When they've stirred up enough interest, we'll consider bids.' He yawned. 'I'm going to bed.'

Straccan looked at the cup without interest, almost with dislike, feeling none of the usual thrill at handling a relic, especially one so notable as this. It had cost two men's lives, thieves though they were, and almost cost Havloc his. But it would fetch a surprising sum of money for Alis and her sisters; there was a world of difference between a small gold cup worth a pound or two and a precious relic worth whatever someone was willing to pay.

He'd be glad to be rid of it.

He hadn't slept in his own bed for months and now he was in it he couldn't sleep anyway, fretting while the hours of darkness crawled on. Where should his search begin? Where might Tostig have taken her, north, south, east or west? And how far? Mentally he drew a ten-mile circle around Shawl, groaning to think of the towns it encompassed. Would Tostig have taken her to a place he knew or a city, such as York? No one at Shawl knew anything about the man, his origins, his family. Straccan remembered him as having the speech of the area, not exactly that of Shawl folk but like enough. That was no help.

He would have taken her somewhere he considered safe from that ranting priest, somewhere the Church wasn't likely to find her. Probably not a town, then, and certainly not a convent.

It was almost dawn.

'Oh God, Mary Mother of God, help me find her!'

He punched his pillow for the hundredth time and took up the other strand of his anxiety: what to do about Gilla's future.

'Father?'

He sat up in bed. 'Gilla?'

She had brought a candle; it lit her face and bright hair, edging them with gold as she stood at his bedchamber door.

'What is it? Are you sick?'

'No. Can I come in?'

'Come here.'

She set the candle on the aumbrey and scrambled up onto his bed, tucking her bare feet under her. He reached to grasp one small slender foot and found it cold as stone.

'Where are your shoes?' he asked, wrapping the coverlid round her.

'I forgot them. Father, I think I can find Janiva.'

'What? How?'

'I can scry for her.'

He drew in a long, long breath and let it slowly out. She could do that; it was an ability she shared with Janiva. Last year when Gilla was kidnapped, the witch Julitta de Beauris had sensed that power in her and forced her to use it against her will. Later Janiva had taught her how to manage the gift, if gift it was.

Uneasily Straccan said, 'I don't know, sweetheart.'

'I can do it.'

'Now?'

'Yes. It's easier when everything's quiet.'

He reached for his bedgown and wrapped himself in it. 'You need a bowl of water.'

'No. It works better for me with the candle. I just look at the flame.'

She sat cross-legged in the middle of the bed, and he watched her as she watched the flame.

'Janiva,' she whispered, 'Janiva, where are you?'

The flame wavered, steadied and grew until it filled all her vision, thinning as it did so to become a circle, a ring of fire through which she saw . . .

. . . a high cliff, miles wide, with a streak of white like a forked branch across its stone face. She saw it from afar and from above and, like a flying bird, swooped down towards it. Now she could see trees, bushes, a narrow path, a walled enclosure, a stone hut built against the cliff face. Although it was night she saw everything clearly but without colour.

'What place is this?' she asked, and again saw the great scar, or whatever it was, on the rock face, shining so whitely that it dazzled. Then she was staring at a candle flame, nothing more.

'Draw it,' Straccan said when she tried to describe it, and while it still glowed in her mind's sight she took the charcoal he offered and scrawled the mark on the bedsheet. An upright stroke, with two branches slanting upwards from its right side. Straccan copied it carefully onto a wax tablet.

'I don't know where it is,' Gilla said. 'It's very big, the cliff rises in steps and there's a waterfall. But Janiva's there, in that house.'

'I'll find it.' Straccan hugged her. His tears ran into her hair. 'Get dressed, honey. I must wake Peter, get him to send a copy of this to every one of my agents, and to every town in the kingdom. Someone will know where it is. We'll find her, sweetheart. We'll find her!'

Read here an exclusive extract from *The Glee-Maiden*, Sylvian Hamilton's enchanting new mediaeval novel, continuing the epic adventures of Sir Richard Straccan, bone-pedlar, available in 2004

The travellers came to the priory on the wings of the worst snow-storm in living memory (living memory being Dame Ada, who claimed seventy winters, if such a thing were possible).

There were two of them, man and woman. She stood in the crook of his left arm, leaning against him, his cloak around them both. Taller than her by more than a head, he looked down at his treasure with an expression so naked, so vulnerable in its tender-ness that Mother Berenice felt a wrench at her own heart, cured leather though she thought it.

He was a knight, he said. Richard Straccan of Stirrup, a place the prioress had never heard of; and barely were they welcomed in, the lady seated by a roaring fire with one of Dame Lovisa's hot possets, than this Straccan demanded to see the nuns' priest. The prioress sent a novice to fetch Father Tobias from the mew where he was – as usual – fiddling with his sparrowhawk.

The priest looked up, blinking, from the delicate task of imping his bird's broken wing-feather.

'Ah, Hilda! Just put your finger on this knot, will you? That's it.' He pulled the thread taut and snipped it. Hilda, who was afraid of the hawk, stepped back quickly as it stretched a wing and shifted its taloned grip on the perch. Father Tobias made kissing sounds to it and gave it a scrap of raw meat, wiping his hands on the skirt of his gown.

'Please-Father-will-you-come-at-once?' Hilda panted. 'It's urgent, Mother says!'

'Is someone dying?'

'I don't think so. They looked all right to me.'

'Who?'

'The knight and his lady.'

'Visitors? In this weather?' The priest hurried to his room to fetch his satchel with the viaticum, just in case, and followed Hilda to the guest-parlour where the prioress, in some agitation, met him at the door.

'What's the matter?'

'I don't know. He insisted on seeing a priest.' She opened the door. Father Tobias took a deep breath and followed her in.

The woman – she looked no more than eighteen – was sitting by the fire, flushed now with warmth and Sister Lovisa's posset. The knight, a tall grey-eyed man with a scarred face, swung round as the door opened, reaching for his lady's hand, and got straight to the point.

'Father, will you hear our vows? We wish to marry. Now.'